CHASING YOU

KRIS JAYNE

CHAPTER 1

ALEXA

*W*hite. Everywhere. Startling white sunlight blasted my eyes open. More white surrounded me. I blinked, then ducked my head under the cloud of bedding.

This isn't my bed.

Only hotels had bed sheets bleached *this* white. My heart jumped. Where was I? London? That was a month ago. A stopover in New York. A weekend in Vegas. Oklahoma for Christmas.

Dallas. Last night. The slamming New Year's party.

What time is it?

The vodka-induced pounding of my head muddled my mind. I had no clue where my dress was—or my underwear. A heavy ache anchored my legs, and my stomach roiled.

I hadn't allowed myself to get that drunk in years. The hangovers. The stupid decision making. The calories.

Seriously, Alexa. Pull it together.

Melissa, my New Year's Eve accomplice, probably wondered where I was. We had a lunch appointment with good-luck black-eyed peas and collard greens. I could use some luck to pull my year out of the ditch. I was sputtering already, and it was only day one.

First, I had to leave the warm bed, find my clothes, and get the hell out of…wherever I was.

"Mornin', sweetheart."

A masculine, sleep-rasped voice snatched my breath. I snapped upright, then yanked the duvet up over my bare chest.

There he was—smiling, naked, and awake in more ways than one.

His eyes were half open, sleepy, and wanton under a fringe of golden brown lashes. My eyes slid down the lean stretch of muscle and tanned skin next to me on top of the covers.

"Why can't you disappear in a puff of smoke?"

My heart thundered as if I'd finished an hour of wind sprints. Somehow, the words that sprang up in my head had come out of my mouth.

GRAHAM

I woke up steeped in the satisfaction of my New Year's Eve success. The details blurred, but I could practically feel the firm ass in my hand, soft lips on mine, and the tight squeeze on my cock. An easy, pleased-with-myself grin spread across my face.

She stirred, rustling in the cocoon of bedding.

"Mornin', sweetheart."

She shot up. I caught a luscious view of dark-tipped breasts before she clutched the comforter up to her chin. Ginger ale eyes widened at me. She pressed her lips tight, beguiling dimples appearing in her cheeks.

I wanted to banish Miss Prim and bring back the woman who'd bucked and clawed astride my lap a few hours before. She threw her face into her palms.

"Why can't you disappear in a puff of smoke?"

What? Women didn't wish for Graham Ryan to disappear. Ever. I shoved aside my indignation and grinned.

"That's not the magic act I do, but drop the sheet, and I'll show you another trick."

"Then I'll disappear."

She swung away from me, fighting the bed sheets to get her feet on the floor.

"Don't go. Come on."

I touched her back, and she arched away and jumped out of bed. I got a fantastic view—long, naked curves of creamy *café au lait* skin.

"No. I'm not...no."

She scrambled to snatch her dress, handbag, and lace underthings off the floor, then raced into the bathroom. The door snapped shut.

I leaned out of bed to grab my cell phone out of my pants pocket and reorient myself with the world while she attended to herself for several minutes.

The muffled rush of water filled the room—first from the sink and then the shower. A clang of objects against the hard countertop surprised me. How much could she have in that tiny purse?

4 | KRIS JAYNE

And what would she look like in the shower? Rivulets of water streaming down the curves of her naked body. Her back would arch, pushing her breasts forward and up.

My hand roved down to my twitching groin, but then I slapped my thigh and thought about football. The Dallas Cowboys. Quarterback play. Defensive line woes.

I couldn't have her walk out and see me tugging on myself like a horny teenager who'd just seen my first boob. Plus, I still hoped to convince her to stay. I'd need that hard-on.

Then, the door flung open as purposefully as it had been slammed shut. Somehow, she looked polished and bright—even in last night's spangly mini-dress.

"I have to go."

"Why?"

"I have plans. I'm probably already late. What time is it?"

Her dispassionate tone sliced off each word flung in my direction. I sat up and turned the clock on the nightstand toward her.

"10:22."

"Shit." She flipped her gaze around the room, dark curly hair bouncing, then found her shoes tumbled over in the corner. Balancing like a dancer on one leg at a time, she strapped the spiked heels to her feet. "I have to get back to my hotel."

"Give me two minutes. I'll drive you."

"No. I'll manage." She strode toward the door. Another second, and she'd be gone.

"Where do you have to be in such a hurry on New Year's Day? I figured we could relax. Go have breakfast. Or order room service."

She turned to face me. With the morning light dancing

off the silver sequins of her dress, she looked like an angelic go-go dancer. My body stiffened again, which I made no attempt to hide from my guest.

Her eyes darted to my erection and then locked back on mine.

"I told you. I have plans. And I need to go back to my hotel and change."

"Let me drive you. It's the least I can do."

Her hand flew to her hip in a fist. "Since I did you the favor of having sex with you?"

Shit, she was a beast. My interest wavered even as she threw her sparkling hip to the side in an unwittingly sexy way. "I'm attempting to be nice."

She huffed. "Fine. Are you going to shower or something?"

"Yeah. Two minutes."

Game on. So what if she was a little bitchy? Her body was killer, and I'd love another turn.

I bounded to my feet and into the bathroom, not bothering to close the door. I threw on the shower and stepped inside. As soon as I closed the shower curtain, I heard the heavy thud of the hotel room door.

Damn. I didn't even remember her name.

ALEXA

I strutted across the posh lobby of the Ritz Carlton as if taking a turn on a fashion runway—not a walk of shame.

I needed a ride and a coffee and a toothbrush.

When I hit the valet stand, the shining sunlight blinded

me. A headache split my skull like an ax, and my stomach did another pirouette.

"Do you need a cab, ma'am?"

"No. I have a ride on the way." I glanced at my phone, checking the progress of my rideshare. "Two minutes."

I held the phone up to indicate that I was on top of the situation.

"Quite the party last night." The valet gestured toward the lobby bar.

"Apparently."

I scoured my memory for details of my New Year's Eve. Mr. Mystery and I hadn't gone to the bar. We left the house party around one a.m. and checked into a room at the Ritz. Or maybe he already had the room? No. He'd stopped at the front desk. Slips of details surfaced like old receipts in my purse.

What was his name? I knew he'd told me. Ryan something? As far as Possibly Ryan knew, my name was Lola. Melissa and I argued about my using my fake name while inching through the line for the bathroom.

"How are you going to connect with the guy if he doesn't know who you are?"

"He's only looking for a party. A party doesn't require a name."

Melissa had pressed up to her tiptoes to shout into my ear. "That guy is smoking hot. And he's into you. You could do better than a one-night stand."

"I'm not going to have a one-night stand. We're just dancing."

The bathroom door had opened, and Melissa headed inside. "Whatever. Let's get more of those fruity shots. Those are really good."

MY stomach wrenched at the memory of the sweet, alcohol-laden mini glasses of hangover. As soon as I got back to Austin, I was doing a cleanse.

I fell into the back seat of the ordered car and willed myself not to throw up. I had a stellar rider score, and I intended to keep it that way.

CHAPTER 2

GRAHAM

*R*ather than stew over the skid marks Lola scorched into the hotel carpet, I called my best friend, Jonah, to check on his sorry ass.

Jonah's girlfriend was pregnant, and he wasn't sure the baby was his. Pretty sorry business if you asked me, but my friend was in love—crazy, turn-down-a-New-Year's-screw-with-a-hot-girl love.

Jonah had stormed out of the New Year's Eve party in a shitty mood, and I figured I could at least make sure the guy hadn't done something stupid—like drunk dial the woman or go all John Cusack in *Say Anything*.

We agreed to meet for a late lunch at a greasy diner near downtown. Maybe the fat would soak up the alcohol that left my mouth dry and my head with a low-pulsing pound.

Jonah was already seated in a bright red, vinyl booth, with water and coffee. Red, white, and grey tile covered nearly every surface of the restaurant, no doubt because it would be easy to scrub the place clean in the event they decided to do so.

The lingering smell of fried everything hung in the air, and my nose scrunched. "Nice pick."

"Look at this." Jonah pointed to the menu. "Hash browns covered in nacho cheese and bacon. That's New Year's Day food."

I slipped into the booth. "If you say so. How're you doing this morning?"

"Okay, actually."

His upbeat tone scared me. "Did you talk to Shannon?"

"Not yet. But I will. I want to work things out with her."

Forgiving a woman for cheating on me? And maybe getting pregnant with another man's baby? I couldn't do it. Ever. But my friend looked happy. Excited, even.

Telling him to snap out of it lingered on my tongue.

Jonah sipped his coffee. "Whatever you have to say. Save it. I don't need advice."

"If you're sure…do what you've got to do."

"Thank you."

"Look, it's your life. I hope it works out."

I knew when a cause was lost.

Jonah grinned. "Thanks, man."

The waitress headed over with another glass of water. "Let me figure out what I'm going to eat."

After we ordered our breakfasts of cholesterol and sodium, Jonah pressed me for the details of my evening. I recounted what I could remember with the tone of a kid who had eaten his favorite cookie but was mad he couldn't have another.

"All in all, it was a good evening, I guess. She was smokin' hot."

"Did you get *any* details?"

"I was trying to remember. I think she said her name was Lola."

Jonah laughed himself breathless. "Really? Lola?"

I shrugged. "That's what she said."

"Glad you had a good time with Lola." Jonah capped off his snide tone with air quotes around the name.

"That I did. Even if she was kind of a witch this morning. Jesus, she was hot." I pounded my fists lightly on the table.

"You mentioned that." His friend's words were as parched as my throat.

I took a long sip of ice water. "I wonder how she got her invite?"

Someone must know who she was. I could probably find her on social media. Pictures from the party were already filling up my newsfeeds.

"Who cares?"

"No one. I'm just curious. Maybe you're right. Maybe her name isn't Lola."

"Of course it isn't. No one's been named Lola since the 1920s. Was she eighty?" Jonah snickered.

"Screw you. I'm being the good guy. All supportive and shit, and you're busting my balls."

"Sounds like that already happened this morning. Did she take them with her in her purse?"

I nearly popped back that Jonah was one to talk, but didn't want to needle my friend. Jonah's situation was serious, but mine wasn't.

"I have to admit. I wouldn't mind getting another taste of that."

"Dude, it doesn't sound like she's interested in a repeat."

"You didn't hear her moaning all night."

Jonah faked a gagging reflex. "Thank God. I don't need images of you humping in my brain."

"You might learn something."

"Doubtful. You going to track her down or what?"

"Not necessarily. I may see if we have mutual friends online."

The faux casual high pitch in my own voice made me cringe—as did the smug, mocking look in Jonah's eyes.

I didn't necessarily care if I saw "Lola" again, but if I *could* track her down, I'd take another run at her. The night was fun. She was Maxim Hot 100 hot. And I knew I could make her wish she'd stayed for room-service breakfast and bloody Marys.

I sniffed again at the pungent odor of hot grease permeating the diner.

I already wished she had.

CHAPTER 3

ALEXA

"How ow was the party last night?" my cousin, Taryn, ladled black-eyed peas into my bowl and then Melissa's. We sat on bar stools at Taryn's kitchen counter.

I made it back to my hotel and changed clothes while my friend dragged herself out of bed and got ready. I refused to answer any of Melissa's questions so I wouldn't have to repeat the tale for Taryn. The less I talked about it, the better.

"Fun. What I remember of it. I started doing shots, which was a massive mistake. Slamming booze doesn't agree with me."

Melissa reached over and lifted a piece of cornbread out of the pan on the counter. "How many vodka sodas with lime can you drink?"

"It's the cleanest drink I can have. You get your zero-calorie hydration along with your booze. Ask for extra limes to get some vitamins. Sip slowly."

Taryn added collard greens to our peas. "You don't sound like you were sipping slowly last night."

"Those sugary drinks always do me in. This food will do me good. I need greens, too. Even if it's all swimming in pork fat."

"Pork fat is the signature part of the dish." Taryn topped each bowl with a square of bread and slid them toward her guests. "Other than the drinks, what else? Were there any single guys there?"

"And now we get back to the key point of the evening." Melissa rubbed her hands together, her ebony, shoulder-length bob swinging as she twisted excitedly in her seat. "You left the party with that guy, and I want details."

"You left with a guy?" Taryn screeched.

I picked up my fork and launched into the story. "I was dancing with this guy and doing shots. He had nice moves and a sexy smile. He smelled like bergamot. Really clean."

"Clean?"

"His smell. He was shorter than I am, but that might have been the heels. He had nice forearms."

Melissa slapped her forehead. "Forearms?"

"This is what I remember. I liked his forearms, and he had strong fingers. Then, it was midnight. Everyone was counting down, and he slipped his hand behind my neck and laid one on me."

I paused, remembering the kiss—not a simple New Year's peck. His lips were soft and strong. The kiss was gentle, but intense. And it went on and on. I cleared my throat and continued. "After *Auld Lang Syne*, another song came on, something kind of slow. And we danced."

"You were into him." Taryn jabbed her fork at me.

"He was hot. I'm not gonna lie. We danced, and then, it was getting later. He asked if I wanted to get a room. I said yes."

I shrugged. A tiny twist of a smile crept onto my face.

"What's his name? Who is he?"

"Ryan? I don't remember. And he said something about construction, I think. But he can't be a construction worker. Possibly Ryan's hands were well-kept."

"That's what you're calling him, huh?" Taryn laughed.

Melissa shook her head. "This morning, you could have gotten his number. Did you even ask? Maybe he would have taken you to breakfast."

"I didn't ask for his number, and he offered breakfast— even mentioned room service." I winced. "But I couldn't get out of there fast enough."

"Why?" Taryn probed.

"I may have woken up and told him that I wished he would disappear in a puff of smoke."

Melissa's cackle nearly knocked her off her stool. Taryn stared, mouth agape.

"How could you say that out loud?"

"I didn't mean to!"

"Was that before or after the breakfast invite?"

"Before."

Melissa howled. "Then you still could have gotten his number. Was the sex bad or something?"

"No. It wasn't."

Possibly Ryan had known what he was doing in the bedroom—how to touch me, how to kiss me. And he'd been so sure of himself, confident, but not cocky. If all sex were like sex with him, I might never leave the house.

Taryn tapped her index finger on the counter in front of my bowl. "You know, you could still find out who he was. Do you remember the room number? Call the hotel. Leave him a message."

"No. These moments pass for a reason."

"That's what you said about Mr. London. These moments pass because you make no attempt to hold onto them."

Over Thanksgiving, I ventured to England to visit a friend going through a difficult divorce. While trying to set Carrie up on a dating app, I'd found a match myself—a sexy, but intense, Brit named Adam Gadsby. We had a brief, memorable fling, and now he called me occasionally.

I indulged his flirtations, figuring they would go nowhere with the two of us on different continents. I put him off each time he pledged to visit. Adam kept wanting to jumpstart something serious, which nearly gave me a rash.

Hell, at least Possibly Ryan seemed pretty light-hearted about the whole thing.

"I'm not looking for that right now."

Taryn groaned. "Then when? Will you ever?"

"I don't know. If it happens, it happens."

My cousin was not one to wait around for what she wanted. She locked in. That's how she'd ended up with her husband, Jeff. They met. She liked him, so she started seeing him exclusively. Soon enough, she knew he was the one. Lock and load.

I assumed one day, I'd meet the guy who'd make me feel like settling down. At some point. In the future. Eventually.

Taryn continued to chastise me. "You have to know that's what you want because there's always going to be someone new."

"If he's the right guy, then the thought of someone new won't thrill me."

Melissa sighed. "But you have to open yourself up to the possibility. You have to give a guy a chance."

"What was I supposed to do?" I dropped my fork and waited. Taryn stepped in with an answer.

"Give the guy your number. Get his number. Go to breakfast. Make arrangements to see him when you come back up to Dallas. The list goes on for ways to take the next step."

I screwed my mouth sideways. Next step? *Meh.* The thought thrashed my stomach as much as lemon drop shots. I had the warm memories of Possibly Ryan and Mr. London, and that was enough.

CHAPTER 4

ALEXA

*W*ith my New Year's adventure behind me, I slid back into my committed relationship with work. I walked into my gym three weeks later early enough to get in a workout before heading to my office.

I attacked the rowing machine, the treadmill, and the shower. Then, I stopped at the front desk and greeted my receptionist, Holly Lawrence, with an endorphin-fueled smile.

"Let me know when the guy from Bass and Carmichael gets here."

Holly looked up from her computer screen and tucked a lock of bright, bottle-red hair behind her ear. "Ten a.m., right?"

"Yes. Some guy named Graham Ryan. He's one of the partners."

"I'm going to miss Michael. I can't believe he sold the building so quick. Did you even know it was for sale?"

"No. He didn't even warn any of us. Before Christmas, he sent all the tenants an email saying he'd sold out to this other real estate company. I just hope the new owners don't screw up our expansion. Michael assures me that the new company can handle anything, but already, they've ignored some electrical things we need."

Melissa and I partnered up for more than parties. Together, we were turning Starlight Fitness into Starlight Fitness & Spa—leasing and transforming the space next to my gym. Melissa, a massage therapist, would run the massage and aesthetician services while I managed the fitness and personal training business.

"You'd think a big developer like that would be able to handle something that basic."

The lack of response from our new landlord threaded my tone with exasperation. I hoped the ownership change wouldn't stall our plans for grand opening on July 1.

"Anyway, I'll be in my office waiting."

"I'll buzz you as soon as he gets here."

I strode past the rows of emptying cardio equipment. My customers arrived in predictable tides. The five a.m. crowd rolled out as the six a.m. clients flooded in. Now, at just past seven, the gym population dropped until the smaller wave of stay-at-home parents came in after dropping kids off at school.

I pushed open the door to my small office and put my gym bag on the credenza sitting between two narrow windows in the corners. Planted at my desk for the next couple hours, I reviewed the week's personnel schedule and other regular tasks, keeping an eye the clock.

By ten fifteen, I wondered if the guy would show. I rang Holly.

"Still a no show, Alexa. I swear, as soon as he gets here... Oh," Holly's voice dropped, "there's a guy coming in. Wow. He's hot. Gotta go."

I didn't care how hot the guy was. I prayed for competent and amenable.

Bubbles of laughter floated down the hall, and Holly strolled in with a man trailing behind her. I couldn't see him, but the receptionist stopped in the doorway and wiggled her eyebrows.

I jumped up and walked to the door, preparing my most congenial smile.

"This is Graham Ryan. The new landlord. Mr. Ryan, this is the owner, Alexa Stevens." Holly's tone was bright as she stepped aside.

Dear God. Possibly Ryan.

Flames of embarrassment licked at my face, but didn't melt my frozen smile. "Thanks for bringing him back, Holly. If you could get back to the front..."

The desk clerk backed away, leaving us to stare at each other.

My X-ray imagination saw "Mr. Ryan" as he was on New Year's Day—sensual cords of muscle and a saluting cock. My surging pulse beat in my ears and in my core.

I blinked away the vision of him naked and focused on his luxe-labelled, but unremarkable, blue oxford shirt and navy slacks.

Never mind the wavy chestnut hair, the gold-brown eyes, the strong cheekbones, and the square jaw. Never mind he looked as if he'd been drawn in a comic book. Never mind the slanted smile that had once hovered between my thighs.

"You found your way home. Good." Graham punctuated his words with a verbal jab.

My throat seized, and I forced a breath to speak. "Yes. I did."

I returned to my desk, but didn't sit down.

"I was a little worried."

"For two weeks?"

"Closer to three, and anyway, I wondered. Never thought I'd see you again. You live here in Austin, then?"

I nodded. "I guess you do, too?"

"I do. I was in Dallas just for New Year's."

"Same here. So, that explains that." I paused to take a long breath. "Look, if it's all the same to you, I'd like to keep things professional. We have business to discuss."

Graham flinched. I longed to sit down and start the meeting, but didn't want to crane my neck up at the broad-shouldered man who suddenly seemed too big for my office.

"You're dismissive."

"What?"

"You decided you were done with me on New Year's Day and just left. You've decided to ignore what happened and just declare that I will, too. What if I have feelings for you?"

"After one night?"

"You've never heard of love at first sight?"

"I've heard of it, but I think it's bullshit."

"Now, that's not language that keeps things professional."

The broad grin accompanying his quip straightened my spine. I leaned over, gripping the edge of my desk, before moderating an even, indisputable tone. "You are not in love with me, so don't play with me. We had an evening together, but that's over, and I would like to move on. Whatever you may think, I take my business seriously, and I'd like to discuss what I'll need from you."

Snide humor raised the pitch of his voice. "You need me."

I folded my arms. "As a landlord. I'm expanding Starlight Fitness, and we're in the middle of construction. Can't we behave like adults?"

His amber eyes widened, and he put up a surrendering hand. "Sure. Of course. I apologize. It's just a shock seeing you."

"Likewise. Now, feel free to have a seat. Do you want anything to drink? We have coffee, tea, and water in the office, or I can get you some fresh juice from next door. We have a good relationship with the smoothie place."

We sat down opposite one another, and Graham tapped his hands on my desk. "No, thanks. I just met with them, and they treated me to some fresh-pressed juice. I'm very hydrated. So, what do you need?"

"There are some changes to the structure that I worked out with my previous landlord. We had a separate written agreement, and it's not clear to me how the change in owner-ship is going to affect our timeline."

"All legal agreements that were made with the tenants have to be honored, so if there was construction promised and deadlines set, we'll follow through."

Graham waved his hand as if my concerns weren't an issue.

"You say that, but in the past two weeks, there was elec-trical work that was supposed to be done, and my contrac-tors are having trouble getting access to what they need in the building."

Graham pulled out his business card and slid it across the desk. "Send me an email with the specific issues, and I'll personally make sure you get what you need."

My shoulders unwound a little. "Thank you."

"Any other issues?"

His wide brown eyes bored into me, and my breath had to crawl out of my chest. "Not at the moment."

With our business wrapped up, I could get him out of my office. The anticipation of it made my knee shake.

"Good. I'm having these tenant meetings so we can introduce ourselves and put faces to names."

"Done. I have a face for the name. Graham Ryan."

I didn't know why I thought he'd said his name was Ryan. I must have misheard him. It *had* been loud at the party.

"And Alexa Stevens. Not Lola. That's what you said, right?"

"I don't know what made you think my name was Lola." I forced my lie, light and dismissive, through my tightened throat.

"Regardless, it's good to see you again. Maybe we can have dinner."

"I don't think so."

"Ah, keeping it professional."

"I think that's best."

"There are professional business dinners."

"Is that what you want? To get together and talk business?"

Graham's fixation on my face flipped my stomach. "Why don't you give me a tour of your facility?"

"Uh, sure."

CHAPTER 5

GRAHAM

I followed Alexa out of the employee area and into the gym itself.

My "Lola" was Alexa. Alexa Stevens. A tenant.

Small, small world.

The sway of her hips jerked my eyes to her ass like the gravitational pull of the sun, and being back in her orbit gave me a charge.

And judging from her reaction, she wasn't nearly as immune to me as she wanted to be. Shock wasn't the only thing widening her velvety eyes and making her jumpier than a frog on meth.

Alexa would pretend we were all business, but I knew better.

She walked with purpose—her back ramrod straight—and barely looked at me as she began our tour in a crisp tone.

I'd let her do her "business" thing. For now.

"The space isn't as large as many national chains, but we have top-notch cardio equipment."

She pointed out the two rows of machines—six treadmills, three ellipticals, and three exercise bikes. A rowing machine sat in one corner next to an area of cabled weight machines, a pull-up station, and free weights with benches.

"That's the area for strength training, obviously."

Every piece of equipment was spotless and top-flight. I probably paid double for the slick, meat-market gym where I had a membership, and it wasn't nearly so well appointed.

I had a feeling this was a direct reflection of the gym's owner. Alexa liked things in order, which surprised me.

The woman I met on New Year's Eve had seemed like a free spirit. This woman? Not so much. But that did explain who she became the minute the sun came up.

She led me through the weights area to peek in on a pilates class.

"We have clients who have been with us for years. They love our classes and our personal fitness and nutritional planning. We have a nutritionist who comes in once a month and does classes. Everything is tailored to each client. We've even trained some fitness competitors."

With her avoiding eye contact and turned toward the studio, I got another prime view of her backside. I hovered a step behind her—the air between us charged and magnetic.

Her curly, dark brown hair clustered in a fluffy, low ponytail, brushing between her shoulder blades. The softness of her electric blue sweater made my fingers tingle. I gripped my hands tight at my sides and followed her form down to her close-fitting, black knit pants.

She could be a fitness competitor herself.

Alexa whipped back around and caught me looking. She smoothed the hem of her pullover, and her mouth pinched.

I darted my gaze around the gym to keep from snickering in her face. That wouldn't help my pursuit. "What's included in your expansion?"

Her lips parted, pressed shut, then parted again. "We're putting in a dry sauna and a whirlpool with an extra shower area between the lobby for the spa and the gym. They'll connect via a hallway." Alexa gestured toward the wall. "The glass doors will be here."

"And the spa?"

"We'll have four massage rooms and two rooms for aestheticians. We toyed with adding a mani-pedi area, but decided against it. There is space in the back of the building to add something like that later. For now, we'll use the room as extra storage. I can take you over there if you like. It's not connected yet, so we have to go outside."

"After you."

Next door, the surging whine of power tools greeted us. The various rooms were framed, but not finished, and the floors were stark concrete.

"Careful where you step."

The space was nearly as large as the gym, and she pointed out where everything would go in the lobby and in each unfinished room.

"It's not much to look at right now. Our drywall can't go in until they finish the wiring and plumbing. That's the issue I mentioned earlier. There's something that has to connect in with the power to the building, and we can't get into the building's wiring closet. Or something. I'll have my contractor detail the problem and email you."

I could see how marketing the businesses together would

be a natural fit for her brand—whole-body wellness, catering to the clientele, and personal service.

"This is very ambitious." I couldn't keep the chirp of surprise out of my voice.

Alexa smirked. "Thank you?"

I rocked back on my heels. "I mean it as a compliment. I wouldn't have guessed...I don't know. Maybe I should shut up now."

"Let me guess. You wouldn't have thought I was a responsible adult."

Sarcasm added heft to her blunt indictment. Maybe for a moment on New Year's Eve, I'd thought she was an aimless party girl, but I suspected that she was more than that by the time the hotel door slammed shut.

"No, actually. I could tell you were a woman in control. Shoulders back. Chin up. Looking me straight in the eye."

As if taking direction from me, she straightened her back.

"I used to model. Posture was everything. So, any more questions about the expansion or the gym?"

I chuckled. "No. No more business questions. I have some questions about your modeling, but I need to get to my lunch appointment. Maybe another time."

She was clearly done with me, and I did have places to be.

Alexa walked me back outside, and I stopped on the driver's side of my Lexus SUV.

"Thank you for the tour. Let me know if you need anything."

"Will do."

She extended her hand for a shake, but I clasped it between my hands and held it there. I craved the reaction I could get from her.

She gave her hand a yank, and I dropped it.

"You said you have a lunch meeting."

"I did. I do." I opened the car door slid behind the wheel.

"Then, I'll see you around." She turned and rounded the front of my massive vehicle to head back to her gym.

I shouted after her. "Bye, Lola."

I laughed. She walked faster, and I couldn't stop myself from laughing again.

CHAPTER 6

GRAHAM

*B*efore I pulled away from Alexa's gym, I tapped her name into the search on my phone, bringing up her social media, her gym's website, and some old, sizzling modeling photos.

I cataloged the new information in my racing mind.

For three weeks, I'd asked every partygoer I knew if they remembered her. And poured through party pictures online. And ignored why I wanted to find her so badly.

Seeing her today answered the question.

Women loved me. They told me I was handsome and charming. Never had a woman walked out after a night with me content to never look back. Alexa's dismissal galled me.

A tantalizing memory of her smiling up at me at the New Year's Eve party stirred my lower regions. Those dimples of hers might be the only sweet thing about her.

I should let it go.

On my way to the northwest Austin steakhouse where I was meeting my partners, I called Jonah.

"Jonah Moran."

"I found her."

"What?"

"It's Graham. Remember the chick from New Year's?"

"The one you nailed? How?"

"Random. She doesn't live in Dallas. She lives here. I walk into a meeting today and boom. There she is. Alexa Stevens."

Jonah snorted. "I told you. No one is named Lola."

"Whatever. That's not the point. The point is that I've finally found her."

"Are you going out with her again?"

"Uh, not yet. She's a little uptight about dating her landlord. I can wear her down."

"Listen to you all excited. She must have cast quite the spell."

"No." My voice clipped. I was not bewitched by some random hookup.

"You sound *really* excited."

An ancient Toyota Tercel swerved in front of me, and I laid on the horn, braking and checking the next lane for escape. "Jesus. No wonder that guy has to duct tape his bumper on."

"Don't let this Alexa agitate you into an accident."

"That had nothing to do with her. It's just some shitty Austin driver." I released my tight grip on the wheel and relaxed into the leather seat.

Jonah's voice taunted me. "But you want to see her again."

"It's my quest, man."

"A quixotic revenge fuck?"

"I'm going to be way more successful than Don Quixote.

And it's not a revenge fuck. It's a cathartic walk down memory lane."

"Alexa Stevens. That name sounds vaguely familiar."

My friend's pondering tone made me white knuckle the steering wheel again. "Please tell me you don't know her and haven't slept with her, too."

Crossing swords with my friend would creep me out.

"I don't know. It's not like I have a spreadsheet with every lay I've ever had. Text me a picture. I'll let you know."

The image of Alexa tangled in the sheets with Jonah hit me like a sucker punch. Jonah and I had shared some wild times, but never a woman. Never. No. Alexa was mine. Okay, maybe not *mine*, but certainly not Jonah's.

"Forget it."

"No. Let's sort this out. Maybe we can compare notes."

"Fuck you."

Jonah's evil snicker faded. "Why do you care? I thought you were just going to bang her again and move on."

"That, I will do."

"Huh. Yeah."

"What?"

"Nothing. I wish you luck in fucking this girl out of your system. But, you know, you could always date her. You sounded like you had a really good time that night. Maybe if you got to know her, you might like her."

I cackled. "I'm not you, Jonah. I'm not looking for a white picket fence, and trust me, she's not any more interested than I am in anything long-term."

"Alright. If you say so. Still, text me a picture of her."

"Creep."

"No. I just want to lay eyes on this woman who's got you all twisted up. That's all."

"Google her. You can find her online. She was a model."

"You've already looked her up, then."

I could hear Jonah's smirk. Heat crept over my face, and I thanked God I was talking to him over the phone. "I was wondering how we were connected. How we ended up at the same party."

"Now who's the creep?"

"Shut up."

"Is this the only reason you called me?"

I tried to think of another topic on my agenda and failed. "Yeah."

Ripples of Jonah's laughter flowed through the phone line. "You are whipped, my friend."

After hanging up, Jonah's suggestion that I might like Alexa more than another handful of screws worth vexed me.

"Shit."

I flew past my exit and pounded my fist on the wheel.

I was not whipped. This was just a matter of pride. *Disappear in a puff of smoke, my ass.* We'd see who was begging whom to stay in the end.

~

ALEXA

I put the disconcerting reunion with Graham Ryan behind me and spoke with the contractor to get an overview of our electrical issue to send a note off to the new landlord. Then, I changed into my workout clothes and taught two pilates and yoga classes.

By seven o'clock, my stomach grumbled angrily, sending me next door to Viva Sandwiches & More before I drove home. Since I hated cooking, Toby and Sarah Larson's shop provided many of my meals—morning smoothies, lunchtime sandwiches, and soups and salads to go for dinner.

"Alexa!"

A rambunctious, dark-haired nine-year-old charged toward me and threw her arms around my waist.

"Hey, Poppy!"

The gap in Poppy Larson's grin made me smile.

"You lost a tooth."

"I did. I got five dollars for it."

"Boy, the Tooth Fairy is getting really generous these days."

"It wasn't the Tooth Fairy. It was my mom. You don't still believe in fairies and the Easter Bunny, do you?"

The little girl turned up her nose.

"Of course not. Everyone knows that only Santa Claus is real."

"Oh, my God. You can *not* be serious."

"I'm totally serious. Didn't Santa bring you some great gifts over the holiday?"

"Yeah," Poppy snorted. "Sure."

"Don't ruin the fun for her, Poppy." Toby emerged from the back of the restaurant with a cleaning rag and began wiping down the counter. "You need some dinner, Lex?"

"Yes, please." I perused the menu alight over Toby's head. "I'll take the low-carb chicken wrap with a side of snap peas and hummus."

"Coming right up." Toby reached for the low-carb tortilla wrap and filled it with a handful of mixed greens and diced grilled chicken.

"Sarah here?"

"No. She'll be back in a bit to take Poppy home. She had a meeting with the juvenile diabetes people. She's getting the details on how we need to structure the fundraiser so we can make sure the donations are tax deductible and all that other money stuff."

"Perfect. I have a ton of ideas of what we can do for the event."

I had volunteered to put on a fundraiser for the Juvenile Diabetes Research Foundation. The cause had become dear to my heart ever since Poppy was diagnosed a year ago.

Her parents managed her condition carefully, allowing her to be the exuberant, healthy child shimmying around one of the café tables in the front of the shop. The Foundation had been a huge help to Toby and Sarah, and they wanted to give back.

"Great. I may have found you some help for that."

"Really?"

"Yeah. This morning, the new landlord came by and saw the store display about the benefit. We got to talking, and he said he'd love to help any way he could. I'll bet he has a lot of connections."

"That's nice of him." My even tone gave no hint of my underlying irritation at Graham's potential involvement.

"I know. I really liked him. I was worried at first about dealing with the big management company, but I feel much better now. Have you met him?"

"Yes. He came to the gym right after his appointment with you."

I fiddled with my wallet, pretending to look for the debit card I already held between my fingers.

"What? You didn't like him? Sarah adored him. Maybe a little too much." Toby slipped into an imitation of his wife. "'He's much better looking than Michael.' I think she must have said that four or five times after he left."

"It's a business arrangement, so I can think of qualities more important than being hot."

Toby's eyebrows slid higher. "But you do think he's hot? He wasn't wearing a wedding ring. Not that I noticed that. Sarah did. I think she's plotting."

"What?"

"You know how she's always on the look out for guys to fix you up with."

I frowned. "I don't need her to play matchmaker for me and the landlord."

"Already on it, then?" An amused feminine voice drew my attention to the front door. Sarah hustled in, hoisting her large handbag higher on her shoulder.

"No. Not on it at all. You two don't need to start."

"Oh, come on. Why not?" Sarah asked.

"We're in business together."

"Oh, hardly. It's not like this is a company where you'll get canned for sexual harassment or something. And you've dated guys who've come into the gym before."

I cursed silently. True. But Graham? *Been there, done that.* Of course, I wouldn't tell Toby and Sarah. That would only encourage more foolishness.

"I appreciate the consideration, but I'll stick to finding my own dates."

Sarah erupted in laughter. "That's a polite way to tell us to go to H-E-double hockey sticks."

"That's Hell, Mom. I can spell hockey sticks." Poppy rolled her eyes wildly with one hand on her hip.

"With that, I think your order is ready." Toby chuckled.

"Great. Excuse me while I bolt." I plopped my card down on the counter.

"Should I give Graham your contact information for the fundraiser?" He passed me the bag of food and dangled the receipt in my face. I snatched it from Toby's fingers.

"I'm pretty sure he has it."

"It's nice of him to volunteer to help, though. Don't you think?" Sarah pressed on.

"It's important for him to establish good relationships with the tenants," I offered.

"I thought he was a nice guy. And he's much better looking than Michael."

"So you've mentioned," Toby piped in.

"Oh, you don't have anything to worry about." Sarah smiled at her husband and smacked her lips together for an air kiss before turning back to me as I began my retreat. "And *you* could do a lot worse."

I didn't feel compelled to respond to my friend's entreaty. Maybe I could do worse than Graham. A repeat performance might even be fun.

My gut quivered.

Excitement? A warning?

I couldn't tell.

I grabbed my dinner and waved goodbye.

CHAPTER 7

ALEXA

*R*olling over, restless, I threw off my covers. Darkness and quiet settled over my house and the entire neighborhood. I found the button on top of my alarm clock, tapping it twice to brighten the light. 2:16 a.m.

Dammit. The surge of irritation at being awake only made my situation more dire. Now wide awake, I lay staring at the ceiling for a few minutes before deciding I might as well get up and get something done.

I threw on my fleece-lined slippers and trudged over to my desk. With all the activities going on at the gym, I was going to have to pull back my class schedule or find new instructors.

I flipped open the computer and brought up the spreadsheet with a list of classes and newly proposed times. As I tapped away, a social messaging notification appeared at the top of my screen.

What are you doing up at this hour?

London Adam.

Me: Couldn't sleep so I gave up tossing and turning and decided to work.

Within a minute, my cell phone rang.

I paused before picking it up. "You didn't have to call to keep me company."

"I so very rarely have the opportunity to talk to you at a reasonable hour—or at least, reasonable for me. It's too bad you're not here. The weather in London has been unseasonably balmy."

"Maybe I'll make it back someday. Who knows? Now that her divorce is nearly final, Carrie is toying with the idea of moving back to the States."

"Surely you have other reasons to be visiting London besides Carrie."

"Of course. The London Eye. The Tate Modern. London is full of sights."

"Funny. It seems if I'm ever going to see you again I need to go ahead and make those plans to visit you in Texas."

"Sure." I tossed the word out like a distraction to facilitate an escape. "Now is a terrible time to visit, though. We have so much going on with the gym and opening the spa. Maybe you could come over the summer. Or the fall is nice. It's much less hot by September-October."

"Not nearly soon enough, but we'll see. Other than work, how are things? Every time I talk to you it's nothing except the gym and spa and what you've got going on business-wise. I hope you're leaving time to have some fun."

I thought back over the previous weeks to New Year's

and knew Adam didn't likely have that kind of fun in mind for me.

"I'm getting out of the office and the gym once in a while. No need to worry. What about you? Are you working on any new paintings?"

"I had my friend in again to sit for me. You saw my paintings of her when you were here."

I had indeed. His "friend" was a stunning, leggy woman who enjoyed being naked. They dated years ago and allegedly that was over, but the running around his apartment naked wasn't nearly over.

Whatever. It was none of my business. Maybe a dalliance with the mysterious naked woman would calm Adam's ardor.

"Fantastic. You have to send me some pictures."

"Will do. Well, I'll let you get back to your work and, hopefully, back to getting some sleep. I'll get back to you with my travel plans."

"Sure."

I said goodbye to Adam and turned back to my computer. He kept pressing for a visit, and I kept putting him off. Eventually, he had to get the hint.

The complications of an overseas relationship weren't in my future. Neither were the complications of a relationship with my landlord, as tempting as that was. Simplicity—that's what I wanted.

~

ADAM

I vacillated between surprising Alexa or giving her advanced notice before I arrived in Austin.

One week into the New Year, a client sparked my interest in an upcoming trip to Texas for the technology and media conference at South by Southwest. I aimed to make that happen.

Before I got back to my artistic work for the afternoon, I needed to make one more phone call.

"Sandra, hello. It's Adam."

"Adam, love, how are you? I was about to call you. I know you've been waiting for the final word on Texas. I can tell you for certain now that we're a go."

The energy of anticipation surged through me. "Fantastic."

"Your proposal was spot on, and you're right. It's best that you go personally to oversee the implementation. And, frankly, it will save me a trip. I love America, but with my husband and my kids, the idea of two or three months over the pond doesn't thrill me."

"No problem. That's why I'm here. Consider me an extension of your team."

"Contact my administrative assistant, and he'll make your travel arrangements. We already rented a corporate apartment downtown for the festival and afterward. You'll likely want a car, as well."

"I'll contact Rafael and book my flight."

I wrapped up the call with an ear-to-ear smile at having convinced her to extend my engagement with them for a few months. More time billing *and* more time with Alexa.

I scraped the back of my fingertips down my jawline. I had yet to shave or shower. Instead, my current work-in-progress called me to the canvas early that morning without any substantive break.

The conversation with Alexa replayed in my mind.

My old friend, Martina, sat for me again, as she always

did every time she passed through town. Usually, once she stripped naked with the grey light of London washing her body with shadows, we took a pass through my bed sheets as well.

Not this time. Since meeting Alexa, I'd been able to think of nothing else but the scent of her left on my pillow and the small movements of her body as she shifted and sighed while I sketched her.

She continued to tell me it wasn't a good time for me to visit, but knowing how skittish she was about starting a more permanent relationship, I put it down to her interminable cold feet. I'd warm them when I got there.

I pulled the vision of her in my mind and pushed it into the brush I held in my hand. This painting was a larger, nearly abstract version of the sketches I did of her when she visited in November.

Unfortunately, she insisted on taking them with her back to the States. Not working from my drawings left me dependent on memory. I knew the shape of her, but I had to reconfigure her form in my mind and my brush each time I conjured her. My neck stiffened.

Lowering the brush, I closed my eyes and drew in a slow, hefty breath before gradually forcing it out between my teeth. I opened my eyes.

Envisioning her on the canvas wasn't enough. I wanted to see her.

Maybe I should surprise her? No. It was better to let her know that my arrival was at least a possibility. Then, I would call her after I landed. Best not to give her time to push me off with another excuse.

When she saw me, I could pick up where I left off—breaking down the walls between her and the love I knew she wanted. I just had to use our chemistry and my powers of persuasion.

CHAPTER 8

GRAHAM

*A*lexa's gym was a twenty-minute drive from home. I passed two other major gym chains, including one where I already had a membership, on my way.

None of that mattered.

Her gym was where I'd been working out for the past couple of weeks—even though it meant getting up a half hour earlier.

I braced my hands on my knees and slid to a faux standing position on the leg press machine. My eyes fixed on the door to the studio.

Half an hour ago, a buzzing hive of about fifteen women followed Alexa into the wood-floored side room. The schedule at the front desk said she'd be teaching a hybrid pilates and yoga class for another fifteen minutes.

I lowered back into a pseudo-squat and then pressed up again. After my set, I moved over to the lateral pulldown machine to work my back. Eventually, I made my way around the room, getting a total body workout that left me more antsy than exhausted.

The door to the studio swung open. Women poured out in a gaggle of sweat and chatter. Above the din, I heard a familiar rolling laugh and abandoned the weight equipment, grabbing my towel, keys, and water bottle.

Alexa caught sight of me as I powered toward her. She didn't smile, but she didn't run. She stopped dead in her tracks by the water fountain and paused before refilling her stainless steel canteen.

"Do you have a membership here? I don't remember an application with your name on it coming across my desk."

"Well, do you keep track of every new member? Maybe you missed me."

"I don't think I would have missed you."

I lifted the corner of my mouth, chuckling. "You caught me."

"Did Holly let you in?" Alexa pursed her lips. Her eyes drifted to the front desk.

"Don't blame her. I told her you said it was okay for me to try things out."

"You could have asked, and I might have. Now, I have to throw you out." Alexa gave an exaggerated sigh and shook her head. "Hold on while I call the police. This is theft, you know."

I mentally rubbed my hands together and tried to look doe-eyed. "How about I buy a membership now? Would that clear my ledger?"

"You don't already belong to a gym?"

"That's not your concern. I'm willing to become a paying client."

"We reserve the right to refuse service." The slightest humor in her voice delighted me. My chest swelled.

"You're banning me?"

Alexa's nostrils flared, but a tiny smile flickered on her face. "Come to my office."

Alexa took off, and of course, I followed. When she got to her office, she turned, holding open the door and throwing it shut behind me.

"Why are you here?" She gestured for me to sit down, but stayed standing, leaning against the edge of her desk. If she thought I'd let her peer down at me, she had another thing coming.

I draped my towel on the back of the chair and widened my stance, just a few feet from my sparring partner. "I wanted to check things out." I gestured toward the gym with my water bottle and keys.

"We did that the other day."

"Okay. I wanted to see you again."

I shot her an unflinching, flirtatious smile, which she met with a daunting glare.

"Why?"

The way her lips bowed on the word supercharged my pulse.

"You seem the secure type. I'm sure you know why."

"I don't like your using my business to pry your way back into my pants." Exasperation rose in her tone and heightened the color in her cheeks.

The effects of pushing her buttons gave me a twisted thrill. I'd never enjoyed annoying another human being more.

"I didn't say anything about your pants. I only said that I wanted to see you again. To ask you out. My getting into your pants is on your mind, not mine."

She crossed her arms, stone-faced. I countered her demeanor by moving a step closer.

She rocked back on her hip, then stood and walked around to put the desk between us.

I pressed forward with my case. "You owe me a breakfast —or the meal of your choice. That would make it up to me for so rudely running out on New Year's Day."

"I thought we agreed not to discuss that."

"Nope. You said you didn't want to talk about it. I said nothing of the kind." I shook my finger at her, then dipped my chin to look up at her with a pleading expression. "One meal. Let's have dinner."

"Dinner, now?" She sighed. "You're my landlord."

"That's an excuse."

"I don't mix business and pleasure." Her gaze fled from mine, and I grinned.

"Never?" When Alexa didn't respond, I tried again. "Come on."

Her mouth twitched near a smile, wariness and amusement wrestling on her face. "Fine."

My prepared arguments died with her capitulation and tripped up my tongue.

"W-what are you doing tomorrow?"

"I have plans already."

"Hot date?"

"Yes, actually."

She raised one brow and stared, not blinking. I wasn't sure I believed her, but she'd given in, so I let it go. "Friday, then."

Alexa shook her head. "I'm meeting with Toby and Sarah after work to discuss plans for their charity event."

"Great. I told them I'd help. I'll pick you up."

"No. I'll be heading there straight from work. I'll meet you there."

I could feel her grasping for control and vowed to stay agreeable. "Perfect. Afterward, maybe we can grab a drink or something."

"Sure. Now, are you going to join the gym and get legal or not?"

"You're still going to take my money?" My hand flew to my chest in mock outrage.

"I'm a businesswoman."

She pulled out some papers from her filing cabinet and waved them at my chest. I took them, pinning the paperwork between my fingers and my water bottle.

"I'll fill them out today and drop them off when I come in tomorrow."

"Be sure to fill them out correctly so we can run your credit." A jovial display of teeth appeared and then quickly disappeared under her stern expression.

I cackled. "Yes, ma'am."

Her curt nod sent me strutting out of her office.

One date was a start, but I'd get more. I could feel her waffling. She was as curious about repeating our night—sober and with full awareness—as I was. Game on.

ALEXA

I dropped into my chair, forgetting how sweaty I was. As I shifted, my skin peeled off the leather seat.

A date with Graham? Why hadn't I just said yes?

He looked incredibly sexy standing there in his muscle T-shirt, wet and sticking to his pecs. Sweat darkened his hair to

bronze, and one curl looped down on one side of his forehead like Superman. Messy, sweaty, and with a seductive
smile—the vision had almost overwhelmed the part of me
that thought this might be a bad idea.

What also didn't make sense was why I'd made up the
part of having a date tomorrow. All I had to do was say no,
and instead, I lied and earned Graham's knowing smirk.

Maybe I could find something to do. The last thing I
wanted was for him to think I'd lied.

I clucked my tongue and stared at the ceiling.

I met a guy named Sam at Melissa's boyfriend's birthday
party in September, and in a "what the hell" moment, I gave
him my phone number. We went on one date, and for several
weeks, he had flirted with me. I laughed and put him off. He
cooled the flirting around the holidays.

Sam only wanted to get lucky, and I knew from the first
time I met him that he would never get to see me naked. But
a fun night out with another guy would keep me from
obsessing over Graham and ensure I wasn't a liar to boot. I
picked up my cell phone and sent a quick text to Sam.

Me: Meet up tomorrow for drinks? Logan's? 6:30?

I turned my phone over and over in my hand. What was I
doing? A minute later, my phone shook twice in rapid
succession. First, I got confirmation of my date with Sam,
and then, a message from Graham popped up.

Graham: Talked to Sarah. See you Friday. Can't wait to
see your beautiful nipples

Seriously? I tapped my phone, ready to tell Graham not to
bother, and it buzzed again.

Graham: DIMPLES!!! Voice recog needs work.

Eruptions of laughter bent me sideways. I accepted his excuse with some incredulity, but if it were an excuse and he was an asshole, I had to give it to him. He was at least a quick-thinking asshole.

CHAPTER 9

ALEXA

*A*s soon as Sam lanked toward me in front of Logan's the following night, I regretted having made the date. Not that he wasn't handsome. He was—even if he wasn't my type.

Pale with strawberry blond hair, I wondered how he survived the blazing suns of a Texas summer. He probably had to dip himself in a vat of sunscreen three times a day.

But he was tall—towering, probably, over any other woman who wasn't six feet tall herself. Six four? No, probably six five. He moved well for a guy his size. Maybe he'd played sports.

He perked up upon seeing me, silencing my mental critique.

"Hey, Alexa, you look gorgeous."

"Thanks, Sam."

He leaned forward to hug me hello, and I bobbed backward, keeping the embrace at arm's length.

"It looks pretty crowded in there. We should hurry and get a table."

We shuffled awkwardly, side-by-side, toward the door.

Once inside, the wave of noise washing over us offered me the opportunity to not speak. Sam gestured toward a booth in the corner, and I followed.

Texting him out of the blue was impulsive, but who knows? Maybe I would discover something to help me forget my landlord who seemed intent on worming his way into other areas of my life.

The waitress came over and took our drink orders. Not wanting to head straight for liquor, I skipped my typical vodka soda and asked for my favorite red wine instead. Sam requested a fancy lager after his first two choices weren't available on tap—much to his consternation.

"It's not like the beer's that obscure. It just won an award as Austin's best new India pale ale." Sam shook his head, brows knit together.

"I have to admit that I know nothing about the local brew scene. It sounds like you're pretty into it." I brightened my expression, encouraging Sam to continue.

"I toyed with the idea of doing a small batch brew. But, you know, the day job gets in the way. It's probably not going to happen."

"I guess I'm lucky that I get to do what I love. What do you do again?"

"I'm a radiology technician at the hospital. It's not that I don't like what I do, but I have a thousand ideas about other stuff I might like better. I see a lot of sickness and a lot of scared people. It gets depressing," he moaned.

"I can see that." I didn't know where to take the conversation once the thought of sick and scared people was in my head.

Sam sighed. "So…how was your holiday?"

"Good. I went to see my parents up in Oklahoma at Christmas, and I stopped in Dallas on the way back for New Year's. My cousin and her new husband live there."

"Oh! What'd you do for New Year's?"

More like…who did I do? "Melissa and I went to a party."

"She didn't spend New Year's with Kyle?"

"He drew the short straw at work and had to do the overnight shift, covering the ER. She met me in Dallas instead."

Kyle was an orthopedic surgeon. He hadn't been happy about having to ring in the New Year setting bones under fluorescent lights.

"Damn. Worst job ever."

"I guess. Kyle has always enjoyed his work."

"No." The vociferous syllable gave me a start. "It's awful. Covering the ER is the worst. Especially at night, and especially on holidays. People get drunk and get in horrible accidents. People get pissed off and shoot their relatives. It's humanity at its worst."

"Wow. Sounds pretty bad…but, anyway, that's what I did for New Year's Eve. I went to a party in Dallas."

I shifted in my seat to get a better view of the rest of the bar and, hopefully, the waitress' arrival with our drinks. I might need a glass of wine the size of a bathtub to get through this date.

"Sorry. Working at the hospital gets to you."

I flashed a smile like an emergency flare. "No. It's fine. I get it."

Sam grinned, reaching across the table and patting my hand, which stilled in response. "You had a good time?"

I shuffled my feet and banged my knee against the heavy wooden table leg, biting my lip to keep from cursing. I breathed through the pain and refocused on my date. "Yeah. It was a good time. What'd you do over the holiday?"

"It was pretty lame. I was in San Antonio with my mom, my stepdad, and my baby sister—half-sister. She's only fifteen, and Jesus, she's a bitch."

I flinched, and Sam reddened. "I mean…It's just, you know, she's a teenager, and so cranky and negative."

"I can see how that would get annoying. I'm going to run to the restroom. I want to wash my hands before we eat."

Jumping up, I grabbed my purse and skirted through the crowd to the back of the bar and through a swinging door adorned with a cowgirl doing a jig. I stepped around the two women in line and headed for the sink, waving my hand furiously in front of the automatic sensor to get the soap to dispense and the water to turn on.

For the first time in a long time, I took the time to sing the alphabet song in my head, scrubbing the germs and delivering myself a mental pep talk.

He wasn't so bad. A little negative, maybe. His job probably had him stressed out. He needed time to decompress. I lifted my head and stared into my own ginger-brown eyes. *Give him a chance.* I flicked my hands into the sink and reached for a paper towel, slowly drying my hands.

Reflexively, my hand dipped into my purse to check my phone messages.

Graham: How's the date? Does he stand a chance?

I stuffed the phone back in my bag and squared my shoulders. Hiding out in the bathroom was bad enough. I wouldn't start texting some other guy.

When I returned to the table, my beautiful glass of Pinot awaited me. I seized the stem. "I love this wine," I murmured, bringing it to my lips. I let the lightly tannic liquid rolled over my tongue for a moment, before swallowing. "God, that's good."

Sam gawked, and his pinkness intensified. "You like wine."

"I do. I've just started getting into it. I've been a cocktail girl for a long time."

"Wine has always seemed kind of pretentious to me. No offense. Beer is so everyday man. It's…democratic."

Damn, this guy had no clue. All he had to do was say anything else like, "What do you like about it so much?" or even, "I've never been into it, but everyone has their taste." But, no, liking wine made me a pretentious snob. I fought off the nearly inescapable urge to fake a phone call and flee toward some imaginary emergency.

"Huh. I've never been a beer drinker. We should eat."

I motioned to our waitress who bounded over.

"Y'all ready to order?"

"Give me a second." Sam flipped the menu over.

"I'll have the grilled chicken sandwich on a whole grain bun. No mayo. No cheese. And can I maybe get some slices of avocado on the side and the mixed green salad instead of fries? Dressing on the side."

"Got it." The waitress turned to Sam as I handed in my menu.

"Oh, well, I'll have the swiss mushroom burger. With fries."

The young woman surveyed us both, and I caught her smug smile as she walked away.

"I forgot. You work at a gym, right? You do the whole health thing." He flipped the back of his hand at me as he spoke.

"I try."

"Where does red wine fit in all that?" Sam snorted.

"One glass isn't going to hurt anything. Normally, I might have a vodka soda if I'm getting my drink on, but red wine with dinner is usually perfect."

"Red wine and chicken? I thought the wine snobs wouldn't dare."

I ground my teeth and huffed. "Those rules don't really matter. Drink what you want. What tastes good to you. That's what matters. It's very *democratic*."

"Whatever floats your boat. But you don't have to order a salad to impress me."

"Trust me. I'm not trying to impress you. I'm not even sure why you're being so...snide. Just because I ordered a salad?"

"Did you even ask if I was ready to order? You just get the waitress over here and start ordering. It's like you're the guy. *I'm* the guy." He thrust both thumbs toward his chest.

A chuckle escaped me, then I noticed the wash of fuchsia on Sam's cheeks. "You're not serious."

Sam planted both forearms on the table and leaned in. "I'm not the kind of guy to sit back and let a woman take over. What would you expect?"

I turned the corner into I-don't-give-a-fuck territory and picked up speed. "Someone who can handle a hungry woman ordering a meal without his balls shriveling."

"Jesus. I should have known you were one of those high-maintenance women. Avocado on the side. Dressing on the side. No cheese. No mayonnaise. Or is that just a black thing?"

"What?" I screeched.

"Th-the no mayonnaise thing." Sam's eyes got wider as his face grew pinker. Soon, he'd be purple.

"How about I just don't fucking like mayonnaise?"

Sam put up a hand as if to slow me down. "Whatever. I'm not trying to be racist. I honestly thought that was a thing, maybe."

I ignored his ramblings about black people and mayonnaise because I was done. I pulled two twenties out of my purse and threw them on the table.

"That should cover my sandwich and the wine."

"You're leaving? The food is still coming."

"Take mine. My treat. Have a nice night."

The staccato beat of my delivery smacked the fight—and the words—out of Sam. I heard nothing behind me as I stormed out of Logan's and down the two blocks to my car.

Sliding behind the steering wheel, I exhaled. How had that gone down the toilet so fast? I pressed the start button and put the car in gear. It didn't matter. Life was too short not to bail on nonsense.

Hell, if I was going to spend the evening arguing, I could have done that with Graham. The thought exploded in my mind, and I raced to put out the fire.

CHAPTER 10

GRAHAM

Alexa: Date was a bust. What are you up to?

The surprising text lit up my phone and my mood. Rather than communicate via messaging, I called her.

"Oh, hi. I didn't expect you to call me."

"You wanted to know what I was doing. I was sitting here licking my wounds because one of Austin's most stunning women put me off until this weekend."

In truth, Sierra was coming over later, when she finished slinging drinks at a whiskey bar downtown—slender, wicked Sierra with purple streaks in her jet hair and a matching pair of butterfly tattoos on her hip bones. I viewed them as placement markers for my thumbs.

I wondered if Sierra was her real name. Given the unnaturally large globes on her narrow-ribbed chest, I figured that at some point she'd been a stripper. She had the talent. She often showed up at my house and began peeling off her clothes as soon as I opened the door. Sierra would fuck me into a coma and be gone by morning, which is how I liked it. Most of the time. For some reason, Alexa's accommodation of that still irked me.

My evening entertainment wouldn't be over until extremely late—probably not until 2:30.

"You're full of flattery this evening. You must be lonely." Her low voice swayed toward me over the phone.

"Without you? Always. Where are you?"

"I just left Logan's. I was going to head home, but I'm all geared up to be out."

"Is your date still at Logan's?"

"I have no idea. I'm not going back there."

I pictured some poor schlub left slump-shouldered and pathetic to drown in tap beer as Alexa sashayed away. His loss. "Where do you live?"

"Why?"

"I thought I'd be a gentleman and meet you somewhere near your house."

"Oh. There's a wine bar just off Lamar before you get to Barton Springs. In a house."

"I know the one." Like a lot of places in that neighborhood, it was hipster heaven, but it was relatively chill and we'd be able to talk.

"I could be there in ten minutes."

"It may take me twenty, but I'll meet you there."

"Great."

Did she actually sound excited to see me? I would have to toast the schmo she dumped for the evening. Poor bastard or lucky bastard? The woman always gets to decide.

~

THE UNSUSPECTING HOUSE turned wine bar was tucked in an increasingly high-toned neighborhood near Zilker Park.

I surveyed the long room to the right of the front door and didn't see Alexa, so I walked straight back. The heels of my dress shoes thwacked hollowly on the wood floor.

A couple with blond dreadlocks sipped burgundy wine at the bar and assessed me as I entered—from the crisp French blue shirt, tucked into belted and expertly creased trousers, to the offending loafers. They exchanged smug snickers.

Slipping into the back room, I saw the spiraling curls of my first date for the evening at a small round table in the corner of the room, facing the door.

"I probably should have changed," I announced, dropping into the chair next to her.

"You do kind of look like a banker."

Alexa stretched her jean-clad legs, adjusting her flowing cotton top in a cornflower blue and sage green print.

"I had meetings, and it's not like I'm wearing a tie."

"In Austin, you look like a banker."

"Maybe I'll start working on my dreads."

Alexa scrunched her nose. "Confession? White people in dreadlocks freak me out. I don't know what's going on there."

"They're hip. White people can't be hip?"

"You're free to do whatever you want. This is America. *But*," she popped the word for effect, "it still freaks me out."

"Duly noted. Scratching dreadlocks off my list of style choices."

The waitress saw me and headed our direction.

I looked at Alexa's glass. "What are you drinking?"

"An Oregon Pinot Noir. It's delicious."

She pulled her glass to her lips and tipped the garnet liquid into her mouth. I loved the taste of wine or whiskey on a woman's lips. Boozy kisses warmed your insides.

She caught me staring and grinned around the rim of her glass.

I mulled the tasty mix of Pinot and Alexa. "It looks delicious."

"What can I get you?" The waitress squeaked her question in one of those high-pitched, little-girl voices.

I pointed to Alexa's drink. "I'll take what she's having."

"Good choice. Would you guys like to get a bottle? You can take it with you if you don't finish. We'll cork it up for you and bag it."

"Yes."

"That's okay."

Our conflicting answers muddled together.

"Bring the bottle." I turned to Alexa. "I'll take it if you don't want it."

"I'm just not going to drink that much. This is my second glass."

"Already?" I hoped Alexa didn't always slam her drinks.

"Not my second here. I had one on my shitty date. Or half of one. That's how bad it was. I left my alcohol."

"Ahh. That's a crime. I'm sorry." I tilted my head in feigned sympathy, watching Alexa's dimples flare.

"You're not in the least bit sorry."

"Hey, I'm trying to comfort you in your time of dating need."

The sweet smile she flashed me had me thinking some not-so-sweet thoughts. I cursed my luck for already having a late-night dance partner. Of course, Sierra was a sure thing. Nothing about Alexa was sure—even with the smile and the low seduction of her voice.

"I know. Thanks for meeting me out."

"Any time." I returned her smile and tapped the table. "How was your Christmas?"

We chatted about our families and the holidays until the waitress arrived and poured his wine. A few sips plus her light mood encouraged me to get some answers to some nagging questions.

"What were you doing in Dallas over New Year's?"

"I think you know what I was doing in Dallas over New Year's."

In the low light of the bar, her eyes looked sleepy and seductive. *Easy, man.* I couldn't take Alexa home tonight. Could I? The fantasy came and went. Sharing her—even with another woman—didn't appeal.

"I mean, why Dallas. Just up for the weekend or what? You had to run off on New Year's Day. Where'd you go?"

"My cousin lives there. I had plans with Melissa to meet at her place for lunch."

"Melissa is your business partner, right? Is that who you were with on New Year's?"

"Yeah. That's her. We had to get to Taryn's for lunch. Plus, weren't you and I kind of finished?"

Finished? "I wasn't. I think you noticed that. I wouldn't have minded...you know..." I chuckled. "Buying you breakfast."

The corner of her mouth flickered at the innuendo. "Or ordering room service. You mentioned that. I just...didn't want to extend something into the next day that I didn't figure would turn into anything. I thought you lived up there."

"I used to. I grew up there."

"You were visiting friends?"

"Yes." I sighed. "One of my school friends was going

through a tough situation. Lady related. Then, he got all depressed and bailed on me."

"Poor you."

"Exactly," I chuckled. "Poor me. Don't worry. He got it straightened out. They're getting married on Valentine's Day. He and his fiancée are expecting a baby."

Jonah had called me a week or so after New Year's. Betting on Shannon worked out for him. He was the baby daddy, and they were now living in bliss. Another one of my wing men off the market.

"I'm glad it worked out for him. And you get to put on a suit and buy a gravy boat."

"Nope. He's doing a small, family-only wedding."

"You're wiggling out of being a groomsman?"

"He asked if it bothered me that I don't get to be a best man. They don't have any attendants. Honestly, I don't think his wife-to-be has any family or many friends in the area."

"Odd."

I shrugged. "Whatever he wants. It's funny. We used to run the streets together, and now he's picking out curtains for the nursery. If you knew Jonah, you'd know how insane that is. I'd tell you stories, but we're sworn to secrecy on the juiciest ones."

At times, I didn't know what to make of my friend's sudden domestication. Jonah was so...happy. The security of finding the one turned him into a different guy. I enjoyed myself, but I had never been *that* happy.

Sometimes I wasn't sure I could be.

CHAPTER 11

ALEXA

*F*or a moment, I thought Graham might get sentimental. Only a flash, then the wickedness returned to his eyes.

"My cousin is pregnant," I said. "She's been overtaken with baby fever, but Taryn has always been that girl you knew was going to get married and be mommy. And her husband already had a daughter, so she's been in mommy mode for a while."

"Jonah's wife has a kid too."

"A ready-made family? Crazy, right?" I cringed as if I'd swallowed something foul.

"Totally."

"I mean. I'm pretty sure—" I broke off my thought and laughed.

"What?"

"Are we going to talk about marriage and kids?" I

grimaced again.

"No. What's your favorite sexual position?"

I palmed my face. Graham snapped his fingers. "New topic. You're welcome."

I raised my head. "There's room for conversation between those two topics."

Graham covered the base of the wine glass with his fingers and circled it on the table, swirling his wine.

"Okay. Here we go."

His strong, neatly trimmed fingers worked the glass, and I swallowed hard, hoping his next question didn't have anything to do with sexual positions.

"What's your type? Guys, I think, mostly don't have a type, but women tend to have a type of guy that they're looking for. You all are very specific."

"I don't know." I examined the raw wood beams of the ceiling above as I considered his theory. "I've dated different kinds of guys. They might all be tall because I'm tall. They tend to be athletic because I'm athletic. Other than that, I date all kinds of guys—personality-wise and career."

"So, eighty percent of the guys you've dated haven't all been doctors? I know a lot of women who really zero in. They want to date a lawyer or a guy who owns a boat...or a lawyer who owns a boat."

"It sounds like you've been dating gold-digging women. Doctors, lawyers, and boats? I mean, I will admit I don't want to have to pay guy's rent. But I'm also not looking for a guy to pay mine."

"An independent woman."

"So everyone says. What about you? If I went through a scrapbook of your past girlfriends, would eighty percent of them be blonde or all be kindergarten teachers?"

I wasn't sure I actually wanted the answer to that question. Spending time contemplating the other women in a man's life was not something I did.

"No kindergarten teachers, but I've dated all kinds of women—professional women, cocktail waitresses, women who own their own gym. All kinds."

Graham splayed his hands wide in front of him.

"So, I'm squarely in your demographic? Female and breathing."

He grinned and gave me a thumbs up. "Precisely. I'd be lying if I didn't say that I like beautiful women, but what man doesn't? Personality-wise? Mostly, it's just about chemistry. I know when I meet a woman if I'm going to see her again tomorrow. That's my only qualification."

A shred of my heart sank, but I scraped it up and forced some humor. "Dammit. Now I don't feel special and all."

"Oh, you're special. You're sexy, blunt, but sweet."

"Never in my life has anyone called me sweet." Ever. Sweet wasn't a goal of mine.

Graham stretched his legs under the table, knocking his foot against mine. That sensation spreading up my leg? No. Not sweet. He disagreed.

"What you're doing for Toby and Sarah is sweet."

"They're my friends. I don't know that I have enough wide-eyed optimism or a perky enough personality for sweet."

"If it counts for anything, I meant it as a compliment."

I raised my glass. "Compliment accepted. By the way, it's nice of you to help out with the benefit. You just met Toby and Sarah, and you didn't have to do it."

"They're good people, and I get asked to donate to a lot of causes that aren't as personal as this one."

"Well, it's real *sss-weet*." I put on my most affected

southern accent. Graham took a fake bow in his chair. "It's nice to know that you're not just some Casanova."

"Only on the weekends. And national holidays. But I could be talked out of that if I met the right woman. I'm open."

"But you have no idea who this 'right woman' is."

"I haven't found her yet, and your Mr. Right is out there somewhere, too."

An itch in my chest seemed to start on the inside. I scratched at it with no effect. "I try not to get wrapped up in the idea. It's like a cult. All the married people in the world won't rest until they are no single people whatsoever."

"I'll settle down eventually." The pitch of his voice fell off in defeat.

"You sound thrilled."

"We're both equally thrilled. Maybe it's fate." He took another sip of wine.

I knew better than to mistake his sardonic smile for a sincere one.

I took another fingernail to my sternum and shifted the conversation to cover the details of our early family lives. Graham spent his endlessly torturing his baby sister, leaving me glad I never had a brother.

"I can't believe you set her Barbies on fire."

"I was trying to play fireman. I didn't know the shoeboxes she was using for Barbie's house would be so flammable. Lesson learned. I've never heard my father yell as loudly as he did when he came home. They had to replace the floor in the den and the hallway. It was all one big piece of ruined carpet." Graham spread his arms wide. "Yeah, my parents were not amused."

Wistfulness clouded his eyes, then cleared. I could imagine a young and mischievous Graham getting into all sorts of trouble. Hell, I could imagine the older, roguish man in front of me getting into trouble.

"I missed out on siblings, but I'd visit relatives and hang out with my cousins in the summer. I was always well-behaved."

"Really? You have a streak of the troublemaker in you."

"My bad behavior didn't start until adulthood. Even now, I'm still about ninety percent good girl."

"See? Sweet. You'll have to tell me more about that ten percent." He rolled his wrist over and checked the time. "It'll have to be another time, though. I have an early start tomorrow."

Having to get up early was an excuse for a man sitting on the edge of your bed putting on his shoes. As the conversation flowed, Graham appeared to be more and more interested in me. I hadn't mistaken his flirtation.

I dug through my bag for a breath mint, put off analyzing the minutia of the man's behavior, then signaled the waitress to bring our bill.

"Don't worry about it. I got it."

"Oh, I'm not reaching for my wallet." I popped a Tic-Tac and hooked my purse on my arm. "I just want to go to the restroom before I leave, and I don't want to leave my purse."

Graham let out another laugh that drew the attention of the other patrons and handed the server his credit card. I stepped around the corner to the bathroom.

When I finished, Graham was no longer at the table. I found him waiting for me in the foyer. He held the door as I walked out and followed closely behind.

"I'll walk you to your car."

I nearly argued with him. My car was parked only half a block away. Instead, I pointed the way, and we walked. Our arms brushed with every step on the narrow sidewalk until we reached my vehicle.

"Here we are. You have safely delivered me to my destination, so you can go get your beauty sleep."

He turned and looked down the street. Something told me rest was not the reason for ending our date.

I opened the passenger side door and dropped my purse on the seat. When I turned back around, Graham pressed closer, taking my hands and bringing them up to his chest. He brushed a kiss across the back of each. Caught between his body in the frame of the car, I leaned back, away from him. He paused.

"I wanted to give you a kiss good night."

Since he still had hold of my hands, I gripped them and pulled him to me. I licked the edge of my bottom lip. "So do it."

He stepped off the curb and straddled my legs, forming contact with as much of his body as possible, then slipped his mouth over mine. Each nip at me set off shockwaves. He toyed with my lips, teasing them apart with his tongue. The slow, easy way he kissed me generated more heat than if he'd grabbed me.

I sighed into his mouth and flattened my palms on his chest with the hard muscle underneath warming my fingertips through the smooth cotton of his shirt.

Graham thrust his tongue once more across mine then pulled back. The tingle he infused in my flesh flickered from my lips to my knees.

"I know. Early morning tomorrow."

He rubbed his jawline with his fingertips, breathing heavily. "Yeah, early morning. I'll call you."

Despite the reluctance in his voice, he was down the

block before I could catch my breath. I definitely didn't believe him.

CHAPTER 12

GRAHAM

*R*egret twisted my stomach as I walked to my car. Wouldn't I much rather spend the evening bringing my New Year's Eve memories into the here and now? I enjoyed Sierra, but she didn't intoxicate me.

The sweet taste of Alexa clung to my lips, making me dizzy. I should have canceled my plans.

I looked back over my shoulder. She was already gone. I imagined I could hear the low rumble of her engine fading.

Too late.

By the time I made it home at one in the morning, I thought I'd pop my zipper. Sierra would be quickly disappointed.

I jogged upstairs to the master bathroom, undressed, and jumped in the shower. The water cascaded over my head, and I closed my eyes—remembering.

The feel of a curl around my finger. The way Alexa's

breath came in hot bursts when I kissed her. The scrape of her hands over my nipples through my starched shirt.

The plush ripeness of her mouth. *Yeah.* That cocktail-soaked New Year's kiss tugging on my lips while I unzipped her spangly dress and dragged it down her race car body. Her round ass filling my hands.

I imagined gripping her now. I squeezed my eyes shut and the image of her breasts bouncing against my cheek while we fucked flooded my mind. Good God. She'd been so tight.

Memory fragments skittered through my mind until I found release under the streaming water.

That would do it. Calm me down until I could have the real thing. Well, not the *real*, real thing. I'd sent *her* off in her BMW.

Was she as frustrated as I was? Or had been. I'd be fine once Sierra got here.

I dressed in a slouched, worn pair of jeans and an old, college T-shirt, and tried to relax in my game room, outfitted with a front projection TV and surround sound. I paged through my DVR while downing a beer, waiting for the sound of the bell.

Settling for another woman was shitty, but Sierra and I had a deal. No strings. Just satisfaction—or close enough to it for tonight.

Soon enough, the door chimed, and I let my consolation for the evening into the house.

We exchanged quick hellos as Sierra kicked off her heeled sandals and headed across the foyer and up the stairs to my bedroom. My legs moved on autopilot behind her.

I didn't bother to close the door. She was already peeling her tights down her slim, tanned legs. I watched as she lifted off her shirt.

"You better catch up. It's already late."

Her dark purple lipstick stretched into a smile as she reached behind her and unhooked her bra. Creamy, pale breasts bounced free with surgically perfected roundness. I slipped out of my clothes and reached for her, closing my eyes.

CHAPTER 13

ALEXA

*O*n Friday morning, Melissa and I hunkered in my office over Greek yogurt and fruit with plans to discuss the spa launch.

However, Mel wasn't interested in business. She narrowed one eye like a sniper and aimed her spoon at me.

"How was your date?"

I balked. It was barely worth discussing. "Sam? Miserable."

"Tell me." Melissa lowered the spoon and swirled her breakfast.

"It was bizarre. I wasn't thrilled to go out with him, but I figured it would be fun. I fought through his pooh-pooh personality, and then he snapped my head off for ordering dinner!"

"For the record, Kyle barely knows the guy. He got invited

to the birthday party by another co-worker. We disavow him."

"Good. He's a weirdo," I declared.

"Too bad. There goes your shot at having a Valentine."

"He wouldn't have been my Valentine anyway. We barely know each other. I can't think of anything more awkward than participating in the most romantic day of the year with someone you barely know."

"You seriously don't want someone to smooch on national holidays?"

"I've pretty much had the national holidays covered of late."

I strove to keep the single-lady defensiveness out of my tone. I had more fun in the last few months than some women got all year—married or not—I'd guess.

"Hooking up on New Year's doesn't count." Melissa banged her spoon in syllabic rhythm on the edge of her yogurt cup.

"Yes, but I hooked up on Thanksgiving and on New Year's. Come on. High five."

I raised my hand up and reached over the desk, waiting. Melissa half-heartedly smacked my hand. "But what about someone to snuggle with on Christmas morning? Kyle made me waffles and bacon. We sat around in our pajamas and watched stupid Hallmark movies. I loved it."

"There you go. Too many Hallmark movies. I had a good time Thanksgiving week, and as embarrassing as it is to run into Graham at work, the night was a good one."

"Then why run out of his hotel room?"

I sat back.

Seeing Graham again did remind me of how hot the sex had been—how hot he had been. And still was.

I gripped the arms of my office chair and shook off the

heat that suffused me again just thinking about him. Heat faded, and you couldn't take horniness seriously.

"I wasn't trying to turn one night into a relationship. I didn't know I'd see him again. I took it as a one-time, 'Happy New Year' kind of thing."

"Well, now, he's back. You can see if it could be more."

I laughed. "Everyone wants me tied down except me. Newsflash: I'm the only one who counts."

Melissa circled her finger in my face. "I'm getting you a Valentine."

"That's next weekend. I think it's too late."

"A Valentine isn't just for February. You can snag one any time of year."

"Are we going to talk about the electrical problems next door or keep beating the dead horse that is my love life?"

"I'm trying to give the horse the shock paddles, and you're not cooperating!"

Melissa held up her fists and pumped them forward. The motion knocked her backward a couple of feet in her rolling desk chair as she mimicked an ER move that Kyle may have implemented a time or two. I dissolved into laughter.

I chuckled. "Forget it, but speaking of Graham, he did send building maintenance over to talk to our contractors, and it looks like they were able to do whatever they needed to do in the wiring closet to start finishing the wiring and communications. They should be ready to drywall by the end of the week."

Melissa's eyes brightened. "Perfect. Your next boyfriend has been so helpful already."

"Shut up." I threw a paper clip at my partner, who ducked.

Melissa scooted to the edge of her seat. "Resistance is futile, my friend."

"I'll fight to the death for my freedom. You've got me feeling very Patrick Henry over here."

Melissa's smile dissolved. "Is that really how you see it? You think being in a relationship means giving up your independence?"

"I think that's how it ends up regardless of how I see it. I really don't want to talk about this. We have work to do."

I refused to discuss my stance on relationships with people who could only see hearts and rainbows—Taryn, Melissa, and then, there was my mother. Each took a different tack, but they all had the same message.

Why didn't I give up dating around and find myself a good man? As if good men dropped from the trees like acorns. And like dating around was so terrible.

I thought about London and New Year's, and I enjoyed all the experiences the world had to offer—particularly of the male variety. For every Sam, I found an Adam or a Graham. A unique new moment with a new man always kept me guessing and nearly always satisfied.

At least Taryn and Melissa understood that part of my life. My choices confused and concerned my mother. Brenda Stevens had married my father, Carlisle, when she was only nineteen. They had an unfathomable connection that had managed to last almost forty years despite the challenges like Dad's stressful life as a cop.

Many nights, when he had been out late on duty, Mom's shuffling down the hallway would wake me up.

"I'm just getting a glass of water."

She drank enough water to drown all those nights.

Luckily, Dad had always come home.

My parents' devotion was a beacon for the future, and they had poured all of their attention into me. No man had ever made me feel like that kind of love would be possible.

I scrolled through the list of men I dated. Most of them had been a good time. Some of them had been shit. Either way, I couldn't find my way to forming intense attachments to them. Most of them were fine with that.

I needed to get my mind and the conversation back on track. "We need to make an appointment with the decorator to finalize our paint choices. Do you have any other ideas?"

"Everything needs to be soothing. I'm thinking blues, light greens—peaceful, like the ocean. Sort of like a seaside spa."

"I can see that, or I can also see something that fits a little bit more with our environment. Still green but with neutrals. Woods, water, trees—still nature, but more local."

"You might be right."

Melissa pulled a folder from her bag and opened it on the desk. She spread some clippings from decorator and travel magazines with images of oceanside homes and out-of-the-way spas in exotic locales.

Melissa's voice turned dreamy. "I love the *feel* of them."

I could see why. Even in the 2-D images of magazine clippings, I could feel the sense of peace and centeredness that I also wanted for the end result. "These look great. We need to show all of this to the decorator. Do you think you might have time next Wednesday?"

"Maybe in the afternoon. Let me check my schedule and get back to you. I have a regular client who wanted to reschedule for that day."

"Okay. Just text me or call me." I flicked the corner of a clipping with a finger.

"Sounds good." Melissa made a note in her phone. "What *are* you going to do for Valentine's weekend?"

"Probably nothing. Netflix. Homemade cocktails. I could use some down time."

Melissa said nothing, but wrinkled her nose.

"I'm single. It's what you do when you're single."

"I didn't say anything."

"Uh, huh. And it speaks volumes."

"It's not as if you aren't interested in Graham. You said the sex was good. I don't get you."

"I know." *No one did.*

CHAPTER 14

GRAHAM

Sarah Larson texted me the fundraiser meeting wouldn't start at their house until eight, but not trusting Austin traffic, I left my west Austin home extra early and arrived south of town much sooner than anticipated.

With nearly twenty minutes to spare, I parked in front of Toby and Sarah's and sat in my car, going through work emails. I didn't know them well enough to show up early and knock on their door.

Ten minutes later, the roar and screech of a shining blue BMW zooming to a sudden stop behind me made my head jerk up. In the sliver of the rearview mirror bounced the wild curls of my favorite gym owner. She bounded out of the car, lugging a leather briefcase, and rushed past me.

I got out to follow.

"Alexa."

She stopped and whirled around. "Oh, I didn't see you."

"Hello to you, too."

"Sorry. I'm in my own head this afternoon. Gym stuff and spa stuff."

I hoped she wasn't having any delays with her construction. I'd been on top of my people to make sure we responded to whatever she needed—whatever any of the new tenants needed.

Charlie, the supervisor for Alexa's property, had assured me everything was moving smoothly.

"Let me know if you need anything. I'd be happy to take care of it."

"Oh, no, the electrical issue got straightened out. That's not a problem. It's not—we just have a lot going on."

I waved off the topic and hustled toward the house.

Whatever was on her mind, it didn't involve me.

"Well, I'm here to help. Your construction. The event. Whatever."

Alexa stopped and beckoned me to walk beside her. "It's nice of you to help with this. Have you met Poppy yet? She's adorable."

"I didn't get to meet her. She was at school, but I'm looking forward to it. I love seeing parents with their kids. It gives me hope that the next generation won't be a screwed up as sometimes I think they'll be."

Alexa tittered with laughter. "I know what you mean. Sort of. Although, I've seen some parents that let me know the next generation might be exactly as screwed up as I think they'll be."

"Ahh, a cynic."

"I'm a realist, not a cynic. At least most of the time."

A small smile curled the edges of Alexa's mouth. The glow of the porch light tipped the edges of her curls slightly golden.

She edged in front of me, mounting the steps to the front door. Her hips shimmied a little as she took each step, which made me smile. Life in the gym did her good.

She moved like an athlete, but had the grace of a dancer. Her body exuded power and elegance much like the sleek blue BMW she used to race around Austin. She'd probably accuse me of being sexist, comparing her to her sports car. But, hey, from a guy, that was a massive compliment.

The door to the house peeled open just a crack. A small, wide-eyed face peered at us through the gap. The girl blinked, then threw open the door.

"Hey! Mom, Alexa's here. And she brought a man. Are you her boyfriend?"

Boyfriend? That would drive Alexa crazy, which pleased me immensely. Before Alexa could answer the small child, I piped in.

"Nice to meet you. You must be Poppy. I'm Graham. Your parents have told me all sorts of wonderful things about you."

"They did? That's nice."

"Well, what else would they have to say, gorgeous?"

Alexa stepped into the foyer of the Larson's house and bent down to hug the Larson's daughter.

Toby and Sarah hustled toward the door.

"Hey, guys. So, Graham, you found the place okay, then?" Toby extended a hand to shake mine as we entered the foyer.

"I did. No problem."

"Poppy, Graham is going to help us plan your charity event."

"Oh, are you friends with Miss Alexa?"

"We know each other from work. That's also how I met your parents. They told me all about the benefit, and I decided that I definitely had to help."

Sarah beamed. "It's incredibly generous of you to donate your time."

"It's not a problem, and I plan on donating a bit more than that. Whatever is necessary."

"Daddy said I could have a disco ball."

Toby shook his head. "I said that I'd look into it, but that I couldn't promise. I don't even know where you would get such a thing."

Poppy's mouth twisted the side, and she sighed. "It would be so much fun. Sparkly and twirling around."

She threw her hands over her head and executed a spot-on disco spin. When she caught me looking at her, her plump cheeks reddened. She threw her arms around her father's waist and grinned into his slacks.

I had been to numerous parties with '70s themes. Somewhere in Austin, we could find what the little girl wanted. Who could tell her no? "I think I know where we can find a disco ball."

"You do?" Poppy pushed away from her father's hip, eyes bright.

I bent down to her eye level. "It shall be done, my lady."

Her face turned scarlet again. This time, from an eruption of giggles.

"Thank you."

Toby mussed Poppy's hair. "I'm going to take this one upstairs to get ready for bed, so we'll be out of your hair. I'll be back down once I get her tucked in."

"Good night, Poppy." Alexa blew her a kiss, which she returned.

The father-daughter pair thumped up the stairs. Once out of sight, Poppy's excited voice picked up steam. I couldn't make out the words, only the joy of anticipation. Even though we had just met, my commitment to making the benefit a success doubled. "She's wonderful."

"Thank you. We like her," Sarah replied with a grin. "Shall we?"

The rest of the adults walked to the back of the house and into the Larson's sunroom.

Alexa swung her purse to the floor next to the wicker loveseat and sat. Instead of sitting in the chair angled next to her, I squeezed into the space next to Alexa. I adjusted in the seat with my knees widened in a man-spread that demanded contact with Alexa's legs. She shifted away, and I only stretched my legs wider.

Sarah busied herself arranging a stack of papers on the coffee table, so she didn't react to Alexa's glare and pursed lips.

Alexa knocked my leg with her knee, and I stretched my arm along the back of the loveseat behind her head. She scooted forward and scowled again.

I turned to Alexa as she fidgeted. "You comfortable?"

"Perfectly."

"Great." Looking at her like the Cheshire Cat made her shoot me another chilly stare. I snagged one of her curls as it floated past my fingers. I twirled it on my index finger and let it go.

"Oh, I made coffee and all that. Be right back."

Sarah hurried back into the main part of the house. Alexa rotated toward me.

"Are you going to keep pestering me like a third-grade boy on the playground? If so, maybe we should send you upstairs for an early bedtime, too."

I detected a tick of amusement, so I didn't care that the other ninety-nine percent I heard was irritation. I leaned closer and dropped my voice.

"Maybe. I'm terribly immature. I wish you had actual pigtails. You'd be so cute."

Alexa stared for a moment, then burst into laughter. "I don't do pigtails."

"Too bad. I like having handles."

"Are always such a perv?" She closed the rapid-fire question with pursed lips.

"Wouldn't you like to know?"

Alexa gave me a shove, knocking me against the arm of the loveseat. Then, she straightened up when Sarah returned with refreshments on a wooden tray. I pulled my legs together and rested my palms on my knees.

I could behave—if I wanted to—but I didn't. And, I might never get her to admit it, but Alexa didn't want me to behave. The dance of jade in her eyes scintillated. I knew she could handle me. *Anytime she wants.*

CHAPTER 15

ALEXA

I said goodbye to the last client leaving pilates class on Saturday afternoon and glanced over at a now-familiar sight. Graham stepped off the pull-up machine, grabbed his things, and walked my way, angling his path to cross mine just past the elliptical machines.

"Are you about to get out of here?"

"I have a little bit more work to do but basically, yeah."

"You maybe want to grab a drink?"

I tugged at the ends of the towel draped around my neck. "I'm not up for that tonight. It's been a long week."

In addition to all of the business on my plate, Adam had texted to let me know that his plans to visit Austin were starting to come together.

My fling with Adam caught me off guard last November.

The intensity of our liaison sent me fleeing back to the continent, glad for the ocean between us. Adam came at you like a storm—thunderous, beautiful, and dangerous on the horizon.

Seeing Graham elicited much the same response as well as the same urge to grab my passport and flee the country. Soon, they might both be in Austin, filling up my dance card. The possibilities kept a perpetual quiver in my stomach.

I managed to smile through my mental conundrum, which Graham interpreted as encouragement.

"What better way to relieve stress than a night out with a friend."

"Is that what you are?"

"Of course. Come on." A siren song lifted his tone, melting my resistance.

My cheeks flushed with heat, and I took a sudden interest in a piece of lint on my yoga pants.

"I don't know. I want to avoid a...romantic dinner scenario. This whole thing..." I waved my hand over my head and dropped my voice. "We're not a Valentine's day couple."

Graham's eyes narrowed, more determined than angry. "Come on. It's dinner. Not Russian roulette." He tilted his head charmingly to the side, evaporating more of my resolve. "I'll keep my hands to myself."

Graham stuffed his hands in the pockets of his loose track pants as if to prove his point. His hair flopped across his forehead, framing his expectant brown eyes. How had I not noticed how impossibly long his lashes were? Keeping his hands to himself was looking like less of a selling point.

His lips parted into an easy smile. "Valentine's is tomorrow. Today is *not* Valentine's Day. We'll meet somewhere very unromantic like Tig's. The Irish Bar. They have trivia tonight. It usually gets started around eight thirty or nine. It'll be very un-Valentine's-like fun."

I wavered, and I swallowed my knee-jerk response. More

than friendship was on the table, and the thought of having one more night with him helped me find my "yes."

"Fine. Tig's it is. Besides, I have some other building issues I'd like your help on."

"Nope. We can talk about ourselves and get to know each other. Friendly, informative conversation. No work talk. That's a must, or I'm rescinding the invite. I'll promise to keep my hands to myself."

His playful tone drew a grin from me. "Okay. Friendly conversation." I extended my hand to shake on it. "We have a deal."

Graham clutched his hands to his chest, shrinking back. "Can I touch you? I don't want to violate the rules right out of the gate?"

I swatted at his hand and grabbed it, shaking it back and forth. "Keeping your hands to yourself was your suggestion. Not mine."

"Maybe we can add an addendum to the agreement then." He chased my elusive eyes with his own and caught me.

I smiled. "We'll see. Tig's. Eight o'clock? I need to run home and change."

"Me too. But text me your address. I'll swing by and pick you up—maybe a few minutes earlier. Seven forty-five?"

"I don't usually let men pick me up at my place when I barely know them."

He looked offended, and I felt a pang of guilt. As always, Graham managed to respond with humor.

"Afraid I'll tie you up and throw you in my trunk? I think I could have done that already."

"Charming."

"Let me be a gentleman and pick you up at your door. Flowers in my hand. Shoes spit shined."

"That's venturing close to romance, but fine. I'll text you my address."

I found Graham's cackle and grin oddly relaxing. *I must be getting used to him.* I escaped to my office, focusing on what I had to do before I went home to keep from contemplating that fact too much.

～

GRAHAM

Her small house sat at the end of a winding street near the wine bar in an up-and-coming neighborhood south of the lake. I checked my watch to make sure I was neither late, nor too early.

Satisfied with my promptness, I climbed out of my SUV and made my way to Alexa's door, which was painted a vibrant, sapphire blue. The color reminded me of her perky little sports car.

Next to the bell, I saw a small handwritten note.

Bell broken. Use the knocker.

So, I tapped the brass door fixture three times and waited. A clack of high-heeled shoes on tile came closer before the door peeled open.

Alexa had her hair pulled up in a high ponytail over her head. Rough tendrils fell beside her face, framing her high cheekbones and catlike brown eyes. Her makeup was soft, except for a deep red lipstick that reminded me of cherry candy. I resisted the desire to grab her and taste it.

"Hi. You look gorgeous."

"Thank you. I try."

"You've succeeded just about every time I've seen you." I

braced one hand on the doorjamb and leaned forward. "Are you ready to go?"

"Sure. I'll get my purse." She turned, and I caught the back view of her stunning outfit. The halter top of her jumpsuit left her back completely bare. The fabric dipped down into the curve just above her ass. My eyes trailed back up, and with her hair pulled up, I noticed for the first time that she had a dusting of tiny star tattoos on the back of her neck, stretching down just to the top of her spine.

"Tattoos? I never would've figured you for a tattoo girl."

"Yeah, well. That's kind of a funny, drunken story from college. To be honest, I don't quite remember. I went through kind of a hippie-dippy, crystal-gazing phase. The constellation seemed like a good idea."

"Which one is it?" I squinted to see if I could make out the pattern of stars as she bent over to scoop up her clutch purse off the couch.

"Taurus. It's my sign."

"You believe in that stuff?"

"And what if I do?"

"You don't believe in that." I spoke with sure finality. Her practical side wouldn't allow it.

"Not really. But when you're drunk and nineteen, it's a better idea than a bull's head. Although, in this town, I might be able to pass that off."

She started to face me, but I stopped her with a hand on her shoulder. "Hold on. Let me see."

She straightened and tipped her head forward. Fixated, I traced the line from one star to another with an index finger. "Interesting."

"Hands on me, already. You, sir, are terrible at keeping promises," she murmured at me with chin still dropped toward her chest.

I stopped my hand, but didn't remove it. "You make it hard."

"Do I?" She crooked her neck and looked at me sideways. The corner of her mouth curled like a beckoning finger.

"Difficult." My cheeks warmed along with the rest of me. "I'm beginning to think ten percent bad girl is an underestimate."

Alexa whipped around. "Maybe. What's the verdict? Thumbs-up or thumbs down on a tattooed woman?"

"I've never had a problem with a tattooed woman or any other type of woman to be honest with you. And I like surprises."

Alexa's tattoo surprised the hell out of me. What other markings on her body might I have missed? The next time I had a night with her, I'd have to be sober as a sentry.

I thought of trailing my fingers from her scalp down the sides of her perfectly sculpted face. I'd keep going to her neck, her shoulders, curving around her high rounded breasts and down her stomach. By the time my mind made its way around her hip to her tight, toned ass, I could barely remember why I was there in the first place.

"So, dinner...I went ahead and reserved a table at Tig's. Sometimes on trivia night, the tables fill up."

"Great. I hate waiting."

"I'll make a note of that."

I stepped out the door in front of her so she could close and lock it behind her. I stood close, and the scent of jasmine with an undernote of musk wafted toward me, seemingly emerging from the smattering of stars. His mouth hovered inches away from the smooth, decorated curve of her neck. Then, she took one step back and turned right into my chest.

Maybe he should've stepped backward, out of the line of

fire, but instead, I held steady, wrapping an arm around her waist and pulling her into my body.

She gave me more side-eye, and a trickle of laughter escaped her crimson-painted lips. "I know last time we were in this situation, I fell into bed with you. This time, you're actually going to have to buy me dinner."

Alexa spun out of my arms and left me standing on her front stoop. The swivel of her ass taunted me. *Not yet.*

I pressed the key fob in my pocket. The sharp chime of the door unlocking took my concentration away from her body and propelled me forward.

We had a reservation.

CHAPTER 16

ALEXA

"*I*s blue your favorite color?"

Graham and I sat in the center of the restaurant at a two-top table, surrounded by couples. It might not be Valentine's Day, but romance wafted through the room like throat-stinging perfume.

Each table had a single, long-stemmed red rose in the middle and flickering candlelight. I picked at my chicken Caesar salad—dressing on the side—distracted by all the nuzzling at other tables, so Graham's voice startled me. "It is. How did you know?"

"Your car. Your door. And when we got inside in different light, your jumpsuit—it's navy, not black like I thought. Plus, the pillows on your couch. All blue."

I widened my eyes, letting the unexpected pleasure from his insight bloom. "I've always liked blue. Baby blue, navy blue, sapphire, cerulean, all shades of blue. It's peaceful. What's your favorite color?"

"If I had to pick, I'd say green. Honestly, I don't know that I have an absolute favorite color."

"Doesn't everyone have a favorite color?"

"I like different colors for different things. I like a black car, but I like bright colors in my house. Yellow, orange, red."

"Where does green come into it?"

"I like nature. When you said peaceful, I thought green."

"Maybe you like camouflage. It sounds like your favorite color changes with your surroundings. I say peaceful, and you say green."

Graham dropped his fork on the edge of his plate and wiped his face with a napkin. "Some likes change with context."

All the times my friends accused me of commitment phobia, and now I was on a date with a guy who couldn't commit to a favorite color. The irony made me snicker.

Graham swallowed a bite of his Irish stew and shook his head. "Is that funny?"

"A little. You're so noncommittal."

He stared at me over the rim of his whiskey glass and took a swig. "Not always. When I see something that I want, I make sure it doesn't get away."

The boldness of Graham's pursuit left me feeling cornered—which I should hate. But the more he pressed, the more comfortable I got in that corner.

I stabbed a piece of grilled chicken, and Graham chuckled. "Something tells me you're much the same."

"Sounds about right."

"So, what do you want?"

As suggestive as the question could have sounded, I could tell Graham was sincere. "I want to help my clients transform

—their bodies, their health, their lives. I want to give them a new way to experience life."

"No, not in business. What do you want?"

The thought of giving him a personal answer made the hairs stand up on my neck. "That's a heavy question for first date."

"We could talk about the weather. Or the Super Bowl. Or politics."

"I don't know that politics is any better a topic." I waived Graham's suggestions off with the back of my hand. "What I want for myself is the same thing I want for my clients. That's why I'm drawn to helping them that way. New experiences, new opportunities to transform."

"You have a noble streak. That's another thing I wouldn't have expected of you."

A flare of anger burned in my throat. "You mean, like the tattoo? What is it exactly that you expect of me? Now I'm fascinated to know. Not tattoos. Not nobility." I looked down and swirled my red wine. Then, I met Graham's gaze head on. "I'm a scared to think what you thought of me when we met."

"I didn't have time to think much of anything. You were out the door too fast. I've never chased a woman off that quick. Usually, they're content to stick around."

I assessed the emotion in his words, unsure if it was plain hurt or hurt pride. "That really bothered you. My leaving. It shouldn't. It had nothing to do with you. I had somewhere to be."

"We spend an amazing night together, and you hightail it like you're being chased by a ghost. But you say it has nothing to do with me."

"Obviously not. If it were about you, I wouldn't be sitting here."

"Point taken. Would you like something else to drink? We may want to order doubles. Once trivia starts, the servers get pretty slammed."

I took Graham's advice and ordered a double vodka soda for after dinner. The waitress also delivered several sheets of paper and a pencil, so we could record our answers for the trivia contest. Graham began reading.

"We need a team name. Maybe, 'Mistaken Impressions.' My nod to letting my wounded male ego shape my impression of you."

I raised my half-empty glass in approval. "Clever, but you never told me what that impression was."

"I don't know how to say this without pissing you off."

"How about I grant you amnesty in advance for the stupid thing you're about to say?" I struggled to keep my tone light.

"Deal. I think. I thought you were a party girl."

"And a party girl is...?"

"Gets drunk. Only wants sex. And...probably not that serious a person."

I knew that's what he'd thought, but hearing him say it threatened to send rage crashing over the dam of my composure. I sat back and knotted my arms in front of my chest.

Graham leaned closer, eyes wide. "I'm trying to be honest. What else was I supposed to think? Seriously, I had no other information to go on except how fast you left and how good a time we had the night before."

My shoulder blades squeezed my spine straight, and I exhaled through my teeth. "I guess you're right." That wasn't *all* I was, but his assessment was probably true. My affirmation loosened the cords in Graham's neck. "You really thought I was going to bite your head off." I finished my wine and watched him sit back and adjust himself in his seat.

"I don't think most women would be too pleased about

what I had to say. A lot of them like to pretend they're more serious than they actually are."

"And a lot of men pretend that they don't like us that way, but in my experience, they do."

Graham shrugged. "It all depends on what you want out of the relationship. I don't mind getting serious, but it takes time. I dated a woman several months ago, and we'd only been out on two or three dates when she ambushed me at her apartment with a surprise dinner with her parents."

I blew the edge off my irritation with a laugh. "That's pretty gutsy. How did it go? Were her parents impressed with you?"

"I guess, but it was awful." Graham swiped a palm over his grin, sputtering his first words through manicured fingers. "Her mother kept winking at me and giving me sly thumbs up."

He punched the air enthusiastically with the gesture and a crazy smile. "When her parents left, I asked her why she did that to me. She didn't think it was a problem. 'After all, we're getting serious.' I disagreed, and that was all she wrote."

"Not all women are in a hurry to lock a man down." Argument turned up the pitch in my voice.

"I see. So, what do you want?"

"Good times. Interesting conversation."

His lids lowered over his darkening brown eyes. "Friendly conversation. Isn't that what we decided?"

"Yes."

"We can be friends, right? Regardless of what's gone on before."

"I can manage that. Does that mean this isn't a real date?"

"It's a date, but it's good that we're on the same page. You're getting me all liquored up, and I don't want you to take advantage of me."

"And what? Have my parents and my grandmother pop up from behind the bar? Maybe there's a minister back there too, and we can get hitched before dessert."

Graham shivered as if I'd doused him with ice water, then laughed and took tug of whiskey. "Are you getting dessert? You're eating so healthy. It makes me feel guilty."

"Order what you want. I am probably going to skip dessert since I'm drinking."

"There must be something someone could offer to tempt you out of your hard-core eating habits. What's your diet kryptonite?"

I squinted, grasping for my dietary weakness. "I like candy. I'm especially fond of Skittles. I also like M&Ms, Reese's Pieces—all the tiny candies that you can eat by the handful and blow your diet. I make sure to keep them out of the house, except for emergencies."

"So much discipline. It's impressive."

"It's practiced discipline. Back when I used to model, I couldn't afford to let my diet go to hell. Gain too much weight, and it's money out of my pocket. I've always been a very serious businesswoman—slash party girl." The mildness of my tone softened the dig.

"I have a weakness for almost everything. Potato chips, French fries, burgers, ice cream. I'll do candy. Snickers bars might be the world's most perfect food."

"I think quinoa might have something to say about that. Or kale or blueberries. Super foods, Graham. You've got to get your super foods."

"But Snickers satisfies."

"There are other, less fattening ways to satisfy."

His eyes and smile turned wicked. "Really? Tell me more."

"A nice hot, wet...bowl of oatmeal, for example. Fiber is very filling."

Graham's grin widened as he scrunched his brow and shook his head. "Disappointing."

Before I could respond, the screech of a microphone too close to a speaker turned everyone's attention to one end of the bar. A shaggy-haired guy in a flannel shirt fiddled with a switch on the mic, then tapped it. He introduced himself and launched into the rules for trivia.

"At the end of each round, we'll come by and collect your answer sheets, and if we miss you, go ahead and bring it up front. Tempting as it is, no phones. No cheating. Remember, it's all in good fun."

CHAPTER 17

GRAHAM

*O*ur fields of random knowledge complemented each other, yielding a perfect score through the first two rounds of trivia. What Alexa didn't know about the Beatles, I could answer instantly, and she surprised me again with her grasp of all things scientific. The periodic table, the solar system, and anatomy—Alexa handled all of the topics with ease.

"Do you go home at night and study science books?"

"I read things and watch science shows on TV." Alexa moved her empty cocktail glass to the edge of the table for the passing busboy, and her pencil rolled off the table. "Then, it's like any of these ridiculous questions. You've collected random factoids along the way, and half the battle is being able to pull them out of your ass when required. I have good ass-to-brain recall."

Of course, I knew that she had a good ass, but the brain

part still came as a surprise. I let the matter drop, though. Expressing continued shock that she wasn't some bimbo would only get me into trouble.

Her hair swung to one side as she bent down to pick up the pencil. My eyes went to the sweep of her neck, bringing to mind her stellar tattoo. At some point in the near future, I'd trace those stars with the tip of my tongue. Contemplating it made me rearrange myself in my seat. Thank God, I still had a napkin on my lap.

The waitress cruised by our table to drop off new answer sheets, and the emcee started round three with a few pop culture questions.

"Question four: What 2016 presidential candidate declared in a 1991 interview with *Esquire* magazine, 'You know, it doesn't really matter what the media write as long as you've got a young and beautiful piece of ass?'"

I didn't wait for discussion before writing down Donald Trump. Alexa flinched and wrinkled her nose.

"What an absolute pig." She stiffened and shot a cold look across the table. "I can't stand him, and I find his success totally depressing."

I racked my brain for a way to humorously change the topic. "Maybe instead of talking politics, we can debate religion. Where do you stand on the infallibility of the Pope?"

Alexa didn't smile, but her shoulders slackened. "I'm not Catholic, so you can probably do the math."

"No Catholic school?"

"Nope. I am a proud product of the Oklahoma City public school system."

"Too bad. I'm a fan of the outfits."

She threw a chip at my head. I deflected it, then picked it up and ate it.

"I went to private school, but not Catholic. Unfortunately,

my school was all male. We missed out on the cute, plaid skirts altogether."

"I suppose that's one good thing from single-sex education. The girls can worry about their education and not horny, slobbering boys in the hallway."

"I'll have you know that I never once slobbered." I tilted a smile at her and popped another chip in my mouth. Alexa shook her head.

"I'm not so sure. I think I may have seen a little spittle on New Year's morning."

"Maybe so." I leaned closer and grumbled in a low voice. "You gave me quite a lot to slobber over."

"You have a one-track mind."

"Not true. I'm perfectly capable of multitasking, but when I'm around you, one of those tasks is always going to be getting you back into my bed."

I steadied my eyes on her. I wasn't sure how the conversation had taken this turn, but once it had, I was all in. If anyone would appreciate the direct approach, it would be Alexa.

"You're ruining the illusion that this is just a friendly date."

"There are varying degrees of friendly. Tell me you wouldn't enjoy turning up the heat. You don't normally wear a backless jumpsuit for dinner with friends, do you?"

"I might."

Her brow and her mouth took prim angles. I wasn't going to let her get away with pretending like she didn't want me as much as I wanted her.

"Bullshit. You wanted to look sexy for me. Well done, by the way."

Under my challenging gaze, a slight flush creeped up her neck and settled in her cheeks. I reached across the table and ran my fingers over her wrist. Her eyes widened, but she didn't look away.

"Did you hear the last question?" she asked, her voice wavering.

I took hold of her hand and circled my thumb in her palm. "No. I've suddenly lost interest in trivia."

"I think it was something about the Rolling Stones. I thought you might know the answer."

"We're really going to sit here and finish trivia?"

"Yep." She curled her fingers around my thumb, locking my hand to hers.

"That's a bummer. I thought I was making progress."

"Toward?" Her voice trailed upward as she squeezed my finger harder.

"You. Me. Getting out of here. I'd love to show you my place."

She opened her hand and pulled it back. "I bet you would. Not tonight."

"I think you're afraid you might like me more than you want to admit."

"Huh. I like you, and that's why I won't go home and sleep with you?"

"Very contrarian, but yes."

She tapped her pencil on the edge of the table and flipped the answer sheet over and back. "The logic of that is so flawed I can't even begin to address it."

Alexa turned toward the front of the room, focusing on the man delivering the questions, but I didn't let it go.

"You're content to leave behind a trail of smoke puffs?"

I shouldn't keep challenging her, but something inside me kept charging forward like Napoleon.

Alexa flipped to face me. "I didn't mean to say that out loud."

"But you did. And you thought it, so what does it matter?"

"I would think a guy who rejects marriage-minded women like a virus would be okay with that."

"I don't mind a woman who wants to get married. I think it takes time to see if that's where a relationship is headed. That's all. I'm open to wherever things lead."

"I'm not closed off to the possibilities, despite what you might think."

My jaw tightened. Did she even know she was lying? We could be halfway to my place by now and on our way to finding out if we were as deeply compatible as I suspected.

Instead, she sat looking perturbed, clutching her pencil like it was a wand she wanted to wave and make me disappear.

A pang of frustrated regret wound through me.

"It's too bad."

"What?"

"You can be so free and easy with yourself—except when it comes to how you feel."

"Free and easy?" Her voice popped like a guitar string on a bad note.

"You know what I mean. I'm just saying—"

"I get what you're saying, and I think we should change the subject."

"I didn't mean to imply—"

She waved her hand at me dismissively. "Forget it. Let's focus on the game. I think we still have a shot at the five hundred bucks."

I had underestimated her competitive streak. The five hundred bucks didn't happen, but we came in second and split two hundred and fifty. After collecting our prize money, she blazed her way outside and left me scurrying behind her to catch up.

"Alexa. I honestly didn't mean anything by what I said."

She turned and tilted her head, eyes narrow. "I should hope not. You and I are two sides of the same coin, and you wouldn't want to be a hypocrite."

Her flash of temper raised the hairs on my arms. "No. I wouldn't."

I stepped close, practically standing in the same space. She didn't retreat.

"Is that an apology?"

I took her breathy question as an invitation. "More or less."

She began to lick her bottom lip, so I bent my head and captured her tongue. Her softness instantly made me hard.

I plunged through her parted lips and wrapped my arms around her, gripping her ass. Through the drapey fabric, I felt her thong—thin straps running over her hips and disappearing. I snapped one side.

She punched my chest and broke out of my arms. "How old are you?"

I laughed and shoved my hands in my pockets, straining and relaxing to release the energy wound in my shoulders.

"I couldn't help myself."

The rise and fall of her chest steadied. "Can you at least look me in the eye while you try to defend giving me a wedgie?"

I stared straight at her face. "You gave yourself a wedgie. Isn't that what thongs do?"

"I can't do this with you. You...You're like a child."

"Oh, come on. We're having fun." The pitch in my voice turned up an octave.

She gripped her handbag, spun, and stalked off.

I shouted after her. "I drove. How are you getting home?"

"I'm a big girl, Graham."

She didn't turn around, and I took a few steps to follow. "But…Wait." She kept walking. *Fuck it.* She *was* a big girl.

I watched her flounce away, knowing I hadn't played my hand well. But seeing her display of passion, even passionate displeasure, kept my quest alive.

CHAPTER 18

ALEXA

*A*s if having two shitty dates in a row weren't enough, I checked my voice messages on my way out the door on Monday and got another not-very-welcome surprise.

"Alexa, hello."

The soft, warm tones of Adam's British accent made my stomach tighten.

"It's Adam. I know we haven't connected on a time for me to visit, but as it turns out, I'll be coming to the States for work in March. To Austin, no less, for the South by Southwest conference. I'm working with a client presenting there, and then I'll be staying around in Austin for a couple of months for work. I absolutely have to see you while I'm in town. I won't take no for an answer. Ring me back. Talk to you soon."

Oh, hell. Two months? Or would it be longer?

I told him we might reconnect. I intended that maybe we might, but in the end, I didn't have time for long-distance relationship with a guy six time zones away.

Now, soon to be zero.

Dread assaulted me. I couldn't stop him from coming, but I could be clear that I wasn't interested in starting up anything serious—if that's what he had in mind.

I cataloged the ways to have that conversation on my way to work, stopping at the sandwich shop for a yogurt and some coffee—although my agitation had me plenty amped.

I stormed into my office and saw Melissa's shiny black hair bent over her breakfast in front of the desk. We had an early morning meeting.

"Oh, my God! You'll never guess in a thousand years who called me last night."

My huff made Melissa pop her head up. "Graham?"

I fell into my office chair and took the lid off my coffee to blow on it before taking a sip. "No. *He* has no reason to be calling me at night. Adam. From London. He left me a message saying he could be here for South by Southwest."

"South by? What is it he does for living again?"

"He works in technology. Some kind of consulting. It *is* an international conference. That's not necessarily strange. I just don't know what to do with him running around town. And he's demanding to see me and everything…"

"Demanding?"

I sipped the coffee slowly, unsure if it might still be too hot. "It's not so much like that. He asked to see me, and he knows how I am. He said he wouldn't take no for an answer. He knows he has to push me."

"Maybe love is in the air. Commitment might be in the water." Melissa beamed at me and circled her hand dramatically in my face.

"What's up with you?"

"I was wondering if you'd notice. I have news of my own."

"What?"

"Oh, my God, Alexa! Look at my hand!"

I focused on the back of the hand steadied at eye level, spotting the gleaming addition. "Holy shit! You got engaged!"

"Yes. Kyle proposed last night."

I jumped out of my office chair and ran around the desk, throwing my arms around Melissa's shoulders. Tears glossed her eyes.

"Sorry. I'm still getting emotional every time I talk about it. He took me to Chez Nous for dinner and proposed right before dessert. Kyle got down on one knee and read me a poem that he wrote. He was so sweet!"

Melissa's voice broke, and she dabbed at her eyes with her napkin. I handed her another.

"I'm really happy for you guys. I could tell things were heading in this direction, and honestly, I'm so happy for you."

"Thanks, Lex. I know all this romantic stuff gives you the heebie-jeebies."

Normally, Melissa might be right, but I loved seeing other people happy. Melissa was such a romantic, and it was nice that Kyle delivered the goods with the proposal. "No, it's great. Have you told your parents?"

"I did. I called them after we got home. I thought my mother was going to faint. Once I hit thirty unmarried, she got nervous. In my family, the women marry young. Thirty-six ain't exactly young."

I frowned. We were nearly the same age. "It's not *that* old."

"Tell that to my mom. Over Christmas, she handed me an article about how hard it is to get pregnant after thirty-five. Hint, hint. If by hint, you mean a donkey kick to the chin.

She was probably crossing herself and lighting candles at the church every day."

My own mother was barely any better. Links to articles about the difficulties of pregnancy or tips about how to get a man passed through my email box on a regular basis. I had gone from chastising her for sending fear-mongering babble to simply clicking delete whenever my eyes passed over one.

I still didn't know if I wanted to have children, and in the back of my mind, I knew, fairly soon, it might not be up to me.

"Congratulations. Now you can get her off your back, and you get a great husband, too. Kyle is wonderful. You're lucky."

"I know. Hey, I've kissed enough frogs, and it's time for my prince. You too, by the way."

"They haven't all been frogs. They just haven't all been princes either. Have you set a date?"

"I wanted a summer wedding, but we don't have time this year. And I don't want to wait until next year, so I'm talking myself into fall or winter. A wedding at Christmas would give my family from Mexico more time off to come up for the wedding."

"Your bridesmaids can wear Santa's helper outfits."

I'd look cute in a red velvet mini. Melissa tipped back in the chair and roared.

"Oh, no. I have to do this traditional all the way. My mother will have my head. And Kyle's head. And the heads of anyone within a hundred-mile radius." She shot forward and pointed at me. "I'm counting on you to be one of my bridesmaids. I'll need someone to keep us all from getting too serious. Plus, you're the woman to plan one hell of a bachelorette party."

"I am that woman. You can count on me."

Melissa detailed her preliminary wedding plans. I hadn't seen her this bright and happy in a long time—maybe ever. Love and good news agreed with Melissa, and it felt a bit contagious. My partner's energy began to sink in as we settled down to go through our construction expenses.

Excitement about our new venture fluttered in my chest. "This could work."

Melissa snickered. "Don't sound so surprised. We're two women who know what we're doing."

"I know. It's still astounding when it starts to all come together. It's like, 'Oh, my, God. We're really doing this.'"

"Oh," Melissa looked up from shuffling through her papers. "The construction supervisor stopped me on my way in, he said we need to get the management company's okay to repaint the exterior when we're done."

"I'll take care of that today. Shouldn't be a problem."

"Of course not. You can get your boyfriend to handle it."

"Do *not* start that again."

I scribbled a note to call Charlie Kaiser, who worked for Graham, avoiding Melissa's eyes, which were bright with scheming zeal.

"But I love the look you get on your face every time I bring him up. Annoyed. Haughty. A tiny smile."

I put on my grimmest visage. "I'm not smiling."

"You could be. I don't know why you're fighting this."

With a sigh, I launched into the story. "The Adam situation wasn't the only news over the weekend. Graham and I met for dinner on Saturday."

"For Valentine's Day?" Melissa's tone arched with intrigued surprise.

"No. Just for a…date. It was a date, but it had nothing to do with Valentine's. We're hardly sweethearts."

"Did it not go well?"

"It did, at first, but we ended up in a fight, and then he basically called me a slut."

Melissa squinted, dubious. "What exactly did he say?"

"He said I give myself away free and easy. Except for my feelings."

"Okay. That's a little rude, I guess."

"You guess?"

"Look, Lex, if the shoe fits..." Melissa shrugged. "He was stating a fact. A fact that I've heard you say about yourself a million times."

I glared.

"You have! Don't get mad at me!"

"He's one to talk."

"Then, you're perfect for each other." Amusement tinged Melissa's quick retort.

"You really don't think I have a right to be upset?"

"Upset, yes. Terminally pissed off? No. Tell him that you didn't appreciate it. Have a conversation. He'll probably apologize, and then you can move on. No guy is going to be perfect all the time. They screw up." She tossed her hands up. "All the time, they screw up."

"That, I know."

Melissa gathered her papers and shoved them into her vegan leather satchel and grinned. "Do what you want, but my wedding will be a lot more fun if you bring a hot date."

"Why bring a date when I can meet a hot guy at the wedding?"

"Like who? You've met all of Kyle's friends and had no interest in any of them. Most of his relatives are female. And you know all of my friends. It'll be slim pickings."

"I'm sure one of you has a hot cousin buried somewhere."

"Or bring Adam. From the picture you showed me, he

was incredibly handsome and looked incredibly into you. I can't wait to meet him."

"I thought you were all about pushing me toward Graham."

"I'm pushing you toward happiness. You like Graham."

I met Melissa's suggestion with the denial of an interrogated murder suspect in my eyes. Melissa wasn't having it.

"You do. And you seemed to like Adam, too. I don't know which guy is right for you. Find out! See where it's going—either one. Pick one."

"What if the answer is neither?"

Melissa's glance pooh-poohed that idea. "Then, you'll be flying solo at my wedding. Sad, sad. You're too gorgeous to be dateless."

"Jesus." I snorted, getting up to toss my empty breakfast container in the trash.

"We need to get next door to meet with the decorator. Try to at least consider the idea that you could have something real with one of these guys."

I harrumphed and grumbled, which made Melissa curse in Spanish.

"Only you could have two hot, successful men after you and find a reason to be dissatisfied."

I chose not to respond. The conversation annoyed and fatigued me. I didn't see why I had to pick door number one or door number two. Sometimes on *Let's Make a Deal*, you're better off going with none of the above—before you end up with a jackass.

CHAPTER 19

ALEXA

I avoided Graham's calls and texts all week, but I couldn't duck him forever.

Graham and I had a meeting on Friday evening to check out a venue recommendation from Taryn for the fundraiser. The event coordinator walked us around the property before leaving to take a call.

I stood on the edge of the ballroom, mesmerized by the beautiful expanse of lawn and the glint of the lake beyond it. I made a note to mention the place to Melissa.

"This would be a great place to have a wedding. You have the ceremony outside, and then move inside for the reception. Or maybe set up tents and keep everything outside."

"Are you planning a wedding?" Shock took Graham's voice up nearly an octave.

I ran my tongue along the top row of my teeth and

pinched my mouth shut to keep from saying something I would regret. "Melissa got engaged to her boyfriend, Kyle."

"Oh, tell her I said congratulations. That's great."

"I'm sure she'll appreciate that. I'm thrilled for her."

Graham snickered. "I figured you might be in mourning. Your friend becomes one of the fallen. I know what that's like."

"You know, I'm not nearly as against commitment as you think that I am. I'm happy when the people who want that get it. Hell, I even got engaged once."

"Really? So what happened there? If you don't mind my asking." Almost immediately, Graham shook his head. "Forget it. It's none of my business."

"No, it's fine. I thought I wanted to get married, and I thought I knew who I was marrying. It turned out I was wrong on both counts. It wasn't the right time or the right guy."

"That happens."

"Have you ever even been close to getting married?"

"I've never been engaged—not even close. I guess I thought about it with my college girlfriend. You know how it is when you get close to graduation and all your friends are starting to propose and your girlfriend's looking at you? I considered it, but I was too young."

"She was okay with that?"

"Nooo, she wasn't." Graham drew out each word. "We got in this huge fight. Half her friends got engaged, and she expected me to come through with the ring. I told her why hurry, we're only twenty-two. She didn't see it that way."

His jaw flexed, and I waited for him to work his way through a pensive pause. "She got married a year later to the father of one of her sorority sisters. He was maybe forty-seven or forty-eight. Old. Or it seemed so at the time."

"That's still pretty old be dating a twenty-two-year-old. Plus, one of your daughter's friends? That's gross."

Graham tossed out an arid laugh. "She really wanted to get married. And she got what she wanted. Plus, back then, I couldn't have given her a Porsche for wedding gift."

"No one ever dates an old guy who's poor. Your wealth better climb with your age if you want a pretty young woman on your arm."

Graham stared out the floor-to-ceiling window. I moved closer until we were shoulder to shoulder, taking in his stern profile.

"I have no idea what Matthew—my ex fiancé—is doing now. I doubt he ever got married. Or if he did, he's already traded her in for a new model. He was very into women maintaining, you know, their beauty, their figure. God forbid a woman have a baby and gain a little weight."

I ran a hand through my hair and shook my head as if trying to shake the thoughts out. "He used to make the most vulgar jokes about what happened to a woman after she had a baby. He told me he'd have to make sure to get me a surrogate, so I wouldn't have the baby myself."

Graham snorted. "He sounds a total asshole."

"He was joking. I guess. My parents absolutely hated him, which they didn't tell me until after I broke off the engagement. My mother said she was trying to be supportive. My father said he never would've let me get married to that guy. They've been married forever and are completely happy with each other. I'd never want anything less than that."

"My parents stayed married too. I don't know that they were always so happy with each other. They seemed happy enough."

"What does that mean, 'happy enough?'"

Graham brought his gaze back into the room, settling on

me. "My father was married before, but his first wife left him. Then, he met my mother, and they dated. My mother got pregnant with me, so they got married. I don't think either one of them were the other's first choice, but they love each other."

"How do you know?"

"My mom got sick a few years ago with early stage Parkinson's disease. My dad was so devoted to her. The way he looked at her. He brought her these little gifts to make her smile. He did his best right up until the end."

I wrapped my arm around his. "That's sweet. I'm sorry to hear about your mother."

Graham patted my hand. The softness in his eyes made my heart squeeze. The thought of losing a parent made my bones shiver.

"My parents were college sweethearts. My mother never seriously dated anyone but my dad. He's been her entire life. It's hard on her. He's a cop. He doesn't patrol anymore, but still...my mom is counting down to his retirement at the end of the year. I can only imagine what it would be like to lose a parent. That's...I don't even know what to say."

"It's okay. It's not easy. No matter how old you are, but I can't imagine feeling that fear of losing your parent as a kid. At least I was an adult before I had to think about that."

"I try not to think about it at all. He's a detective now, so it's better." I nearly continued but found I had nothing else to say on the topic.

"You mentioned Oklahoma City the other night. Is that where you're from?"

"Yes. My dad is on the force there."

I shifted from leg to leg, dodging eye contact with Graham to avoid breaching the wall I mentally erected as we spoke.

My childhood had been a good one, and I hated talking about the downsides of what my father did for a living. Contemplating what can go wrong and saying it out loud were taboo in my house.

"Do you two have any other questions?"

The sudden inquiry from the event manager made me to jump away from Graham as if we'd been caught necking under the bleachers. I stuttered, and Graham assured the hotel representative we were fine. After his smooth reply, we made our way back out to the parking lot.

I reached my car door and then felt Graham's hand on my elbow. His touch both calmed and excited me.

"Listen, about the other night, I'm sorry for what I said. I didn't mean to make it sound like I was judging you. I think you have every right to do what you want with me or anyone else."

The combination of his imploring apology and the bright twilight sun behind him crinkled my brow. Half of me wanted to jump in the car and peel out. The other half soaked up Graham's touch like a thirsty plant.

"You don't have to apologize. You were basically telling the truth. That's how I've been in relationships, but that doesn't mean that's all I'll ever want. I'm open to more if the guy warrants it."

I intended that to be my conciliatory, parting note, but his jaw tightened.

"And I don't?"

This time, I reached out and squeezed his upper arm. Graham tensed at the contact. A charge of tension and excitement passed between us.

≈

GRAHAM

This conversation should have made me run the other direction. Alexa presented a confused mix of wanting reassurance and commitment out of a man while offering little in return. I should recognize that for the nightmare it was, but I couldn't. I felt more determination than aversion.

"I don't know if you do or you don't."

"I might, then."

She fidgeted with her car door handle. Nervous humor crept into her voice. "You might. I don't know. I'm not good at this, to be honest. I practice not bothering to look for more than that."

"That's too bad."

"I need to get going."

I accepted her unconvincing mutter as if she meant it. "Okay. So, I'll see you around?"

"Probably. Look, I don't mean to make it sound like...I don't know. Like I'm not interested or that you're not worth my time or however it sounds. I mean it when I say I'm not good at this."

"At what, exactly?"

"Building more. Relationships."

The utter confusion on her face beguiled me. I could show her what more looked like—if she let me.

I moved toward her and brushed her chin with my thumb, settling it in the divot under her bottom lip. My other hand slipped behind her neck, feeling the soft fuzz of her hairline under my fingertips. I leaned in, but didn't kiss her.

"This is more, right now. No rushing into bed. No rushing out the door. Just standing here together. Now."

Her breath heaved, and I pulled my right thumb forward

under her jaw. Her pulse beat against it, faster and faster. My eyes met hers. Her lids lowered in expectation.

"Kiss me."

I held back."No."

As the moment expanded, her lips parted. Her tongue slid over her bottom lip and back again before she caught the edge of the plump flesh between her teeth. The movement almost undid me, but I kept my jaw snapped shut and went back to staring at the sparks of jade in the brown of her eyes.

She pressed forward, touching her forehead to mine. Her mouth opened wider, but only to release a huffing laugh, then a whisper. "How long are we going to stay like this?"

"However long you'll let me."

"Okay then."

She lifted her chin and moved her lips lightly over mine. Her breath mixed with my own, and the sensation pulled the blood away from my brain and to a lower, less thoughtful place. I held my breath.

Not giving her what she wanted only encouraged her. She extended the tip of her tongue to my lips and traced halfway around the bottom one before the desperation of desire overtook my control.

I grabbed her by the hair and thrust my tongue into her mouth, breathing again and like it was for the first time. The taste of her awakened memories of her body clenching mine, and I lost myself.

I dropped my hands to her hips and gripped her closer, pressing my clothed erection between her legs and advancing until her ass stopped against her car.

Her hands closed around my head, urging me deeper into her mouth. Her sweetness and fervor electrified every nerve in my body. Then, as suddenly as we came together, her palms shoved me backward, and I had to let her go. Her warmth left me.

One soft brown gaze met another.

"I'm hungry," she declared. "Buy me dinner?"

"I could make you dinner at my place, but you live closer."

"You can pick something up on the way to mine."

"Deal."

I stepped away from her.

She stood like a statue, hand poised on her car door. Leaving her frozen, I weaved through the lot toward my SUV and jumped in, feeling an urgency that scared me.

CHAPTER 20

ALEXA

J tested the limits of my sports car to get home. I showered at record speed, pinning my hair up in a plastic shower cap so I wouldn't have to spend half an hour blow-drying it. I skipped redoing my makeup and threw on a T-shirt and jeans over a matching set of lace underwear in deep lavender.

The woman staring back at me in the mirror turned, posed, and declared herself ready for prime time.

When Graham knocked on the front door, my legs stiffened with nervous energy as I approached it slowly, breathing deeply.

I leaned on the open door. "Hey. What's for dinner?"

Graham gripped the handles of the paper bag with two hands as he came in. "A steak and veggie dinner and a salmon and veggie dinner. I know you like to eat healthy. Take your pick."

I bent closer to get a view of my dinner. "I'll take the salmon."

"I did okay, then?"

Graham moved the bag to one hand and tipped up my chin with his other index finger.

"Fishing for compliments?"

"I went in search of food. I want to know if my lady is pleased."

"Not yet."

"You smell like the tropics."

"I showered."

"Now I feel like a pig. Would it be presumptuous to ask if I can shower real quick?"

"You don't have to take a shower."

I took the bag from him and dropped it by the couch. The need for proper refrigeration crossed my mind, but I didn't care. Graham smelled of sweat and a day's work, and my pulse revved like my BMW.

I spread my fingertips over his chest and leaned into him, lips parted in sure expectation. Still, the pressure of his mouth on me gave me a thrill.

Tiny shocks of joy rolled through me, swirling into the pit of my stomach. I trembled, and he wrapped his arms tighter.

Had this been what he felt like on New Year's? I hated that the evening blurred every time I thought of it—especially now, experiencing him again.

His tongue rolled softly over mine. With my arms pinned between us, I longed to run my fingers through the gentle waves of his chestnut hair.

The sensations of his kisses threatened to knock me into oblivion, but I pulled it together to unbuckle his belt, then bring my hands back up to his chest. Warmth infused me, and the world around me dissolved. Only the sweetness of his mouth and the beating of his heart against my wrist anchored me in time and place.

Graham dropped his arms and pulled away from my mouth before recapturing it with a quick succession of kisses that tugged my lower lip between his teeth.

I took advantage of my freedom and scraped my fingers down his abs and over his zipper. His solid flesh shifted under my fingertips as he pressed against me, his forehead on mine.

"Forget steak. I could eat you for dinner."

His soft, whiskey-colored eyes sharpened on me. Then, he kissed me hard and found the hem of my T-shirt. In a flash, he exposed my laced cleavage to his ravenous eyes. Nips of his teeth traveled the swell of my breasts, slowing around each curve.

When his teeth found my nipple through the wet lace, my left knee buckled, and I fell into him.

"My bedroom is down the hall." The direction rasped out of my desire-tightened throat.

"Lead the way."

I plucked open the button on my jeans and slid the zipper down as we raced down the hallway. We reached my bedroom, and I stopped in front of the quilt-covered bed. Folding myself over, I pushed the denim down my smoothly muscled legs.

Graham moved beside me and traced the scalloped edge of the panties stretched across my ass. I looked up at him as he pinched the lacy fabric in one hand and a condom in the other.

"How much would you hate me if I tore these off?"

I straightened and peered at him sideways.

"No panties need to die."

I pulled them carefully down over my hips and legs and stepped out of them, hooking the lacy wisp of fabric on my fingertip. I turned and waved them in his face.

"Be kind to the lingerie."

He snatched them and hurled them into the corner of my dimly lit room. I cocked my head to the side.

"Come on. I'll be kind to yours."

Graham thrust his hips forward. "I'm not wearing lacy underpants."

"Let's see. You never know." I snapped the waistband of his black boxer briefs. "Too boring. Those have to go."

Graham pulled his pants and underwear down and kicked them to the side, then lifted off his shirt. I took in the sharp line of his shoulders and the narrowing of his defined chest to firm abs.

The tiniest push and Graham fell back on the bed. I climbed on after him, legs folded underneath me at his side. Liquid infused my body—my limbs fluid, my mouth watering, my core clenched and wet.

My trail of kisses started in the center of his chest. I drew my tongue across his pecs and stopped over his left nipple. My teeth returned the biting favor while I grasped his erection in my hand and gave it a long, squeezing tug.

Graham tangled his fingers in my hair to lift my head, but I stayed fixed with his hard nipple in my mouth and the satin iron of his cock in my hand.

He pulled on the back of my head, and I turned. My gaze traveled up his heaving chest to his eyes peering at me.

"Is there a problem?" The question came at me in a low grumble.

I tightened my hand and pulled, stopping to stroke his slick tip with my thumb. His belly rippled and hardened with a sharp intake of breath.

Graham pulled harder on my hair. "Here's what's going to happen. I'm going to put this on." He waved the condom in his left hand. "And then, I'm going to flip you on your back."

I shook his fist from my head and stretched beside him. "You have to be on top, huh?"

I voluntarily rolled to my back, laughing as he nudged my legs apart. Then, he straightened up on his knees and tore the wrapper open with his teeth.

"This is better."

"Sexist."

"Probably."

He unrolled the condom down his impressive length and dropped to one elbow, widening my knees with the weight of his hips.

"You'll love it." He thrust into me, hard and fast.

I did.

He pressed to the hilt again and ground against me before crushing my mouth with his. A ripple of his tongue accompanied each long thrust.

Rational thought and my resistance to this man evaporated. All I could taste, smell, or feel was him—the tug of his hands in my hair, his back rolling under my fingers in rhythm as he plunged, and the scratch of the hair on his legs against the smoothness of mine.

Each time he drew out of me, I took a moment to catch a breath before he crashed into me again. Graham buried his face in my neck, punctuating his motion with a series of groans that grew deeper and deeper.

The friction of our bodies locked together in motion, first coiled sensation in my core, tighter and tighter, then it snapped, unraveling threads of pleasure in my blood. My orgasm pulsed, heating my face and curling my toes.

"God, Graham!"

He let go. Forehead to forehead, he stared directly into my eyes and thrust longer and slower once, twice more. Every muscle in his body went rigid and then, he fell against me.

"Fuck, that was amazing." He slapped the side of my thigh and grinned. "Tell me you didn't love it."

Shockwaves twitched from my clit up my belly even though he'd stopped moving. I vowed not to return the satisfaction. "Not bad."

Sweat beaded on his hairline, and he touched the tip of my nose with his. "You're a liar."

"Maybe." A satiated sigh escaped me. "Probably."

His lips played with mine until I opened to him and our tongues rolled together. Tiny shivers shot through me again. I ran his short, silky hair between my fingers.

My mind began to coalesce again even with the new onslaught of awareness. I was a liar, and he spoke the truth. Amazing.

CHAPTER 21

GRAHAM

"I want to do this again with you. Again and again."

Alexa remained silent and pulled the tie on her short robe tighter. Every time she reached forward to stab a piece of food on her plate, it gaped open. I raised my chin and kept my eyes on her face.

"You're not getting rid of me so easily."

"I don't want to get rid of you." Her admission swelled my bare chest with victory.

"Good. I love a chase, but catching you is more fun."

And keeping you.

The thought died as quickly as it rose in my mind. Keeping was out of the question. She didn't want that, and I didn't know what I wanted beyond another round with her in bed. Sleeping with her to get her out of my mind might take a little longer than anticipated, which was just fine with me.

"Yeah, it is." She nibbled on her grilled zucchini, still staring at me until she must have realized it and looked down at her plate.

She wanted me more than she'd admit to herself, which was crazy. Why not just go with it? However long this thing between us lasted, it was bound to be a hell of a lot of fun.

I took another bite of my flank steak. Its chewiness kept me from saying anything else, and she wasn't in a talkative mood. We ate in near silence for another couple of minutes. I looked around her kitchen.

"I should find the rest of my clothes." I'd only slipped on my boxers when hunger drove us from the bed.

"You should stay a little longer. The food is giving me more energy." A lure in her voice hooked me, sending the blood rushing to my crotch.

I coughed to keep the meat from going down the wrong way. "Whatever you say." I took a gulp of red wine.

"Good." She stabbed another vegetable and popped it in her mouth.

We made small talk until she finished her dinner and downed the last of her wine. Then, she stood and slinked over to me, saying nothing.

I stood and took her hands in mine, draping her arms over my shoulders. I thought she was going to kiss me on the lips and licked them in preparation.

Instead, feathery kisses brushed from my chin to my ear. She suckled my neck, biting—no doubt leaving a hickey for me to explain in the morning.

Her touch covered me from neck to hip—fingertips, palms, and the occasional thumb strumming my nipples. The burn of wanting her intensified, pushing me to the edge.

"Let's go."

I pulled Alexa around the corner and back down the

short hallway of her small house. Once in the bedroom, I grabbed her face and kissed her before guiding her backward on the bed.

She stretched her arms overhead slowly and extended her legs, pointing her toes. I yanked the sash of her robe, and it fell open.

Creamy mocha breasts tipped with brown mounded on her chest above a length of hard stomach and a generous expansion of hip.

I slid my hands between her knees and separated them. Our mutual desire thickened silence between us as I descended between her legs.

I BURIED my face between Alexa's breasts and had just reached for the juncture between her legs when I started wide awake and pissed off. I always woke up in the best parts of my sex dreams.

The soft sighs of the woman sleeping next to me ruined my hope of a middle-of-the-night romp. I considered following through on the invitation to stay the night, but a half-hour later, I lay flat on my back, three cups of coffee and two energy drinks worth of awake. I needed my own bed.

I glanced again to my right. Half of the symmetrical lines and curves of her face, smashed into the pillow. Her eyelashes fluttered, and I held his breath, wondering if she would wake up. She stilled and stayed sleeping.

My mind tossed me back to the last time I saw her like this. I chuckled to myself and rose from the bed.

Her desk sat against the far wall, opposite the bed—a small mess of papers and unopened mail. I located a sticky note and a pen and scribbled. Turning back to the bed, I smoothed the paper onto the pillow.

I almost straightened up and hightailed it right then, but I couldn't help it. I took one last sniff of her hair and dropped a soft kiss on her brow, not wanting to wake her. She didn't move.

God, she was beautiful.

I gathered my clothes and closed the door soundlessly behind me. Then, I dressed in her living room and walked away.

∽

ALEXA

Playing the genie and granting your wish. Poof.

Then, he topped off his fucking note with a smiley face. Like that was cute.

I crushed the lime green square in my hand and threw it across the room, directly into the trash can.

"Two points for me," I growled.

Leaving in the middle of the night without speaking to me? After saying he wanted to see me again and again and talking about wanting to catch me? After I invited him to stay the night? I never did that. Ever.

"Asshole." I punctuated the moniker with a swift pillow punch.

Did he think turning my careless words into a running joke would amuse me? Maybe it was funny.

I flopped onto the bed, face in the sheets. It didn't *feel* funny.

CHAPTER 22

ALEXA

"Hey, Alexa. You have a delivery up at the front desk. Reee-ally nice." Holly's envy stretched her words.

I dropped my office phone back into its cradle and plodded to the gym's check-in desk. At reception sat a vase of roses so dark, they looked tinged with black.

I grinned. Maybe Graham knew he'd been a pig and was sending apology flowers. Should I call him or make him sweat? I landed on making him sweat until at least the afternoon before calling him to thank him.

I pulled the vase toward me, out of Holly's grasp. "Thanks."

"Do you need help? It's a giant vase."

"No. I got it," I replied and floated back to my desk.

I had to dig through the foliage and baby's breath to

locate the pearlescent envelope bearing my name. Flipping it over, I tore it open.

Can't wait to see you in a few weeks. Thinking you every day until then.
Adam

Disappointment shot through me so fast, it made me dizzy. I shoved the card back into its pronged plastic holder and moved the flowers to the low bookcase under the window behind me.

I spent the rest of the day trying to ignore them, but every time I turned, I caught them taunting me out of the corner of my eye.

Shit. I slapped my palms over my eyes and huffed, elbows planted uncomfortably on my desk. I had no reason to expect anything from him. I said I wanted to keep things light, and that's what he was doing.

And that was okay. I had to get a handle on myself. We had an incredible night together. He'd likely call me again for a repeat. I'd say yes. *Let it go,* I admonished myself.

After a couple of hours, my phone alarmed. Time for me to get ready to teach my mid-morning Saturday kickboxing class. Then, after lunch, I had a pilates-yoga class, then barre. The schedule reminded me that I needed to hire a new instructor.

An hour of roundhouse kicks and uppercuts helped exorcise my anger demons. Sweaty and less on edge, I headed to my office for a recovery drink and a sandwich. I swung through the double door and down the hallway. A familiar set of square shoulders faced my desk.

Graham must have heard me coming because he turned and grinned.

"I hope you don't mind my stopping by. I remember you told me you had a break for lunch, so I took a chance."

"I wasn't sure I would get to see you today. You left quite a trail of smoke behind you early this morning."

His welcoming smile slid into a grimace. "You didn't think the note was funny. I should've known better. Maybe that wasn't such a good joke."

"So, you did intend it to be funny? I suppose I'm glad it wasn't just some twisted revenge."

"I drew a smiley face. Are you mad?"

Yes. I still fumed though I couldn't explain my raw nerves, so I lied. "No, it shocked me a little, but I knew you were joking. Maybe we should give up on waking up together and having it be anything other than strange."

"Or... Maybe third time's a charm."

His suggestion wound desire into the tension in my gut.

Normally, I'd punish a guy for pulling a stunt like that and let him stew, but looking into Graham's pale-bronze eyes, my fortitude for punishment dissipated.

"So, did you bring me lunch or what?" I drew my fingers across his shoulders as I walked around him and then the desk to sit down.

"I brought you an energy smoothie from next-door. Toby says this is the perfect thing to propel you for your afternoon classes."

Great. Now, Toby and Sarah would know Graham was buying me lunch and visiting me during the day. The questions would come at me fast and furious the next time I saw either one of them.

"I'll take it. I mixed up a recovery drink, but I can drink it this afternoon." I grabbed the drink and took a long sip. "This can't be the most exciting thing you have planned for Saturday. What else you have going on today?"

"Well, I ended up having to work a little bit this morning. A water tank burst at one of the other properties. Charlie needed my approval for additional expenses, and the tenant was furious that it took an hour for the plumber to get there. The place flooded and...never mind. You don't need to hear about all that. Needless to say, it was a mess. Plus, I had a ten a.m. tee time and had to cancel."

The call of the fairway had to be at least one reason why he bailed on me in the middle of the night. Disgruntlement ate at the edges of my mood again.

"You men and your golf."

"It's not just men who play golf. You've never played?"

"I have. I used to play pretty regularly, but I gave it up. Not my thing."

Matthew had loved golf and insisted I learn. I took golf lessons for almost two years and managed to get my handicap down to an acceptable level from the ladies' tees. Of course, I hadn't played in years, and I knew regular play was the only way to keep from embarrassing yourself. I said a silent prayer Graham wouldn't ask me to go play golf.

"We should play some time."

"Sure," I replied in the light tone I used to let men think they were getting their way. Like with Adam. His arrival loomed as did the flowers over my shoulder. I unconsciously took a gander at them, which was a mistake.

"Nice flowers. It's not your birthday or something is it?"

"No, uh, those are from a friend. For Valentine's Day, I guess."

"That was a week ago."

"I know." I had no explanation to offer Graham for Adam's behavior.

"A male friend?"

"Yes. I saw him briefly last November. We weren't even

really dating. He doesn't live here, but he's coming to town soon. He wanted to let me know."

Rather than avoid Graham's narrowed gaze, I looked at him straight and didn't blink.

GRAHAM

My heart raced with unjustified fury. Alexa and I were just connecting, so I had to expect there would be one or two other guys in the wings. Still, seeing another man's flowers displayed in her office stung the ego.

I searched her impassive face for some clue as to how attached she was to Red Rose Guy. She stared back, giving me nothing.

I smirked. "Beautiful. Incredibly cliché, but beautiful."

"You think you could've done better?" Her obvious joy at my discomfort added a roguery to her smile.

"You are not a clichéd woman. I would've gone for something more exotic. I mean baby's breath? Come on."

"I think they're lovely."

Lovely? The primness of the word on Alexa's lips caused a burst of laughter to erupt from my chest.

"Sure you do. When is Mr. Cliché arriving?"

"I'm not entirely sure, but he's supposed to be here for South by Southwest."

"Does he work in the entertainment industry?"

The thought that this could be some oily bigwig who knew Alexa from her modeling days made me crazy.

"No, he works in technology as a consultant."

A consultant might be worse than some overly tanned executive.

When I didn't say anything, Alexa continued. "I met him when I went to visit my friend in England at Thanksgiving. He's British. And he's also an artist. He paints and sketches."

I envisioned a pale, long-haired hippie with bad teeth.

"He sounds fascinating, but I don't want to spend lunch talking about some other guy—especially one as uninteresting as this one sounds."

"Your jealousy is kind of exciting."

"No jealousy." I waved my hands to sweep away the notion. "Frankly, I can tell you're not that into him."

"What on Earth makes you say that?" Alexa leaned back and crossed her arms.

"Number one, you're not even sure when he's arriving. If you were that excited, you'd be counting down the days. Number two, since you're not counting down the days, his sending flowers is only bound to annoy you. I know you well enough to know that. You're not his girlfriend. And number three, you called them 'lovely.' Lovely is a word old women use when they're trying to be nice about ugly children or friends they secretly can't stand. You don't use 'lovely' to describe anything related to a guy who makes you hot."

Alexa emitted a soft rumble of laughter. "Wow. Wouldn't you make an excellent detective."

"I'm a keen observer, but no worries. I can handle some 'lovely' competition."

My cocky assertion drew a smile from her. Maybe she found it stimulating—more stimulating than some stodgy British guy. I'd bet the guy had snaggleteeth. And rickets. Or was it scurvy? How rude would it be to send a basket of limes to the guy's hotel?

Alexa blew off my snide remark. "You men and your pissing contests. Am I a trophy now?"

"It's nature. I'm a man, and I can't help puffing out my

chest when I hear that some other man is after one of my ladies."

"One of your ladies? Maybe I should be puffing out my chest. Or I could pee on your leg."

I knocked back my head and erupted in laughter. "I know a guy who'd pay you to do that."

"Who the hell do you hang out with?" Her top lip curled up in disgust even though she laughed.

"I have a varied assortment of friends."

Alexa palmed her face, shaking her head. "Is there anything else we need to discuss? Unlike you, who seems to have unlimited amounts of time for gallivanting, I need to get back to work."

"Gallivanting? I'm checking in on one of my most valued tenants."

Alexa blew me a raspberry. "Get out of my office."

She flipped her index finger toward the door and gave me a stern look. I laughed and stood to leave.

"So bossy. I know a guy who'd pay for that, too."

CHAPTER 23

ALEXA

*O*ver the next three weeks, I counted down the days, but not necessarily with anticipation.

After our initial conversation, Graham never mentioned Adam again or asked when he was coming. With South by Southwest starting over the weekend, he had to know Adam's arrival approached.

I couldn't tell whether arrogance or envy kept Graham from acknowledging the arrival of...my old lover? I didn't know what to call Adam.

"Lover" made me cringe. Much about the situation gave me an acid stomach. That afternoon, I worked out my nerves by finishing my kickboxing class with furious combinations of hooks, jabs, and round house kicks before the cool down.

"Damn. You kicked our asses today," wheezed Hannah, one of my loyal clients. The woman dropped her hands to her knees, bracing herself and gasping.

"Working through some bad energy."

Shortly before class, Adam left me a voicemail to let me know he'd landed at Bergstrom Airport. The anticipation in his voice provided the nervous energy for my workout.

When I got back to my office, I called him back. He wanted to have dinner.

"I assume you want to get to your hotel and freshen up." I hoped the casual persuasion in my voice would cut off debate. "I'm still at work, and I don't know when I'll be able to get out of here. I taught classes this afternoon, so I have some office work to finish."

"Well, I'd love to see you tonight, if you have time."

"How about we make plans for tomorrow?"

Graham had challenged me to a pool tournament. Competitive, I told him to bring it on. Knowing the flight from London would arrive after five p.m., I hadn't expected to see Adam today.

Silence lingered on the phone line, followed by a hiss. Sigh or a tick in the phone connection—I couldn't tell. "Alright then. Tomorrow at eight o'clock? I'll make reservations somewhere."

"That works. Just let me know where, and I'll meet you there."

"You could just meet me at the hotel, and we can go together."

"It depends on where you make reservations. With the festival traffic, meeting you there simplifies things. During South by, it's tough to even get a pedicab. The streets are crazy."

"You certainly would know more about that than I do, so I'll let you know where I make the reservation. You can meet me there."

I felt as if I had to pull acquiescence out of him. That didn't bode well.

~

"YOUR SHOT, MY LADY."

Graham gestured toward the cue ball after missing a tough bank shot to the side pocket. I chalked my cue and surveyed the table. I had two relatively easy looks, but one might better position me to sink the other on my next shot.

I lined up my stick and quickly fired, nailing the solid blue ball in the perfect spot. It dropped in the corner pocket, and the cue ball rolled into alignment with the solid yellow. I sank that one as well and fist pumped at my competition.

"So, when is Red Rose Guy getting here for the conference?"

If he thought surprising me with a question about Adam would throw me off my game, he underestimated my focus. His mistake. I banked in the six and examined my next shot.

"He got here today, actually."

"And you didn't welcome him?"

"He's settling in at the hotel, and I'll see him another time."

I smacked the next shot too hard, scratching. Graham chuckled as he walked away from me to the end of the table to collect the cue ball and pick his next shot.

"Sounds lovely."

"Smart ass. It's not a big deal. It seems silly not to meet up with him since he's flying all the way here from London."

"We're keeping things easy, right? You don't know me an explanation."

I stood my cue stick on the floor, leaning slightly against

it. Although I didn't have to justify myself, I still wanted to explain. "No, but you seem to have questions."

After making his first, Graham fired his second shot wide and the cue ball careened all the way back to the other end. He laid his stick across the edge of the table.

"I'll admit that I'm curious. You met him at Thanksgiving, and he's coming to visit you now, but you seem nonchalant about it."

My eyes met his with a challenge. "Would you like me to be more excited about it?"

"Nope. So you're not…dating him?"

"No" I said. "And I didn't invite him here. He's in town on business. We're friendly. It's not a big deal."

"It's a big enough deal that you felt compelled to tell me. You could have said nothing, and I would never have known."

"I wouldn't say 'compelled.' You asked about the roses. I answered your questions. There's no reason for me to be cagey about it."

He picked up his stick and let it slide through his fingers, banging it on the floor. "Okay."

The subject of Adam clearly irritated Graham. I supposed a little natural human jealousy was bound to crop up.

I took another solid off the table, then shot well wide of my target and put my hand on my hip. "I hope you aren't grilling me thinking you can distract me."

"If I were, I'd be failing, wouldn't I?" Graham moved around the table, evaluating his position. On one side, he had to turn and sidestep past me in the narrow space.

I angled away to give him more room, but he stopped, pressing toward me. I backed up against the table, and he leaned in.

"Is this more or less distracting than my line of questions?" he whispered.

The twisted sparkle in his eyes made me laugh. His thick thigh pressed against my zipper. Even though I thought about riding him like a horse, I kept my legs firmly together.

"Neither. I'm not distracted by you at all."

He bent toward my ear. "You sure? I'm trying pretty hard here."

"I can see that." I rotated my hips away from him and walked to the end of the table. "I do have some questions for you."

"Shoot."

"Do you really know a guy who would pay to have a woman boss him around?"

"Seriously?" He pinched the bridge of his nose between his fingers and laughed until he was nearly breathless. "Yeah, I do."

"How do you even find something like that out about somebody?"

Graham drilled one of the stripes into a side pocket and straightened up.

"There was a guy I worked with. We were out of town together on business, and in the morning, I was downstairs at breakfast waiting for him. He didn't show. After a while, I got concerned because he wouldn't answer his cell phone, and I couldn't get him on the hotel phone either. I convinced the hotel to let me into his suite. Lucky for him, I went in alone. He was gagged with his hands behind his back tied up in zip ties. I had to use toenail clippers to chew through the plastic and cut him loose."

My blast of laughter drew curious stares from a handful of people playing at the next table.

"He kept saying, 'You can't tell anybody. Seriously, you

can't tell anybody.' I promised him I wouldn't. I asked him what his deal was. He said that he likes to hire women who specialized in bondage and domination stuff. And, I mean, this guy was a bigwig. A real power player in development and politics. He said it helped him relax to have a woman take control."

"The men who hire dominatrices are mostly really rich powerful guys, right? I just kind of assume that."

"I couldn't tell you. I'm not really an expert. I only know the one guy."

"You don't know a guy who hires women to pee on his leg?" I shook my finger at him as if I caught him in a lie.

"Oh wait, I know that guy, too."

"Different guy?"

"Yeah, different guy. That was a guy in college. I think he just watched too much weird porn."

"I'm beginning to wonder about you. Part of the measure of a man is the company he keeps."

He pointed his stick at me in emphatic denial. "Hey, I don't keep company with these guys. I only know them. I keep company with guys like my friend, Jonah. Settling down and becoming a family man. Maybe on our next date, I'll bring references."

Graham focused back on the game, positioning his stick and firing. The cue ball bounced off the rail and straight at the eight ball.

"No, no, no," he groaned, leaning the opposite direction as if he could will the ball away from the hole. "Shit."

"That was quick." I sauntered over and smacked him on the ass. "You have my sympathy. Let's rack them again."

I grabbed the triangle and suppressed a mocking laugh, knowing better than to make too much fun of a man when I was kicking his ass.

CHAPTER 24

GRAHAM

*A*fter our lopsided games of pool, we settled in at the bar and waited for Melissa and Kyle to join us. Alexa's friend called as we were wrapping up to see if she wanted to hang out.

I ran to the bathroom, and when I returned, Alexa's petite, dark-haired business partner was holding hands with a stocky blond guy who had to be her fiancé. We exchanged introductions and found a table.

"What have you guys been up to tonight?" Melissa asked.

"Someone was killing me at pool, and now I owe her drinks."

Melissa gave Alexa a high five and shook her head at me. "Her dad taught her to play pool when she was, like, four or five years old. She's a pool shark. She suckered you."

"You were hustling me?"

"You're the one who suggested we go play pool. I'm trying

to be an agreeable woman." Alexa batted her eyelashes and folded her hands, propping them under her chin.

Her attempt at demure set the whole table tittering. I sat back in my seat.

"I hope Alexa passed along my congratulations, Melissa."

"She did. Thank you. Kyle and I are so excited."

"How long have you been dating?"

Kyle stroked his chin. "We've been together…almost three years now. We kinda started then stopped, and then started up again."

"Yeah, there is a gap in there of four or five months."

Since they'd brought it up, I figured it was okay to ask about it. "Why the break?"

Alexa smacked my knee under the table with the back of her hand. Her admonishment wasn't as surreptitious as she'd hoped. Melissa laughed.

"It's fine. I had an old boyfriend who came back. I was stupid, but it all worked out in the end." Melissa dropped her head onto Kyle's shoulder and squeezed his hand.

I stiffened. I couldn't imagine how embarrassing it was for Kyle to have his girlfriend up and leave to chase some old boyfriend. Obviously, she came crawling back at some point.

The other couple exchanged an amorous glance.

"Graham and I were looking at venues a few days ago and found a wonderful spot. It overlooks the river and has indoor and outdoor space. I meant to send you those pictures, Melissa."

"You and Graham are looking at wedding venues?" Kyle gasped and sputtered. His beer sloshed as it slipped out of his grasp to the table with a thud.

"No," she and I vociferated simultaneously.

Melissa set the record straight before her fiancé coughed up a lung. "I think it was for the juvenile diabetes benefit Alexa is helping out with for Toby and Sarah. Am I right?"

"Yes. You'll love it, and it's not nearly as expensive as I thought it would be."

Alexa fished her phone out of her purse and climbed off her stool, walking around to stand shoulder to shoulder with Melissa and page through the photos. With the women hunched over the phone, I stared at Kyle who sat opposite me, trying not to think about my last inappropriate inquiry into the other guy's life.

Kyle drummed the table then pointed. "Melissa tells me that you're their landlord?"

"I'm a partner in a commercial real estate management and development company. We purchased their building. What do you do?"

"I'm an orthopedic trauma surgeon at University Medical Center."

I whistled. "Wow. I can't imagine the stress."

"It's tough, but I love the pace of it and the variety, just not the hours, which suck. I'm already taking extra shifts for colleagues so I can call in some favors and take a honeymoon. Melissa has thrown down one rule. We are having a honeymoon, longer than a week. My wedding gift to her is making that happen."

Talking about making his fiancée happy put a glowing light in Kyle's eyes. Whatever had gone on before, Kyle had clearly put it behind him. I wasn't sure I could do the same.

"Are you talking about our honeymoon?" Melissa nudged Kyle with her elbow. "I'm making a list of places I want to go. I can't decide between Europe, someplace with a beach, or maybe something unusual like an African safari."

Kyle reached over and stroked Melissa's hand. "My vote is for the beach. I want to sit and do nothing. If we go to

Europe, we'll be running around all day. I'll need a vacation from my vacation."

"I know. It's just all the places I've ever really wanted to go are in Europe. We could find a place to sit and relax in Italy or the south of France."

After sitting back down, Alexa perked up. "I love southern France. You could stay near Nice and visit Monaco. I have a friend who owns an apartment there. She rents out on occasion to friends. I can get the information if you'd like."

"I love that idea," Kyle exclaimed. "It's a nice compromise. By the way, how was London? I don't think I've seen you since you got back."

I glanced sideways at Alexa, who stiffened next to me. "London was nice."

"It's another city on Melissa's list." Kyle popped a tortilla chip in his mouth.

Alexa shifted in her seat. "If you're thinking honeymoon, I would do Paris, Barcelona, or somewhere in Italy before London."

"You can scare up a romance any place—even London." Melissa shot Alexa a pointed look and a pleased-with-herself smile.

Alexa's eyes widened as if willing her friend to be quiet.

"Did you find London romantic?" I widened my eyes, striving for sincerity.

Alexa downed half her vodka soda before shrugging. "Not especially. I can think of a million places I rank ahead of London in the romance department."

I put an arm on the back of her stool and leaned in. Drawing close to her made my skin dance with pulses of heat. "What's the most romantic place you've ever been?"

She cast her eyes to the ceiling and tapped the side of the glass. "I hiked Machu Picchu with a boyfriend once. We were dirty and smelly for days, but there is something romantic about being up in the mountains—even if we were in a tent."

"You don't strike me as a camper."

Alexa met my incredulous squint with a bemused eye roll. "I've been camping dozens of times. I love being outdoors. You'd be surprised at all the things that I'm into."

The crotch of my pants strained at the implication of her words. She flushed a little, realizing how what she said might've sounded to me. Melissa giggled, and Kyle cleared his throat.

"I look forward to finding out." I bumped the side of her leg with my knee, twice, maximizing the friction.

Alexa pursed her lips. "You have a filthy mind."

She loved it, and I wasn't going to let her get away with pretending like she didn't. "I don't know what you're talking about. If there's any untoward connotation to what you said, that's on you."

"Nice. You sit over there looking like an old lady fanning herself against the heat of the Devil with her church hat, but I think we know who the dirty bird in this conversation is."

She poked my side, and I snickered, grabbing her hand. Her soft skin electrified my fingertips. "Church sounds like a grand idea. We could use a little bit of the Good Word to straighten us out."

Alexa switched her finger between us and waved away the thought. "Us? I go to church, thank you."

Melissa snorted. "When was the last time you went to church?"

"I'll have you know I went Christmas Day. My mother wouldn't have it any other way. When was the last time you took communion?"

Alexa's friend tipped her dark head forward, letting a curtain of thick, ebony hair hide her face. "Sorry. You're breaking up." Her voice raised as if she weren't sure if the rest of her companions could hear her.

"Looks like we're all going to hell." Kyle cackled.

"Probably." I took another drink and whispered to Alexa. "Maybe I can come to your place tonight. We can discuss our sins."

Alexa kept looking across the table at our companions. Her hand slipped over my knee and up my thigh until her fingers wedged in my crotch.

She didn't turn her head. "You know what they say. I may be going to hell, but at least all my friends will be there."

If I was destined for fire and brimstone, I could think of worse things than earning my way there with Alexa.

I RACED behind her to her house and jumped out of the car, making it to the door just as she pushed it open.

The thunk of her purse dropping to the floor was followed by the click of the light. I wrapped my arm around her.

"You're going to have to let me go if I'm going to take my shirt off," she said.

I didn't let her go. I pulled her closer and grabbed the hem of the shirt at her hips and yanked it up. Her arms lifted with mine, and I snatched it off her head and threw it somewhere.

She put her hands on either side of my face and kissed me. Alexa opened her sweet, full lips on my mouth and stroked me with her tongue. The long, slow pressure of her mouth might as well have been on my cock because it pulsed against my thigh.

Her bra or my jeans? My fingers solved the conundrum

without my mind activating, undoing each hook and pulling the silk and lace to her elbows. She dropped her arms and let it fall. I moved forward to bring her arms and hands back to my body, and the bra caught on the toe of my shoe. I kicked it somewhere.

I palmed her breast, feeling the weight and pinching her nipple.

She gasped into my mouth.

I pulled away from her suckling kiss.

"Turn around."

I swept her hair away so I could taste the stars dotting the back of her neck while taking both breasts in my hands, thumbing the peaks, rolling them in his fingers, and squeezing until she arched her back, breathless.

Her ass ground into my crotch.

"Bedroom." I could barely hear her husky voice.

I didn't have the patience to make it down the short hall to the bedroom. I walked her over to the couch and unfastened her jeans.

Alexa took over. She kicked off her shoes and pulled her jeans down, bending over to reveal her round ass perfectly displayed in pair of silky boyshorts. I ran a hand over her left cheek.

Smack.

She laughed, so I did it again.

She twisted around, still giggling. "Stop it. Take your pants off, already."

I followed orders, but stopped to pull out my wallet and grab a condom.

Alexa stood there, luring me in—her smile soft, her nipples hard, and her skin golden brown in the light of her living room.

Slipping one hand into her hair, I pulled her head back

and kissed her relentlessly hard while I roamed my other hand down her belly into the silky lace she still wore.

I raised my head so I could see her face. Her eyes closed while her mouth circled open.

"Oh, God, yeah."

I lowered her onto the couch, our bodies knocking off pillows as we positioned ourselves. I stayed anchored with one foot on the floor, and Alexa kicked one leg up onto the back of the sofa.

I played with her slick folds, making sure a finger always stayed on the tight nub topping them.

My cock strained toward her. I thought of giving in and sinking into her soft, wet heat. But her breath shortened. Her eyelids flickered. Her moaning turned desperate.

I moved my fingers faster, sliding over her and slipping two fingers into her tightness while strumming her with my thumb. I found her most sensitive spot and stroked her there.

"Oh, fuck."

She squeezed my fingers so tight, I wondered how I'd ever fit my cock inside her.

I tore open the condom and put it on, ready to find out.

ALEXA

I eventually dragged Graham off the couch and to the bedroom for rounds two and three of the evening. We collapsed in a heap with my tangled sheets.

I lay on his chest and ran my hands over the scatter of light brown hair swirling from his pecs to his belly. His stomach rose and fell in a rolling rhythm that slowly synced with my own breathing.

I wanted him to stay the night.

Staying in that exact position, feeling his heart thump against my cheek, felt like heaven even if it paved my way to hell.

I raised up and kissed his nipple.

Graham tucked his index finger under my chin and got me to look up at him. "What are you doing tomorrow?"

The low rumbling question pulled another moan from her. This one, unhappy. I didn't believe in hell, but it might be something like this.

"I have a thing." My voice came out hollow and strangely high.

Right now, in his arms, I would not mention Adam. Nor could I get out of seeing him. Could I?

Shit, shit, shit.

I silently wished for a remote control to take me back thirty seconds. I started to tell Graham I could cancel.

"A thing." His tone dropped. It wasn't a question. My chance had passed. Graham scooted away and onto his side.

I rolled onto my belly. My eyes flipped up to him, infused with as much but-I-want-to-see-you as I could muster. "I can move things around."

His eyes clouded. He tugged on a few spiraled locks of my hair, then stroked and squeezed my arm.

"I better get going." Graham kissed me on the forehead, swung his feet to the floor, then turned back. "Maybe I'll stop by for lunch one day."

"Do that. The rest of the week is wide open. Just call me."

He grinned. "I will."

Then, Graham stood and strode out of my room, leaving me to stare at his naked, muscled behind.

A magma-deep yearning to run after him erupted in me, but a languor in my limbs kept me pinned to the mattress. It wasn't the bone-squealing sex. It was indecision mixed with the fear that comes from standing on the edge of the unknown.

I missed him, and he was still knocking around my living room. The sounds of him in my house would be intimate and comforting if I didn't know he was pulling on his clothes and heading out the door.

CHAPTER 25

ALEXA

*A*dam picked one of Austin's toniest steakhouses for dinner.

The foyer buzzed. The festival crowd already swelled even though the events didn't start until Friday. A peal of jazz piano trickled toward me as I entered the bar. A tendril of hair escaped my high ponytail, and I smoothed it behind one ear.

I went back and forth with what to wear to my non-date. Thankfully, Austin didn't require you to get dressed up. I'd gone for long, lean denim, heeled, rhinestoned sandals, and a flowing silk top that said pretty, but not sexy.

Pulling my shoulders back and lifting my head, I perused each face around the mahogany-paneled room. I hadn't seen Adam for months, and a shiver of excitement betrayed my intentions.

The traitorous emotions brought to mind last night. I

hadn't heard anything from Graham all day. His quiet departure from my house left me shaking with self-recrimination. I shouldn't even be here.

But I was.

I spotted Adam in the throng of people. Since he hadn't seen me yet, I hung back for a moment to take him in.

Thick, dark hair and caramel skin came from his Indian heritage on his mother's side. Someone next to him must've said something funny because his wide, bright smile sparked in the dim light. He stood a head taller than the man with the joke.

Even though I hesitated, I anticipated the warmth of his deep brown eyes.

I propelled myself around the bar and approached him from behind, reaching up to touch his shoulder. He spun around, and I found myself wrapped in a tight embrace before I could even say hello.

I thought back to my last moments in his London apartment, which involved pulling myself out of his arms following a passionate night and, then, morning.

"Alexa!" His silken voice stretched out the "ex."

"Adam, how are you?" Secured in his hug, I had no choice but to wait until he released me. He gave me one more squeeze before doing so.

"Fantastic. Last night, I went to dinner with clients, and then, we took in some live music. Unbelievable barbecue and great bands. It was grand. You should've come out."

I ignored his entreaty. "Glad you're enjoying the city. Who are your clients? If you can tell me, that is."

"Prospect Tech. It's a small software firm headquartered in Ireland. They're opening an office here. I'm helping them set up their systems and some other terribly boring things. How about you? How's business?"

"Business is good. We're moving from construction into decoration and finish out on the spa in the next several weeks. We're hiring staff. I need to hire at least one more fitness instructor, so I can focus on the business and more personal training. Things are clicking along."

I glanced over to the bar, contemplating my drink order. Adam stroked my upper arm with his thumb. "What can I get you to drink?"

"A Tito's and soda with two limes would be perfect."

"Tito's?"

"It's vodka. They'll have it."

Adam ordered for me and then turned back.

"My building is under new owners, but they've been easy to work with so far. Their rep...has responded to anything that we need."

My cheeks grew hot. The bartender slid a bubbling tumbler toward me on a napkin.

"Excellent." Adam eyed me and exhaled. "Enough about business. What else do you have going on?"

I sipped my drink. I only had two things going on: the gym and Graham. "Melissa, my business partner, is getting married."

"Wonderful. Am I going to get to meet her?"

"At some point, I'm sure." I gulped my vodka cocktail.

"How far is your gym from here?"

"Over the river, kind of through the woods, on the other side of Zilker Park, but not far—except for all the traffic."

"Is that where you live?"

"Close. I'm between First and South Congress. I bought a house there when I moved back from New York. It's nothing fancy, but I love the neighborhood. I can walk to some phenomenal restaurants and bars and Amy's Ice Cream. You have to have it while you're here."

156 | KRIS JAYNE

"I'll put that on the list."

I tapped a fingernail against the stem of my glass. "How long are you in town? You sounded up in the air on that the last time we spoke."

"At least a couple of months. Maybe into the summer. We'll see. How ever long it takes to have a successful engagement," Adam answered and rubbed my shoulder. "It's so good to see you again."

Now.

"You, too, but Adam, I should tell you that I'm seeing someone. While it's great to see you, I hope you're not expecting a repeat of what happened in London."

A brief cloud shuttled across his eyes, but he smiled it away. "I see. If you're seeing someone and you're here with me, it can't be that serious."

"It's not about him. It's just that I'm not available. We can hang out while you're here. I'll show you around, but that's it. We need to keep this on a friendship level. I want to be clear."

He drew his full bottom lip between his teeth and stared off over my shoulder. "I see."

"I hope so. I don't want any misunderstandings."

His hand gripped the brass railing on the bar, turning his knuckles pale before he released it. "We're clear. No worries. I'd love to meet your friends—all of them."

"Sure." Adam and Graham crossing paths? Before panic choked me, I threw it off. I'd manage them...somehow.

ADAM

The news that Alexa had a new lover burned, but it wouldn't dissuade me. She said it wasn't a serious relationship, which meant she could drop this other guy as quickly as she found him.

I signaled for the bar bill and set my course on moving to our table as soon as the hostess collected us. The press of patrons as the bar filled up frustrated attempts at in-depth conversation.

The bartender nodded at me and hustled to the register. I flicked my eyes back to Alexa, who waved a twenty dollar bill at him.

"Absolutely not." I swatted her hand away.

"No. I'm not going to let you pay for my drink after the conversation we just had. It wouldn't be right."

"I can be a friend and pay for your drink."

"I know, but I don't want you to."

Alexa leveled her green-flecked brown eyes at me, unblinking. Her obstinance impressed and irritated me equally, and I found the challenge of her resistance sexy.

"We can split dinner if you'd like, but I'm paying for your drink. Let me. My manly pride demands it, and you wouldn't want to wound my masculinity, would you?"

Her gaze steeled, then softened. She slipped the money back into her purse with an amused smile slanting across her face. "Of course not."

"Good."

I tossed my own bills down on the bar. After dinner, I'd make sure the waiter settled the bill on his credit card before bringing it to the table. Tonight was on me. If I expected to draw her away from this other fellow, I'd have to take charge, and despite her protestations, I knew that was the way to go.

"I'll bet our table is almost ready. Let's check at the hostess stand."

I looped my arm around hers and guided her through the

foyer, enjoying the appreciative looks other men gave as she passed.

Having this alluring woman on my arm was more than worth a steak dinner.

~

ALEXA

Rather than get a steak the size of my head, I ordered grilled fish and steamed vegetables. Adam declared that he couldn't come all the way to Texas and not get some proper beef, so he ordered the Porterhouse.

"Have you gone off steak and that for good?"

"No. I just try to limit how much beef I eat. Steakhouses always give you these huge cuts of meat—twelve and sixteen ounces or more. And the leftovers are never as good."

"Aha. You're not a...what do they call it...a pescetarian then?"

"No. I can't cut out whole food groups. The minute I tell myself no, I start to obsess."

"I can see that about you. You have a rebellious nature."

"Is that a good thing?"

"It's a challenge." Adam's eyes darkened with intensity. "I enjoy taking on challenges."

He locked in on me resolutely as he did every time I saw him. Was I a challenge to be won? What happened after that?

Graham had all but called me a trophy when the subject of Adam first arose. Maybe I had a type after all. Matthew had seen me that way—as a shiny object to be won.

"I'd prefer to just be a woman."

"A good woman is a challenge."

"A bad one is easy?" I edged forward in my seat, catching my linen napkin as it almost slid to the floor.

"An uninteresting one is easy. Not sexually—I wouldn't want to be accused of having a sexist double standard. I appreciate complexity in a woman."

"I like my men simpler, I think." I chuckled, drawing laughter from Adam and easing the tension in my shoulders. He could be so serious. What I had taken as intriguing depth in London struck me now as exhausting.

"Fine. Let's be simple. This weather is already dreadfully warm. I fear that by summer I'll be melting."

"Yes. You will be. Stay inside in the afternoon, drink margaritas, and you'll be fine. I warned you. May through September are miserable. How long are you going to be in Austin anyway?"

"At least until May."

Shit. I'd assumed he would be here for the festival and maybe a couple of weeks more. Until May? I forced a smile. "Then, you'll be getting out just in time."

"If I don't extend, then yes."

There was no reason for the dread I felt. I'd been honest with him, but the thought of him hanging around into the summer, looking at me with that expectant depth in his eyes, made my stomach knot. "You'll set up the office, and then what?"

"I help manage systems integrations. If I stay on until that's completed, I might be here through the summer."

"Do yourself a favor and escape before then."

"You can't be ready to send me packing already?"

In the face of Adam's unwavering scrutiny, I searched the room for our waiter, shaking my glass of melting ice. Where was the drink I'd ordered when we sat down? The slight, bow-tied man caught my roaming gaze and signaled that he'd be there in a minute.

"Of course not. Just joking about the weather."

"Are you attending any of the festivities in the next week?"

"We'll see how my schedule goes."

How it would go was that I would be clearing the deck for Graham. Maybe he was a little peeved about my "thing," but I could think of a dozen ways to make that up to him.

Adam pouted. "That's too bad. I have passes to see The Strokes on Tuesday."

I shook my head. "I can't make The Strokes. You should go, though. They're great. I saw them at ACL last year."

"That's another music festival?"

"Yes. Austin City Limits. It doesn't have as much of all the other stuff going on. It's just one big outdoor concert series in the park."

The arrival of our waiter with drinks and appetizers distracted Adam from responding.

"Here you go. Sorry it took me so long. Your food will be out in a bit."

"No problem." Adam smiled, dismissing the server. "I might see if I can unload the tickets, then."

"Don't do that on my account. I'm sure you can find one of your clients to go. Or go by yourself. You won't be the only one flying solo."

"I'll think it over. But if you can go, give me a call."

"Sure."

I squeezed my two limes into the clear, effervescent liquid, which I prayed had more vodka in it than my first round.

Adam ran his thumb along the full, sensuous line of his

bottom lip. The loud ringing of a mobile phone at the next table shocked me out of my contemplation of Adam's mouth.

I enjoyed my trip in November—especially my time with Adam. Maybe...Why not? *Stop!* Knowing Adam wanted more from me than I could give him answered my question.

Plus, there was Graham. He made me laugh, and I wanted more nights like last night. I couldn't turn myself into a piece of meat being tugged at between two alpha dogs.

I turned my attention to the goat cheese salad in front of me and ignored the burn of Adam's ebony eyes.

CHAPTER 26

ALEXA

*H*iring a new cardio instructor pushed everything off my plate. I'd advertised the opening on several job sites and in the local paper.

Of the two dozen candidates who'd contacted me, only two had the basic qualifications and sounded reliable enough to interview in person. One was free to come in that evening to talk in person.

At five thirty, Holly knocked on my door.

"Alexa, this is your five thirty. Trista Halpern."

"Trista, hi." The trim, muscled woman gave me a hard-gripped handshake. "Have a seat. Thanks, Holly."

Trista wore a body conscious pencil skirt and crisp white shirt with heeled sandals in an animal print. She sat erect in her chair and crossed her legs—emphasizing their tone and bulk. Her figure suggested body building—probably competitively.

"Thanks for coming in on short notice."

"Not a problem. When I read about the opening, I was so excited. I wanted to come in as soon I could." Her smokey voice vibrated with enthusiasm.

"How long have you been teaching group classes?"

"Seven years. I worked at a couple of national chains up in Dallas and then got my own studio."

"Oh, you ran your own gym."

"It was more of a yoga and fitness studio. We had free weights in the studio, but no cardio equipment or anything. A friend and I taught classes and ran the place together. I had to leave when my mother got sick. She lived here—or in Round Rock. I've been here the last couple of years, teaching at a chain."

"Lived" made me redirect the conversation.

"I see that you're still there? What makes you want to leave one of the big boys?"

"I miss being able to work with customers more individually. I miss recognizing all the clients and knowing them by name." Trista's words skipped rapidly as she spoke.

I nodded, hopeful that if I hired the woman, she wouldn't want to run her own studio again. Two years ago, an instructor quit and took some clients with her. Of course, many of them came back. Teaching classes and running a business are two different things.

Still, Trista's experience might come in handy. I had visions of turning over some of the course scheduling if she worked out.

We chatted more about Trista's certifications and her yoga practice before concluding the interview.

I bounded toward the office door. "I have one more candidate to interview, but I'll be in touch by the end of the week. Call me if you have any questions."

After walking Trista up to the front, we shared another firm handshake.

"Trista?"

My interviewee and I turned sharply. Graham walked over, jaw slackened.

"Oh, my God! Graham!"

Trista flung herself at his taut, sweaty form.

"What are you doing in Austin?" Graham's pitch rose as he spoke.

"I moved back down here two years ago. My mom had cancer. She passed away a few months ago."

"Oh, Trista. I'm so sorry to hear that. She was a sharp, funny lady."

"She was..." Trista's voice turned wispy for a second. "But, hey, it's good to see you. Do you work out here?"

"I do. I—" Graham flicked his eyes over to me, observing the scene with an unwelcome stiffness in my spine. "My real estate company bought the building. That's how I found the place. I've been coming here for a few weeks now."

"Well, maybe I'll see you again, but I guess that's up to Alexa. I'm applying for a position here."

"Oh, you've gotten around to hiring a new instructor."

It took me a couple of seconds to realize Graham was addressing me.

"Yes. I've been putting it off, but I need to cut back my teaching schedule."

"I—"

"Well—"

"So—"

The three of us fumbled over ourselves to speak. I broke in again.

"Like I said, Trista. I'll be in touch this week. It was great meeting you." I smiled and stared, and Trista gave Graham a sideways glance.

"Great. I'll see you around, Graham."

I watched Graham watch the other woman's toned behind exit the building.

"You know her, huh?"

"Yes. In Dallas. I haven't seen her in ages. At first, I wasn't even sure it was her."

"And here she was."

"Wow. Trista Halpern. That's a real surprise."

He stared at the door and shook his head as if to dislodge a memory. The mix of shock and goggle-eyed pleasure rankled.

Finally, Graham refocused on the woman still standing in front of him—me.

"And she's about to start working here?"

"I haven't decided yet. I have some other candidates to see."

"I remember going to her studio for yoga. Her clients loved her."

"Good to know."

Did he have some kind of fetish for women who work in fitness? I thought back to the joke he'd made about dating women who own their own gym. Maybe that hadn't been a joke.

"Well, I'm going to grab my things and head home. Have a good workout."

"Hey, how about we meet up later?"

I glanced at him sideways as I pretended to be fixated on the class sign-up sheet at the reception desk.

"Can't tonight. I'm looking forward to getting home, kicking back, and relaxing."

"I know how to relax." He dropped his voice to a gravelly whisper.

"You'll have to find a way to relax yourself tonight." *Or find someone else. That shouldn't be hard.* The spike of jealousy made me feel foolish. "Maybe later in the week?"

I let my chest rise as I inhaled and pulled my shoulders back, willing a pleasant expression on my face.

"I'll call you then."

"Do that."

Then, I left Graham and his quizzical brow behind me and marched back to my office to collect my things.

CHAPTER 27

GRAHAM

*M*y urgent, Pavlovian response to my ringing phone nearly sent me sprawling naked and wet across the Italian marble of my bathroom. I didn't recognize the Dallas number popping up, but answered it anyway.

"Hello?"

I snatched a towel off the rack and stepped carefully into the carpeted master bedroom.

"Graham! You still have the same number. I thought I'd take a chance."

"Trista. God, it was a surprise to see you today."

"I know. Me too. How are you?"

"Great. Things are good."

A sick feeling settled over me. Why would Trista want to talk to me after all this time?

"I'm glad. I thought I'd call and catch up."

"Oh, great."

The last time I'd seen Trista, tears trailed salty streaks down her cheeks, and she called me a bastard who was wasting her time.

After a year of dating, she raised the prospect of moving in together—a thought that had never occurred to me. I responded with surprise.

"Why would we want to live together? Things are good as they are."

I'd barely had time to duck before her glass came flying at my head. The conversation devolved from there, and we broke up. I tried to contact her again and work things out, but she wanted none of it.

In the end, I wrote Trista off as another woman wanting to rush into a level of commitment that didn't match what we felt—just because she had some timeline in her head that matched up with how fast her friends were moving in with their boyfriends and getting married. Not the girl for me.

"So, how are things with you?" I asked.

"Getting back to normal since my mother passed away."

"That's right. Trista, I'm sorry. I know how hard it is to lose a parent."

"Yeah. It was hard. That's why I moved back." Her quick intake of breath whistled over the phone line. "Anyway, I was thinking maybe we could catch up in person sometime."

Oh, dear. That wouldn't do her employment chances any favors. Regardless of whether Alexa and I were exclusive, I couldn't date one of her employees. "I could go for a drink."

"Okay, yeah. Want to meet up tomorrow?"

Jonah was driving down to hang out for the weekend. We could make it a trio for Friday happy hour. "Sure, I have a friend coming into town, so I hope you don't mind a third wheel."

Another silence met my comment, and I wondered if the line had dropped. "Hello?"

"I'm here. Yes. Okay."

"Great. You remember Jonah, don't you?"

"Yeah. It'll be great. I can catch up with him too then."

"Perfect. How about Logan's, six o'clock?"

"See you there. Good seeing you, Graham."

A friendly hangout might not be what she had in mind, but that's all I had for Trista. I still had a small scar from the shattered glass of our last encounter. I didn't need the drama.

CHAPTER 28

ALEXA

*T*he next afternoon, Melissa had less interest in business and more interest in pestering me about meeting "this mysterious Adam."

"Every time you say that, it sounds like you're talking about the original, biblical man. Like he's slithering through the woods and going to offer me an apple."

I tapped a pen on the edge of my desk, cradling the phone with my shoulder. Melissa took advantage of our call to drop in another plea.

"That would be Satan, not Adam. You really could use a trip to church." Melissa laughed. "I'm curious."

"I know you are. How about tonight? We can meet at Logan's."

"I think Kyle is working late, but I'll be there. Can you meet early, like at six o'clock?"

"I can. I have to check with Adam. And I think I'll see if

Toby or Sarah can come. The more the merrier."

Melissa expelled a single, disbelieving chuckle. "You just want the buffer of a group."

"Yep."

GETTING to the bar by six meant rushing out the door and hurrying through traffic. I snatched my purse out of the passenger seat and rambled down the sidewalk toward the bar. The happy hour crowds mingled, and it took me a while to locate Adam's dark head standing by the bar. Then, I saw Melissa in a corner booth.

I maneuvered toward Adam and gestured toward the back corner. He headed that direction, and I trailed behind.

I squeezed between two partying strangers, only to be blocked by a group who'd pulled together two tables. I doubled back around a post, wondering if the fire marshal might show up and shut everything down.

My eyes stayed focused on my destination in the back corner, and I ran right into the back of a guy. His beer tipped, spilling half of it.

"Oh, my God. I'm so sorry." I fumbled to find napkins, but a familiar voice caught my attention.

"You're normally so coordinated."

I whipped around. Graham dabbed at his wet shirt with a small, square bar napkin.

"God, Graham, I'm so sorry. It's so crowded, and I lost track of where was going. Let me see if I can go get a towel or something."

"Don't worry about it. Most of it ended up on the floor. It's not that bad. And it's his drink anyway." Graham stopped wiping his shirt for a moment and pointed at his friend. "Jonah, this is Alexa."

The tall, lean, and very blond man whose beer I had ruined extended his hand. "Hi, nice to meet you. If I'd stuck with whiskey instead of ordering a pint of beer, this might not have happened."

I shook his hand and smiled, chagrined. "I'm sorry. I wasn't paying attention."

Something on Graham's phone had him temporarily preoccupied, so Jonah had to make small talk.

"I've heard a lot about you, and it's nice to finally meet you."

I hoped the blood rushing to my face wouldn't be too obvious. I could only imagine what Jonah had heard. Graham finally looked up and shoved his phone back in his pocket. "He drove down from Dallas for some meetings and is staying for the weekend."

I glanced over to the corner where Melissa craned her neck to see what had gotten her friend's attention. I held up a hand to signal for her to wait and stepped toward Graham and his friend.

"It's nice to meet you too. Congratulations, I hear you're expecting. Or at least that your wife is." I stumbled over my words. For the first time in a long time, I wished I still lived in New York City where randomly running into people that you know was an oddity.

"Thanks. We're really excited about it. Are you here with friends? You should join us."

Out of the corner of my eye, I saw Graham wince.

"Although, I guess you probably already have a table," Jonah backtracked, glancing at the reaction on his friend's face.

"My friend, Melissa, got us a table."

I turned away, but then, Adam planted himself beside me.

"I'd wondered what waylaid you. Hi, I'm Adam."

As soon as the British man spoke, a light of recognition turned on in Graham's eyes.

"You're her visitor from England. How are you finding Austin?"

"It's been lovely."

The cocky amusement in Graham's laugh only wound the tension in my gut tighter. I racked my brain for something to say to get Adam back over to the table with Melissa. Instead, to my chagrin, Melissa dodged bar patrons and walked our way.

The inevitability of all of us socializing hit me, and I relented.

"Adam, this is Graham. His development company owns the building where I have my gym."

"Ah, you're her new overlord."

"Landlord," Graham snapped, smiling. "Things are quite congenial between us."

Jonah coughed and developed an inordinate interest in whatever sporting event flashed on the television above the bar. Melissa's eyes rounded.

"Our table is still available, Alexa." She gestured over her shoulder with her thumb.

"I don't want to crash your guys' night," I proclaimed.

God bless Melissa for trying to break up the clusterfuck that was this encounter. It didn't work.

Jonah tilted a grin at me and my compatriots. "Not a problem. Aren't we waiting on a friend of yours anyway, Graham? We have a big table right here. The more, the merrier. Are you expecting anyone else?"

"No. Toby and Sarah aren't going to be able to make it," I responded.

"We've got six seats right here." Jonah pointed at the table.

Graham pulled out the stiff-backed stool at the bar-height table and slid into it. Resigned, I went to the other side of the table and sat opposite me. Adam and Melissa took seats on either side of me, Melissa on my right. Jonah cast a dubious look at the crew and then sat next to Graham across from Melissa.

"Who are you expecting?" Melissa asked.

"Trista."

"The woman I just hired for my open instructor position?" I asked like I didn't know the answer.

"I didn't know you'd hired her."

"I called her this morning and offered her the job. She starts on Monday."

I darted a fierce look in his direction.

"Good for her. And for you. She'll be great. Anyway, she wanted to meet out and catch up. Since I was coming out with Jonah anyway, I thought she could join us."

The verbal backbend Graham did to explain why he was meeting up with Trista gave me a small thrill. Then, I felt sick. The evening couldn't get more awkward— especially once Graham turned his attention to my overseas visitor.

"Adam, Alexa tells me that you work in technology. You're here for South by Southwest?"

A deep frown formed on Adam's face that he tried to sweep away with a forced smile. I wiped my damp palms on my pants.

"I'm working with a software company that's opening an office here, so I'm actually going to be here for a few months."

Graham blinked rapidly as he took in the news that British Adam wasn't going home anytime soon. I swept my gaze between the two men and took a settling breath.

Why should I be nervous? No doubt, Graham kept checking his phone to see when Trista would arrive. We both had impromptu meet-ups with an ex. Plus, Graham and I had a clear understanding.

Socializing with all of us at the same time was a circus act, but we were all adults.

"If you need someone to show you around, I'd be happy to. I know Alexa's been quite busy with work," Graham suggested.

"Thanks for the offer, but I've been getting around just fine."

"Alexa said that you were a consultant, so what are you doing at the tech conference?" Melissa drew Adam's attention away from Graham.

"I connected my client with an expert on the future of artificial intelligence in gaming. He's presenting on a panel, and we're meeting with him. I'm hoping to bring him into the project. His participation could help my customer garner extra money in their next call for investment."

Jonah broke in, excited. "What is it exactly that they do? I run a private equity firm that invests in tech companies. We always have our eye out for new opportunities."

Adam moved around the table to have a deeper discussion with Jonah about his projects, leaving me and Melissa to chat with Graham. However, just as I opened my mouth to speak, Graham's phone rang and he stepped away from the table.

Melissa dipped her head toward my ear. "This isn't awkward at all."

A moment later, he stepped back to the table.

"Something came up, and Trista's not going to be able to make it."

"Oh, really? That's too bad," Alexa replied, infusing my voice with as much sincerity as I could muster.

"It is. She knows Jonah from when we all lived in Dallas. It would have been nice for us all to catch up."

"How long have you known Trista?"

"Oh, man. Eight or nine years? She still had her yoga studio."

"Is that how you met?"

"Yes. I had an ex-girlfriend who is really into yoga, and she used to drag me to class. We broke up, but I kept going to yoga. Then, Trista and I got to be friends."

Graham might not want to admit it, but obviously, "friends" didn't capture the full essence of their relationship. Trista had looked at Graham the way a starving junkyard dog looks at a bowl of kibble.

Each of his relationships sure followed quickly on the heels of the last—one practically leading to the other. I hoped I hadn't made a mistake hiring Trista, then decided it probably wouldn't matter. He had better sense than to sleep with the boss and the employee.

"She does seem friendly."

"She is. It's part of what made her really good at her job. You'll be glad you hired her."

"I hope so."

Adam broke away from his conversation with Jonah after exchanging business cards. "Sorry to spend so much time talking business. I feel like I've been neglecting you."

A knot formed between my shoulder blades when Adam draped an arm on the back of my chair. I scooted forward. "We were talking about Trista, my new fitness instructor. She and Graham were friends in Dallas. And I guess you knew her too, Jonah."

"I did. I haven't seen her since she and Graham broke up."

Graham grimaced, and Jonah snickered, seemingly delighted to bust his friend.

"It was years ago. I'll have to tell you the story some time." His eyes bored into mine and then flicked to Adam.

Jonah grinned broadly. "You and Trista can tell us together when she gets here."

"She can't make it. We're going to meet up tomorrow."

My left eye twitched. I reminded myself that I didn't own Graham. He could do whatever he wanted.

"How about a game of pool?" he asked.

Adam shook his head. "I'm not one for billiards. Do they have darts? Every proper pub in England has darts."

"Sorry to disappoint you. No darts. Alexa owes me a chance to redeem myself. I went easy on you last time, darlin'. I didn't know I was dealing with a pool shark."

"If that's what you need to tell yourself in order to feel better about my whooping your butt, then bless your heart, darlin'. What about you, Melissa? You up for a game?"

"No. Kyle's going to stop in for a little bit before his night shift. He'll be here in a few minutes, and I don't want to miss him."

Graham slid off his chair and headed toward the pool tables, stopping shoulder to shoulder with me. His eyes slanted with mischief. "I guess it's just you and me."

"I'll join you," Adam piped in before I could respond to Graham's unspoken challenge.

CHAPTER 29

GRAHAM

I hadn't taken it easy on Alexa during our first turn at pool, but I knew I could play better. Something about having Alexa's puppy dog, Adam, sniffing around sharpened my vision and my shots.

"You've been practicing since the last time we played."

Alexa plucked the cube of blue chalk off the edge of the table and circled it around the tip of her pool cue. The slow and deliberate movements put alternate visions of her hands at work in my mind. I focused on her eyes to eliminate the distraction. Tonight, I would not get shamed at the table.

"Nope. Just bringing my 'A' game. Your shot."

Alexa lined up a wicked bank shot and sank two more stripes one after the other. The cue ball rolled to a stop in perfect alignment three inches from her next target.

Adam applauded and doubled over in rapturous laughter. *At least I'm not afraid to play the game.*

I fantasized about spearing the Brit through the chest while Alexa easily dropped the only remaining striped ball in a corner pocket. Just like that, even with my best effort, the rout was on. I dropped my chin to my chest and shook my head.

"You're evil. I think you've been touched by the devil. It's black magic."

"I do have an aunt in New Orleans who tells fortunes and sells voodoo dolls." She waggled her fingers and cooed spooky noises at me before turning all business again. "Eight ball, side pocket."

I closed my eyes, not needing to look. The smack of the cue and the soft thump of a single ball dropping and rolling in the depths of the table. My left eye cracked open. "Was it the side pocket?"

Alexa met my eyes stone faced. "Of course it was. Want to play again?"

I laid my pool cue on the table and smacked the felt.

"Not before I have another drink. Do you want another vodka soda?"

"Sure."

"I'll get your drink. Two limes?" Adam raised an eyebrow at me.

"Yes, thank you."

"I'll take a Macallan 18, neat." My smooth smile achieved its desired result—a contemptuous pout from the Brit.

"I'll be right back."

Adam jogged up the two steps to the main bar area and disappeared around the corner. I couldn't help but comment. "He likes you."

"I guess. I've told him that I'm not starting anything up with him again."

"So it is 'again?'"

Alexa paused and met my eyes directly. "It would be, except that it's not. What about you and Trista? Is that 'again?'"

"Does 'never again' count? We had a pretty bad breakup. I'm not going down that road again."

"Then watch out. I think she has other ideas."

"How do you know?"

"The way she threw herself at you the other day."

I shrugged. "No. We hadn't seen each other in forever. That's all."

"Good. Because sharing a man with one of my employees isn't on my 'to do' list. It's bad business."

Her jealousy had nothing to do with business, and it delighted me more than I wanted to admit.

"Point taken. And while we're issuing warnings, watch out for that one."

"Adam?" Alexa chuckled.

"The looks he's throwing me...I don't like him."

"Whereas, you're looking at him with peace in your heart?" She laughed again. "Both of you are just being macho. I'm not taking either one of you seriously."

I skirted around the table until I was close enough to reach out and draw my fingertips down her bicep. "That hurts. I take us quite seriously."

She stepped back and squared up to me. Her height matched mine, and I realized how often I depended on my greater physicality to draw a reaction from a woman.

Amusement brightened her eyes, and I leaned closer. A clean, floral scent filled the air between us. Perfume? Or maybe shampoo? Either way, I dipped my face behind her ear and inhaled. I reveled in her smell and her sudden intake of breath.

She turned her head and whispered in my ear. "Enjoy it. This is what a winner smells like."

I fell back with laughter and sat on the edge of the pool table. The half-moon of her pearlescent smile warmed my insides. I'd never thought of a woman as cocky before, but that's what she was.

Alexa smacked my thigh with the back of her hand and stepped back, rolling her pool cue between her hands. "Rack 'em up."

"There you go being bossy again. God, the money you're leaving on the table. As a businessman, it so hard to watch."

"What, are you a pimp now? The way you talk and you with your crazy friends, maybe I better watch out for you."

"Hmm. Yes. Keep an eye on me." I jumped up, grabbed the pool rack, and began pulling the balls out from the end of the table. Alexa squinted at me with faux suspicion, glaring and laughing.

I slid my fingers into the bottom of the loaded rack and slid it along the table to get it in position. "Shall I break?"

"Have at it."

I lined up the cue ball and leaned over. Right as I took a shot, Adam loudly announced his return. The cue ball skittered, tapping the lead ball in the wrong spot, and the balls moved no more than a few inches.

Adam sat the three drinks he triangulated in his hands on the nearby table and glanced at the still-clustered balls in the center of the pool table. "Tough go there, mate. Maybe give the lady a try at it."

Alexa took her drink off the table and tossed me a sympathetic look. "Go ahead and re-rack. Your shot got interrupted."

I had no choice but to take the redo and ignore Adam's baseless bravado. "Why don't you play this round, Adam?

Getting in the game is more fun than looking on from the sidelines."

Sizing up the Brit, I knew that if the asshole had any skills at all, he would take great delight in mopping the floor with either one of us. "Why don't we play in teams? Alexa can see if Melissa wants to join us."

"Sounds good. You and Melissa versus me and Alexa." Adam spoke as if his suggestion settled the case.

"Or," Alexa began, "we could go with a battle of the sexes."

I eyed Adam. Be on the same team with that jerk off? I wanted to argue, but Melissa stepped down into the side room with the pool table, clutching her cocktail.

"Just in time. You and I are going to take it to these guys in the next game." Alexa pulled a stick off the wall and handed it to Melissa, who froze. Her neck tensed, not moving, while her eyes flung back and forth between me and my rival.

"O-kay. I hardly ever play, and when I do, I suck. So, I guess that makes sense."

I hid my smile. "Excellent idea. This way, the teams can be balanced. Adam doesn't play much and neither does Melissa."

I pulled another stick from the wall and handed it to Adam, then slapped him heartily on the back. The bare teeth of the Brit's taut grin stiffened my spine.

I stepped toward him, unflinching. "I'll break."

"Perfect." Alexa bowed her head with Melissa's, chuckling.

Adam chalked his cue stick, still fixated darkly in my direction. I squeezed him out of my peripheral vision and snapped the break shot quickly, accurately. The balls scattered wildly across the felt.

I would have to keep an eye on Alexa's new suitor if she wouldn't.

CHAPTER 30

ALEXA

I hated the term "Girls' Night Out." It always sounded like some housewives escaped their chains in the basement for the evening. Nevertheless, my friends and I enjoyed the happy hour specials, dubbed "GNO Saturday" at one of our favorite sushi restaurants downtown.

We toasted with our half-price sake, grateful our long week was over. I reveled in the fact that I had taught the last of my Saturday classes. Bringing Trista on board would be a godsend. I crossed my fingers that it would work out.

"To getting work off my plate."

"Here, here," Melissa cheered.

Holly lifted her small ceramic cup of hot sake. "I've got good vibes about Trista."

"Me too. I hope she likes it and sticks with Starlight. The worst thing about aerobics instructors is how flaky some of them are. The good ones are great, but the bad ones..." I dropped my forehead to the table three times.

"Same with massage therapists."

"Maybe it's a universal human thing," Holly proffered.

"Maybe." I shrugged. "It's crazy. All you want are good employees who show up when they're supposed to and don't suck."

"Remember that one girl you hired after Nina left?"

"Luna."

Holly snorted. "Looney more like it."

"Yeah. That should have been a clue. I don't know what she was on."

Melissa downed her sake and refilled her cup. "Or if she needed to be on something. Isn't she the one you caught having a threesome in the hot tub overnight?"

I grimaced. "She used her key to get into the gym with her friends. I found them passed out the next morning tangled up like a sex pretzel."

"Thank God for bleach." Holly shuddered. "But you know, we catch people screwing at the gym every once in a while. It's gross. I don't understand it."

I did – sort of. "The blood gets pumping. A lot of them are really fit. Hormones get raging. People start screwing. Every gym I've worked in has had the same problem at some point."

Holly kept shaking her head. "No. Still disgusting."

"Gyms are pick-up joints," Melissa explained. "That's where I met Kyle. The gym in the student center when we were in college. He had the worst pick-up line. 'I got stopped by the police on the way here. He told me it was illegal to carry these guns.'"

"No!" Holly shouted.

"He flexed and everything. It was so bad."

I squeezed my eyes shut, shaking my head. "I can't believe he recovered from that."

"Somehow, he made it come across as cute. We started talking, and there you go." Melissa flicked her hand in the air and then stared at me. "It just goes to show that first impressions don't have to last."

I gulped my drink. Just because Melissa and Kyle were bounding toward a happily ever after, didn't mean I had to be. Graham and I had a completely different deal.

"How are things with Graham?" Holly asked.

"There aren't really 'things' with Graham. We've gone out a few times. It's not serious."

Her face relaxed in relief. "Good."

"Why?"

Holly caught her bottom lip in her teeth. "I—I've seen him chatting up a couple of other women at the gym, and I heard Shauna talking with Bridget. She said she thought she was making progress with him. Ever since he joined, half the single women started circling like there's blood in the water."

Melissa jumped in. "She could be exaggerating. You know Shauna."

I breathed through the instant tightening of my diaphragm. He was a good-looking guy, and like I said, gyms were a hot bed of hookups.

"He's a flirt. We're not exclusive or anything. That said, I don't want to get into a catfight with a client over him. I'll ask him and see what he says."

"I almost didn't say anything."

I smiled. "Don't worry about it. We're not serious."

CHAPTER 31

GRAHAM

I agreed to meet Trista again at Logan's—just the two of us. I arrived shortly after seven and squeezed up to the bar, which was packed wall to wall. With no seating readily available, I joined the throngs hovering and waiting for the people who had seats to give them up.

After a few minutes, I noticed a man asking for the check while his female companion gathered their things. Rather than take a chance, I tapped the guy in the shoulder and asked straight out if I could have their seat.

"There are a lot of people waiting." The man glanced around the bar.

"Can you do me this favor? I'm waiting for a friend. A friend of the female variety…"

As I suspected, the guy did the bro-code thing and set me up to impress my lady friend with my ability to score seats. The couple left, and I staked my claim—much to the irrita-

CHASING YOU | 187

tion of several people around me. I didn't care. I hated waiting.

She arrived about fifteen minutes later as the mob grew impatient with my occupation of two seats.

"Hey, you! It's so great to see you."

Trista attempted to give me a hug, which didn't quite work since I was seated in the bar stool. She settled for curling her hands around the back of my neck and pulling me cheek to cheek.

She wore the same perfume she always had—a designer fragrance that smelled of cinnamon and musk. It always made my nose itch. I stifled a sneeze as she climbed into the stool next to me.

Her short, black skirt climbed up her thighs. The outfit showed off her strong, defined legs, which flowed down to a sexy pair of open-toed platform pumps. "Fuck me" shoes if there ever were a pair. She wore a red halter top, tied behind her neck with an inviting bow. The blouse plunged in the front, and as she positioned herself on the stool, her breasts pushed together, swelling nearly to the point of spilling. I cast my eyes away and caught the attention of the bartender.

"What do you want to drink?" I looked at my non-date sideways.

She peered over into my glass. "What are you having?"

"A glass of Cabernet."

"Sounds good."

I ordered her the same and launched into small talk.

"Did it take you long to get here? The traffic has been a mess."

"I guess. I hardly even notice anymore. I'd been living out in Round Rock, so anytime I had to come into the city, it was a nightmare."

"You're not still there?"

"No. I sold my mom's house and moved to East Austin."

I read her face for signs of whether she would want to talk about her mother. I knew from experience that sometimes you just wanted to stay happy.

Trista smiled and flipped her hair.

I'd keep it light. "I still can't believe that part of town is now the trendy place to live. Back in the day, all you wanted to do was avoid East Austin."

"I love it. I'm glad to be back in the thick of things. What about you? Where do you live in these days?"

She crossed one leg over the other below the knee, brushing her leg against mine. Her smile puckered in invitation.

I swallowed hard. "The other side of town. In West Lake."

"Nice. Posh." Trista giggled. "You're making me regret that I ever broke up with you."

Her hand brushed my thigh, and I turned, catching her fanning her lashes at me.

My crotch tightened, and I pressed my heels into the bar stool.

Our tumultuous relationship always seesawed between her not being able to get enough of me and then nearly throttling me. Trista ran hot—surface of the sun hot—and ice cold.

I wasn't doing that again.

"That was probably for the best." I laughed. "As I remember it, we didn't want the same things."

"You still don't want to get married? Or have kids?"

"Those are big questions."

"I'm just curious." Trista picked up the red wine newly delivered in front of her and swirled it gently, nosing the glass.

I couldn't respond to Trista's inquiry. Not because I was

incapable, but because the answers would never be applicable to her. When I was younger, I took screaming and yelling and passionate make-up sex as a sign of great feeling.

I couldn't contemplate marriage and kids sitting across from a woman so tempestuous.

"I'm not ruling anything out if I meet the right woman."

"You've matured. That's good news."

"I suppose I have." *Have you?* I wouldn't ask her that question. "What else is been going on in the past seven years?"

"I sold my half of the studio to Trina. From what I hear, the business has really taken off. I think she's opened a couple of extra locations."

"You don't keep in touch with her?"

"We lost touch," she answered curtly. *Hot and cold.*

"Do you miss having your own business? You always loved being in charge of every aspect of the operation."

"I did, but running everything is exhausting. Mostly what I miss is the personal contact with clients. I'm excited to start working at Starlight Fitness. Alexa seems like she'll be a great boss. Do you know her well?"

I poured over Trista's blank expression. Innocently asked question or a mining expedition? She sipped her wine and continued to gaze at me with wide-eyed interest.

"I haven't known her long. We bought the building back in January, and that's when we met."

"Oh. I thought you two seemed friendlier when I ran into you at the gym that day."

Her innocent eyes blinked at me, but I realized her game. "We've gotten to know each other since I started working out there. From what I've seen, you're right. She's a good boss, and you're lucky to work there."

"Cool. That's good to know. How's your dad?"

I welcomed the new line of questioning. I caught her up

on the goings on of my family and the few friends we'd once shared. Once we ordered dinner at the bar, I relaxed. Trista quit pumping me for information about my personal life, and I remembered how much fun she could be when we were't entangled in a messy relationship.

After we ate, we surrendered our bar seats to other people who wanted to grab dinner, moving closer to the entrance as the throngs pressed toward the bar.

"I miss this." Trista tipped her face up toward me. A man passed behind her, and she made a big show of being bumped, throwing her body against mine and bracing herself with her hands on my shoulders. Not sure if she were really about to topple over, I grabbed her around her waist.

I righted her on her feet and my hand slipped down, trailing over her firm ass. I couldn't go there again, but damn, she still had a rocking body. Feeling a little nostalgic, I held my hand there, smiling down at her.

"I do, but I don't."

She tossed her hair back, which thrust her breasts up and gave me a tantalizing view. Oh, the mistakes I'd once made. I gave her backside another quick pat, looked up, and froze.

The last person I needed to see me right now walked in the front door. The statuesque woman blazed at me with rage-filled eyes. *Oh, shit.*

CHAPTER 32

ALEXA

I spotted Graham as soon as I walked into Logan's. His hands slid down the back of a firmly built woman and then settled squarely on her ass. The woman in the skintight outfit and "fuck me" pumps laughed. Graham's familiar smirk shined down on her. Not until he lifted his eyes and met mine did he push the woman away.

"Oh, shit."

The expletive got the petite, but muscled, woman to turn around and blanch before blushing. I approached them with calm resolve.

"I see you're getting to know my new instructor. Oh, wait. That's right. You two already know each other." I pressed my lips together and tried to keep my nostrils from flaring like a longhorn bull.

"Look, Alexa, this isn't what it looks like. I was telling Trista that she and I are just going to be friends."

"Really?" Trista and I expressed our disbelief at the same time, causing me to shake my head.

"You know what, Graham. I can't even be mad. You and I aren't exclusive. That's clear. So, it's none of my business. Except it is. She does work for me, but that's not your problem." I turned heel and returned to my friends.

Holly reached out and squeezed my arm. "Let's just go somewhere else."

"No. We came here to have a drink, and that's what we'll do. He could do whatever he wants."

"There are hundreds of bars within spitting distance of this place," Melissa pointed out.

I dropped my voice. "I'm not giving him the satisfaction. Who else wants a cocktail? I'm going to the bar."

I didn't wait for my friends' approval or continued sympathies. A woman on a mission, I forced my way forward and made eye contact with the bartender.

"Can I get three tequila shots please?"

While I waited for the drinks, Graham and Trista huddled together, sparring. Or Trista was sparring. Graham had that patronizing, "Just calm down, sweetie," look that men get when they've messed up, but want you to believe you're overreacting. Trista sniped one last time and then fled.

The bartender poured three golden shots and left my tab open. Drinks in hand, I scrambled back to my friends and passed out my wares.

"Bottoms up."

I slammed the tequila shot like I hadn't since my last year of college. I should have been more specific with regard to the quality of the tequila because the pungent burn hit me like a one-ton pickup.

"Alexa, please. Let's talk outside."

Without turning to look at Graham, I spat out a, "fine,"

and walked outside, knowing he would follow. When I heard the footsteps behind me come to a stop, I whirled around.

"Honestly, Graham, you can do whatever you want. But I thought we had this conversation. Yesterday. How could you expect this not to bite you in the ass? Correction, bite me in the ass. Or Trista. This is my business. You are astoundingly fucking selfish."

"I'm not sleeping with Trista, and I wasn't going to sleep with Trista."

"So, feeling her up in the bar is what then?"

"I wasn't feeling her up. She stumbled, and I caught her and we kinda laughed. I literally was just telling her that we can't go back to where we were."

"Is that why you were leering at her tits?" I threw my hands to my temples and then to the sky. "Don't answer that. I don't have the right to tell you what to do with your life. I just wish you gave more consideration to how what you were doing affects everyone else. But, I guess, you're not that guy. I know that now."

"I'm sorry." Graham's pleading eyes searched mine for understanding, and I gave him none. "I let my little head have more control than the head on my shoulders. I shouldn't have been touching her like that if for no other reason than I knew she wanted to start things up again, and I don't."

"I'm not talking about this anymore. I'm hanging out with my friends, trying to have a good time, and you're blowing my buzz."

I took a couple of strides back toward the door, and Graham changed his tack.

"So, you're hanging out with your ex and introducing him to your friends. You expect me to be okay with that, so I roll with it. But one freaking moment with an ex-girlfriend and you flip out."

His indictment turned me back around and sent me storming toward him.

"I wasn't groping Adam. And I introduced you to him because he and I are nothing, and it wasn't a big deal."

"You introduced me to him because you had no choice. And he's practically in love with you, so you need a way to back him off. You used me to deflect him. Don't kid yourself."

I huffed and looked past him, down the street. "Deflecting is making this about me when you're shuffling things around so she doesn't show up yesterday and you two can canoodle tonight one-on-one on your date."

I blasted him, all the while chastising myself for not walking away. Our relationship wasn't a serious one, so why get into this big to do with him? *Walk away.* But I couldn't.

"It's not a date."

"Like our not dates?" I smiled to stave off a grimace. "It's fine. Really. We both know what we wanted. Right? We got it. Now, it's over."

"Got it. That's good to get straight." Graham's words snapped. "But please tell me you're not going to take this out on Trista. She had no idea that you and I were seeing each other."

I felt like gagging at his protectiveness of another woman. "Of course I won't. That's the whole point. I don't want anything personal interfering with my business."

"Good. I wouldn't want our thing to make things hard for her at work. She's a good person, and she's good at what she does."

"Wow. She should have listed you as a reference."

"Alexa—"

"Forget it. Good night, Graham."

CHAPTER 33

ALEXA

*T*equila shots are a fast track to regret.

I could sense the sunlight through my eyelids before I threw off the covers and stumbled around my house in search of water. Vodka sodas never left me feeling like I'd licked the bottom of someone's shoe and then clubbed myself over the head with it.

After storming back into Logan's the night before, I doubled down on the party and downed two more tequila shots in short order. Melissa and Holly joined in out of sisterly solidarity.

"We can't let you drink alone. That would make this sad," Holly had declared before ordering the next round of shots— lemon drops. "But one more tequila shot, and I might lose my sushi."

Our raw fish dinner at the Japanese restaurant a few

blocks away was maybe the worst preamble to tequila-fueled drunkenness ever, but that escaped my mind as I ordered drink after drink.

Steeped in alcohol, we decided we needed to go dancing, so we took a pedicab a few blocks over to a nightclub. I remembered standing in line outside with the thumping bass pounding through the muraled brick wall. Holly recognized the bouncer and shimmied her way to the front, springing us from the line to the VIP rooftop.

Bumping bodies and free drinks courtesy of various men took us into the early hours Sunday morning. The next logical step was to grab a breakfast of sorts from the Tex-Mex food truck serving all-night migas around the corner. Melissa bowed out, going home to Kyle and a passable amount of sleep before heading to a late church service.

Holly and I rallied and filled up on a mashup of eggs, tortilla chips, and salsa, rolled in corn tortillas with a side of crispy potatoes and onions. The meal may have saved me from the worst of the hangover, even if late-night eating meant I'd have to white-knuckle it through a workout at some point.

But for now, I needed water. And lots of it. Simply being vertical made my temples pulse with pain. I filled a liter-sized water bottle and guzzled it before heading to the couch. I paged through my phone messages and saw numerous texts and two voicemails from Melissa.

"Morning, Mel," I grumbled when my friend picked up the phone.

"You're alive! I was beginning to wonder if I needed to swing by your house and make sure you weren't passed out face down on your lawn."

"It's not so bad as that. I took a rideshare home from the

taco stand. Of course, that took over an hour and probably cost me an arm and a leg with the surge pricing."

"How's Holly?"

"I haven't talked to her this morning, but she texted me when she got home. I'll see her at work tomorrow—hopefully. Of course, I'll also see Trista at work tomorrow. That should be fun."

I closed my eyes and circled my fingertips on my temples. None of that was Trista's fault, but it would make her first day on the job incredibly uncomfortable. Regardless of what Graham had said, his proclamation that he didn't want to date her clearly came as a shock.

"Do you think she'll quit?"

"I don't know. Most of me hopes that she stays on. Professionally, I really think she'll be great. A tiny sliver of me, though, would love to duck the whole issue and have her no-show me."

"You don't mean that."

I sighed. "No, I don't. I'll manage it the way that I always do. Rip the Band-Aid off with the horrible conversation and then move on."

"Have you heard from Graham?"

"No. He hasn't called or texted or anything. I wouldn't expect him to. Him, I definitely want to no-show. If he has any pride whatsoever, he'll never set foot in my gym again."

"Offer him his money back."

"I never actually processed his application. I can just tell him to go away. You think that would be childish?"

"I think it's practical."

"Enough about all that. Are you going to church today? It's Palm Sunday."

"I was, but Kyle wants to sleep in. Plus, I feel kinda dingy going to church with tequila seeping from my pores." Melissa moaned. "Why did you do that to us?"

"Stupidity. I used to drink tequila every weekend, all weekend, and bounce right back. That's not exactly happening this morning. Right now, I'm trying to stay horizontal."

"Pull it together. You want to be on your game tomorrow morning."

"I'm so dreading that conversation. The thought of it pisses me off all over again. He's such a jackass to mess with my business like this."

"Only business? You're not usually one to get this emotional over something like that."

I rolled over to hide in the sofa cushion. "I have no other right to be angry."

"You liked him, and he's treating that like it's nothing. You can be pissed off about it."

Guys I dated before had seen other women, and a handful of times, I ran into them at restaurants or events. Typically, it rolled off my back. Graham was different.

My anger bubbled and flowed like lava, slowly cooling to hard rock.

"I don't want to think about how pissed I am because it doesn't matter. He and I are done."

"He made a mistake, but that doesn't have to end everything if you like him. Where would I be if Kyle had written me off because I dumped him to chase Chris? As someone who's benefited from forgiveness, I can tell you I'm a big believer."

"Kyle loved you, and you loved him. Graham and I are not in love."

"Maybe not. I'm going to save you a lecture on how do

you know you're not in love if you don't focus on the person and give them a chance to be the one."

"That's saving it?"

Melissa sighed. "Stay strong and hydrate, sister."

"I'll try. Talk to you later."

As usual, she gave me much to consider, but allowing Graham back into my good graces wouldn't happen. He had to go.

CHAPTER 34

GRAHAM

"I've done some stupid shit in my life, but I've never been caught in the midst of it like last night, man."

I sat across from Jonah at a popular brunch spot near my house. We had a carafe of Bloody Marys on the table along with a hot pot of coffee. I needed both this morning.

"Why don't you try talking to her? In the light of day, she may have calmed down."

"You didn't see her. The look in her eyes screamed, 'Done.' She's a stubborn woman."

"Then, be done with her. Didn't this all start out because you wanted to get New Year's Eve out of your system? Mission accomplished."

Jonah popped a mini muffin in his mouth and chewed enthusiastically.

"It did…But I kind of started to like her. She was fun until the yelling started."

"So then, try to explain things to her."

I snorted. "Was my advice to you a few months ago this shitty?"

"Come to think of it, yes. It was. You told me exactly what I'm telling you now. And then you tried to get me to sleep with my ex-girlfriend or some random woman as if that would change how I felt about Shannon. I loved her, and no woman was going to change that. But you're not in love with Alexa, right?" Jonah snatched another muffin and jabbed it toward me. "Move on."

I nodded. Alexa, while interesting, was no more than a passing phase in my life. Last night had been embarrassing more than anything else. I'd get over it. "I still have to have another conversation with Trista. I probably fucked things up for her at her new job before she even started."

"Women can be vindictive."

"I don't think Alexa would take it out on her. She's very hard-core about her business, and if she hired Trista, it's because she was impressed."

"Your squeezing her employee's ass was probably also pretty impressive though."

My head fell back, and I groaned. With my eyes closed, I could see the aura of rage around Alexa when she walked into the bar and saw us. Hadn't she promised not to fire Trista? Or, hell, Trista might just quit? Except that Trista had already quit her old job. If things didn't work out at Alexa's, Trista would be unemployed. How utterly moronic I had been.

"I'll fix it."

"How?"

"Floods of apologies in every direction."

"If you can get either woman to stand still long enough to listen to you."

"I'll manage it. Alexa and I were supposed to meet with that couple I told you about—the ones with the diabetic little girl. We're fundraising for them. She'll have to talk to me at some point, and Trista...I'll just have to call her."

"You really started to like her?"

"Trista?"

"No, Alexa."

I rubbed my fingers over my stubbled chin. Thinking I would work my way through my feelings by sleeping with her was a miscalculation. Spending time with her was more addiction than catharsis. Every obstinate look and snide remark triggered the need for more. The woman was so much trouble—maybe too much—but I couldn't get enough.

The thought of admitting as much out loud gave me indigestion.

"We were having a good time."

"You keep saying that she's a good time. There are other women who offer good times. Less complicated women."

"And you're a big fan of less complicated?"

I raised an eyebrow, and Jonah cackled. He'd chosen the most complicated of women—a recovering addict, with a child, and two ex-husbands.

"Less complicated isn't all it's cracked up to be, but I thought that's what you were all about."

"Me too, and Alexa isn't...She's just...Alexa."

I roved a hand through my hair and gripped the back of my neck, having lost the ability to describe the woman or how I felt about her. Jonah's grin only irked me more, chasing me to another topic.

"How's the moving and shaking?"

"I'm making good contacts in support of my Congressional bid and raising a decent amount of money. My father is still angry about my party affiliation. Coming out as a Democrat may have been as horrible to him as my sister coming out as gay."

"Poor guy. He's had a rough couple of years."

Jonah's deeply conservative father had his daughter come out of the closet, his son marry a woman he couldn't stand, his wife file for divorce, and, now, his son goes public as a liberal.

"He has actually. I've never seen him as despondent as he's been about my mother moving out. I think he's still hoping he can lure her back."

"Maybe they'll work it out. Your parents belong with each other. It's hard to imagine one without the other."

"My mother doesn't feel that way. She's never been happier. She got back from a vacation in the Mediterranean with her friends and bought a house in my neighborhood 'to be near the baby.' Shannon is worried she'll be camping out in our nursery. I keep saying at least she's excited."

"That *is* progress."

Jonah's father wasn't the only one who didn't cotton to his wife in the beginning. The prospect of finally getting a grandchild worked wonders on the older woman.

"I enjoy having Mom around more, but don't tell Shannon I said that. I'm supposed to be creating 'healthy boundaries.'" Jonah curled his fingers into air quotes.

"As long as your mom plays nice, Shannon will come around."

"Don't say that. I've been optimistic!"

"Your mom's a nice woman. Or, nice-ish."

Jonah chuckled, then tipped his head in consolation. "She can be—when she wants to. I think she's motivated. Now, if I can only get her to stop dropping hints about names for our baby boy."

My eyes widened in horror. "What names?"

"Francis is a family name on her father's side—as is Cornelius."

"Nice," I laughed. "Classics."

"Yeah, like Ambrose," Jonah sniped, referring to his own middle name.

"Do you have a name picked out?"

"We do. I'm not supposed to tell anybody, so you have to promise not to say anything."

"No offense, Jonah, but your baby is only a topic that comes up when I talk to you."

"Funny." He threw a balled-up mini muffin wrapper at me. "Benjamin."

"Oh. That's nice and normal."

"It is."

A wide smile lit up Jonah's face, signaling his thorough domestication. Over the years, Jonah and I spent many a Sunday recounting wild sexual details of our weekend. Now, here we were talking baby names—and my discontent over a woman.

I slumped. We were *both* getting domesticated. And that wouldn't do.

CHAPTER 35

ALEXA

I left Trista a voicemail to assure her that she still had a job at Starlight Fitness and to schedule a meeting after her first early morning classes. Locked in the employee bathroom, I stared into the mirror and gave myself a pep talk.

Professionalism. That's how I would get through today and the few weeks it would likely take for me to get over the weekend's events. *You put on your game face and be professional.*

Trista sat in front of my desk, back straight and arms to the side facing upward as if she were in a contemplative yoga pose. I relaxed.

"Good morning."

Trista jumped, and she whipped her head around. "Good morning."

"Thanks for stopping in."

I rounded the desk and sat down. "This is incredibly

awkward, so I'd rather just acknowledge that than pretend this is a perfectly normal conversation to have on your first day of work."

The corner of Trista's mouth twitched, almost smiling, so I continued.

"That was an ugly scene on Saturday night, and I'm sorry to have involved you in some silly drama. It won't happen again, and I'm hoping that you'll join the team and enjoy working here."

Having delivered the speech I practiced all day Sunday, I held my breath and waited for Trista to respond. The other woman relaxed her grip on her knees and sat back in the chair.

"I had no idea you and Graham were dating," she blurted. "Nothing happened. He and I were together for a while, but that was a long time ago. Maybe I hoped we might reconnect, but trust me, not anymore. You and he…I wish you luck. Honestly."

"You don't need to worry about that. That's…over. The reason I wanted to have this meeting is to let you know that none of this is going to impact your work here. At least, I hope it doesn't."

Even if I didn't mean it, I knew assuring Trista was my only option. I couldn't very well fire the woman over personal issues. Beyond legalities, I would never want anyone to find me that petty.

"It won't. I promise. The classes this morning went really well, and I'm excited." Trista managed a sincere smile, and we both laughed. "How long exactly before this stops being weird though?"

"I think this one goes down for the ages in weirdness, but how about we start now deciding to let it go?"

"Sounds good. And I'm really, truly sorry for getting in the middle of all this."

"It's not your fault."

No, this was Graham's fault. He's the one who created this sticky situation. He was also next up for an awkward conversation.

I texted him and asked if he could stop by in the early afternoon. Trista would be on the other side of the building teaching, so that time gave us the best chance to not have a repeat run-in as a threesome.

~

GRAHAM

Even though I'd agreed to meet in Alexa's office, I texted her at lunch to move the meeting to neutral territory. We met at a coffee shop halfway between the gym and my office.

I stayed at the shop all morning working, so I could ensure she wouldn't beat me there. My laptop and bag were strewn over the table next to a half-eaten sandwich and empty coffee cup. I got up to throw away my trash and saw Alexa walking through the doors. She noticed me and marched over.

"I don't have much time since we're not in my office, and I have to drive back to meet with a personal training client. Where are you sitting?"

The chill emanating from her could cool an outdoor patio in August.

"In the back corner. You don't want to get a coffee or sandwich or anything first?"

"Nope."

She pushed past me and took a seat at the table I'd indicated. I dropped my trash in the bin and trudged back to the table at the speed of a man walking the plank.

"Thanks for meeting me here." I folded my computer closed and moved it to the side. My steepled fingers looked like a prayer.

"Listen, I'm only here to talk about one thing. I'd appreciate it if you didn't come around the gym. I talked to Trista this morning, and we've worked things out, but having you around will just make everything awkward all over again."

As she spoke, she folded her arms neatly in front of her and kept her face still. No flirtatious humor or teasing bravado. She gave me nothing.

"I see. And you don't want to discuss at all what happened on Saturday? I wanted to have the opportunity to explain again and apologize. I do apologize for creating an awkward situation for you and Trista. I wasn't thinking."

"I appreciate the apology, but it's not necessary."

She scooted back from the table and grabbed her purse.

"That's it?"

"I don't want to cover old ground."

"It's not old ground when we haven't even had the first conversation about it. Can you give me five minutes?"

She tensed up, but swung her bag onto the neighboring chair and sat back down. "Go."

"I let things get out of hand on Saturday, but I had no intention of getting involved with Trista. I'm aware of how sleazy it would be to be involved with both of you. Not to mention the fact that anything between Trista and I died a long time ago. I hate that you walked in at that precise moment. It couldn't have been worse timing."

"Yeah. That's the problem. You got caught. Otherwise, you're right. We wouldn't have an issue. I'd be clueless. Trista would be hanging onto the idea that you were interested in her. No problem at all."

"That's not true. I was telling Trista that there was no jumpstarting a new relationship. And there's nothing going on for you to be clueless about."

"Is that what you wanted to say to me?" She crossed her arms tightly through the handle of her purse, ready to bolt.

"I suppose that sums it up."

"Thanks for understanding about coming to gym. I think this will be easier on everyone."

Alexa sprang from the chair and charged out of the coffee shop, her tight butt swishing side to side. I watched, missing it already.

CHAPTER 36

ALEXA

*M*y hand paused, poised on the car door. I wanted to crawl home and curl up under the blanket on my couch until the sun came up and I had to go to work again tomorrow. Instead, I climbed out of the car and walked toward the Tex-Mex restaurant on South Congress where I agreed to meet Adam for dinner.

The days since my finale with Graham hadn't removed the tight band of hurt and regret that made it hard for me to breathe easy. *Shit.* I couldn't let a guy—especially a player like Graham—have a grip on me like this. I squeezed my eyes shut and clicked the button on my key fob to lock the door.

I found Adam chatting closely with the bartender and sipping on a rocks margarita.

"Hey." Tapping him on the arm got his attention.

"Hello. How are you? The bartender was just telling me where to go for salsa dancing. Have you ever been?"

"I'm good, and I have."

I loved salsa dancing. I hadn't dated many guys who were interested in going. The image of Graham swaying his hips to the rumble of a Latin band made me giggle. Could you salsa in chinos and loafers?

"You enjoyed it. We should go." Adam smiled. "With your friends or whatever. I don't want to be presumptuous."

He held his hand up in what I interpreted as a gallant concession to the fact that I was seeing someone else. I wasn't ready to open the door to Adam, so I didn't say anything about Graham.

"No worries. Although, it is more fun in a group. I may have to recruit some of Melissa's relatives. I went to a party at her place once, and the Navarro clan knows how to dance."

"You can invite Graham."

I shook my head and shrugged.

"What happened?"

I examined the line of liquor bottles behind him, thinking about my choice of cocktail. "Whatever happens with these things. It's not worth talking about."

"Absolutely." Adam held up his margarita, grinning. "I'd toast to exciting new possibilities, but we need to get you a drink."

"I'll get something when we get to the table."

His wide smile coaxed me into a better mood.

Dinner rolled along with easy conversation that kept my mind mostly off of the other man. I introduced Adam to chili rellenos—fried poblano peppers stuffed with spiced chicken, cheese, almonds, and raisins.

"That was amazing. Now, what kind of dessert should we order? I'm in the mood for something sweet." He licked his full bottom lip and drew it into his mouth as he perused the trifold dessert and cocktail menu on the table.

"They have good sopapillas, but I say we close out and head up the street to Amy's Ice Cream. It's amazing and an Austin tradition."

"Sounds perfect."

I motioned for the waiter to bring the bill, and when it arrived, I placed my credit card in the leather bill holder. "My treat this time."

"No way. I'm on an expense account. Let me get it."

I waved him off. "Nope. My treat. You can get it next time."

His white smile beamed. "Okay. If we are in agreement that there will be a next time, I'll relent."

I signed the check when it came back, and we meandered up the street, past storefronts like a music store advertising "RECORDS" in red letters. I peered in at the tattered album covers shielded by plastic from further damage. "I thought about getting a record player to listen to old vinyl again."

"Really?"

"It's mostly nostalgia. I still have some of my albums from when I was a kid. Or my parents do at their house."

"Like what?"

"*Sesame Street Fever. Thriller.*" I chuckled and kicked at a bottle cap underneath my foot. "That's kind of a big leap."

"*Sesame Street?* Like the puppets on television?"

"Yep. I loved listening to Ernie sing to his rubber ducky."

Adam laughed, and we walked on. I wiped my palms on my thighs. The thick night air threatened rain. A man with a mohawk rolled by in his classic car, reflecting the street lights off of its sleek lines in emerald and chrome.

"My dad always wanted to get a classic car from the '50s.

For a while, I thought about getting him a model or something. I know nothing about those old cars."

"That was a Chevrolet Bel Air."

I grinned. "You know about old American cars?"

"I went through a phase where I was obsessed with midcentury design. There's something alluring about the industrialism of those old, heavy machines. There's an artist who paints classic cars, showing off their angles and shiny chrome. God, I can't remember his name. I adore those old cars. That was a fascinating time. Things were more traditional then."

"I didn't peg you as a traditionalist."

"I am. In my own way, I suppose."

I took his arm and stepped to the curb, looking both ways. "We need to cross the street."

We hustled across to the ice cream shop, which consisted of a small stand and a smattering of picnic tables outside. Strains of Latin guitar grew louder on the street corner. The musician launched into a soft, melodious song in Spanish.

"This music is beautiful. We should dance." Adam stroked my hand and patted it. As the music rose on the night air, I gently rocked to the melody.

"Okay."

Adam pulled me into his body. Holding one hand up and wrapping his other arm around my waist, we began to move together. At first, I stepped right when Adam guided me left, but after a couple of missteps, we glided together on the bare dirt between the haphazardly arranged tables.

The rhythm picked up, and so did our feet. Adam released my waist and sent me twirling around, arms in the air. My bubble of laughter mixed with the twangs of the music as I whirled. A few fast strums of the guitar, and the song was over.

Adam drew me back to him. He tucked his chin on top of my shoulder, and his laughter warmed my neck. I grabbed his hands and took a step back.

"Another!" Adam called to the guitarist, and the man struck up another song, faster this time, throwing us into more of a cha-cha. My hips moved instinctively in response to the beat and Adam's motion.

The small crowd enjoying our ice cream began clapping. The lightness of my feet shocked even me as did Adam's ability to keep up as the pace increased. Back and forth, our bodies mirrored each other in perfect synchrony until the music halted.

Adam panted. "That was amazing. We have to make a date to go dancing. All night next time."

"I don't know if there's a place to dance all night, but I'm sure I could find something."

"We still need to order our ice cream. Tell me what's best."

"I like Mexican Vanilla with M&Ms. Let's see what they have."

I led Adam to the line and, when we got up front, surveyed our options. I put in my order and then advised him. "Lemon custard is tremendous. It depends on what you like. Chocolate or vanilla. Nuts. Candy. She's known for the Mexican Vanilla. You can get that and mix in some extras."

"Mexican Vanilla and Snickers."

Graham's perfect food. I crumpled up the thought and threw it away.

The young, dreadlocked woman behind the counter took Adam's money and started making our order. In profile, Adam's shining grin was shadowed, but I leaned into the pull of its exuberance. I was having a good time.

He grabbed our cups of ice cream and motioned with his chin toward the tables.

"Lead the way."

～

"ALEXA. You have another delivery up at the front."

"Can you bring it back, Holly? I'm in the middle of something."

I looked up as Holly rapped on my office door, which stood slightly ajar.

"These are gorgeous. Are the apology roses going to work?"

I waved my receptionist into the room and gestured for her to set the crystal vase on the cabinet in front of the window. The dozen crimson roses spiked with baby's breath could only be from Adam.

"Thanks, Holly, but I'm pretty sure these aren't from Graham."

"No?" Holly gave me a sly smile.

"No. Dollars to donuts, they're from Adam—the guy I met in London."

"The one who was in town for the festival? I thought you and he were just friends."

"I guess." I rubbed the bridge of my nose, squeezing my eyes shut to forestall a growing headache. Holly leaned over the floral display, inhaled, and then shook her head.

"Two guys are after you. Don't look so depressed."

I wrinkled my nose. "It's drama. I hate it."

"What's the drama? Graham pulls that stunt, and I told you all the things I've heard women in the gym saying about him. Tell him to go pound sand and heat things up with flower boy."

I poked absently at the floral offering, so Holly searched through the stems herself. She plucked a tiny note from the forked card holder and handed it to me. "Open it."

I popped open the envelope with Holly hovering.

"Do you want to tell me what it says or am I being nosy?"

"'If ever any beauty I did see, which I desired, and got, 'twas but a dream of thee.' It's not signed." My cheeks tingled with heat.

"It sounds British-y." Holly's tone turned speculative. "Kind of bold not to put his name."

The line sounded familiar, but I couldn't place it. I rotated in my chair and opened my laptop. A second later, I had my answer.

"It's a John Donne poem. 'The Good Morrow.' And, yeah, John Donne is British."

"Romantic and literate." Holly counted the traits on her fingers. "And you said Adam was handsome, right?"

"He is all of those things."

Holly threw her hand to her hip. "You have zero problems."

I stared at the card. "We went to dinner the other night and then walked up Congress to Amy's for ice cream. I had a good time. I don't know what's wrong with me."

I dropped the card onto my desk and rubbed the back of my neck.

Holly slid the note closer so she could read it. "The same thing that's wrong with all of us. We're jaded. We're tired. We're suspicious. Men disappoint us. But this guy sounds like a peach, and at least you know he hasn't slept with half of Austin. With all his running around, Graham might need a penicillin dip."

I frowned. "True."

"Guys like that are good for a while, but when they show their colors, you move on."

"I *am* moving on. That's not even the decision."

"Bring Adam by the gym or out to happy hour. I'll meet him and grill him and tell you what I think."

A stuttering laugh escaped my lips. I could always count on my friends to come through. "Okay. Maybe."

"No maybe. I, at least, want to set eyes on him. You can tell a lot just by looking a guy in the eye."

Yes, you could. From the moment I met Adam, he'd put his focus entirely on me. He had that way about him of being totally present. His gaze and his intentions never wavered. At this point, I should admire him for his consistency alone.

"Alright. Alright. We'll see."

"I better get back to the front." Holly looked at her watch. "Get excited. I can't tell you the last time a guy sent me flowers. Maybe I need to go find a foreigner to get a guy with romantic instincts."

"Hey, American men aren't so bad."

"Aren't they?" Holly tossed over her shoulder as she started back down the hallway.

CHAPTER 37

GRAHAM

"Y ou work out at Starlight Fitness."

I looked up from my computer at the stellar, auburn-haired woman tapping me on the arm. I'd brought my car into the dealership for an oil change and a car wash, taking advantage of the free Wi-Fi in the posh waiting area to get work done.

Her hair spilled over her shoulders is sexy, red waves, which she flipped back while surveying me with interest. She looked familiar.

"Yes. I do."

"I thought I'd seen you there. Shauna March."

She extended her hot-pink manicure toward me, and I shook her hand.

"Graham Ryan."

"I love that place. The owner, Alexa, she's my personal trainer. She's killer."

"I'll bet. She takes her training seriously for herself, so I imagine she's the same with her clients."

"Oh, you've met her?"

"Yes. My company bought her building, so I've worked with her."

"You're in real estate."

"I am."

"So am I. Residential real estate. Let me give you my card."

The sleek, black business card bearing Shauna's smiling face was in my hand so fast I wondered if she didn't keep them hidden up her sleeve like a magician. I recognized the realty group as one a friend of mine started about ten years ago.

"I know the woman who owns your company. Nadine Dominguez. She's married to an old college friend of mine."

"Nadine and Carlos? Oh, my God. Aren't they the best?"

She slapped me on the knee and lowered her lashes. The invitation in her eyes roused my interest. Why not? No sense in crying over spilt milk when another woman presented me with a fresh pitcher for the taking.

"They are. I've known them for years. Nadine found me the house I'm in now."

"Really? Where?"

"Westlake Highlands."

"Nice. There are some beautiful properties over there. I'm looking at one myself. Maybe we'll be neighbors."

"Maybe." I warmed her with my smile, and she flushed. I drew my hands over my knees and sat forward, leaning toward her. "How long have you been waiting for your car?"

"About half an hour. They said it would be forty-five minutes."

"Me too. We should be done about the same time." I made

a show of checking my watch. "My work day is winding down. Would you be up for a drink? I know a great sushi place less than a mile from here, Yukimura. If you like sushi."

"I looove sushi."

Her grin accentuated the deep rouge swept over her high cheekbones. As I examined her face, I finally remembered seeing Shauna at the gym without the warpaint.

I much preferred the bare look—including the sports bra she often wore without a shirt. Other than noting her outfit, I hadn't paid much attention to her at the time. Watching out for the gym's owner consumed most of my focus.

I shot my new target the most charming smile in my arsenal and held up the small plastic disk given to me by the service manager. "Great. Now we're just in a race to see whose buzzer goes off first."

She laughed, and minutes later, our buzzers went off within seconds of one another.

"See you there." Shauna fanned her lashes at me with a smile that I found cloying.

I shook off my aversion. *Get back in the saddle and ride.*

SHAUNA LAUGHED at virtually everything I said. While I liked to believe I had a good sense of humor, no one was *that* funny.

I reminded myself to be grateful for my congenial dinner companion and flicked my eyes every once in a while to the sequined V-neck of her silk blouse. *Nice.* I could do this. I had done this. Many times. I loved doing this.

The internal pep talk meant I lost track of what Shauna was saying until her voice rose and then stopped. Was that a question? The last thing I remembered, we were debating love at first sight, which she insisted was real. She launched into her own dating experiences, and I let her talk.

"It's hard to say." I stroked my chin and dropped my head as if thinking. The bright green line of her green apple martini had dipped low in the glass. "Did you need another drink? I'd hate for you to be thirsty."

"Yes, but don't think you're getting out of answering the question. Everyone has had that one ex who got away, and you regret it. I want to hear your story."

I didn't feel like telling it. Up until recently, I would have argued that I never regretted the end of any relationship. Now, I wasn't sure if my liaison with Alexa counted as a relationship, but I had a sense of loss that nagged at me. Did that count?

Even if it did, I wouldn't be telling Shauna about it. Instead of answering, I flagged down the waitress and ordered her another frilly martini and myself another Japanese single-malt whisky.

"Talk." Shauna zeroed in.

"Maybe it's too sensitive a topic," I replied, half telling the truth.

"That's sweet."

"My personal pain is sweet?"

"That you have someone that you've loved. That's sweet— maybe bittersweet."

"There was a woman once. We started up, had a fight, and it ended quickly. Not much to talk about, but it stung a little. I moved on."

"Such a man. Onto the next. Maybe you just haven't met the right woman yet."

"Maybe."

"You should do something about that." Her lips parted,

and her cleavage seemed to swell toward me. The visual took my mind down another rabbit hole.

"Graham Ryan."

The bark of my name came from my left side—angry, female, and unrecognizable. I swiveled and found the pinched face and blazing eyes of...God, what was her name?

I met the olive-skinned brunette right after New Year's and spent the night at her apartment. The diamond stud in her nose kickstarted my memory. Ruby. I joked that she should have a ruby in her nose instead of a diamond. She, like Shauna, had thought I was funny.

She didn't look amused now. After our night together, I pleaded an early start to work the next morning and bugged out of her place at midnight. She texted to invite me to dinner the next night.

Ruby ran a cookie delivery business—fresh hot cookies delivered within the hour all over the city. Ruby's Goodies. They were tasty. Her cookies, that is.

The rest of her wasn't so bad, either, but once I satisfied my sweet tooth, I hadn't had a craving for more. So, I'd ghosted her.

"I wasn't sure if you were still alive."

Ruby's eyes, dark like tarnished silver, fixed on me as she ground to a halt about two feet away. She gripped her martini glass, sloshing its contents down her arm. The spiked olive rolled side to side.

"I've been consumed with work, Ruby. I'm sorry I haven't gotten back to you about dinner."

"I'm sure." She glared at Shauna. "This doesn't look like work."

"It's not. I'm on a date."

"You're not so busy that you can find some new piece of

ass to screw. Watch out, sweetie, this guy wouldn't know a good woman if she bit him in the ass. But, hey, maybe you're not a good woman. Maybe that's what he likes. Fire-crotched whores."

"Hey, you don't know me! He and I just met—" Shauna started to press forward with her defense, but I raised a hand and stopped her.

I lowered my voice and spoke evenly. "I'm sorry I haven't gotten back to you, but that's not a reason to cause a scene. You think you're making a fool of me, but you're only making a fool of yourself."

"A scene? This is a scene."

Ruby cursed in a language I didn't recognize. My eyes flashed wide before reflex yanked them shut. The speared olive and a bath of mixed liquor washed over my head. After a wave of gasps, giggles, and foot shuffling, someone—probably the manager—insisted that Ruby leave.

I fumbled around the table for a napkin until one was thrust into my hand. I brought it to my eyes, trying to sweep away as much liquid as possible. Eventually, I could open them and see the amused and horrified faces in the bar of the restaurant where we sat.

"I take it that wasn't the one who got away," Shauna said.

"No." I wiped my face again with the small section of the napkin that was still dry then drew a hand through his hair. "We went out once. Only once. I wasn't interested in anything more, and I guess she objects."

I forced a small smile and waited.

"She sounds like a lunatic."

"Maybe so. That came out of nowhere. Did she get some on you?"

"Some. It spilled before she dumped it over your head."

I balled up the wet napkin and flung it on the table. "I'm... God, sorry doesn't cover it."

I counted the number of times a woman had thrown a drink in my face. Four. Now, five.

Jonah used to say I was a magnet for crazies. Of course, I dated some women who were—as my grandfather would put it—crazier than a football bat. But I'd also hurt some of them.

I prided myself on being honest. I never led women to think I was interested in anything more than the here and now and figured that was fair warning. Their expectations were on them.

Still, as I shook off the remnants of the latest incident, I was tired—the fights, the confrontations, the bitterness in their eyes. And me, picking an olive out of my hair.

Shauna looked on with sympathy. "Some women are needy and delusional. But then, some men are pigs."

"I'm not a pig," I asserted as much for myself as for Shauna. "I'm sorry for the drama."

"Not your fault. Let's close out and go somewhere else. We can hit the reset button over some more cocktails."

"Tempting, but I think I'm going to go home and put on some dry clothes." And think. "But I'll call you tomorrow. We can go to dinner this weekend. Have you been to Pulse?"

The trendy eatery had just opened on the east side of town. It had a two-month wait for weekend reservations, but I happened to know the owner. Maybe a posh, quiet dinner could sweep tonight out of Shauna's memory banks—and mine.

"That's sounds nice. Another time, then."

"Perfect. Thanks. And, again, sorry. I was having a nice time."

"Me too. But you better call me." She pointed her finger at

me with her overly sweet grin. "You don't want another pissed off woman on your hands."

I chuckled, wiping my eyes with the back of my hand. No, I didn't.

CHAPTER 38

ALEXA

On my way to my office, I cruised by the fitness studio to see Trista teaching her kickboxing class. Students packed the room, which wasn't a surprise.

Since Trista came on board, Starlight Fitness had seen nearly a twenty percent increase in class sign-ups. There was a waiting list for our new morning bootcamp. Numerous clients stopped me to talk about how much they loved Trista's dynamic energy and kick-butt style.

Class let out, and I caught Trista's eye. I started to go in and chat with my newest employee, but ran into a training client, Shauna.

"Hey, Alexa. I saw the construction guys getting at it early next door. When is that spa opening? I can't wait."

"Still July. We have a little hiccup, but I think we're good to go."

"Trust me. I know how much of a nightmare construction projects can be. Are they dragging their feet?"

"No. It was a permitting thing. I have to get sign-off from the landlord. I need it yesterday, but my rep says it may take a week or more. I'm working on it."

Melissa and I couldn't afford a delay, but the city permit is very specific. I needed a release from ownership. Paperwork and large companies equal bureaucracy.

Shauna bit her lip and stepped closer. "Hey. Who owns your building?"

"Bass and Carmichael. Why?"

"Shoot. You know that guy Graham who works out here?"

"He hasn't been here in a couple of weeks."

"I ran into him, and he said he owned part of the building."

"He does. He's a partner at Bass and Carmichael."

Shauna's face brightened. "So, it wasn't just a line."

"No. Are you seeing each other?" Fatigue at Graham's exploits gnawed at me. He'd moved from the gym owner, to one of the employees, and now to one of my clients—and with several other women in between.

"I had a date with him over the weekend. It was crazy. While we were waiting at the bar, some woman came over and started yelling at him and at me. And I'm, like, 'I don't have anything to do with this. It's just our first date.' So she calls him a bastard and goes on and on. I guess they hooked up, and he never called her back. She tossed a drink over his head and everything."

I pressed my fists against my thighs. "I'd steer clear of that drama if I were you."

"Oh, totally. I mean, we're supposed to go out again, but he's not someone to get serious with."

"Why go out with him at all?"

"You saw him. He's smokin' hot. And he looks like a lot of fun." Shauna shrugged. "He's taking me to that new restaurant in East Austin. It's impossible to get a reservation. He's obviously connected."

"All across the city, it would seem." Lips pursed, I smoothed my ponytail with a tense hand.

"But he really owns the building?"

"He and his business partners. Yes. Listen, I need to get back to the office. I have a ton of stuff to take care of. But I'll see you tomorrow for your training session?"

"Bright and early. It kills me to get up, and you kill me when I get here, but a girl's gotta keep it up, right?" She swept her hand up and down in front of her indicating the body she fought to keep toned.

I forced a smile. "Your health is everything. I'll see you tomorrow."

I stormed away, figuring I could talk to Trista later.

Graham had the attention span of a demented cat in a yarn factory. Sexy, brown eyes and charming smiles. As special as it might feel in the moment, those looks and those grins were for any woman he could find.

I TRIED to avoid meeting at the development office, and on the rare occasions I did, I would sneak past the hallway to Graham's office. Being a coward bothered me less than having to make small talk with him when I was still so angry. And knowing he still got to me only made me more furious.

However, Charlie had called and told me the release I needed was ready, and Melissa had clients. I didn't want to wait for a messenger, so I drove over myself.

"I wasn't expecting this to get done so fast."

"We knew it was important, so management put a rush on it."

"Management?"

That could only mean Graham.

"When the bosses say do it, it gets done. Between you and me, it kind of pissed off the legal department. They want to put the magnifying glass to every dot of ink. But I guess, people have to justify their existence sometimes." Charlie grinned. "Anything else we can do?"

"No. That's plenty. Thank your boss for me." I stood and scooped up my bag. Charlie followed me to the door, opening it for me to step out.

"Thank him yourself. He's in the office today."

"I don't want to bother him."

I stopped, and Charlie's brow lifted in mischief. "I don't think he'd consider a visit from you a bother."

His insinuation seared my cheeks. Did people at Graham's office know that we'd had a…thing? My silent discomfort made Charlie blush.

"Sorry. I didn't mean to imply anything or make you uncomfortable. I've just, you know, noticed you two. I—I'm going to shut the hell up now."

"He and I are friends. I have a boyfriend."

I forced a smile. Was that the first time I'd called Adam my boyfriend? The word put Charlie on his heels, which served my purposes even if it made sweat trickle down my back.

"Oh, well, that's too bad for everyone else, isn't it?" He chuckled to dispel the awkwardness.

"I'll take that as a compliment."

I shook Charlie's hand in goodbye and rushed to the elevator, pressing the down button twice.

"You're in a mighty hurry."

I didn't have to turn around to know who it was, but I did. Graham wore his usual look of sexy bemusement that melted the panties off women within a five-mile radius.

"It's getting late in the day. I'm hoping to get out of here before the traffic gets too snarly."

"Traffic is always snarly."

I shrugged. "Are you heading home?"

He hesitated and glanced at the elevator. "I was. I need to go back to my office and grab my bag. Walk with me?"

Was he pretending to be leaving just to follow me out? A loud ding reverberated off the marble tile. "The elevator is here."

"The thing about elevators is that you can let them go, and they'll come back again later."

He'd been helpful, and I didn't want to come across as irascibly snarky. "Sure. I'll walk with you."

"Perfect. Then, we can stop next door for a drink."

I strode next to him until we stood in front of his office, which shone with glass and chrome. He went to his desk and threw some papers into his messenger bag, which already held his laptop. I hovered in the doorway.

"I should thank you in person for helping out the release paperwork. I appreciate it."

"Not a problem. We want you to have what you need."

"Still. I've been…We haven't exactly been friendly. I wouldn't blame you for letting the normal process grind along slowly."

"I know this is important for you and Melissa."

"Well, thank you. Again." My tone softened.

Graham surveyed me so close, sweat began to trickle down me back. The heat. That's all it was. The Texas heat.

"You know how you can thank me? Let's grab a drink

downstairs. I can apologize some more over tap beer and pretzels."

"I can't."

"I'm really sorry about that night."

"I know. It's not that. It's…" My protestation faded as the entreaty in Graham's eyes grew.

"Adam. You have plans."

"Actually, he's out of town."

"Perfect. Then, you're free."

"I can't."

Reaching a truce with Graham in our business relationship was miles away from seeing him socially. I felt guilty that even a small part of me wanted to go. Adam's dedication should earn him at least enough loyalty that I wouldn't chase Graham's attention.

"I really can't. But I'll see you around."

"Okay. Let's go catch that elevator."

The thread of disappointment in his tone made my breath catch in my chest. That couldn't be. He couldn't be disappointed, and neither could I.

CHAPTER 39

ALEXA

*T*he gravelly rumble in Graham's voice reverberated in my mind, short-circuiting my sleep and leaving me tired all the next day.

I couldn't fool myself. My residual attraction to him didn't mean we had a future. It meant we'd had a past, which was best left behind us both.

Stepping through the door after work that evening, I collapsed on my couch, too tired to even figure out what to eat for dinner when Adam called. We talked for a few minutes, and then he signed off as he always did.

"Goodnight, beautiful. I'll be thinking of you."

Soon, I drifted to uneasy sleep on the couch with Adam on my mind.

My phone rang me awake with a start. I fumbled for the device shaking on my coffee table, unsure of how much time had passed, and blinked to clear my vision. My mother's face and number lit up the display.

"Hey, Mom."

"Alexa—"

The buzz of a noisy room muffled her voice, but didn't hide the strain.

"Something's wrong. What's wrong? Where are you?"

"Everything's going to be okay."

I shot up, clutching the throw blanket to my thundering chest. "What's wrong?"

"Your father..." she began.

The rest of Mom's words blended into remembrances of childhood nightmares. My father had been shot. She avoided saying the words and fell back on, "involved in a shooting," but never, ever, "shot."

"He's fine. He's in surgery. The bullet passed through his arm. It's nothing to worry about. They have to reattach his bicep. That's all. The bone is fine. It missed major blood vessels. It's just the muscle. He'll be fine."

"And Jimmy?" Dad's partner was like an uncle to me.

"He's in surgery, too. He was...it's his lung. Gloria said the doctors are hopeful. You know, Jimmy. That man's probably too stubborn to die. He wouldn't give Gloria the satisfaction. They're always bickering..."

Her voice trailed off.

I pressed the phone to the side of my head to keep my hand from shaking. "Where are you?"

She gave me the hospital details and told me what room they would be in when he came out of surgery. "He'll be groggy for a while, but you should be able to talk to him tomorrow. He'll be fine."

If I heard "fine" one more time, I might look for someone to shoot.

"I'll drive up tonight, I just—"

"No. I don't want you driving in the middle of the night. Leave in the morning. Get a flight, maybe. He's going to be out of it anyway."

I heard a muffled thumping in the background.

"Oh, hell," my mother grumbled.

"What?"

"Hang on," she told me and then talked to someone who'd entered the room. "He's in surgery, and he won't be able to talk to you until late tomorrow, at the earliest."

An insistent male voice spoke sharply, and my mother snapped back. "I know you need to talk to him, but if he's not conscious and clear-headed, you're going to have to wait."

They exchanged more words with Mom getting more obstinate by the second. Then, whoever it was left.

"Who was that?" I asked.

"Internal affairs. They've been circling like sharks."

"Why?"

"Oh, sweetie, your dad fired back at the man. He died. There's going to be an investigation, but that's routine. Everything is going to be okay. I just don't like the IA guy."

"They don't think that Dad did anything wrong, do they?"

"No. Of course not. Don't worry about that."

I fell back against my sofa cushion, tears streaming down my temples into the chenille fabric. "I don't know how you live like this. Knowing Dad could…"

I couldn't say it.

"Because I love him. And this is what he was meant to do."

"It's not worth it. None of this is worth it. I couldn't do it."

"It's a sacrifice, but it's worth it because a single day with him—even if I'm afraid—is better than a lifetime of feeling safe, but not having that love in my life." Mom's voice broke, then came back together with resolve.

Her unshakeable love for Dad was daunting. All it took

was a single moment, and your whole world could crumble. Life gone. The relief and luck I felt at my father surviving while killing another made me queasy.

"Alexa, please don't worry."

"That's impossible, Mom. I'm coming up first thing in the morning."

"Okay. Call me before you leave so I know when to expect you. And be careful driving."

"I will."

My hands shook as I hung up the phone and dialed Melissa and Holly and then my cousin, Taryn. I tried to get Adam back, but no luck. No one answered.

I flopped back on my sofa and closed my eyes, hoping that shutting out the fading evening light would ease the tension headache beginning to squeeze between my eyes. Getting to the bedroom seemed too much to handle, so I wrapped myself in the soft cashmere of my throw, curling into a tight ball on the couch. Imagined scenes of Dad on the job and Mom at the hospital peppered me with anxiety.

When my phone sounded again, I leaped up, afraid to answer. Only, it wasn't my mother.

"Alexa, hey. I had a quick question. I hope it's not too late."

"Hi, Graham. Now isn't a good time. I need to—" Sobs engulfed me.

"Alexa, what's wrong? What happened? Where are you?"

"Home," I choked as I tried to answer Graham's questions, but couldn't get any more words out.

"I'm coming over." The line went dead.

I couldn't see around me through the veil of tears, so I fumbled back to the sofa and collapsed. Half an hour later, I heard a quick rapping on my door. I pushed myself up to answer it.

Graham stood in my doorway, eyes wide and his hair disheveled. "What's wrong?"

My throat trembled, and I stammered. "My mom...She said my dad...was...sh...shot....He'll be okay. That's what she said....Okay."

Nothing I said would make any sense to Graham, but it didn't matter. He encircled me, pulling my face to the crook of his neck. Leaning against him, I could let go. I soaked his T-shirt, and my body shook.

Soon, my breathing steadied, and my eyes were depleted. "Sorry. Come in."

I stepped back and turned to allow room for him to come through the doorway. He approached, and my eyes slipped shut as he stroked my cheek with the back of his fingertips. Relief and desire mixed and made me shiver.

"What happened?"

I didn't answer right away. Instead, I motioned him toward the couch and then sat. I closed my eyes and inhaled, then exhaled, repeating the breath three times before finally speaking.

"My dad and his partner...An apartment...He shot them. Through the door. My dad's in surgery with his arm. And Jimmy. God, Jimmy got shot in the chest...They were almost retired. Both of them."

The weight of terror squeezed the air from my chest, and I closed my eyes.

"I am so, so sorry, Alexa." Graham scooted toward me, wrapping an arm around me.

"I keep seeing him, upbeat and cracking jokes to keep me from being scared. That's what he'd do." Crying choked me again. "I'm...I feel like an eight-year-old."

"No matter how old we get, our parents are still our parents. How's your mother?"

"Busy. Running around. Telling IA to fuck off..." My breath shuddered, yet a tiny smile emerged. "She'd never say that. I'd say that...I have to go up tomorrow."

I kept my face buried in Graham's neck as I spoke, allowing myself to breathe him in and not judge myself. His warmth coupled with the even vibration in his chest when he spoke steadied my emotions. The sudden chiming of my phone made me jump from his arms.

"It's my cousin." I gripped the phone tightly to my ear. "Taryn, oh, my God. Did my mother call you?"

"She did, but I missed it. I just got off the phone with my mother. It's horrifying."

"I...I can't..." My voice cracked, and Graham put a hand on my knee. "I'm heading up in the morning."

"I'll come with you. Stop in Dallas, and we'll drive the rest of the way together."

"Thanks. It'll probably be better if I didn't drive all that way by myself."

Graham cleared his throat and left the couch, heading into the kitchen.

"Is Adam there with you?"

"No, he's out of town. I have to call him. I couldn't get ahold of him."

"Oh, I thought I heard someone. Anyway, I'll see you in the morning. Drive safe. And if you have any trouble, call us, and one of us can come get you."

"It'll be fine. I'll be okay."

I hung up the phone just as Graham returned with a glass of ice water.

"She's going to make the trip with me. From Dallas."

"Do you want some company? I can ride with you."

"No, no. You don't have to do that. I'm pulling it together. I am. I'm my mother's daughter. We do what needs doing." I sat back on the couch, pressing the cold, sweating glass to my temple. "Could you stay for a little?"

"Of course. Do you need help with anything?"

"No. I just need to pack. You can keep me company. Talk to me about something stupid."

"You're in luck. Stupidity is my expertise." Graham's soft grin reassured me. "Did I tell you that my friend's wife is on the *Real Housewives of Dallas*? I can't believe he agreed to have cameras in his house. Her, I can totally believe. Sometimes, I think her big, blonde Dallas hair is ingrown."

I managed a breathy chuckle and went back to the bedroom to pack. Graham followed, regaling me with tales of Dallas' not-so-high society.

Once packed, I dropped onto the bed in a daze. "I can't believe this is happening."

Graham leaned over and pulled my curls out of my face. "You should try to sleep a little before driving."

"What time is it?"

"Just past eleven."

My nerves jangled. "I'm not going to get any sleep."

"Then, lie down at least." He moved my bag to the floor.

I rolled to my side and scrambled back on the bed. Flat on my back, I stared at the ceiling.

"Come on." Graham walked around the bed and yanked back the quilt as far as it would go with me sprawled on top of it. "Under the covers."

I obliged him. He pulled the quilted bed covering to my chin and sat on the edge of the bed. Our brown eyes met and held as he lowered his head and dropped a kiss on my forehead. I closed my eyes, lifting my hand to the light stubble of his cheek.

His lips grazed mine, and I froze, suspended somewhere between yearning and guilt. Graham pulled back and ran the pad of his thumb over my eyebrow. I sighed, and he jerked his hand back as if he'd been burned. My eyes snapped open.

"Good night." He stood, still staring at me.

"Are you headed home?"

Graham shook his head. "I'll be on the couch if you need me."

Relief flooded me. "Thanks, Graham."

"No problem."

Our eyes bored into each other, and I lost my breath. The taste of his kiss clung to my lips. He stepped back and turned. All the things I wished I had the energy to say died in the air between me and Graham's retreating back.

CHAPTER 40

GRAHAM

*A*lexa's couch offered little comfort. I wriggled and stretched and couldn't relax. Except for the surge of the air conditioner turning on, silence blanketed the house, and I wondered if Alexa had been able to fall asleep.

I certainly couldn't. So, I got up and tiptoed down the hall to her open bedroom door. I halted with a creak on the hardwood, feeling like a creep.

She'd flung off the quilt and lay on her side with her knees tucked nearly to her chin. The childlike pose made my chest ache. I hoped her father would be all right. I didn't know what was worse, losing a parent slowly and painfully or suddenly and violently. The heartbreak of both pained me.

I stepped away from her door and ventured back to the living room sofa. The sight of Alexa forlorn was a vision I never wanted to see again. The Alexa I knew stood tall, staring down any challenge and laughing at the notion of defeat. That was not the woman who opened the door to me a few hours earlier.

Nothing compelled me more than the helplessness in her voice when I'd called, but now that I was here, wide awake on the couch at two in the morning, I wondered if I shouldn't have come over.

If Adam had been in town, I wouldn't be here. If she'd been able to reach Melissa, I wouldn't be here. If her cousin lived in town, I wouldn't be here. A surrogate boyfriend and surrogate friend—that's what I was tonight. A stand-in.

I inhaled sharply—her scent of vanilla and musk clinging to my memory. Her warm, tired body against mine had sparked something inside me. Not lust. Not when she shook with fear and tears. Something better. Something worse.

I shouldn't have come. The thought plagued me into a light, unsatisfying sleep until I saw the pop of light from her room down the hall and heard the soft thump of footsteps.

"You're still here."

The pleasure in her voice made me never want to leave.

"Yeah."

I yawned and blinked, trying not to absorb how beautiful she looked in her giant T-shirt, faded denim, and bare feet. She'd pulled her hair up on her head into a lopsided pile. The cloud of curls looked like a billowy hat perched on the side of her head.

"I'm going to make some breakfast and get on the road. You want anything?"

"You're cooking?"

"I can scramble eggs," she said with insistent pride and the hint of a smile.

Apparently, we simply not going to speak of what passed between us the night before. Her emotions got the better of her, and now, she would pretend they hadn't. I had a harder time putting on the act.

"I probably should get going."

"Oh. Okay."

I swung my feet to the floor and grabbed my left sneaker.

"How about some coffee? I can at least make you some coffee. I have an espresso machine. Best espresso within at least a hundred feet or so."

Her humor tugged at the corners of my mouth, and I felt a pull in my gut.

"Another time."

"Okay," she repeated. "Thanks for staying. I was a mess last night. It was good to have company."

I ran a hand through my hair and finished tying my right shoe. "Give me a call when you get to Dallas. And keep me posted on your dad."

"I will."

I snatched up my keys and hurried to open the door. She padded after me, putting her hand on my shoulder. It slipped off as I stepped outside. I wanted to sprint to the car, but turned around instead. Her eyes, tired and slightly swollen, leveled with mine.

"Thanks again."

"It's nothing. I'll talk to you later."

I jogged down the steps and didn't look back.

CHAPTER 41

ALEXA

O ther than the usual crawl out of Round Rock and then again on the other side of Waco, I reached North Dallas in good time. I almost wished for more traffic to consume my mind, so I wouldn't have to think about Graham.

Before heading to Taryn and Jeff's, I stopped to get gas and phoned Adam. A knot curled in my stomach as I steeled myself to go through the story again.

"Alexa, darling. Hello. I didn't expect you to call so early."

I pulled the phone away from my ear to check the time. It was six forty-five California time. "I know. I wanted to catch you as soon as I could. My mom called me last night, and—" I lingered over what to say next and decided to spit it out. "My dad was shot. He's fine. He was only shot in the arm, but I'm heading up there. I don't know how long I'll be gone. Maybe just the week."

"Oh, my God. Is he in hospital?"

"Yeah. They had to do surgery. My mom left a message overnight that he's already in recovery. Thank God for trauma surgeons like Kyle." I paused to catch my breath. "Anyway, I just got to Dallas. I'll let you know if anything changes."

"Okay. Should you be driving all that way? How far is that?"

"About six hours total from Austin. It's not too bad. I'm picking up my cousin Taryn in Dallas, and I've driven this stretch probably a hundred times. Straight up 35. I'll be fine."

"It doesn't seem like a good idea for you to drive that far by yourself."

"I'm already half-way there. Maybe in England the distance a big deal, but it's not here—especially in Texas. I don't have the energy to argue."

"Then, maybe you really shouldn't be driving. And Taryn's pregnant, isn't she? The two of you driving—"

"I've got to go, Adam. I'm on my way to Taryn's, and we'll want to get on the road. I'll talk to you when I get back."

I didn't wait for Adam's affirmation. I tapped the END button on my phone and started the car.

A few minutes later, I rounded the circular drive in front of my cousin's massive home and saw the front door fly open before I could even get out of the car. I opened the car door, and Taryn launched.

"Hey! We're ready to go. Jeff insisted on driving."

"He doesn't have to do that. Who's going to stay with Olivia?"

"Her mom came to get her this morning. It's fine."

Taryn toddled toward me. At seven months pregnant and only five-foot-two, she was beginning to resemble a walking basketball.

I climbed out of the car, reaching across the front console to get my purse. As soon as I turned around, Taryn sidled next to me and hugged me sideways.

"I'm so glad your dad's going to be all right! I talked to your mom an hour or so ago. He's still a little groggy from the surgery, but she said he's talking and joking."

"Did you get to talk to my dad?"

"No. He was resting."

The sound of grinding metal scratched through the air as the iron gate next to their house cranked open. Taryn's husband, Jeff, eased his SUV out into the drive, pulling forward to leave room behind him.

"Do you have a bag?" Taryn asked me, looking through the car window.

"I have a suitcase in the trunk."

His tinted window was slid half-way down. "Let's get it in the car, and then you can pull your car into the garage."

I transferred my luggage to the other vehicle and hopped back in my car, comforted by doing what I was told. Taryn was now in charge, and I could relax.

Jeff guided us through a series of highways until we were on track for Oklahoma City. I stretched my legs across the back seat, propping up against the driver-side door.

"You know what I was thinking of, Taryn? That time you came to visit over the summer. You were maybe seven or eight."

"I remember that. I was seven. You had to have been twelve. I trailed after you and your friends every day, riding bikes or going to the pool. I think I maybe annoyed you."

I laughed. "A little, but my mother made me promise to be nice."

"I thought you were so cool."

"Thought I was cool? I was the bomb."

A trickle of Taryn's laughter rolled into the back seat. I closed my eyes. I could feel the intense heat of the Oklahoma sun on my face and hear the screech of kids laughing as they popped wheelies on their bikes.

"On the weekends, my dad would wake us up really early in the morning to either go fishing or just wandering around the woods. Dad's always been a country guy. He loves getting outside."

"He taught me how to bait a hook. Still, I stunk at fishing. All that sitting still and being quiet. My chatter drove him crazy."

"He loved it. I don't think he had any illusions about catching any fish with two girls giggling and rocking the boat."

"Your mom and dad were like a second set of parents to me. I loved those summers in the big city." Taryn turned toward Jeff in the driver's seat. "Oklahoma City was the big city to me in those days. They had real malls and more than one movie theater. Big-time stuff."

"Mom and Dad loved having you visit. They always wanted more than one kid. I think when you came, they could see what it would've been like to have a larger family."

The car fell silent.

Both sisters, Brenda Stevens and Taryn's mother, Annabelle, had tried for more kids with heartbreaking complications. My parents had a lifelong sadness over the children they'd lost—even as they put on happy faces.

"Mine too," Taryn said after a minute.

She and I didn't have siblings, but we had each other. Now, Taryn was pregnant herself. Seeing her waddling and aglow warmed my spirit.

I let my mind wander to the idea of being pregnant. Taking on a family sounded like nothing but stress.

Recalling the warmth of my childhood memories, however, tickled a part of my brain I'd assumed would lie dormant forever.

Taryn's voice broke into my thoughts. "Family is everything." She twisted in her seat and sent me a sweet, comforting smile.

"Have I told you how excited I am about you and the baby? I'll have to make a trip up to Dallas just to see your nursery. It sounds like it's going to be beautiful."

Taryn and Jeff—though mostly Taryn—hired a muralist to paint a jungle scene on the wall. The sketch featured friendly lions, a fat monkey swinging from a tree, and assorted other creatures.

"It is! We bought our crib the other day and went through the baby shop to pick the registry for the baby shower."

"Micky just sent the invitations out over the weekend. She also sent an email invite to everyone," I said.

Taryn's best friend, Micky, asked me if I could come up early and help set up everything for the shower—mostly to keep my bossy cousin from stepping in and taking over the planning.

"Good. It took me a while to get her all the email addresses she needed for the invitations. And then there's food and games. I finally talked someone into doing a co-ed baby shower."

Jeff had his limits, and he interjected in a tone that walked a careful line of diplomacy. "We'll have to talk about games. I love you, but my friends don't want to pin the tail on the diaper or whatever people do. We should make it more of a barbecue."

I snickered. "Micky and I will make sure that happens. And, we'll make sure Taryn just shows up as the guest of honor."

A loud huff came from the front passenger seat. "I know. It's just killing me."

Since she planned events for a living, I knew that leaving the details to other people would be a struggle for her.

"We've got it under control. Jeff, I promise no silly games. Taryn, relax."

Jeff chuckled. "Good luck. She's freaking out about the shower, the nursery, everything."

"I'm a control freak, and you love it, mister." Taryn smacked him on the leg and then pointed at me. "Let's talk about what's going on with you. How are things with Adam? When do I get to meet him?"

"Things are good. I like him. We're hanging out. It's good."

"You like him? Every time I talk to you, he's done some other incredibly romantic, relationship-y thing. Since you haven't run the other way, I'm assuming that you more than 'like' him."

I sighed. "I do. It's a new thing. I'm giving this a chance."

"The guy from New Year's is totally history?"

"Yes, but not totally, totally. He's still my landlord. We're still working on a benefit for my friends, Toby and Sarah. And, actually," I paused, clearing my throat. "He called right after I got off the phone with my mom and ended up coming over to check on me."

"You invited him over?"

"No. He called, and I was upset. So…he just came over."

Taryn exchanged a glance with Jeff, and I continued. "As a friend. That's all. He was worried."

"You're not interested in him, then?"

"No. Graham is not the best prospect. Adam is… steadier. He's gentlemanly and kind of traditional about romance and courtship. Sort of."

"You like that?" Jeff queried. I could see his eyes bounce up to the rearview mirror.

"He's not *that* traditional. I mean, he's an artist, and he paints nudes. He's traditional in that he wants to date, and he's pursuing me. Who doesn't want to be wooed?"

Taryn gave me a thumbs up. "I'm glad, and again, I need to meet this guy."

"We'll come back up in a few of weeks. Scout's honor."

"Good. Just watch out for this Graham situation. If you're attracted to him, and he's hanging around, it's easy to start thinking that the grass is always greener."

"Trust me, I know he's not greener."

I spoke with a confidence that didn't quite reach my gut. When I forgot that Graham was a player, it was easy to be attracted by his game—handsome, funny, and caring when he wanted to be.

Of course, I couldn't forget he was a player. It would be all too easy to slip back into my usual mode of avoiding relationships altogether.

CHAPTER 42

ALEXA

"*D*ad?"

His coloring shocked me, but Carlisle Stevens' ashen face brightened as I touched his hand. I leaned over and planted a kiss on his forehead, taking comfort in the warmth of his skin.

"Hey, Lexie Lex. Come to join the party?"

"Is that what this is?" My voice cracked along with my resolve to not cry. A burst of teardrops slid down my face, tickling my chin as they hovered there. I snagged a tissue from the bedside table and dabbed them before they fell.

"Every day, it's a party, Lex—especially since you came all this way to see me."

I stroked his cheek and perched on the edge of the stool next to bed, clutching my handbag to my stomach with my other hand.

"You didn't have to go through all this trouble if all you wanted was a visit, you know. You could have just called."

"Good to know. No bullets next time."

My chest squeezed. "I don't want to talk about bullets."

"Me either."

"Where's Mom?"

"She went out to Shakey's to get some real food."

Shakey's had the greasiest, cheesiest burgers in town, always served with a side of crispy, sweet, and salty onion rings in an oil-soaked brown paper bag. I sniffed, almost able to smell the savory joy of fried onions.

"Should you be eating that?"

"Don't worry. She's not bringing me any, and I begged. You'd think in my sorry state that she'd be more sympathetic. She said that you hadn't stopped to eat lunch, so she's getting it for you. It's true what they say. Once you have babies, it's like the husband doesn't exist."

"You're impossible."

I cradled Dad's rough, thick-fingered hand in mine. He looked terrible and fantastic.

His usually caramel skin had nearly all the gold washed out, but Mom had been right. Spirit and humor shined through his dark chocolate eyes. I tried to avoid looking at the arm bent and strapped to his left side by bandages and a sling.

I wanted to ask him how this could have happened. I wanted every detail to determine what went wrong so it could never happen again, but I didn't want to hear it. None of it—the horror of gunshots, fear, and blood. I wrapped my arms around my stomach.

"You cold? I can have the nurse turn up the thermostat." His hoarse grumble made me smile.

"No. I'm not cold. And I wouldn't want to bother the nurse with that."

"I thought your mom said you were coming up with Taryn? And she said something about Jeff. I was half out of it."

"I stopped on the way, and Jeff drove us from Dallas. They thought they'd let me come in and see how you were before we all descended on you."

"Go get 'em. I could use more company and a little dose of Taryn. That girl is like a blood transfusion."

Dad's smile cracked, his mouth slightly whitened along the edges. Twisting around on the stool, I saw a water pitcher and plastic cups in the corner of the room. I patted his hand and got up. "I'll get them. Do you want some water?"

"Yeah. I'm a pint low, I think—even though they got me all stuck up like pincushion with this IV."

"When did the doctor say you could go home?"

"Maybe tomorrow as long as I don't have a fever. I tell you, girl, I can't wait. The air in this place chokes you."

I started to hand my father the cup, but thought better of it and tipped the bendy straw to his gray, parted lips. He raised his head a fraction of an inch and took a few sips, then waved it away. "That's good. Thank you."

He dropped his head back to the pillow and let out a sigh, closing his eyes.

To see my strapping, cop father exhausted by the infinitesimal effort brought a fresh pool of tears to the back of my eyes, and I rushed out, telling him I would bring back his niece and nephew-in-law.

The door clicked behind me, and the dam burst. No sobs came, just rivers of tears frustrating my vision.

"Honey, do you need something?"

I blinked with fury and wiped my eyes. A short, broad man pushing a cart stood before me, and the hallway in each direction looked the same. "Which way is the family waiting room?"

The orderly pointed around the nurse's station at the end of the corridor. "To the right, through the double doors. Go straight, and about half-way down before you get to the elevator, you'll see it. I can walk with you if you'd like."

The man's blue eyes rounded.

"No. I can find it. I'm fine." I smiled to erase the concern rippling across his face. "Really."

The waiting room wasn't nearly as far as the man's description had made it sound, but I was thankful for the directions, nonetheless. At every turn, another stretch of hallways extended in different directions.

Jeff sat next to Taryn on a vinyl couch, rubbing her back as she stretched her legs in front of her. They looked up as I pushed through the door. "Dad's awake, and he wants to see you two."

I traced my mental breadcrumbs back to the room. "Look who I found loitering outside."

Taryn ambled to her uncle's bedside. She patted on his chest. "I can't hug you."

Carlisle placed his right hand over hers and smiled. "I don't need hugs. How are you and my grand-niece or nephew?"

"Wonderful. I'm getting big as all outdoors, but it's the best."

"That one is taking good care of you then?" Carlisle thrust his chin in Jeff's direction.

"I try. She doesn't normally need too much taking care of, but lately, my services are in greater demand. You look good."

The older man snorted. "I look like I'm dead."

"Dad!" I barked. He laughed. "That's not funny."

"Gotta laugh, sweetheart. I'm going to be good as new in a few weeks."

That's what Mom had told me. Right now, seeing him helpless in bed, that was hard to imagine, but I hoped. The man was too stubborn to stay down for long—a genetic trait.

"Don't say things like that when Mom gets back." I chastised him through pursed lips.

"I didn't mean to get you upset, baby girl."

"I'm fine." I sniffled.

"What all did the doctor say?" Taryn pulled a stool over to the bedside. She couldn't sit, so she leaned. Jeff moved behind her and helped lift her onto the seat, bracing her against his chest.

"Rest. Don't go too hard. Get scheduled for physical therapy. The damage wasn't too bad. They had to reattach the muscle. Getting use out of it will take some work."

His fingers wiggled a little in his sling. The tiny movement eased the tension in my neck.

"Is that it? They must have said more than that, Uncle Carlisle?"

"Those are the highlights." He closed his eyes, heaved a sigh, and then opened them again. "I can't wait to meet little Carlisle or Carla. I've decided that you're going to name the little bugger after me, if that's okay."

Taryn stroked his shoulder above the sling. "I love you, big man, but I can't make any promises."

"Right now, we're trying to fend off my mom's wanting to name him Edgar after her dad. Even as a middle name…no," Jeff grumbled.

"She must be excited—getting grandkid number two. One

of these days, before I leave this mortal coil, I'd like a grandchild."

I sighed. "Mom's not even here, and I'm having to listen to this."

Carlisle lifted his brow over wide eyes and lowered his chin. "She's not the only one wondering when you might settle down. She's just the loudest about it."

With Dad joining in on the act, I might have to skip holidays until menopause took my options off the table. Taryn's pregnancy had my mother in a lather. She tried not to push, but her jealousy of her sister Annabelle's grandma-to-be status vibrated off of her in waves—in person, over email, on the phone. My mother's signals could power AT&T.

My dad had no problem amplifying them in his wife's absence. "Don't give me that sourpuss look. You know we only want you to be happy."

Taryn cleared her throat. "Everybody has their own path. If it's what Alexa wants, she'll get it. No doubt about that. How's your partner?"

Carlisle dropped his eyes to the thin blanket covering him to the waist. "Better, from what I hear. He took a shot to the chest. They removed the bullet and fixed him up. He's in ICU. Once I get the clearance, my sister is going to wheel me up there. She'll be here tonight."

My eyes widened. "Is something wrong with your legs?"

"No, but I'm not supposed to be up walking around while I'm on all these meds. They're afraid I'm going to keel over."

"Oh."

The conversation felt like a roundhouse to the stomach, and I thought I might fall over myself.

"I'm going to be right as rain, Lex."

"I know. Everyone keeps saying that."

Taryn gave me a soft smile. "When is that Shakey's getting here? I think we could all use a boost of fat and sugar."

"Not sure that's a solution to anything." I wrinkled my nose. If I gave in to eating my stress, I'd have a belly as big as Taryn, without the excuse.

"Nonsense," Dad roared. "A good burger is the solution to everything."

I forced a laugh and stood to walk over to the sink for a paper towel. A fine layer of sweat shined on his brow. Was he feverish? The monitor next to the bed told me no, but he looked clammy.

I lightly wet the towel with cool water and walked to the other side of the bed from Taryn. Dad's eyes shut when I dabbed at his forehead. He could say he was fine all he wanted, but I knew he needed his family. I couldn't head home until I knew he'd be okay without me.

CHAPTER 43

ALEXA

My parents' kitchen was a time capsule from 1987. That's when my mom replaced the golden laminate countertops with beige ones and ripped out the linoleum in favor of ceramic tile.

They had a newish, white refrigerator only because I insisted and bought them one for Christmas almost ten years ago. I wanted to get them a suite of brand new, stainless steel appliances.

My mother had balked. "All we need is a fridge. And I don't like the stainless steel ones. You can't put magnets on the front."

A cluster of cards, fragments of paper, and random baby photos clung to the refrigerator door. My eyes drifted from the prayer reminders and invitations to church potlucks to the yellow floral wallpaper encasing the room. Its velvet-flocked horror was original to the house, dating back to the year after I was born.

I blinked and looked away as if staring too long might transport me back to the time of big-banged poodle hair and acid-washed jeans.

"Charlene got in okay?" Mom pulled a family size bag of Skittles fun packs from the cabinet and sat down at the oak, butcher block table, tossing over three tiny bags of candy. I tore one open and sorted through it for the red and green ones. My favorites.

"Yes. Of course, as soon as she got there, they started bickering."

"Your father and his sister are a pair."

"She loves him, though, and now, you can come home and get some sleep."

She shook a few of my discarded candies in her palm before popping one in her mouth. "You could have stayed at the hospital."

"I'm supposed to make sure you put your feet up."

"Your father spoils me."

"I know. It's embarrassing."

I leaned over and kissed her hand. The fine bones shifted under ivory skin thinning with age.

Today, she looked older, but even on better days, I noted the progression of time in the hair color going from blonde to gray to golden frost—the platinum shade popular at the local salon. Time always catches up with you.

My phone skittered on the table, flashing at me, and I picked it up.

Graham: Hope your dad is okay. Give me a call if you feel like it later. Anytime. Late or whatever.

My heart lightened.

"Is that your new man?" Mom grinned.

"Oh. No. Just a friend."

"The way you smiled, I thought it must be this Adam fella. What friend is it?" Her crisp green eyes sharpened on me. "Yes. I'm being nosy."

"It's not Adam. It's a guy that I was seeing before Adam came to town. Graham. I mentioned him. He's with the company that bought the building. He called me last night and came over to check on me. I was a mess."

"That's nice of him. ...It's good that you can stay friends." She chewed as slowly as she spoke.

I knew what it meant when Mom's words poured out like molasses. "He and I weren't serious. He's not the serious type."

"Adam is serious about you, then?"

I nodded. "He's been clear about that from the beginning."

"That was okay with you? I'm a little surprised."

My mother shook the bag in her hand and poked through it, apparently absorbed in her selection.

"Me too."

She looked up. "Have you talked to Adam?"

"This morning, before I left. He texted me. I need to call him back. He's out of town."

"So, he *did* check on you?"

"Of course." My terse reply sat somewhere between defensive and accusatory.

Mom sighed. "I'm just trying to sort through your love life. I have to figure things out. You never tell me anything."

"I told you about Adam."

"You never told me about dating this Graham."

"That wasn't worth talking about."

"But he's checking on you."

"We're friends." I spoke sharply.

"Alright. Just asking." Her right shoulder lifted in a shrug.

"What?"

"Nothing. If you're seeing this Adam, I'd like to meet him. You should bring him up, so your father and I can lay eyes on him before he goes back to England."

I said my thousandth prayer for the day, this time, for this conversation to end. "I'll see what his schedule is."

"Good." A tension I hadn't noticed before eased in my mother's face. "What are you going to do when he goes back to England?"

"I don't know. He's here for the next couple months, and he's hinted that he might stay longer. I'll cross that bridge when I get there."

"I like having you nearby. Texas is better than New York and much better than London."

I grabbed her hand and squeezed. "I don't want to go anywhere."

"So, you're moving back to Oklahoma?" She gave a half smile.

"Don't go crazy."

"I don't know why you feel that way about your home town. We're growing. We have excitement like any other city."

I suppressed a grumble. I didn't want to insult the town she loved. "I have my business in Austin. I can't up and leave."

"I know. I'm your mother. I have to keep you feeling guilty about something."

Somewhere, Mom had a Tupperware container of gold medals for guilting children. "It's late. You should get some rest, so we can get back to the hospital early."

I kissed her goodnight, climbed the stairs, and meandered down the hall leading to my childhood bedroom. Framed memories scattered the wall, displaying versions of myself in assorted sizes and with varying amounts of teeth.

I groaned at the picture I'd asked Mom to remove at least a hundred times. My hair looked like a jailbreak of curls throughout my middle school years. Add braces and glasses, and the hideousness stunned me every time I saw it.

"I love that picture. It's exactly how I remember you at that age. You were so cute," she always insisted.

I had no idea what she saw. I could only be grateful that the acne hadn't shown up until the braces came off in ninth grade. That's also when I shot up five inches—almost to my current six feet of height.

The summer before senior year burned away my awkwardness, and I started doing local modeling—for newspaper mailers and department stores—when I was seventeen. Soon, I found an agent and landed larger and larger jobs. Then, after a couple of years at college, I moved to New York to model full-time.

Driving into Manhattan in the back of a rickety taxi, I had taken one look at the endless sweep of towering buildings and knew I'd never move back to Oklahoma. The town had more going on now, but when I was little, it had seemed like a godforsaken outpost. Everything came to Oklahoma City late—music, movies, and fashions.

I wanted fresh and happening. I escaped the first chance I got, first to Texas for college and then to New York, the ink on my high school diploma still glistening.

Pushing open the door to my old room, I stopped and grinned. My Cabbage Patch kid smiled at me from the bed. Even though they had renovated the room and moved a number of things to storage, the doll stayed. I wiggled a finger in Kirstie Lorraine's dimple. The thrill of my eighth birthday surprise flooded back. Silly as the doll was now, it had been hard to come by and not cheap.

I scooted the bag off the bed and flopped back, kicking off my shoes. I brought pajamas, but didn't have the energy to change. Eyes closed, I brought the doll to my chest and tried to remember what it had been like to have it be the pinnacle of satisfaction in my life.

Being an adult complicated everything.

CHAPTER 44

GRAHAM

$\mathcal{I}$ tapped the back arrow on my phone to listen to the voicemail again.

"Hey, Graham. It's Alexa. I'm calling to let you know that my dad is in recovery, and he should be up and around in a day or so. Thanks again for the other night. Things are looking up, and I appreciate it."

I took a swig of beer, relaxing. She would be fine, and I'd served my purpose. I considered calling her back. Part of me just wanted to hear the cheer in her voice rather than distress. Of course, I wouldn't.

Instead, I dialed Sierra. What I needed was to get my mind off of my failed venture with Alexa and onto a sure thing.

When Sierra didn't pick up the phone, I sent her brief message.

Me: What are you up to tonight?

I got up to get another beer and flipped through the TV channels, waiting for response.

Sierra: Not much.
Me: Come over?
Sierra: How about dinner?

My thumb hovered over my phone. Sierra never wanted to have dinner or do anything remotely date-like, but I wouldn't let suspicion drive me to a knee-jerk "no." Right now, some easy conversation capped off with our usual evening sounded like a perfect combination.

Me: Rio de Luna?

I remembered how much Sierra loved Tex-Mex.

Sierra: See you in 30

With the date made, I grabbed a quick shower and headed out.

~

SIERRA BEAT me to the restaurant. I saw her sitting at a high-topped table in the bar. Her spike-heeled ankle boots tapped furiously against the leg of her chair. When she spotted me, she gave me a jittery wave.

I smiled and stroked her upper arm before sitting opposite her. I expected a seductive look in return with a flirtatious wink or flip of her hair. This was a woman with whom I spent most of my time naked. Instead, she cleared her throat and warbled, "Hello."

I frowned. "How are you?"

"Good. Great actually."

I blew out a tense breath. "Really? Good news?"

"Yes. At least, I hope you think so." She paused and downed whatever cocktail she'd ordered before I arrived. "I've been wanting to talk to you."

"About what?"

"Us. Or whatever 'us' there's ever been."

She looked at me squarely now. I mentally braced myself for an emotional onslaught. Did she want to change our relationship from something casual to something more regular?

In the nearly two years we'd known each other, this would be, maybe, the third meal we ever shared. The other two involved either pizza or Chinese delivery. I couldn't remember. I thought that maybe once I'd fed her with chopsticks, but that might've been someone else.

But I liked Sierra. I knew she was smart, and she had a quick sense of humor.

"'Us' is a topic we've always avoided."

"I know, but now we need to have a conversation."

"I'd be open to that."

I shifted in my chair and reached across the table with flattened palms. She pulled her hands back.

"No. Not like that. I met someone a couple of weeks ago. A really great guy. And this thing we do…I can't do it anymore."

I nearly choked my own foolishness. "Oh. That's wonderful, Sierra. I'm happy for you."

I wiped my sweaty palms on my knees.

"You are? That's a relief. I met him and—" She pulled her fists to her temples and exploded her hands, then continued.

"He's sweet and funny and dedicated. He has custody of his son. He's five. I don't know. I just know. You know? It's crazy. You and I? Party girl." Her voice rose, and she pointed to her chest and then swiveled her finger toward me. "Party guy. But it's different now."

The thought rankled me.

"It's not a bad thing, Graham. You and I…I want something more now. I know you're not that guy. I wouldn't even try to put that on you."

"How do you know I'm not that guy?"

Sierra chuckled and leaned over the table, dropping her voice. "Because the only time you call me is when you want a booty call. I'm not delusional enough to think that's ever going to develop into a golden anniversary with grandkids and rocking chairs on the porch. Besides, you and I don't have that kind of chemistry. We're nothing alike. You're corporate. You wear loafers and live in a fancy house in Westlake. I change my hair color every other week and have a neck tattoo. Honestly, outside of the bedroom, I'd make you crazy—in a bad way. And you —"

She laughed again.

"You think I'm square."

"Commercial real estate development? The few times you've talked about what you do, I have to be honest, my eyes started to glaze over. There's nothing wrong with it, but that's not what *my* guy does with his life. It's terminally boring. No offense."

I stifled the offense I did feel. It wasn't about Sierra. She was right. I couldn't take her to a business dinner with her fishnet stockings and quarter-inch eyeliner. Not even in

Austin. What bothered me was a lingering question. Whose guy was I?

"It's fine," I sighed. "What's your guy's name?"

"Larry."

I squeezed my lips together to keep from laughing.

"Don't get smug. It's his name."

"How old is he?"

"My age. He's technically Larry Junior."

"Like the drummer for U2."

She grinned. "Exactly. Only he plays bass. For Solo Disorder. You heard of them?"

I raised my brows in recognition even if I wasn't sure if I'd heard of the band. A lot of the wacky Austin band names ran together.

Sierra lifted her shoulders with such pride. She *liked* this bass player.

"He makes you happy."

"He does. I don't know exactly where it's headed, but I'll never know if I keep fooling around. When you have a chance at love, I think you have to grab it." She blushed. "You probably think I'm a sap."

"I don't. Not at all. I agree. You can't let love pass you by."

My encouragement sent joy dancing across Sierra's face, but depression sank in my chest. The women in my life— disparate group though it was—agreed on one thing: I was not a candidate for a happily ever after.

"No, you can't. One day, you'll meet your perfect woman." She tilted her head to the side. "Like a lawyer. Or a woman who…works in business."

"In business," I chuckled. "That's pretty generic."

"Well, I don't know! A woman who is together and clean-cut and, you know, business-y."

"I don't know that I'm looking for a woman that straight."

She wiggled her eyebrows. "Maybe you aren't. Remember that one time…" Sierra fell apart laughing.

Yes, I remembered. What had the other woman's name been? Cara or Tara? Sara? Something kind of like Sierra. In fact, some*one* kind of like Sierra. Only Cara/Tara/Sara had been blonde. At least up top.

I swiped my hand down my face. And I wondered why these women didn't take me seriously. "I'm not into that scene anymore."

"Since when?"

"I'm getting older and settling down a *little* bit." I held up my forefinger and thumb, gapped to indicate my personal growth.

"I wish you luck."

"Are we still having dinner?" I drummed my fingers on the table and glanced around the bar.

"Yes. We can have dinner. We never have dinner. Dinner is friendly, and I hope we can be friends."

"Of course, we can."

"Good. I'm *so* in need of enchiladas. I'm dying." She stuck her tongue out to the side and made a choking gesture with her hands.

"We can't have that. Poor Larry Junior might not recover," I quipped.

"No, I don't think he would. It's nice."

I mulled Sierra's moon-faced love, trying not to look as shocked as I felt.

We ordered dinner, and then my phone rang. Alexa. My shoulders tensed.

"Take the call. I'm going to run to the bathroom."

I touched the green button and swiped to answer. "Alexa. Hi."

"Hey, Graham!"

"You sound chipper. That's good news."

"It is. Hold on...I'm going to step out into the hall." Muffled voices and the thunk of a door came through the phone. "My dad is still a little goofy on pain meds, but he's telling his terrible jokes and giving my mom a hard time. It's a relief."

"Good for him. And your mom is doing okay?"

"Yeah, she is. She's being bossy, but that's normal. My dad keeps trying to get people to bring him food from the outside. He's not impressed with the Salisbury steak and Jell-O."

"Who would be?"

"I know. It's pretty disgusting. I promised him I'd bring him a sandwich."

"You're a good daughter."

"I try."

A beat of silence constricted my chest. "I got your message. I was going to call you back earlier."

"It's fine. I wanted to make sure I got a hold of you."

Why? I had my suspicions, but what would I do about it? "Thanks. I was a worried about you."

"I appreciate it. Everyone's been so supportive."

Everyone. I coughed. Sierra hustled back toward the table.

"Hey, Graham, you'll never guess who I ran into... Sorry. You're still on the phone."

Alexa's voice clipped. "You're out."

"I'm at dinner."

"With Shauna?"

"Shauna? No. It's my friend, Sierra."

"Sierra."

The tone in her voice made me feel like I'd been caught

with my hand in the cookie jar. "She's filling me in on her new boyfriend, Larry."

"Oh. Larry, huh?"

"Yes."

"Good...hold on. This is Adam calling me back. I need to go."

"Tell Adam I said hello." I managed the words through clamped teeth.

"Sure. Enjoy your dinner."

"I will."

After I hung up, Sierra gazed at me expectantly. "Who was that?"

"A friend of mine. Her dad is a cop, and he was shot a couple of nights ago."

"Oh, my God! Is he alright?"

"He is. That's why she called. To give me an update." I looked down at my phone and set it down.

"Do I know her?"

"Who?"

"Your friend."

"No. I just met her a few weeks ago. Or, actually, over New Year's, but we reconnected a few weeks ago."

"Is she single?"

"No." Resignation broke into my voice.

"And you're not happy about it," Sierra sang in a know-it-all tone.

"Not at all...I mean, I'm fine with it. We had a thing, but it's over."

"Since when?"

"Since she declared that I was a shitty candidate for monogamy or anything serious. Sound familiar?"

Sierra's shoulders sank with pity. "I'm sorry, Graham. I didn't mean to make it sound like that."

I flipped my phone over and over, thumping it on the table. "I'm struggling to grasp this theme of how hopeless I am as boyfriend material."

"I don't think you're hopeless. I never got the idea that it's what you wanted. You're charming. And fun. And light-hearted."

Sierra's pity only made me feel more hopeless. I gripped the hair on the crown of my head and let it go. "Not serious."

"Not in your personal life. Or I didn't think. Listen, what you are is up to you. If you want something deeper, you can have that. It's easy for men. There's no shortage of women looking to settle down."

But Alexa is taken. I resented my fixation. Maybe it was my way of continuing to avoid commitment. I couldn't have her, so she was a convenient target. Except that's not how I'd felt at her house the other day.

When she was in pain, the desire to sweep it away overwhelmed me. I couldn't bear her tears, her misery. I wanted to set her world right—even if that wasn't my job.

I wanted the job.

I blinked, refocusing on Sierra. She leaned on her elbow and stared at me with her chin tilted into her upturned palm.

"Have you told this woman that you want to start something real with her?"

"Sort of. She said I wasn't the guy to get serious with, and I asked her how she knew that. I told her to give me a shot. Who knows?"

Sierra shook her head. "Oh, honey, that's weak. If you want to change her mind, you've got to bring stronger game than that. Tell her how you feel about her."

"I don't even know how I feel about her. I like her. A lot. That's it."

"Why did you call me tonight?" She folded her arms across her chest.

"What?"

Sierra pinned me with her stare. "You heard me."

"Because…" I exhaled and found the courage to be honest. "Because I needed to get her out of my head. I went over to her place the other night after she heard about her dad, and she was a mess. It…killed me. I wanted to fix it, but that's not my job. She flew off to Oklahoma, and she has a boyfriend."

I thought back to the last time I'd called Sierra. I'd also been in the throes of Alexa avoidance.

Sierra smacked my hand. "You can't let love pass you by. You said it yourself. You should at least give it a shot. If you've just reconnected with her, then this other guy can't have been around for very long. Give her a dose of the Ryan charm. This other guy can't match that, right?"

"He's British," I grumbled.

Sierra made a face. "Bad teeth and no fun."

"His teeth are fine. I've met him."

"So what? You have to at least try."

"I guess. You're probably right. I can talk to her when she gets back in town."

I tried to rally the confidence that usually came so easy for me.

"Do it." Sierra flung across the table and slapped my hand again. "Promise."

"Okay. Okay. When I thought about how this evening was going to end, I didn't think it would be with you giving me a pep talk to go chase another woman. Now, bringing another woman to the party? Maybe."

"Lothario. We're not doing that anymore. Remember?" Sierra shook her finger in my face. "You're going to have to get your mind right if you're going to convince this woman that you're serious. What's her name?"

"Alexa."

"Ooh. Sexy."

"Yes. She is."

Sierra clapped her hands together. "I love it. We're going to get you into a relationship. An actual relationship."

"We'll see."

CHAPTER 45

ALEXA

*M*uch to his delight, they moved Dad home on Tuesday morning. He settled in on the couch, and at noon, he put in his request for a hearty barbecue lunch.

I wondered aloud whether that was the most healing food and was quickly shouted down.

"If your daddy wants barbecue, then I'm getting him barbecue. A man should have what he wants in his own house," Mom proclaimed.

His smug smile told me not to argue.

After lunch, I helped him to bed for a nap and returned to the center of the house: the kitchen table.

My phone clattered on the table again. "People are calling and calling."

"Go ahead and take it. Maybe it's your Adam."

"He's not mine, Mom."

"Well, why not? If you like him." She flicked her hand at me. "I don't understand you girls these days."

"Mom, there's nothing to understand...I...I'm going to take this upstairs." I excused myself and climbed the stairs to my old room.

"You sound quite tired," Adam remarked after our greetings.

"I am. It hit me all of a sudden."

"I'm flying back tomorrow morning, scheduled to change planes in Dallas, and I thought I might fly up to Oklahoma instead of back to Austin."

My temples squeezed in pain. "You don't have to do that."

"I know I don't, but I thought I could help out, and I'd love to meet your parents."

Stress. That's what Adam's suggestion sounded like. I couldn't deal with introducing him to my parents right now, and I felt sick having to tell him no.

"Now isn't a good time."

"I'd like to help."

"I know, but we're still getting Dad settled and back into a routine. It's not the best time for me to introduce you. He's not at his best."

"I imagine not. I understand that. I don't have any expectations. I want to be there for you and your family."

"You don't know how my mother is. If she has guests, she'll feel the need to be running around and making you comfortable—cooking and entertaining. She won't be able to help herself. My dad's the same way. It's too much right now. In a few weeks, we can come back up."

"I'm sorry if I'm pushing. I'm still upset that I wasn't there when you got the news. I hate that you had to deal with it by yourself."

"I dealt with it. And," I heaved a sigh and continued, "I

wasn't totally by myself. Right after I talked to my mother, Graham called about the benefit, and we talked. The next day, I got to Dallas, and Taryn was with me."

"Graham?"

"I couldn't get ahold of anyone else then, and he helped me out."

"How's that?"

"He came over and kept me company while I packed."

"And you're just now mentioning this."

I could hear Adam's snarl.

"I didn't think to mention it before, but you said that I was alone. I wanted to be honest."

"Unbelievable."

"I didn't ask him to come over. He heard how upset I was. I could barely speak, so he just came over. He was being a good guy."

"He is *not* a good guy. He runs through women like a pint through a drunk." Adam's furious huffing kept the line from going silent. "Why would you encourage him when you know how he feels about you?"

"Graham has a thousand girlfriends and isn't sitting around mooning over me."

"I don't want you seeing him anymore."

"Impossible. We're doing this event for Poppy. Period." Adam's imperious demand sparked my stubbornness.

"Working on a charity event doesn't need to involve seeing him socially or having him at your house."

"You're overreacting."

"Am I? You're my girlfriend, and you continue having a regular relationship with your ex-boyfriend—"

"We went out, but Graham was never my boyfriend."

"You forget that I saw you together. The two of you were

more than casually dating. And now, I hear that while I'm out of town, he's at your house consoling you."

Hearing the facts laid out from Adam's point of view softened my stance. I got jealous over Trista, and Graham and I weren't in an exclusive relationship.

Why was I clinging to my "friendship" with Graham? The truth—and my own hypocrisy—sank in.

"I get it. I should think about how it looks to have him at my house. I wasn't considering your feelings."

"Thank you. And the benefit planning? I don't like the time you spend alone with him. It's not appropriate."

"I made a commitment to my friends, and I won't back out. You'll just have to trust that I'll keep my contact with Graham...on topic. Okay? Let's change the subject."

"Gladly. How is your father?"

"Better. Tired. He's glad to be home. It'll do him good."

"How much longer are you going to be up there?"

"Probably through the weekend, and then it depends on my mom. She says she has everything handled, but I don't want her to get overwhelmed. She's not as young as she used to be."

"Then, we'll head back up in a few weeks."

I scratched my cheek. My father's opinions could be brutal, and I still felt too unsure of my own feelings to invite his unflinching scrutiny of my relationship with Adam.

I never wanted to introduce guys to Dad. Meeting the parents was so...serious. Of course, that's exactly why Adam wanted to meet them. He wanted to know that I meant it when I said I was giving them a chance. I wanted to leave behind the comfort of keeping a man at arm's length.

"That sounds like a plan."

"Perfect." Adam's pleasant charm returned. "I need to ring off. Get some rest."

"I will."

"Goodbye, sweetheart."

I found my smile. "Bye, Adam."

CHAPTER 46

ALEXA

*a*fter a few more days in Oklahoma, Mom began to manage more around my help than with it. I headed back to Austin relieved to be extraneous.

I made myself useful back home by agreeing to keep Poppy for a night so Toby and Sarah could celebrate their anniversary with a romantic dinner.

At six thirty, I closed up my business office and walked next door to the sandwich shop. Bells on the door jangled as I swung the door open. Toby appeared from the back, trailed by the man I'd been ducking since my phone conversation with Adam.

In the last day, we had yet another contentious conversation over Adam's joining me while I babysat. I mentioned that Adam might come over, and Sarah had asked that he not be there.

"It's nothing personal, but we don't know him. I'm sure

he's fine, but we don't allow Poppy to spend the night with people we don't know."

I understood and told Adam that he couldn't come over. A pout threaded through his voice. "I wish you could include me more in your circle of friends, then maybe Sarah wouldn't be uncomfortable. I hate that."

"We'll see them at the benefit. And maybe I'll invite everyone over for dinner—Toby and Sarah and Melissa and Kyle."

"I'd love that. A couples' dinner." Adam's voice lifted.

"I'll give you a call tomorrow, and you and I can have dinner."

"Sounds good."

I exited the call with Adam's mood high before I could say anything to sour it.

"Alexa, hi!" Toby bounded over and gave me a warm hug. "How's your dad?"

I slapped Toby on the arm as he released me. "Better. Recovering. Getting back to the usual, which is being coddled by my mom."

"I'm glad to hear it." The chipper rumble of Graham's voice whipped my head around.

He was dressed in his usual sharp, pressed pants and starched shirt, but managed to look warm and casual. The look in his eyes put a flutter in my throat.

"Thanks."

The patter of feet from behind the counter gave me a welcome distraction from Graham's burnishing gaze. Sarah followed.

"Hi, Miss Alexa."

"Hi, Poppy. You ready to spend the night?"

"Yes. I brought my own pillow." She held up the flattened, hot pink rectangle, then hugged it back to her chest.

Toby picked at the corner of Poppy's treasure. "She loves that old pillow. I have to block out thinking about what's living in it after all these years."

"It's my favorite." Poppy flashed a gapped smile and closed her eyes as I tousled her hair.

"You lost another tooth. Was the Tooth Fairy good to you?"

She played along with a grin. "Five dollars again. My friend Riley gets ten. Dad said that's because her parents are divorced, and her dad feels guilty."

Poppy giggled as Toby turned crimson. "I didn't know you heard that."

"Ahh, the bribery of the weekend parent. I missed out on that as a kid," Graham lamented.

"I think it's worth it to have parents that stay together." Sarah grinned at Toby, who nodded and picked up Poppy's overnight bag.

"Speaking of parents staying together, we better get going. Your mother and I need to close up here and get home to change for our date."

I pointed my key fob through the storefront window to pop the trunk for Toby, who took Poppy's deflated pillow with him as well.

Sarah checked the register. "What do you have planned for tonight?"

"I thought we'd grab dinner. You pick, Poppy. Burgers, pizza, whatever you want. Then, I have some movies back at the house and a brand new deck of Uno cards."

"Pizza! Fanelli's!" the little girl declared.

Graham lifted his hand to high five her. "Fanelli's is an excellent choice. They have the best pizza."

"You should come, too, Mister Graham."

Graham gave me side eye and didn't answer. Not sure what to say, I froze.

"He may have plans, Poppy," Sarah interjected.

"Actually, I don't."

He turned full face toward me with a lopsided grin and roguish spark in his eye.

"I was hoping for a girl's night." I pretended to pout, hoping it would get me out of the dilemma. Toby came back in, and after surveying the scene, fled to his office to finish up "paperwork."

Poppy pressed her case. "But he doesn't have anything to do. It'll be fun."

I sent Graham my most pathetic pleading look, and he ignored me. "It will be. Are we leaving straight from here?"

"That was the plan."

"Why don't we go to the bathroom one more time before you go, Poppy?" Sarah beckoned her daughter.

"But I don't have to go."

"Better be sure. Come on." Sarah eyed me as she led Poppy to the bathroom.

"Hey, Graham—"

"You don't want me at dinner? I thought we could talk—about your dad, how things are going..."

I shifted my weight from side to side, gripping my handbag. The ingratitude of tossing his support out the window shamed me, but so did the underhandedness of having dinner with him after the promises I made Adam. The latter forced my hand.

"I can't have dinner with you."

"Why not?"

I sucked in a spine-steeling gulp of air. "I'm not comfortable with how...we...with our socializing like we have. With Adam, I just...it doesn't feel right."

"You and I are friends. That's it. I thought that's all this was."

"It is," I replied, brightly.

"What's the problem?"

I pressed my lips together, slowly exhaling. I didn't get a chance to respond to his question. Graham tipped his head to the side, eyes wide. "If your boyfriend doesn't trust you, I'm not the problem."

"It's not a matter of trust. Would you be happy if you were dating a woman and she kept having dinner with an ex-boyfriend?"

"I was never your boyfriend. You've reminded me of that repeatedly," he snapped.

I jerked my head back in alarm. "I think the agreement that we weren't serious was pretty mutual."

"Yes. It was. So, what's the problem now? You've gone through a serious situation with your parents, and I want to see how you're doing. What's the big deal unless you think there's something between us that there shouldn't be?"

"No. No. I just—Adam is sensitive about it. He wanted to hang out tonight, and I already told him no because I'm babysitting. To then spend the evening at dinner with you wouldn't be right. I'm sorry. Can't you tell Poppy that something came up?"

Graham's jaw flexed. "Okay."

We stared in heavy silence, waiting for Poppy and Sarah to come back. After a minute, I called out. "Are you done, Poppy?"

Sarah came through the double doors with a befuddled and perturbed Poppy in tow. "I didn't have to go."

"That's okay. We should get going."

"You're coming with us, Graham?"

"I'm sorry, Poppy. I remembered something that I need to

do. I can't make it, but some other time. I promise." He held up two fingers in a Boy Scout promise. "I'll see you all later. Or most of you."

The look he threw me had the odd impact of raising the hair on my arms while heating me from head to toe. Sarah switched her eyes back and forth between us.

"See you around, Graham." She turned her attention to her daughter as he stormed out. "And I'll see you in the morning."

I led Poppy toward the door. "I'll bring her by the house around nine."

"Perfect."

After loading the little girl into the back seat of the car, I slid behind the wheel. Graham sat in the car next to us on his phone with someone—maybe calling one of his many side pieces.

For once, I hoped that's what he was up to. Otherwise, the guilt of excising him from my life after the concern he'd shown for me carved a hole in my heart.

DESPITE GRAHAM'S SNIDE REMARK, I did see him—just two days later. We met with a donor to nail down a sponsorship for the silent charity auction and a few items for bid.

"An evening cruise on Lake Travis and two golf packages at the resort. Those should fetch good money." I beamed as we walked out of the man's office building. "Thanks for coming with me. It helps to tag team these things."

"Not a problem."

I pretended not to hear the bite in his words. While he'd been nothing but cordial and even congenial during our meeting, up to the last minute before and, now, immediately after, Graham remained taciturn.

"We need this push before Saturday. I can't believe we only have a few days left. I haven't thanked you for taking care of all the details while I've been out of town."

"You don't have to."

"I feel like I do."

"You're welcome," he growled.

I stopped him with a hand on his elbow. "I'm sorry if I hurt your feelings the other day. With Poppy and dinner."

"So, you admit that I have feelings? That's progress."

"Of course, I do. You do." I touched his arm again, and he yanked it away and stepped in front of me.

Fury emanated from him in waves. "We never actually have *the* conversation. Do we?"

"What?"

"You and I are not just friends. We have never been just friends. I don't know what we were or are, but it's always been more than that. We pretended like that wasn't the case because we're both cowards. Now, we're pretending that's not the case because you're doing whatever it is you're doing with that British fuck. All the while, I can't shake the feeling like that's all a mistake."

A tsunami of emotion poured over me. His. Mine. It crashed into me and threatened to pull me under.

"I don't know what you want me to say."

"Nothing."

He took my cheeks in his hands and lifted my chin with his thumbs. His kiss came at me so quickly, I didn't have time to protest—even if I would have. In my most honest moments alone, I'd never admit that I wouldn't have.

The shock of his lips on mine was in the tenderness. The urgent softness of his tongue playing with mine slowly unwound my resolve. Why? Why fight this? His hands held me at the most receptive angle for his attentions.

My arms slackened at my side, sending my purse to the sidewalk with a thud. His mouth roamed, slowly, deliberately hunting me down until I was cornered by the undeniable fact that I wanted him as much as he wanted me.

I shouldn't. Right? He did this to all of his women. All the women. Their faces hovered in the margins of my psyche. Did they all feel like this when he kissed them?

Impossible.

He kissed me like there was no other woman in the world. No other people. If we were the last people on Earth, our kiss couldn't have been more intimate.

His hold on my jawline fell away and only our lips touched. He suckled my bottom lip once, then twice. Then, nothing. A slight breeze lifted the blanket of warm evening air. The skin abandoned by his hands and mouth chilled faster with the loss of contact.

"Open your eyes."

I hadn't realized they weren't open, and opening them didn't chase the blindness of desire. Maybe it was the mixed-up light of twilight, but I still couldn't see. I blinked, and Graham spoke.

"Tell me you don't know that you and I have something you couldn't possibly have with the Englishman."

"Or that you don't have with anyone in your stable of women?"

"I don't have a stable of women. I dated. Sure. Maybe I dated a lot, but when I was with you, I was with you. The thing with Trista was a moment. A dumb moment that I would have forgotten immediately if it hadn't lost me you. Adam can't give you what I can."

"What are you offering me?"

"The chance at something spectacular."

"With you?"

"Why not with me?"

"I don't know anymore."

Graham claimed my mouth once more.

My body clenched as desire coiled in my belly, and he knew.

"Exactly."

I blinked again and looked around. The plain of the cement parking lot with its herds of cars came into focus.

"I can't keep doing this, though, Graham."

"Doing what?"

"Jumping out of a relationship every time it starts to get serious. I never give anything a full chance. It starts to get real, and I bail."

"That's what you did with us. Now, you can fix it. Come back to me."

"Is it? Or is that what I'm doing now? A few kisses, and I'm going to toss over a guy who genuinely cares about me? He's never shown anything but total commitment to me. It's not like I don't have feelings for him. I do."

Graham's eyes chilled to hardened amber. "Feelings like you do for me."

I couldn't answer that while I could still taste him. "I have to go."

"Stay." He took me by the wrist, forcing me to raise my head. "Let's go somewhere and talk."

I pulled away, breathless. "I don't know if I'm stepping off a ledge and flying or falling." I pressed the heels of my hands into my eyes, then dropped my hands to my side. "I need space to think. I can't do that with you looking at me like you want to swallow me whole. It's too much."

"I know. That's the point. This," he switched his index

finger between us, then tapped the divot at the top of my breastbone, "is too much to ignore."

"I know, but that doesn't mean it's enough."

"How do you know if you don't try?"

"I'm trying now. With Adam. It's so easy for me to run away. That's what this would be. Running away to you. I have to finish whatever it is with him. I have to see where it goes. For once."

Graham stuffed his hands in the pockets of his trousers. His chin dropped to his chest for a minute before he lifted his head and looked at me through the tops of his lashes.

"Then you finish it. I hope it works out. But I bet it won't. Because of this." He drew a curve around the corner of my mouth with his thumb. "Any time he touches you from now on, it won't feel the same to you. I hope I've ruined you for him as much as you've ruined me for any other woman."

He leaned into me, his breath whispering on my lips. "You think about that when he kisses you."

He took a step back, still staring at me, then turned and walked away.

Bereft in his absence, I struggled to find the strength to put one foot in front of the other and leave our moment in the past.

CHAPTER 47

ADAM

"*I* want to make you dinner."

I called Alexa early, knowing that was the only way to catch her before her five a.m. workout after which she plunged into her daily routine.

Over the past several weeks, I'd learned to make my claim on her time as soon as possible before her work, her friends, and myriad distractions could take her away from me.

"That sounds perfect. Do you want to come to my place? I have a slightly better kitchen than the one at your corporate apartment."

"How would you know? You hardly cook." I laughed, delighted to tease her about her lack of domesticity. My mother would be appalled when they met. I'd been raised to consider a woman's homemaking skills of the utmost importance. I had no such qualms, but then a mother would never see the other charms a woman brings to a relationship.

"Why waste all that time and energy shopping and cooking when there are so many restaurants with takeout? I'm a believer in efficiency and convenience."

"The consultant in me is very impressed. I'll be at your place around eight."

"See you then."

"Goodbye, my lovely."

The faint sigh of pleasure I received after my sign-off gave me a charge that lasted until I rang her doorbell hours later. She welcomed me inside, and I lugged my bags of groceries into my immaculate and hardly used kitchen.

"How was your day?" I unloaded chicken and vegetables from the paper bags and glanced around for Alexa's knife set. It was usually on the counter next to the stove.

"Good," she replied. "What are you looking for?"

"Knives, so I can prepare the vegetables for the stir fry."

"Over here. The housekeeper must have moved them." She hefted the wood block of cutlery from the counter on the other side of the refrigerator.

It amazed me that she bothered to have help for her small house where she lived alone, but I knew that also fell into the category of why should she waste time on that when she had a business to run. She possessed a single-minded focus and eliminated any activities that didn't contribute to her bottom line.

I pulled the largest chef's knife from the block and began breaking down heads of broccoli, carrots, and onions. She peered over my shoulder, arms folded.

"Can I help with anything?"

"You can make yourself useful making rice."

"Did you buy some?" Alexa twisted her face in thought, glancing at her pantry.

"I did. I know not to make assumptions regarding your provisions."

"I know. I'm a sad case when it comes to homemaking. My high school home ec teacher would give me an 'F' for sure."

I snorted. "So, you did receive some instruction along the way?"

"Believe it or not, I have. My mother is a regular Martha Stewart, too. She tried her best. I can cook pretty well when I try." I thrust out her chin.

Could she? I let her confidence quell my doubt. "If you can cook, you might be perfect." I bumped her with my hip. "Next time, you'll make dinner, then."

"Maybe next weekend. Once the benefit is over."

"And if you're a disaster, we can order pizza. Fanelli's to the rescue. "

Her face lit up with laughter, then froze, and she looked away.

"What's wrong?"

"Nothing. I...had a long couple of days."

"Anything you want to talk about?"

"Nope. The usual." The brightness in her tone strove to fend off my question. She put her arm around my waist. I reflexively tensed. She was hiding something and covering it with affection.

I had a nose for subterfuge.

"Construction is coming along, right? You resolved that permit issue."

"The management company put a rush on it."

Alexa pulled away from me and began picking at the vegetables on the counter.

"I guess being friendly with one of the partners has its advantages."

As the words flew out of my mouth, regret scourged me. I vowed not to bring up Graham, no matter how much the man's involvement with my girlfriend vexed me. Talking about the guy always made Alexa defensive, which only angered me more.

"Graham wanted to be helpful."

I sliced a carrot with such force, a few of the pieces propelled off the cutting board to the floor. I hated hearing the jerk's name on her lips. It reminded me that she'd probably whispered it as the man made love to her. Or maybe she screamed. The syllable echoed in my head.

I shouldn't have to contemplate Graham's presence in her life. She should have ceased all communication when I asked her to. Maybe she didn't hang out with him anymore, but there was still contact.

Graham owned part of her life as long as his company owned her building. That wouldn't change unless she moved her business elsewhere, which she wouldn't do unless I gave her a reason to move herself.

The thought occurred to me repeatedly that I'd love to have Alexa come back to London with me. I knew the impracticality of the idea. She was intractably independent and focused on her business. In many ways, her gym was as much a competitor as Graham Ryan.

I wondered what it would take to be number one in her life.

"What does it matter? I have a business to run." She snaked an arm around my waist. "You don't have to worry."

I glanced over to the stove. "Put a lid on the rice. It's boiling."

"Oh." She whirled around and grabbed the lid to the pot.

"It's a good thing I'm watching." I grinned at her.

She gave me a slanted smile in return.

CHAPTER 48

ALEXA

I kept smiling throughout dinner and trained my mind on my dinner companion. Letting my attraction to Graham's charm cloud my thinking was too easy. Adam had his own charm, and I vowed to let him win me over.

"It's so sweet of you to cook me dinner. Your skills in the kitchen outshine mine by a mile."

"Or a kilometer."

I chuckled. "Sure."

I gathered up the dishes and pans and began rinsing everything for the dishwasher. What I couldn't put in the dishwasher would wait until the housekeeper came in the morning.

"It doesn't bother you to leave them in the sink overnight?"

"Nope. What are they going to sprout fangs and kill me in

my sleep?" I hissed and showed my teeth like a vampire, laughing.

"No," Adam answered sharply. "I just thought we'd go ahead and wash them tonight."

"Uh uh. I've had a long day, week, month. I'm going to sit on the couch and clear off some programs from the DVR. Or we can watch a movie."

"A movie. I don't know that I could stand to sit through… What's that show you watch? True housewives in wherever."

His tart tone dripped with contempt, so when he moved closer, slipping an arm around my waist, I stiffened.

"I can't defend it, so I won't try. I just like them. Sue me."

"They're outrageous."

"I know. That's the point. We don't have to watch that." I pulled out of his arms and headed for the sofa. "We'll pick a movie."

I plucked the remote from the coffee table and sat down. Adam hovered in the archway between the kitchen and the living room. "What kind of movie?"

"I don't know. Let's see." I flicked on the TV and paged through the guide to my movie channels. "If we don't find one here, then we can look on Netflix. Come sit down."

I patted the cushion next to me.

"I'll be in shortly."

He disappeared, and moments later, the clang of pots and pans blended with the sound of running water. Seriously? They'd get cleaned and put away in the morning. I flipped to my DVR, figuring I might as well watch something else before the movie since Adam insisted on playing housemaid.

Half-way through an episode of *Days of Our Lives*, he sauntered in and sat down, edging closer. I fought off irritation and let him.

"Is this a soap opera?"

"It is."

"I think I've seen this on in England."

"Probably."

I pulled out my iPad and opened the Netflix app, waiting to see if he had more commentary. "What do you want to watch?" I asked, handing him the tablet.

He swiped and swiped before grinning. "How about *Basquiat*?"

A wrenching pain pulsed between my eyes. "I was hoping to watch something light. Something funny."

"It's a beautiful movie."

"He lived in a cardboard box, then descended into drug-addicted madness and died before he was thirty."

"That's a rabidly unfair summary of his life. His art was transcendent."

"I know, but I don't want to be depressed. Not tonight."

I took the tablet back and began scrolling through the comedic options for something intelligent enough for Adam, but that wouldn't leave me searching for cyanide capsules. "What about some stand-up? They have lots of comedy specials. Look, this guy is British."

"He's a…" Adam waved his hands. "Okay."

I smoothed my tone. "If you don't want to watch him, just say so. I've seen this guy before, and he's hilarious. You'll like him."

"Whatever you want to watch is fine. Honestly, I know what a hard time you've had. We should see something fun."

I relaxed into Adam's side. "Thank you."

The comedian managed to pull some laugh-out-loud moments from Adam, erasing my headache with the closeness of shared jokes. My head tipped on his shoulder, and I dug my bare feet between the sofa cushions to warm them.

"Do you want to watch something else?" He muttered the question into my hair.

"No."

His stubble scraped my forehead as I turned into his neck and took in his strong, warm scent—cedar and something floral. Woody and slightly cloying. The memory of Graham's clean scent sprang up, and I pulled back to see Adam's face. Adam.

He locked the ebony depths of his eyes on me, and he dipped his head. I kept my eyes open as our lips met. The long fringe of his lashes fluttered. He moaned into my mouth. The insistence of the kiss passed the point of passion, and I pushed on his chest to give myself more air.

Lifting the hem of my shirt, Adam fluttered his fingers down my belly and began to work the button on my jeans. My heaving breath froze in my chest. All the heat in my body escaped through my pores, standing every hair on end.

"What?"

My eyes snapped open. He hovered over me with the glow of the TV screen saver flickering over the side of his face. His dark eyes smoldered, but left me chilled.

"I can't do this right now."

"Whatever you need. I I—" He snapped his mouth shut for a second, then continued. "I care about you."

My cheeks burned, and an itch crawled up my legs. I crawled backward on the sofa and swung my legs to the floor. He hadn't said it, so I could move past it. Sweet Jesus. He'd only been in the U.S. a few weeks.

I found my sweater and pulled it over head. "My brain is so tired."

"It's okay."

He moved to me again, wrapping me in an embrace. As he kissed me on the forehead, his hand slid behind my neck, squeezing it between his fingers. The massage should have worked out the tension, but the unspoken word lingered in my shoulders, robbing me of relief.

I put my hand on his chest and pressed him back, silently cursing my reaction. Adam wanted me. Entirely. He sent flowers. He cooked for me. He kissed me with an unquenchable desire.

Thoughts of Graham stalked me, but I had to erase them. He said he wanted me now, but how long might that last? Now, for the first time, I wanted something lasting. It's what I needed. Knowing it and feeling it, however, didn't go hand in hand.

CHAPTER 49

GRAHAM

The ballroom sparkled under a canopy of lights draped like a circus tent toward a twinkling ball in the center. I walked in with my last-minute date, Candace, and smiled. I loved that we'd given Poppy her disco ball.

Candace was Walker Carmichael's idea. Or Walker's wife's idea. Mrs. Carmichael might be the only person on the planet to bring Walker to heel. I admired her—and feared her as would anyone with an ounce of sense.

"My wife has been hounding me to find prospects for her friend's daughter—namely you. I told her I wasn't sure what your status was, and I didn't want to pry. But if you're single and available, how about I give you the girl's number?"

Why hadn't I just told Walker no when he threw his wife's friend's daughter at me? Scrounging up another date hadn't been on my to-do list, and lately, my roster of regular date options had thinned. That suited me fine.

"I've met her, and she is a lovely girl," Walker urged. "Or woman, I suppose. I have to cure myself of calling every woman under forty a girl. Helena swears you'll find her delightful."

"It's a nice offer, but I wouldn't want any misplaced expectations to cause issues with your wife." I had exhaled, proud of my carefully crafted diplomacy.

"No pressure at all. Just a date, and only if you want to. I find these events more tolerable with a companion. Don't you?"

Walker had a gift for making a suggestion sound like a command. I had nodded and shrugged.

"Her name is Candace Levitt. Her mother, Ginny, and Helena were sorority sisters at Texas years ago."

"I'll take her number. We can meet for drinks, and then see about the benefit."

So, I had drinks with the woman. As it turned out, we had met before. I'd dated one of her old friends. Our mini-date went well enough, but I knew this wasn't the woman for me. I knew who I wanted. She was tall, with a halo of curly hair.

Candace had too much makeup and too much Texas flash packed into her five-foot-four ex-cheerleader body. She was more Dallas than Austin. I wouldn't have invited her except that Walker's wife had already mentioned it to her.

"I'm so glad you asked me to go with you."

I hadn't, but I didn't want to hurt her feelings.

Now, we made our way shoulder-to-shoulder through the wide hotel hallway. Candace shimmied in her gown and gave me a predatory look poorly disguised as coy. I ignored it.

"I feel bad that I have to leave you as soon as we get here. Before everything kicks off, we have to run through the show one more time."

Candace placed an understanding hand on my forearm. "It's okay. Seriously. I talked a friend into buying a ticket, and she's meeting me here early for a drink in the bar. You'll find that I don't need a lot of babysitting."

Glittering butterflies secured Candace's up-do, catching the light as she swiveled her head to take in the room. The sunny blonde hair lifted off her shoulders showed off her elegant neck and drew my eyes to the cleavage-enhancing sweetheart neckline of her shimmery red gown. I flung my gaze back up to her eyes, but not before she noticed my attention and swayed toward me.

I swallowed my sigh. A pair of meticulously presented, distractingly large breasts was hard to ignore, and I was afraid Candace took it as a greater indicator of my interest than I'd intended.

She craned her neck to look up at me through a fan of long eyelashes that I thought might be fake. I wasn't an expert, but they looked even longer than when we had drinks a couple of days ago.

"Where should I come find you when the doors open?" She looped her arm around mine.

Over her head, I saw Alexa gliding toward us in a gilded sheath that draped from every curve. She was alone. A tug on my arm reminded me that Candace had asked me a question.

"Meet me at the front left table right in front of the stage. I'll be there at seven-thirty sharp."

"Perfect. See you then."

The blonde spun around and walked away, shaking everything her mama gave her—which wasn't much from behind.

Alexa passed Candace and glanced sideways at her without turning her head. I braced myself for her commentary.

"You ready? The showrunner texted me that they're ready for us. Toby and Sarah are on their way. They just parked."

She slipped her cell phone back in a bronze satin clutch. Her eyes leveled with mine without any visible irritation or curiosity.

"Great. Where's Adam?"

"I didn't think there was any point in having him here this early. He's coming later. Was that your date?" Her sweet smile betrayed nothing.

"Yes."

"I thought you said you didn't have one."

"I didn't. My business partner's wife wanted to fix us up."

"What happened to Sierra?"

"I'm not dating Sierra. Never was. I thought this would be more fun with a date. Walker—you'll meet him tonight— suggested that I ask Candace. As it turns out, we'd met before through a friend of hers."

Alexa blinked rapidly, and her nostrils twitched briefly into a flare. I pulled my shoulders back and pursed my lips to stop a grin.

"She's lovely."

I couldn't hold back a cackle.

"What's so funny?" Alexa's question snapped.

"'Lovely?'"

"She is, in fact, a lovely woman. You don't think so?"

"She's not as cute as her friend was," I joked and then grimaced. "That's just a joke."

Alexa blew out a disgusted air.

"I'm only kidding. I joke about this stuff, and maybe I shouldn't."

Alexa only brushed past me and stalked toward the stage. Her fury told me I wasn't out of the running by a long shot, but I'd have to control my mouth. Drawing attention to my previous exploits wasn't helping my case.

CHAPTER 50

ALEXA

*O*nce the attendants flung open the doors and our guests streamed into the ballroom, I went into full-on charm mode, glad-handing and coaxing the dollars out of the patrons. But getting into the spirit proved harder than I anticipated.

Over the course of the evening, Candace rubbed Graham's shoulders, squeezed his arm, and wiped non-existent crumbs from the corner of his mouth. The effusion of intimate touches didn't let up. I half-expected her to stuff her hand down his pants and get it over with.

To think that I spent the previous few days wondering if I'd made a mistake.

"She's attentive," Sarah sipped her champagne. She and I exchanged mocking glances.

"That she is. I'm sure he enjoys it."

"Really? It looks to me like he's enduring her. He stiffens every time she goes near him."

"I'll bet."

Sarah laughed into her champagne flute. "That's not what I meant."

"I don't like her," a young, high voice declared behind us.

We jerked around to see Poppy standing there.

"She seems nice," I lied.

"I like you and Graham," Poppy insisted.

"I have a boyfriend. Adam. He's nice. He went to get us more refreshments."

Or booze. Adam went to get me a much-needed double vodka soda with lime.

"He's weird."

"Poppy!" Sarah exclaimed. "That's not nice. Apologize."

"Sorry, Miss Alexa." The little girl's voice sang.

I smiled at Poppy. "That's okay. I'm sure he seems different because he's from another country, and you don't know him very well. Besides, you don't have to like anyone you don't want to."

"We should invite you and Adam over for dinner," Sarah suggested.

"He'd love that. He feels like he doesn't know my friends very well. Having us all get to know each other would be great. Maybe I'll host."

Sarah giggled. "You're cooking? I'm busy that night."

"I'll surprise all of you with my kitchen skills. I'll invite Melissa and Kyle, too. Trista has a new boyfriend. Maybe she can come over."

"Are you going to invite Graham and Candace?" Poppy asked.

"I don't know. That's a lot of people. My house isn't that big."

Sarah poked me in the shoulder as Toby leaned over and kissed his wife on the cheek. "Everything looks great, Alexa. You guys did such a great job."

"Thanks."

"They make a great team," Sarah remarked.

"Stop it."

Toby laughed. "I'm not here to start trouble. I wanted to ask my baby girl to dance."

Poppy jumped up and grabbed her father's hand. "Let's go."

She pulled her father toward the dance floor. I turned back to my friend.

"Look, I like Graham. He's a great guy in a lot of ways. But as much as he says he's interested in me, every time I see him, there's a new woman in the mix. It only proves why I'm making the right decision."

"If that's how you see it, then I'm happy for you." Sarah couldn't sound less convinced.

"It is. I hope Adam comes back soon. I'm supposed to meet Graham in a few minutes to start tallying up the take."

Sarah circled her eyes around to the dance floor, watching Toby twirl Poppy. "I'm going to go dance with my peeps."

I waved her on and reminded myself why we were there. Tonight was about Poppy, not my drama.

Soon enough, Adam returned, and I gulped half of my vodka soda as soon as it hit my hand.

"Thirsty?" Adam glared.

"Very."

"Let's dance."

He stroked his thumb up the inside of my wrist, making me shiver.

"I can't now. I'll save a dance for you later. I promise. The silent auction closed, and we need to add everything up so we can announce it at the end of the night."

"That must be why Graham is bearing down on us like a Navy destroyer."

Sure enough, Graham hurried over with a stack of papers. Rather than get caught in an Adam-Graham face off, I stood up.

"I'll be back in about half an hour. Maybe forty-five minutes."

Adam's eyes darkened as Graham approached. "You sure you don't need any help?"

"No. We know how it's all organized. It'll go faster if we handle it."

I bent over and tipped Adam's face up with my finger, softly kissing his lips. His mouth opened, and he strained upward just as Graham arrived. I patted his cheek and stood.

The new arrival glanced sideways at Adam and adjusted a cufflink. "Sorry to interrupt."

"No problem. Be back soon," I assured my date.

I marched with Graham out of the ballroom and down the hallway to the staging room, abuzz with volunteers from the local juvenile diabetes charity. I grabbed my laptop with the files we needed, including our donation spreadsheet.

"I can't concentrate in here," Graham said. "Let's find another room."

"There's the room next door the A/V guys were using for storage, but I don't think there's a place to sit."

In response, Graham stacked two chairs and gestured toward the door with his head. "Lead on."

CHAPTER 51

ALEXA

*N*ext door, Graham and I settled into a free corner, putting our papers and the computer on top of a tall, metal case and sitting on opposite sides. We split the stack of silent auction sheets and began tallying. He tapped away, using his cell phone as a calculator. "Poppy looks like she's having the time of her life."

I thought of how Poppy owned the room and smiled. "She absolutely is. You should see her circulating. Sarah took her around to all the tables. Her charm is probably responsible for most of the take tonight."

He chuckled. "Do you know what she asked me?"

"For a check? She's not afraid to ask for the sale," I giggled.

"No. She asked me why you weren't my girlfriend."

"I'm surprised Poppy was able to do that with Candace glued to your side."

"When I agreed to bring her, I didn't know how… exuberant she would be."

He gave me a chagrined smile.

I dropped my pen. "Agreed? What kind of deal did you make?"

"No deal. It's just that Walker's wife wanted to fix us up, and as soon as he heard that I wasn't with anyone, he pounced. He's the senior partner at our firm, and even though we're partners, he's kind of my boss, in a sense."

"So, he's pimping out this girl and you agreed?"

"No. It's not like that, and I think in this scenario, I'd be the one getting pimped out."

"Interesting. Well, if the fishnets fit." I intended to deliver my dig with humor.

Graham's face stormed. "Ahh. I'm a whore."

My exasperation came out as a growl. "No. But seriously. There's always a new woman with you."

"I'm not dating all the women that you think I am. I know a lot of people. And if I *were* dating different women, isn't that perfectly normal? I wasn't aware that your not wanting me meant I was supposed to live like a monk."

I turned my attention to my calculator. "You're right. It's none of my business. Candace seems…like a lot of fun."

Graham peered at me and put down his pen. "That doesn't sound like a compliment when you say it."

"Why should you care what I think about your date any more than I care what you think about mine?" I frowned and threw up a hand. "I can't believe I'm even comparing whatever is going on with you and the flavor of the week to me and Adam."

"Wow." Graham smirked.

"What?"

"Can't you just let it go with, 'I'm choosing Adam,' and

leave it at that? Why do you need to get bitchy on your way out the door?"

I snorted. "I'm a bitch now. Fantastic."

"No. You're *being* bitchy."

"Then, it's a good thing we're not together. I wouldn't want to annoy you with my bitchiness."

The urge to needle him attacked out of nowhere, squelching my loathing of my own snide remarks.

"I really care for you, you know. I don't know why I even give you the satisfaction of knowing that. I suppose I'm still trying to convince you that I was sincere," he said.

I sighed and closed my eyes. His tone and his words chiseled away at my heart, but I couldn't keep doing this to myself. The waffling back and forth. I'd made my choice. Graham "cared." Perfect. How *lovely*.

"I get it. Okay? We should both move on."

"We should. So, leave Candace alone. She's a nice enough girl."

I thought about the girl's "girls" spilling out of her dress and forced myself not to make another rude comment. The wellspring of irritation bubbling inside me had no place, and I had no right.

Instead of continuing down that path, I sorted the silent auction sheets. We worked in silence, noting the winners and adding up the bid totals.

He looked up after going through his last slip. "I've got just over a hundred sixty-two five. You?"

I punched more digits into my calculator and hit the equal button. "Almost seventy-seven thousand."

I took Graham's tally sheet and put the numbers together. "$239,189."

"That's a great take. How much did they get in ticket sales?"

"Just under one hundred and eighty-two thousand." I located the pre-event total and tapped away at my calculator. "181,900. So, a total of $421,089."

I grinned, and Graham managed to return a smile.

"That's amazing. I'm thrilled for Toby and Sarah."

Putting our sniping aside, we discussed how to announce the results to the attendees and who else we needed to add to our thank you list. Graham took notes.

"Who was the top bidder from the auction? We should mention them. Or maybe the top three."

"Roger and Britta Connery. They bid on the Paris trip. Then, Camilla Strong. She won the yachting trip. Then, oh, Adam. He bid on the golf weekend at Pebble Beach."

"You hate golf," Graham reminded me.

"I do. But I love California, and I think there's also a spa."

Graham rolled his eyes.

"Now who's being bitchy."

"No one. I apologize. I hope it works out with him."

"Thank you. I think it will."

"Do you really, Alexa?" He slapped his hands on the table. "Forget it. We've had this conversation. I don't want to have it again. Good luck."

"No." I lifted my chin in obstinance. "He *loves* me."

"And you love him?"

"I do," I shot back, doubling down with a confidence I didn't feel.

"Truly?"

"I...do. I—" I cut myself off before I said I "cared" for him. The words stuck in my throat.

"You love him, but you melt every time I come near you. I kiss you, and you can't see straight. That scares you, so you've chosen him because he's safer."

Graham stood up and turned away from our

makeshift desk, scooping up his dinner jacket and shrugging it back over his broad shoulders. His whiskey eyes settled on me.

A tremor at the corner of my eye was the single sign of my quaking rage. I stood and smoothed my dress, holding my shoulders at a defiant angle and charging around the makeshift table.

"What does that mean—'safe?' Because I know where I stand with him? Because he's a one-woman guy? What you call safe, I call reliable. You make loyalty and commitment sound like a problem."

"That's not what I mean. He's safe for you because he hasn't made it into your heart. And he won't."

Graham closed the small distance between us. His eyes locked with mine. "He doesn't make you feel like you're stepping off the ledge and flying, does he?"

The warmth of his proximity dried my mouth. I could smell him—clean and citrusy—and swallowed, desperate to quell my body's predictable reaction.

"I want to trust the man I'm with, and you see that as settling. That's how I know you're not the guy for me, Graham."

"Trust is about how you feel. I can't control that."

"No. It's about what you do. Who you are."

"When have I ever made you feel like I wouldn't commit to you? I've told you that I want to be with you."

Graham touched the tip of his index finger under my chin, and my face heated. The bottom dropped out of my stomach, and I felt like I was falling—not flying—with nothing to hold.

So I clung to my story. "Am I supposed to be comforted that you've taken a temporary leave from sleeping your way through the Hill Country?"

"I don't know, Alexa. Should Adam feel comforted that you have?"

My fear whiplashed into anger. "Fuck you, Graham."

"You'd like to. Wouldn't you? You should just admit that's what you want. Let's go from there."

"You're telling me what I want is a guy who has to be brow beaten into monogamy?"

"A guy who's willing to embrace it if it means I get to be with you."

"I don't believe you." The heat of my desire melded with rage.

"You don't want to believe me because then you might let yourself fall in love for real."

"My feelings for Adam are real, but I don't have to convince you of that."

I peeled away on unsteady legs and glanced toward the doorway.

"Of course you don't. You have to convince yourself. Good luck with that, by the way. How long before your true colors show and *you* bail on *him*? Just because your biological clock may be ticking, watching your cousin have a baby and Melissa get engaged, doesn't mean you have to rush things with this guy."

"Nice. You think I'm that much of a simpleton? Well, then, forgive me if I don't want to waste my waning years of usefulness as a woman on you."

I pushed past him, down the hall from the work room. The sounds of the party grew louder as I turned through the double doors into the banquet hall. Crowds of people swirled, and the band screamed. My chest constricted.

Standing out in the sea of humanity, Adam waved and caught my eye. I ping-ponged my way to him.

"I need to go outside for a few minutes and get some air."

I plucked my mobile phone out of my purse. I had about twenty minutes before Graham and I announced the auction winners and gave our thank you speeches.

"I'll come with you." Adam glanced over my head, and his jaw tightened. "What's going on with Graham?"

"Nothing."

"So, he's stormed out here after you about nothing?"

My gaze roamed over my shoulder. Graham had followed, but then stopped, staring at me and Adam. A faint shake of my adversary's head, and he disappeared into the crowd.

"We had a disagreement over some of the final details, but we've worked it out. Look, I'm a little tired. Let's step out on the patio and take a minute."

"Of course."

Adam grasped my elbow and led me toward the door. I followed silently, glad that the sliding metallic screech of electric guitar made speaking nearly impossible.

The heavy door swung shut behind us, blunting the thump of music inside.

"He upset you."

I forced a smile. "No. He didn't. I'm fine."

Adam pulled me to him and kissed my temple. "You should stay away from him."

"Except for the fundraiser and the building situation, we hardly talk. Now, this is done."

"Good. I don't like to see you upset."

The plush softness of his lips on my forehead calmed my nerves.

"I'm not. It's been a long day."

"You aren't going to see him anymore? You shouldn't."

"I don't know, Adam." I sighed and shrugged. "I'll see him when I see him. It doesn't matter."

"It does to me. I don't like the way he looks at you. He's still making a play for you." Adam slipped his hand under my hair, holding the back of my neck between his thumb and forefinger.

"Not anymore, he won't."

"Something *did* happen."

"No. Not really. I told him before that we were only going to be friends. He understood that way before tonight." I pulled away from Adam and smiled again. "I don't want to talk about Graham. Let's talk about our upcoming vacation —assuming that you're taking me as your plus one."

Adam's gleaming grin cheered me. "Absolutely. Do you golf?"

"No, but I'm sure I can find something to do."

I wrapped my arms around Adam and nuzzled my face in his neck.

"I'm sure we both can."

He squeezed me tight. His iron grip on my waist had mixed results in dispelling my troublesome mood. *Hold on to him,* I encouraged myself. That's all I had to do.

CHAPTER 52

GRAHAM

The minute Candace reached behind her and unzipped her scarlet dress, I wished she would disappear. Maybe in a puff of smoke.

We had stopped at a couple of bars after the benefit before catching a ride home. My chin fell to my chest as I thought about how I'd have to go get my car in the morning. I could practically feel the bourbon and tequila sloshing inside my skull.

I could blame the alcohol for how I ended up sitting on the edge of my bed, watching a woman I wasn't sure I even liked take her clothes off. Or I could blame the bone-deep bruises on my ego.

Being a sore loser only added to the shame. Sure, I'd lost Alexa to that British control freak, but if that's what she wanted, I couldn't help her. She'd see what a mistake she was making, and I wouldn't be there to hold her hand. Her loss.

That petulance led me to the moment where a half-naked woman swaying her hips like a willow in a windstorm left me cold. My body's disinterest was equal parts humiliating and affirming. Sure, having the deflation of my ego made manifest in my listless cock hurt my pride, but on the other hand, it proved I wasn't quite the asshole Alexa thought.

After all, bringing Candace home was a mistake. What I wanted was to tangle my hands in the cloud of Alexa's hair and bury myself in her all night. The booze-soaked thought bobbed in my mind, rousing my nether regions.

She eyed my burgeoning erection and smiled. "Hello, Mr. Happy."

I flinched at the cutesy talk, briefly deciding to send her home, but she stepped over to me and knelt down, slipping her hand inside my boxer briefs to free me. She closed her hand on my cock and stroked upward, swirling her palm around the tip.

My teeth ground together. "You know this is just for tonight, right?"

I wanted to be straight with her. The last thing I needed was her running off and crying on Helena Carmichael's shoulder.

"Fine by me." Her hot breath tingled. I closed my eyes.

A vision of Alexa's dress sliding off into a gold pool at her feet materialized in my brain. Dark, peaked nipples. I could imagine tasting one. But I couldn't and probably never would again. Reality doused the spark of my arousal. In a show of will, I pushed Candace's open mouth away and rolled to the side to get my dick out of her hand.

"What's the problem?"

"I can't do this."

She sat back on her heels. "Are you worried about the Carmichaels? Don't be. I'm not going to start planning our wedding and then whine because you broke my heart. I just want to have fun, and you do too. I can tell. You're a party guy."

The echoing indictment of me deflated what had been left of my hard-on. Candace reached for me again, and I grabbed her wrist. "Don't. I'm done."

"I can see that, whiskey dick."

"Put your clothes on."

Her snarky pout sealed the deal. I stood up and put my uninspired penis back in my underwear. "Do you need me to call you a taxi? Or order you a car?"

Candace stepped into her dress and pulled it up over her shoulders. "No. All I need is for you to zip me up."

I obliged and walked her out of my bedroom and down the stairs to the entryway. It might be ten or fifteen minutes before she got a driver at this time of night. I'd have to extend my hospitality a little longer.

"Do you want something to drink?"

"No. I'll wait outside."

"You don't have to."

"I'm not going to sit in your house awkwardly staring at you. I'll save you that embarrassment."

I shrugged and opened the door. "Suit yourself."

Her heels clacked over the threshold of the door, and she stumbled, but righted herself before I had to catch her. A drunk woman tripping through my yard didn't sound like a good idea.

"You alright?"

"I'm fine. I'll stand here and wait. The car will be here in," she paused and tapped on her phone, waiting a bit, "twelve minutes. Close the door."

I welcomed the idea and slammed it shut, waiting until I saw her throw herself into the back of her ride before heading back to bed. Glad to be alone, I conjured up old memories and new fantasies starring Alexa.

That pleasure was something I could do by myself. Using Candace as a blow-up doll wouldn't make me feel better.

Then, I felt like a fool. I had thrown a warm, willing woman out of my house. What had Alexa done to me?

CHAPTER 53

ALEXA

$\mathcal{T}$he days after the charity event rolled on slowly. I put the drama out of my head and invested in finishing the spa expansion and giving Adam my remaining time and energy.

He kept pushing for a trip to meet my family, and I figured a good compromise over going to Oklahoma was a trip to Dallas to see Taryn and Jeff. Two weekends later, we left early Saturday morning and headed up I-35.

We arrived at lunchtime, and Taryn made us a creamy lemon chicken with pasta and a salad, which much impressed Adam.

"From what I gather, Alexa's mother is a wonderful cook. You are a wonderful cook. What happened with you?" he asked, shooting a grin at me.

"I'm missing the gene to want to cook."

Jeff twirled a last bite of pasta on his fork. "Alexa has cooked before. She might be sandbagging to get you to do it."

"Ahh. A trickster. Well, we'll have to do something about that. If you want to keep your man happy, you're going to have to work on your domestic skills."

Taryn's nostrils flared. "It's never been her thing. Not all women are domestic."

"True. Maybe that's why she's still single. Lucky for me."

"Yes, lucky for you," Taryn snapped. "May I take your plate?"

I jumped up from the table in the sparkling kitchen. "I'll clear the table. You don't need to be on your feet."

Adam stood as well. "I'll help as well. I would hate to be a poor house guest. We'll clean up."

"You guys don't have to worry about all that," Jeff countered. "Just put them in the sink with the pots and pans. Our housekeeper will be back in tonight."

"Are you sure?" Adam asked.

"Absolutely. Instead of doing dishes, how about I show you the new putting green I mentioned. I have some clubs you can borrow."

"Okay. Fantastic." Adam turned to me, who scooped up more dishes. "Come with us."

"You know I'm not much for golf, and Taryn is in no shape for it. You guys go do guy time."

"I want to catch up on girl talk with my cousin anyway," my cousin piped in.

Adam's eyes narrowed.

"We promise not to talk about you too much. Go!" she insisted with a grin.

"Arguing is futile. Trust me," Jeff added.

The men took off, and I cleared the table, then sat back down and braced myself. "Alright, what do think of him?"

"You said he was really into you. That's clear."

"That's not an answer."

"You like him. I can tell that. He's very handsome."

"Still not an answer."

"I don't know."

I squinted at her. "You're picking over your words like you're trying to find gold nuggets in a pile of shit. You can't tell me that you have no opinion."

"Nice image. Thank you for that. Do you want some coffee?" She thrust herself out of her chair and lumbered over to the espresso machine.

"Just say it."

"He leaves me cold. And that whole thing about your domestic skills. Not cool."

"He was joking."

She snorted. "He was joking in that way that's supposed to sound like joking, but you really mean it. Shady."

I pushed back, not wanting to sound too defensive. "Obviously, if it bothered him that much, he wouldn't be with me."

Taryn's huff was silenced by the clatter of the coffee maker. She filled two cups and carried them back over to the table. "What happened with the guy from New Year's? Have you talked to him since your fight?"

"No."

"Was it that bad?"

"I told you what he said. He was completely off base. Calling me bitchy. Telling me that the only reason I'm with Adam is because my biological clock is ticking and I'm desperate for a man to commit. Utter bullshit."

"Okay. Easy. Jesus. He was probably just mad."

I chewed my bottom lip, then sipped my coffee.

"If it's not true, Lex, why get worked up? Or was what he said more true than you'd like to admit?"

"It's not true. Graham has a wandering eye—and some other wandering body parts as well."

"Fine, but are you serious about Adam?"

An "of course" popped in my mind—almost too quickly—but stalled on my tongue. I dug deep for what was true.

"He's attentive and romantic. And I don't have to push him to want me and only me. It comes naturally for him. That matters. I can trust him. I would always have been wondering about Graham and waiting for his head to turn."

"Did you have that conversation with Graham? It sounds like he wants to give it a shot, and you ran away."

"I didn't run away from Graham. I ran toward Adam."

"Just because Graham isn't the right guy doesn't mean Adam is. None of the above is also an option."

"I know, but—" I started to argue, but seeing Adam appear from around the corner trapped the words in my throat.

"Sorry. Jeff pointed me in the direction of the bathroom, but I took a wrong turn."

"Down the hall. First door on the right."

"Perfect. What are you two chattering about so intensely?"

I pasted a smile on my face. "Taryn is giving me advice. She's always ready with advice."

He opened his mouth, clearly about to follow up his line of questioning, but thought better of it. "First door on the right?"

"Yep."

His eyes stayed fixed on me for a moment before he turned heel for the bathroom.

"Change of subject," Taryn announced in a drawled whisper, then continued. "What are you doing for your birthday?"

"Melissa and Trista are throwing me a party at Trista's."

She pouted. "I hate to miss it."

"You wouldn't have fun anyway. They're getting kegs and liquor. You'd be the one sober person at the party."

"Yeah. That's no fun. Am I a total alcoholic that I miss drinking? I'm dying for a glass of champagne."

"Having a baby is a thing to celebrate."

"Exactly! We'll see. I've been reading, and some mothers pump and dump."

My nose turned up. "I have no idea what that is, but it sounds repulsive."

"It's where you drink and then use the breast pump, but you dump the milk for a few hours after so you don't give it to the baby."

"What is that from drunkmom.com?"

"Funny."

I taunted Taryn with my ability to drink whatever and whenever I wanted until Adam found his way back outside.

"Now. What was I saying?" Taryn asked.

"None of the above is an option."

"Exactly. Something to keep in mind."

I rolled the warm coffee mug between my hands. "You really don't like him."

Taryn reached across the table and took my hand. "I've got to be honest. No. I don't. But if he makes you happy, I'm happy."

"He does," I asserted, as my cousin's dubious look challenged me. "He *does*."

CHAPTER 54

ADAM

*L*unch the next day brought about forced smiles and congeniality. I thought my face would crack.

Fuck Taryn. How someone as strong as Alexa could let her interfering cousin boss her around baffled me. Loud and insufferable, Alexa's cousin was exactly what I found repellent in most American women. The woman had an opinion about everything, and a voice like the shriek of a hillbilly barn owl.

I considered nominating Taryn's husband, Jeff, for a Nobel Peace Prize. Of course, Jeff had begged off from our mid-morning brunch adventure in favor of "work" and needing to pick up his daughter from his ex-wife's house later in the afternoon. His choice left me abandoned and in the company of the two women.

As I sipped my overly sweet cocktail, I tried to not to

curse at the auditory intrusion of chimes clanging at me every few minutes.

"I love the chimes. They're motion-sensing, so they go off when runners pass by," Taryn explained.

Alexa looked around and tipped her head back, sunlight on her face. "It's such a beautiful day. I love it when patio weather comes out to play. Every spring and fall almost make up for the summers." She leveled her chin. "Almost."

Taryn scrunched her face and stuck out her tongue. "Ugh. I can't even think about summer. Let me believe that this eighty-degree weather is going to last."

"Maybe you can enclose your house with a giant bubble, and then you can make it comfortable year-round," I suggested.

I still hadn't gotten over the monstrosity of Jeff and Taryn's home. Seven bedrooms? It was close to obscene. I took another sip of my drink. The house was fine. Clearly, Jeff had the money. I remonstrated myself. I shouldn't let my feelings about its female occupant turn me into some kind of socialist.

Her words looped in my mind. *None of the above is also an option.* She had no idea about Alexa's relationship with me. We were perfect for one another. Alexa would see that in time.

I forced air into my lungs and then out. I had to calm down. For better or worse, Taryn was family. Quelling her influence on Alexa wouldn't be easy, but it would be impossible if I let my contempt for her build and bubble over.

"I'm so lucky that I get to see you this weekend and in two weeks. You should come up early and hang out the whole week."

"Tempting, but I can't."

"I know. You've got the business to run."

"Things are getting easier now that I've hired Trista. That girl is a dynamo. She teaches two and three classes, six days a week. Best hire I ever made."

I found this the perfect time to interject. "Things aren't awkward between you?"

Alexa had told me about Graham's prior relationship with Trista after I pried the reason for the break up out of her. It hadn't been an easy task, getting her to admit that Graham was little more than a womanizer.

"Not at all."

I examined her face for whatever a look or a flicker might tell me. Nothing. I relaxed.

"So many female friends."

Despite my best efforts, I couldn't suppress the derision in my tone, but then my mind wandered to a vision of Graham and Alexa in a tangle of limbs and bed sheets. I gritted my teeth and forced my fists to open.

She had no reason to see him anymore. Alexa assured me that she had no business contact with the guy. Allegedly, he hadn't been at the gym in weeks. *She cut things off with him.* I repeated the mantra.

"I forgot to ask you how your party planning gig went last weekend."

Alexa's inquiry for Taryn broke through my rumination.

Taryn launched into her response. "Great. We had a small hiccup when a couple of servers didn't show up, but I called Shannon, and she helped me find a couple of replacements."

"Shannon is Jeff's first wife," Alexa explained, then turned back to her cousin. "She worked at a restaurant, right?"

"She did. She stopped working, though. Waiting tables and being pregnant don't mix."

"But the business is going well?"

"It is. For now. I'm taking things easy." Taryn rubbed her

hands over her bulbous belly. "My munchkin is my top priority."

Alexa cackled. "You're going to be a great mom. You're already skilled at turning every conversation back to your kid. You're in the mommy-verse now."

"I know! I'm totally turning into that woman. I love it though, so you're just going to have to get used to it."

Taryn's high-pitched voice accelerated through every sentence. I downed my drink, hoping the alcohol would dull my hearing. Alexa's lower voice gave me a break as they chattered.

"This is what you've always wanted, and now you have it. I'm thrilled. I'll gear up for many afternoons of boring conversation about Diaper Genies and pre-school waiting lists."

"Nope. We won't have any talk about pre-school waiting lists. No need. Jeff and I already secured the kiddo a spot." Taryn patted her stomach.

Alexa laughed, then looked more closely at the grin affixed to her cousin's face. "Oh, my God! You're serious!"

"Totally. Have we not met?" Taryn rolled out the question in her syrupy drawl.

"I have to go to the bathroom and reconsider our entire relationship."

Alexa stood and stretched her lithe body, then disappeared inside the restaurant, as Taryn continued her inane prattle over the competitive world of pre-school placements.

I beckoned Taryn closer and dropped my voice. She leaned over the arm of her chair, eyes wide. "Can I talk to you about something for a minute?"

"Okay...What?"

"Alexa truly is thrilled for you, so I know she won't say this to you. But I think it's important. For Alexa."

Taryn then leaned back in her chair, arms folded over her rounded belly. I continued.

"I think all of this baby talk is starting to get to her. Not that she's not happy for you, but she feels this pressure right now from her parents and from herself. With all of her work commitments, she doesn't know when or if she's going to be able to have a family. It's a lot. And seeing you...Hearing you talk about all of this. It's been a strain."

"If she had a problem, she would tell me." Irritation hardened her gaze.

"No, she wouldn't tell you. She wouldn't want to make you feel bad."

"But you don't mind." Taryn's blue eyes narrowed like shards of broken glass. I had expected this kind of resistance.

"Not if it means doing what's best for Alexa. I know you're not sure about me and my intentions, but I love her, and I have her best interests in mind."

"Sweetie, I don't think one way or another about you. If Alexa cares about you and she's happy, then I'm happy. I'm not the one who has to be sure."

A razor-edged look of amusement and dismissiveness settled over her face and sliced into my self-control. The insinuation was clear, but I pushed down the anger and stayed focused. Taryn needed to back off.

"All I'm saying is that the pressure she gets from her friends and from her family to settle down plus your having a baby and her business partner's getting married...It all adds up to anxiety. You know how Alexa is. She would never admit that any of this got to her."

"No, she wouldn't." My words seemed to find their mark. Taryn's head tilted in contemplation. "I never thought Alexa would ever feel anxious about what's going on in my life. She's always so happy with hers."

"She is happy. We're happy. But she's not getting any younger, and she wonders whether she'd even be able to have a family."

"Alexa?"

Taryn glared at me, ready to argue. I looked away and into the restaurant. Alexa wound her way through the tables toward the patio.

"I think maybe it's better to give her some space on the whole baby thing. She's coming back out. Please don't say anything to her. She'd be mortified that I said anything to you."

The sharp-eyed blonde stared at me. "I'll do whatever is best for her."

CHAPTER 55

ALEXA

*T*wo days in Dallas left me feeling behind when I returned to work even though Melissa assured me everything was progressing.

After checking in with Melissa on the construction and then with Trista on the class schedule, I focused on a piece of personal business—Taryn's shower. The day before, Taryn's friend, Micky, left me an odd voicemail.

Taryn didn't think I needed to come up early for the shower as planned. It sounded to me like Taryn was taking on more for the party than she should. Taryn the control freak might need an intervention.

"Alexa, hi. What's up?" Micky greeted.

"I got your voicemail. I wanted to make sure everything is okay. Taryn isn't doing too much is she?"

"No." Micky's voice had that little dip that you hear when

someone has more to say, but they're trying to keep their mouth shut.

"Something's up. What's the matter?"

"I'm not supposed to say anything."

"Let's just skip to the part where you tell me."

Micky waded into her answer slowly in a high-pitched tone. "Taryn asked me not to bother you with too many details about the shower. She knows you're busy with work."

"I told her it wouldn't be a problem. I don't get it."

"I didn't either, but I got the feeling that it would give Taryn more anxiety if you were still doing a lot than if I just handle things. I don't want to stress her out." Micky hesitated, then her voice pitched. "Maaay-be you should call her."

"I will, and you can count on me to drive up Thursday like we planned. Let's still meet for breakfast on Friday and go over what needs to be done."

"Okay. Promise me that you'll talk to Taryn beforehand. I don't want her wigging out."

"Calling her right now. Promise."

I rocked back in my office chair and dialed. After a few rings, Taryn picked up the phone. "What's up, cuz?"

"That's what I wanted to ask you. Is everything okay?"

"Everything's fine. Jeff and I went to the doctor yesterday, and we're all good. Why?"

I breathed deep to settle my fluttering stomach and tapped a pen on the desk like a metronome. "I talked with Micky. She said that I didn't need to come up early. Are you worried about my work situation? Because things are handled."

"Oh, hell. I wanted to keep things easy for you."

"Are you sure that's it? The last few times I called you and asked about the baby, you change the subject. You know you can tell me anything, right?"

I stilled my seesawing pen, waiting for Taryn's long string of silence to end.

"Look, I talked to Adam, and he said you were feeling a lot of pressure and that you might be anxious about... Whether you might ever have a baby or just where your relationships are headed and...I know I've been so focused on baby, baby, baby."

"What precisely did Adam say?" I threw my pen, and it skipped off the edge of the desk. My skin tingled with fury.

"He said that all my talk about babies added to Melissa's getting married might be making you feel bad about where you were in your life."

"Why in God's name would you believe that?" Disbelief launched my voice higher.

"How many conversations have we had lately about your wanting to settle down now? It feels like maybe you have been a little...I don't know. Dissatisfied. He made it sound like you and he had some conversations about this, and that you didn't want to say anything because you didn't want to hurt my feelings."

"That never happened. Yes, I've questioned my relationships, but how that translates into I'm not happy about the baby or don't want to help you with the baby shower...That's just bullshit. I can't believe he'd say that to you."

Taryn's pitch shifted near a squeak. "I didn't believe him at first but the more he talked, I started thinking. Plus, with everything going on with Uncle Carlisle, I didn't want to add anything else to your plate."

"I'll manage my plate just fine. And Adam too, while I'm at it. I can't believe him."

Even if he thought I was so dissatisfied with my life that I couldn't bear to hear about my cousin's good fortune, why would he think it was his place to have a conversation with

Taryn behind my back? Any conversation I needed to have, I could have myself. Anyone who knew me would know that.

"I'll tell you what I told Micky, everything is fine and I'll be up that Thursday night. You don't need to worry about me. I'll always be there for you. Even if I had my own stupid issues, I never let that get in the way of helping you."

Taryn's drawl slowed. "I don't mean to mean you feel uncomfortable or pressured or anything. I want you to be happy."

"What makes me happy is to know what's going on with you. I don't know why Adam would say that I didn't want to hear about the baby. But you and I are good. Baby talk me away!"

Inexplicably, a lump formed in my throat.

Taryn sniffled. "I know. I should have just talked to you. I can't wait to see you. I love you."

"Love you, too. See you then."

I hung up the phone and leaned back in my chair, aghast. Despite the urge to call Adam immediately and demand an explanation, I took a beat.

This was a conversation best had face-to-face.

I sent him a text to see if he could meet me at my house at seven. He replied back with a thumbs up and a smiley face emoticon.

We'll see how long that smile lasts.

MY LEG BOUNCED NERVOUSLY as I squeezed a wedge of lime into my Tito's and soda. Terminally punctual, Adam should arrive in a few minutes.

I looked over to the vase of black beauty roses sitting on my end table, looking darker in the shaded, early evening light of my living room. I reached over to the other table and clicked on the lamp.

When I called to thank him after the latest flower delivery, I moderated my tone, reserving my outrage for our discussion in person. I wanted to be able to read him when I asked about what he'd told Taryn. If he detected strain in y voice, he didn't let on.

The staccato of his knock on the door sent my heart racing, but I stilled my leg and stood up.

Flipping open the door, Adam's perfect smile highlighted his face, which was shadowed by the roof overhanging my porch.

"Hello. Those roses look more beautiful than I'd imagined. The deeply colored flowers are my favorite."

I stepped aside in the open doorway to let him in.

He leaned in to give me a kiss but stopped short, searching. "What's wrong?"

"You want to have a seat? I can get you a drink. What do you want?"

"Nothing for now. You seem upset."

My breath shortened. I paced to keep my legs steady. "I talked to Taryn today."

"Oh?"

"Sit down."

I stopped and pointed to the overstuffed side chair, but Adam chose the couch. I perched on the edge of the chair and sipped the cocktail I made in preparation for this chat. "Are you sure you don't want something to drink?"

"Do I need one?"

"That depends. How well can you explain why you told Taryn that talking about the baby upsets me and makes me doubt my life?"

Beneath the burnished gold of his skin, a blush emerged on his cheeks. "That's not exactly what I said."

I kept my voice even, but my leg began to shake again. "Then, what did you say?"

"I told her that you were going through a lot, and that she needed to be sensitive to that."

"Taryn doesn't need lessons on how to deal with me. We've been friends our entire lives. She's family."

"I only wanted to help." His accent took on a whining tone.

"I don't need any help. Why would you think that I would want you to interfere with my relationship with my cousin? She's one of my best friends."

"Is she? I'm not sure she cares about your happiness the way that you think. I know she's your family, but she seems more interested in lording over you with her obscenely wealthy husband and that eyesore of a house. Telling you what to do. Who you should date. I'm not the one interfering. She is."

"What are you talking about?"

I asked the question even though the vitriolic fury of his words already provided the answer.

"I heard her. Pushing you toward Graham. Telling you that you don't need to be with me. It's disrespectful."

"It's her opinion. And she's entitled to it, and frankly, it's none of your business."

Adam's face puffed with rage. "How is it none of my business when she's trying to get between us?"

"The only one wedging himself into a relationship is you between me and Taryn. I get it if you don't like what she said, but that doesn't mean you go behind my back and drop poison in her ear."

"I see," Adam hissed his "s."

I pitched forward, chin up. "I hope you do. If you have a problem with something, come to me. Don't run around to other people making things up."

"She's working against us. And why? So you can start things back up with that philandering...I don't even have a word for what he is."

"You're blowing the whole thing out of proportion."

"Am I? 'None of the above is an option.' She wants to keep you single and alone, so she can be the darling. I wouldn't be surprised if she's sabotaged other relationships you've had by planting seeds of doubt to keep you from being happy."

"This is crazy! You're twisting what she said and...God, you're being ridiculous."

Adam surged off the sofa and hovered over me. I pressed against the chair cushion, glaring up at him.

He leaned over and ground out his words. "This is what you do. This is why you can't hang on to a relationship. A man shows you some consideration, and you turn it into a flaw. I love you, and I want to be with you. That is not ridiculous."

My awareness of his bulk sinking toward me put every cell of my body on alert. My toes curled. My skin prickled. My vision narrowed on his snarling face.

To put distance between us, I scrambled up from the chair and planted my feet in a wide stance, the left slightly in front of the right, with my palms facing him.

"Calm down. I don't understand how we got from zero to insanity in a nanosecond. You're overreacting."

"I'm not overreacting. I'm reacting." Adam took a long stride toward me, stopping just a foot away from being nose-to-nose. "I swear you wouldn't know true love if it slapped you in the face."

I stood firm. My fingers curled into fists. I brought my

arms in close to my body and dropped my chin. "You underestimate me. I know what love is supposed to look like, and this isn't it. You need to leave."

Adam swept his open hands in front of his chest and stepped backward. His sudden downshift only made my heartbeat jump faster. "I'm sorry. Let's talk about this. We should talk about this."

"No. Go. We don't need to say anything else to each other right now."

When he didn't move, I barked. "Out, Adam. I'm not kidding."

"I can't leave until I know that you and I are going to talk about this." A grating calm edged in his voice.

"You leave when I say 'leave.' I'd like you to go voluntarily, but if you won't do that, I can make other arrangements."

Angry energy sprang up in my legs. my phone was somewhere in my purse, but I had an alarm system keypad at the front door and in my bedroom. Both had panic buttons.

My stance and tone finally penetrated Adam's fog. His shoulders and chest deflated. "I'm leaving. I'm leaving. I'll call you."

I sidestepped to the front door, keeping him on my periphery, and threw it open. Adam marched toward it, opening his mouth to speak, but I glowered at him.

"Not another word."

He left, and I closed and bolted the door.

What the fuck?

CHAPTER 56

GRAHAM

*J*eans or slacks? A nice T-shirt or something else? What else did I have besides dress shirts?

I retrieved another option from my closet and returned to stand in front of the full-length mirror in my bedroom. Holding up a multi-colored Robert Graham sport shirt—swirled with paisley and a faint dragon print—under my chin, I wasn't sure. Too loud? Too metrosexual? Why had I bought this thing in the first place?

"You're acting like a teenage girl," I chided in the empty room.

The shirt joined the other discarded options on the bed, then I reached again for a light grey, linen button-down, deciding to wear jeans and slip-on sneakers and call it a day. I rolled up my sleeves and put my game face on.

When Trista invited me to Alexa's birthday party at her

house, I RSVP'ed "yes" immediately with an embarrassing level of excitement.

"She mentioned to me yesterday that Adam wasn't coming, so I thought you might want to."

"She and I aren't a thing anymore. I'm surprised you're even inviting me. I wouldn't think she'd want me there."

Trista shrugged. "I think she would."

"Should I bring anything?"

"Your own booze if you want something particular. I'm not shelling out for fancy single-malt so if want top-shelf anything, that's on you. But that's it. She specifically said no gifts."

I decided on a mid-range bottle of bourbon from my liquor cabinet. I would never bring a single-malt Scotch to a house party. Some asshole might put it in their Diet Coke.

Then, I shoved my wallet in my back pocket and grabbed my keys and my gift for the birthday girl. I wouldn't show up empty-handed.

I wasn't the only one who disregarded the no-gifts policy. Once I stepped into Trista's backyard, I spotted a table covered in cards and a handful of tissue-papered gift bags next to one offering up various forms of barbecue.

"Looking for me?" Trista smacked me on the arm.

"I am," I lied. "I have to say hello to the host. Where do I put this?"

I held up the bourbon.

"In the kitchen, there's a counter with all the drinks, mixers, and cups. Can't miss it. Gifts and cards over there. She'll open them in a few."

"Thanks, but I'll hang onto this and give it to her myself."

Trista snickered.

"What?"

"I love seeing you like this. It's like witnessing a miracle."

"With a birthday present?"

"No. God. You know what I mean. Forget it. She's over there by the margarita machine if you're interested." Trista flicked a finger toward a table in the far corner of the yard.

"I hate frozen margaritas."

"No…never mind. When you come back out, find me at some point. I want to introduce you to my new boyfriend."

"Absolutely."

She punched my bicep and then wandered off, shouting to other guests. I headed into the house to fix a bourbon on the rocks. The booze counter was as easy to find as advertised. I set the gift bag temporarily on the counter and plucked a red plastic cup from the stack, questioning my adulthood before turning around to look for ice.

Our eyes flew together like magnets.

She wore an azure blue halter top and short denim skirt, which showed off the dark caramel length of her strong legs. I followed their lines down to her bright pink toes in leather sandals. Her curls were loose, and her eyes widened.

"I didn't know you were going to be here."

"Trista didn't tell you?"

"I gave her a few names for the guest list. She and Melissa did everything. I didn't realize—"

"Do you want me to leave? I don't want to ruin your party."

"No. Don't. Stay. It's fine."

"I don't have to worry that Adam might take a run at me?"

"He's not here."

My tongue practically itched to ask why, but there was a world of explanation in those three words. I exhaled and grabbed another party cup.

A cooler filled with ice sat on the floor at the end of the counter, so I turned to scoop some into both cups.

"You don't have a drink." I grabbed one of the many bottles of Austin-distilled vodka lining the counter and began mixing her a cocktail. My gaze swept up and down the counter. "You may have to go without lime."

"I brought some. They're cut up in the fridge."

"Aren't you the regular Girl Scout? Arriving all prepared and shit." I hoped my attempt at humor would unravel the tension I saw corded in her neck.

"I'm dedicated when it comes to my cocktails."

Alexa opened the refrigerator to retrieve the limes and set them on the counter while I poured myself a generous portion of bourbon.

"Happy birthday, by the way. I got you a little something." I gestured to the blue sparkled bag on the counter.

"People don't seem to know what no gifts means. But, thank you."

She plucked it off the counter. "Should open this now? Or with the others?"

"Now."

She rifled through the obligatory tissue and pulled out a flat cardboard box. As she lifted the lid, the muscles in my legs tightened.

"Very cool." I exhaled at the sight of her smile. "An Oregon Pinot wine-of-the-month club. Thank you."

"You seemed to like it."

"I did. Thanks." A skittish laugh bubbled out of her. "I guess I already said that."

I squeezed a lime into Alexa's cup and handed it to her, then lifted my own drink. "Cheers."

We brushed plastic and drank.

"You're almost done with construction. That must be a relief."

"It is. We'll be open in a few weeks."

"Planning a grand opening?"

"Yeah. Um, we just sent invitations out to some key clients for an exclusive spa party. We have reps from our organic skin care line coming in to do facials and demo the products. We'll do a yoga for relaxation class. It's shaping up."

"I'm glad."

"Thanks for all your help getting things done on time."

"You're welcome."

"How are things with you?"

"Par for the course. I hear your dad's doing well."

One of her carefully arched brows dipped, creating a little wrinkle in her forehead.

"Sarah told me."

"Oh. Yeah. He's doing much better, actually. Internal affairs just cleared the shooting. He's basically on leave until his retirement. My mom couldn't be happier."

"That's a relief. I'm glad." I ran out of tolerance for the elephant standing idly in the corner. "It's none of my business. I'm sure you'll say that, but no Adam at your birthday?"

The look in her eyes could have chilled our drinks. "Do you miss him? I could call him."

"Oh, yes. Please." I swallowed a stinging punch of whiskey.

"It's nothing. Sometimes you have issues. We'll work it out."

She swiveled her head toward the back door, lips firmly shut. The ice crunched in her cup as she shook it and took another drink.

CHAPTER 57

ALEXA

*W*hy did he need to press me on this now?

I longed to run screaming from the room to avoid the line of questioning, but my legs didn't move. Graham kept staring at me. No smugness or self-satisfaction. I detected more concern even, than curiosity.

"We had a disagreement."

"It looks like more than that."

"I can't talk about this with you."

"Why?"

"It feels disrespectful to discuss this with the one person that I know would drive Adam crazy."

"I don't care what drives Adam crazy." His declaration rolled out in a steady, low-pitched rhythm.

I stopped dancing away from Graham's eyes. "What boyfriend wants his girlfriend's old lover hanging around? I don't blame him for that."

"What *do* you blame him for?"

"Don't go there, Graham. Adam...he cares for me. He wants to be with me, and I'm not going to mock him for the thing that drew me to him in the first place."

"I'm not mocking him."

I moved to brush past Graham and leave. He touched my elbow, and I halted.

"I'm sorry. I worry about that guy."

"Why?"

"There's something in the way he is with you that's too... much. He's possessive."

I scratched an imaginary itch on the nape of my neck.

"You see it, too. I don't know what he did, but my guess is that I'm right on the money. Be careful with him, okay?"

"You don't need to worry about me."

"I know, but it doesn't stop me."

His eyes darted away. He sighed and rested his hands on his hips. I stared at his profile—the tightness of his jaw extended into his neck. I longed to touch him and ease his tension. Resisting the magnetic pull between us expended more energy than I had.

"I need to get back out there. I'm supposed to open my presents. Thanks for this." I held up the wine certificate and turned toward the door.

"Alexa, wait."

I kept walking and felt a tingle from my scalp to my heels. Then, the sensation faded. I looked back as I closed the door behind me to go down the steps to the back yard. Graham was gone.

Drink in hand, I wandered across the lawn. The swooshing churn of the margarita machine mixed with reverberating conversations and atmospheric indie rock. The darkening yard frustrated the search for my hostess until a sudden pop of colors twinkled above. Criss-crossing strands of lights stretched away from the roofline, creating a trellis of color befitting Christmas.

"I've heard of Christmas in July, but May is a bit early."

The familiar voice made me spin around, smiling and giving the tall man a hug. "Hey, Kyle."

"Happy, happy birthday!"

"Thanks!"

"Hey, Birthday Girl, come open your presents."

I found myself in the center of my partygoers opening gifts to a chorus of laughter. My friends had ignored my request, but most of them did so with a heavy dose of wit and sarcasm. I immediately donned the plastic tiara, which read, "Diva," and then opened up one of the many bags of candy and sweets.

"It's like y'all won't rest until I have diabetes."

"You can't eat healthy all the time!" One of my clients shouted from the back of the crowd.

"Thanks for coming, everyone. It's been a tough few weeks, but if it's taught me anything, it's how important it is to have friends and family and to tell them that you love them while you can."

"Oh, God. Are you going to get weepy on us?" Holly grumbled loudly.

"Hell, no. I'm going to toast all of you who came." My eyes settled on Graham, who skirted the side of the yard. He hadn't left. I smiled. "All of you. So, raise 'em up, people. This party is about to go off. Cheers!"

Everyone whooped, and several of my old college friends hollered the obligatory, "Hook 'em." The music cranked, and Trista led people out to an open expanse on the lawn to start dancing.

I kept finding Graham and saw him making his way over.

"I'm heading out in a bit, but I wanted to tell you that I'm sorry if I made you uncomfortable earlier. It's your birthday. I shouldn't have brought up Adam."

"It's a hard topic for you and I to avoid, but I'd like to. I know how you feel about him. I appreciate your concern, but I just can't go there with you. Okay?"

"Done."

"Good. I am glad that you came. The last time we saw each other...things got ugly. Can we agree that we both said some stupid things and kind of acted like children?"

He grinned. "Something we agree on."

"Why don't you stay? The party's just starting."

"Tempting, but I think I'm going to call it a night." Graham touched my bare shoulder, and my knees jellied. "Work out what you need to work out. And I'll see you around."

He stepped back, downed his drink, spun, and was gone— the imprint of his hand still tingling on my arm when I turned to the rest of the party goers and joined the celebration.

CHAPTER 58

ALEXA

*a*dam kept his physical distance, but his presence dogged me through dozens of phone calls and text messages. I ignored him for three more days before replying simply via text message that I needed more time.

> **Adam:** I can come over and cook dinner.
> **Me:** No. Don't come over. We can talk next weekend.

I couldn't sort through the jumble in my head and my heart with Adam smothering me with demands for communication.

On Monday, after training back-to-back all afternoon, I skipped out on work and picked up an industrial-sized bag of Skittles and a bottle of vodka. I didn't often indulge my desire to pig out and check out, but tonight, this seemed like the perfect recipe.

I came up my street with the music blasting enough to force out my persistent anxious thoughts. Just when I thought that it was working, I spotted Adam's rented charcoal gray sedan parked on the curb in front of my house.

Rather than parking in the driveway, which could be seen from my living room window, I pulled up to the curb a few houses down. Once in "Park," I snatched my phone from my purse and called Melissa.

"Hey, Alexa. What's up?"

"I just got home—or nearly home—and Adam is parked in front of my house."

"You're kidding! Is he in the car?"

"I don't think so. I'm down the street, but the car looks empty. But he couldn't be in my house. I never gave him a key."

"Then, where is he?"

"I don't know. I can't imagine what he's doing here."

"Do not get out of your car. Don't go in the house."

"He wouldn't do anything crazy."

Melissa's voice wound tight, shifting her normal tone. "Chica, you sound like the white girl in the movie who hears a noise and wanders into the basement with a serial killer on the loose. Call the police."

"I can't believe he would do anything crazy." I fixed my eyes on my driveway. "Maybe we're overreacting. I'll just see if he's in the house. I won't go in. I'll just open the door and check."

"What if he's not in the house? What if he's just waiting in the bushes?"

"He's not waiting in the bushes. I don't have bushes big enough to hide a full-grown man." I twisted around to get a better view of my front yard. I couldn't see anything from this vantage point. "I'll call you back."

CHASING YOU | 349

I climbed out of my car and ventured slowly down the street. His car was empty. My front door was closed. I scanned my yard, including my stubby bushes, but found no signs of Adam. Then, I caught movement in the living room window. Somehow, he'd gotten into my house.

A wave of rage nearly pushed me inside to find his crazy ass and demand an explanation. Two steps up the drive, and I heard Melissa screaming in my head. I turned, prepared to sprint back to my car.

The creak of my front door swinging open spun me back around.

Adam stood in the doorway with a kitchen towel thrown over his shoulder. I froze.

"How the hell did you get in my house?"

"I had a key."

"I never gave you a key."

I questioned the wisdom of engaging in a dialogue with him, but as long as he didn't move, I figured I'd be fine.

He leaned one shoulder against the door jamb. "I found it when I was here cooking dinner. I locked up when I went to the store and forgot to put it back."

The only time he'd gone to the store was when I was home. Did he think he made sense? Who lifts someone's house keys?

A person with serious boundary issues and a screw loose.

"I'm going to walk down the sidewalk back to my car, and I want to watch you leave my house, close the door behind you, and get the hell away from me. If that doesn't happen, I'm calling the cops."

I circled around to keep Adam's car between us, which meant walking down the center of the street. I kept a fraction of him in my peripheral vision as I scurried. When I reached my car, I turned around and saw him standing in the yard.

"I'm not joking," I yelled. "Get your shit and get out of my house."

He didn't move. His fists fixed at his hips, and he took several steps toward the sidewalk. I dialed 911.

"911. What's your emergency?"

"My ex-boyfriend showed up at my house, and he refuses to leave."

I gave the dispatcher my address as I got back in my car and started the engine. I stayed on the line with the 911 operator, giving her a blow-by-blow as Adam went back into the house, then came out with his keys. Just when it looked like he was going to get in his car and leave, he strode up the street toward me.

I put the car in gear and accelerated down the street. Rolling down my passenger-side window, I slowed as I passed him.

"The police are on their way, so if you don't want to get arrested and deported, you better leave."

I circled the block once and saw him sitting in his car. I pulled off again. When I came back around, his car was gone. However, I still didn't want to go into my house until the police showed up.

It took ten minutes. Finally, a police cruiser pulled down my street and stopped at my address.

"The police are here. I'm pulling up in my blue BMW."

I parked behind the police car and got out.

"Ma'am, is this your house?" One of the officers, a thickly muscled man with a crew cut, kept his hand on his holster and faced me squarely. A skinnier officer who looked like he couldn't be more than twenty-two or twenty-three flanked him, also with his hand on his hip.

"Yes. I'm the one who called 911. He left after I called you.

I haven't gone back inside. I don't know what he was doing in there."

"Do you have any ID on you? Something with your address on it."

The suspicion in his voice pissed me off, but I resolved not to get myself in trouble—even though *I* had called the cops.

"I live here, so yes. It's in my car. Do I have to go get it?"

The stouter one eyed me for a second, from my head to my feet. "No. You stay here with Officer Brigham while I check inside."

He hadn't been inside more than two or three minutes when he came back out and gave the all-clear. Officer Brigham walked me up to the door. The older cop stood in the center of my living room, swiveling his head.

"It's like Valentine's Day exploded in here. And he was your ex-boyfriend?"

"He is now. We'd had a fight."

Rose petals fluttered on the floor as a burst of wind swept in from outside and caused the scores of helium balloons to swirl on their strings. The scent of heavy spice assaulted me. I felt certain I would never eat curry ever again.

"If I did this for my girlfriend, there's a lot of things she'd do, but the list wouldn't include calling the police."

"I didn't get your name." My piercing tone could have popped every balloon bobbing in my living room.

"I'm Officer Donovan." He walked toward me to shake my hand. I kept my arms folded.

"Well, Officer Donovan, when I tell a man to leave me alone and I tell him not to come over and he comes over anyway and breaks into my house, I'm calling the police."

The younger officer cleared his throat. "You should probably have a look around and let us know if anything is missing."

I went room by room and examined each from floor to ceiling. Other than the food on my counters and a simmering pot—plus all the sickeningly romantic decoration—nothing else looked out of place.

My phone buzzed in my hand.

"Why were you at my house?"

Officer Brigham waved his hands, mouthing for me to hang up. The distance provided by speaking to Adam over the phone emboldened me.

"I thought we could hit the reset button and go back where we started."

"I told you I needed space. I told you that I didn't want you coming over. And you show up, unannounced, let yourself in and do all this. Where is my house key?"

"I dropped it in the yard."

I wasn't sure I believed him, but it didn't matter because I was getting the locks changed before nightfall. "I don't understand this. I don't know what all of this stuff is."

"You wouldn't." An edge of fury crept into his voice. I needed to hang up.

"It's not romantic if it creeps me out. And *this* creeps me the fuck out."

"I—" He began to argue, and I tapped the END button on my phone.

I looked around my home and wondered when and how I could ever feel at peace here again.

I HAD to open the windows to carry the smell of my would-be dinner out of the house. I dumped the contents of the pot simmering on my stove into a trash bag and immediately took it to the curb.

Melissa came over to help me wash and scrub to get my kitchen back to its original condition. The clatter of pots and pans mingled with the sharp pop and hiss of every balloon I stabbed with my office scissors.

It took a little over an hour, but eventually, we cleared the evidence of Adams's break with reality from the house.

"I really think he thought he was being romantic." I scoured my living room floor for deflated pieces of rubber.

"You're giving him too much credit. This shit is *loco*. No sane man hijacks a key to a woman's house and breaks into cook her Indian food."

"He cooked this for me the first time I went to his flat. He said he wanted to take us back to where we started. Not saying what he did was okay. I'm just trying to figure out what he was thinking."

Melissa snapped the dishwasher shut and turned it on. Then, she flung her dishrag into the sink. "I need you to look me in the eye and tell me you know this was batshit."

I dumped the remnants of the murdered balloons into the trash and looked my friend in the eye. "It's completely nuts. Inexcusably cray-cray. I know that. It just came out of nowhere."

"Not exactly. That controlling crap with Taryn. Plus, every time you talked about him it was just about how locked-in on you he was. He was fixated. You're probably the whole reason he came to Austin in the first place."

"Under any other circumstances though, isn't that romantic? He flew all the way across the ocean just to spend time with me. I guess it's all champagne and roses until your house smells like turmeric and ginger and you have to call the police."

I managed a small smile as I surveyed my now-clean house emptied of the crazy.

"What are you going to do now? He's still in town for several more weeks."

"I'll have him served with a protective order. Hopefully, that will be enough to get him to come to his senses. If he pushes his luck and gets arrested, I would think he'd be deported. He can't want his client to find out about this."

"Make sure to tell Holly and all the front desk people that they should call the police if they see him."

"God, this is so embarrassing."

I flung myself into my kitchen chair and buried my face in my hands. I waited for the tears to come, but they didn't. Strangely, no emotion came. No anger. Not even any fear. Just a swirling emptiness inside me.

"Don't be embarrassed." Melissa bent over and draped an arm around my shoulders. I reached up and patted her hand. "And don't let this get you down about finding the right guy. He's out there."

"Is he? One thing Adam was right about, I don't think I'd know love if it walked up and slapped me in the face. My radar is way off."

I dug the heels of my hands into my eye sockets and rubbed.

"Is that your phone?"

The ring tone sang to me faintly from the other room. Melissa told me to stay put and retrieved my phone from the other room. She glanced at the screen and handed me the device. "He keeps calling. You should block his number."

Fatigue drew a long sigh from my chest. "I don't even know how to do that. Do I have to call the phone company?"

"You can and maybe you should, but you can block him now on your phone."

Melissa bent down so she could show me what to do.

"See, I tap on his name and scroll down. There it is," Melissa pointed to the screen and tapped. "'Block this caller' and then 'block contact.'"

"Thanks."

I released a long, uneasy sigh. Blocking calls, protective orders, and police reports. I'd have to call my parents. Defeat and dread saturated me.

Mom was going to have to peel my father off the ceiling. Bullet wounds or no, he would want to rush to Austin and tell Adam where he could go. I'd wait. They had enough going on, and this would only make them worry.

A shiver trickled up my spine as I surveyed the kitchen and through the archway into the living room.

"Why don't you pack a suitcase and come stay with me for a few days? We can lock the house up and set the alarm. Just for a few days, so you're not here by yourself before you can serve Adam with papers."

Part of me refused to let Adam chase me from my own home, but now was not the time for pride. I squared my shoulders and maintained an unwavering confidence in my ability to handle Adam if he showed up again. Still, I understood the foolishness of inviting the drama.

"Let me throw some things into a bag." I hesitated before standing up. "Are you sure Kyle won't mind?"

"Of course not. He cares about you as much as I do. Come here."

Melissa circled both hands toward herself, prompting a welcome hug. The tight squeeze comforted me while, at the same time, concentrating my will. After taking care of the protective order and getting the locks changed, I would come home. The sooner I got back to the easy life I had before this mess, the better.

CHAPTER 59

GRAHAM

a crowd of high schoolers chattered and cackled, filling every table in the sandwich shop. Stopping to pick up dinner, I had to dodge a teen bouncing between tables from one unimpressed, whispering girl to another. His cringeworthy antics reminded me how desperate the lovesick can get. It didn't look great on a guy.

The kid danced backward with zero self-awareness and ran smack into my chest. The boy spun around, red-faced and stuttering.

"S-sorry, man."

"You might want to watch where you're going." Nothing like a grim, paternal tone to scare the shit of a teen-age boy. Two young girls fanned their eyes at me, tittered, and whispered to each other. The boy, no longer preening, slid back into a seat, dejected.

So much drama.

"Hey, if you guys can't hold it together, you're going to have to leave." The stern threat from Toby quieted the room.

"Graham, what can I do for you, sir?"

"Can I get a couple of chicken salad sandwiches to go?"

"You have company tonight?"

I waved off Toby's suggestive question. "Nah. Just getting an extra for lunch tomorrow. Nothing so exciting. What's going on with you?"

"Nothing much. Planning Poppy's birthday party. We're doing pony rides and getting a magician. Expect an invitation. I'm also doing some promotional stuff for the spa. We're printing up some coupons for her clients."

"How's she doing?"

"Alexa?"

"Yeah."

"Alright. Of course, she's been lying low since the whole Adam situation came to a head."

"What Adam situation?" My neck tightened at the obvious seriousness of whatever this 'Adam situation' was. "Is she okay? I mean, she has to be. I talked to her at her party the other night."

"You were there? We must have missed you."

"What's going on with Adam? Obviously, something, but she swore it wasn't serious."

"Oh. This was after her party, but I shouldn't say anything if she hasn't."

"Say anything about what?" Sarah joined her husband behind the counter.

"The whole thing with Adam."

"There's not much for us to do anyway except keep an eye out for him and call the police if we see him hanging around the gym."

My mouth went dry. "The police? Did he hurt her or something?"

Sarah's face flamed. "She's fine. She didn't tell you?"

"No. What happened?"

"You should ask her. If she hadn't already mentioned it to you, I don't think we should— I mean, we should stay out of it." Her eyes slanted with sympathy, but her mouth stayed shut.

"Hold on." I pulled out my phone and dialed Alexa. Each ring of the phone turned the screws on my chest, squeezing and shortening my breath.

"Graham, hi."

"Are you still in your office?"

"Yeah. I just finished with a client. Why?"

"I'm next door. Can I stop in?"

"Er, sure."

I paid for the sandwiches, plus one of the energy smoothies Alexa liked, and hurried to the gym. My mind ran wild. I combed through the few snippets I gleaned from Sarah and Toby. Sarah hadn't denied that Adam had attacked Alexa. She had only said that Alexa was fine.

Reaching her cracked office door, I knocked and entered when she called to me from her desk.

"Hi."

"Hi. I come bearing refreshments."

"Come in."

I dropped the smoothie in front of her and claimed the seat opposite her.

She sighed and straightened in her chair. "That's not why you're here. What's wrong?"

"That's what I wanted to ask you. Toby said something happened with Adam, but he wouldn't tell me what."

Alexa's expression shuttered closed, and worry propelled me forward.

"Adam," I prompted. "Just tell me because I'm imagining the worst scenarios."

"We had an argument—before the party. I told him I needed time to think things over. He kept calling. Pushing. A few days ago, I came home from work, and he was at my house—or in it. He'd taken my spare house key and let himself in. I don't know what he was thinking. The whole thing was so strange. He was cooking me dinner, and he decorated the whole house. I guess it was supposed to be romantic. He—"

"He broke into your house?"

"Took my spare key and helped himself inside."

She ran her hands through her hair, squeezing her temples.

"Did he hurt you?" I held my breath, and my stomach pitched.

"No, but...I've never seen him that angry. He got angry before, and it scared me a little. That's why I wanted to take get away for a few days. He couldn't let it go though. He was just...I don't even know how to describe it."

"Obsessed. Controlling and obsessed with you."

She leveled her eyes with mine. "I'll say it. You told me so. You saw it. I didn't."

I slid my hands across the desk, aching to be closer, but anchoring myself in place. "I don't have any I told you so's. Honestly, even I thought maybe I was just jealous."

Alexa closed her eyes for a few seconds before speaking. "I'm trying not to think of it. He got my temporary protective order. In a couple of weeks, it'll be permanent."

"Is that going to be enough to keep him away from you?"

"I think so. I blocked his number on my phone, so he started calling the gym. The calls have stopped since he got served. That's a good sign."

She managed a meager smile that didn't reach her eyes. My protective streak raged. "He's here on a work visa. Maybe we could get that revoked."

"I'm not trying to ruin his life. I just want him to respect my space. If he does that, I don't care what he does."

Doubt tugged at me, but I didn't want to agitate her. "I'm sure your dad can help you sort this out." At least, she had someone she trusted to look out for her.

"He would. I haven't said anything to him yet."

I swore. "You need to tell him. He can help you talk to the police and tell you what you need to do."

"He's still recovering, and there's nothing he's not going to tell me that I don't already know at this point. If I say anything, he and my mom will be down here in a heartbeat. I'll let them know in a few weeks after I get the permanent order. Until then, they'll just worry."

"Where are you staying? You're not still at your house."

"I stayed with Mel for a couple of days, but once I knew he had the order, I went back home." Alexa returned my astounded glare. "I had the locks changed, and I have an alarm system. Plus, he hasn't done anything except break into my house with balloons and flowers and make me dinner."

"You and I both know that it was more than just making you dinner."

"I know!" Her chest rose, her tank top tightening then relaxing. "I'm sorry. I don't need more advice right now. I'm trying to put one foot in front of the other and move on."

I leaned back and ran a hand through my hair. "I'm sure

you don't need another man pushing you try to tell you what to do. But I'll be worried until that jackass gets back on an airplane and flies home to the motherland."

"You and me both, but we can't always get what we want."

"No, but that doesn't stop us from trying does it?"

Alexa stared at me, silent.

"You haven't heard anything else from him?"

"Not since the order. I really think that's enough to scare him. He can't afford the embarrassment of getting arrested."

"If he's capable of thinking about consequences, maybe." I lightly pounded my fists on the desk. "Staying at your house by yourself. That just...It doesn't seem like a good idea."

Her jaw flexed. "It's my home. I'm not going to let someone scare me out of my home."

"You've been okay there?"

She clasped her hands behind her neck and sighed. "I'm fine."

"Really?"

"It's a little creepy. I drive up to my house, and I half expect to see him standing in my doorway, looking...not like himself. Sometimes, I get all the way there, and then pull off and go...anywhere else for a while."

"That fucking guy."

"Yeah. It's over though."

The unease in her eyes wasn't over. The stiffness in her shoulders. The tremor in her hands when she talked about him.

"Are you headed home now?"

"I was planning on it."

"Let me take you to dinner."

"I don't know, Graham. You and I—"

"A friendly dinner." I smiled at her.

"Friendly, huh?"

"Always."

She exhaled. "Okay. Can we pick someplace quiet? I have a teeny tiny headache."

"I know just the place."

CHAPTER 60

ALEXA

*a*n hour and a half later, I sipped a sparkling water and looked at Graham over the table at a quiet French bistro. My longing to avoid going home landed me in the uncomfortable situation of dodging the expectation in his eyes while trying to squeeze a nervous flutter out of my gut.

He drummed the table. The noise of it got lost in the crisp white table linens as the patio mister hissed and spewed a cooling cloud over our heads.

"Are you going to Poppy's birthday party? Toby invited me. I hear there's going to be a pony." Graham's voice pitched higher with forced levity.

"Wow. Maybe I should have let Toby and Sarah plan my party. All we did was get a little drunk and dance. You missed out on the best part of the night, by the way. Trista got up and sang Miley Cyrus karaoke-style."

"What song?"

"*We Can't Stop.* We didn't, either, until three in the morning."

"Sorry. I missed it."

"But a pony sounds like fun. I think there's also going to be a magician."

"They're going all out." He laughed. "They're really good parents. I don't know that I could do that kind of job with a kid."

"Sure, you could. You're good with Poppy."

"Yeah. I'm not really a kid person, though, I don't think."

"What makes you say that?"

"A few interactions here or there are quite different from the day in and day out of making sure your kid doesn't turn out to be an asshole."

"If you care enough, you'll do what it takes."

"Are you ready to take that on?"

I pressed two fingers to my temple. "No, but don't tell my mom. As an only child, I bear the sole responsibility of giving my parents grandchildren. That it might not happen would be too much for them to take right now."

The levity I intended fell flat. I didn't think I would ever have children—a fact that would devastate my mother. I gazed up at the sun, letting the light filter through my sunglasses and hopefully purge my brain of its wayward thoughts and stop my leg from shaking under the table.

"I'm sure they understand. You all seem close."

"We are."

"But you're not going to tell him about Adam?"

"Nope. Not yet. Dad doesn't need the worry. And neither does my mother."

Graham leaned his chin onto the heel of his hand, propping himself up on his elbow. He appeared to stare at me, but the mirrored reflection of his sunglasses hid his eyes. I crossed my arms to deflect the energy pouring off of him.

"You think I should tell them."

"I think you should be more concerned. Going back home? He broke into your house."

"I changed the locks."

"Still."

"What am I supposed to do?"

"Stay with friends. Melissa or Sarah and Toby."

I had imposed enough of my craziness on friends. "Adam knows where they live. He knows where I work. I can't hide."

"That's what worries me."

"But what other choice do I have? I have to keep living."

Graham jumped back in his seat and crossed his arms. "My property has a security gate."

"I can't stay with you. That, I cannot do." My voice and my knees shook.

"Okay. If you're sure."

"I am." I took another drink. "Change of subject."

"To what?"

I shrugged. What could we talk about? The weather? Giant, lumbering elephants parked themselves on the edges of every conversation, staring and blinking as if ready to trample us both at any moment. "Work. The spa is opening soon."

"I don't want to talk about work."

"Then what?"

Graham rubbed his thumb in the divot above his chin. "You and me."

"No. And you promised we wouldn't have to talk about that."

"When did I promise that?"

"You said this was a friendly dinner."

"I said I wouldn't push you into something romantic."

"Exactly."

"I took that to mean I'm not allowed to kiss you senseless like I've wanted to ever since I saw you at your party. Or—what I'd really like to do—carry you off somewhere safe where it's just the two of us. That probably makes me sound as crazy as Adam."

He raised his tumbler to his mouth and drained its contents. At the mere suggestion, I could taste Graham on my lips—sweet and with a hint of whiskey.

"No. You're not Adam."

"I'm here for you. Let's leave it at that. You want something stronger than Perrier?"

His grin couldn't loosen the shackle of fear constricting my chest. I hated turning into an emotional minefield.

I missed the ease of not caring—not wanting anything more than flirtation and a cocktail. I thought Adam was the one who'd changed things for me. No.

Graham had been right. About my fear. About Adam being a distraction. About how letting my heart go with Graham scared me more than Adam ever could.

The why of my cavernous fear danced outside my mental grasp, taunting me.

"Order me something. I'm going to run to the restroom."

I left my purse at the table and fled inside, chased by my own confusion.

CHAPTER 61

GRAHAM

I signaled to the waiter.

"Another bourbon for me and a vodka soda with lime. And can you bring extra lime?"

"Sure thing."

Our back and forth felt surreal. Why had I brought her here? Oh, yeah, I wanted to see her. I wanted to spend time with her. I wanted her to know that I cared about her.

Bang up job I was doing. She practically sprinted to the bathroom.

I had to lay off. Give her space. How much? I didn't know. I only knew I didn't want to be another Adam.

Alexa slipped back into her chair, and with the shifting shadow on the patio, she took off her sunglasses.

I didn't say anything. I watched her—beautiful as always, but with fatigue weighing her eyelids and creasing her forehead. I was staring, and our eyes locked.

Alexa's voice floated through my contemplation. "You're lost in thought."

"I am. This election season has me baffled." I ran a hand through my hair, letting it rest on the back of my neck before dropping it to his lap.

"Politics, then?"

"Why not?"

"I think I'd rather talk about my crazy ex-boyfriend."

She flashed the no-time-for-this-nonsense look that I loved.

"We all have crazy exes. I had a girlfriend slash my tires once."

"What did you do?"

"Why are you assuming it's my fault?" I pouted.

"I didn't mean it that way," Alexa giggled. "What did you do after she slashed your tires?"

"Oh. I called the police. They talked to her, and she agreed to make restitution. I never did get that check from her. I should have pressed the issue as a matter of justice."

"Sometimes, it's better to let it go."

"True."

The waiter reappeared with our drinks, Alexa pulled her glass closer, arranging it carefully on the napkin. "I had a neighbor in college who made a bonfire out of her ex-boyfriend's clothes on her front lawn. She ran around screaming like a lunatic. Luckily, I had a fire extinguisher."

"That's very prepared. I don't think I've ever had one in the house."

"My father made sure that I had all of that stuff when I moved into my first apartment. He was afraid I might leave the stove on and burn down the house."

"That's silly. Doesn't he know that you never turn on the stove?"

Alexa stuck her tongue out at me. "I've cooked before."

"When? When was the last time you cooked?"

"George W. may have been president, but still, I have the capacity."

"I have my doubts."

"Are you going to lecture me about my terrible home-making skills?"

"I wouldn't dream of it. Nothing says you have to be little Susie Homemaker. Everyone has their area of expertise."

"How evolved of you."

"I'm the very model of a modern gentleman."

"Of course you are. Are you going to launch into music from *The Pirates of Penzance*?"

"Huh?"

"You now, that song from the musical about being the very model of a modern major general. Knowing about all matters mathematical and what not."

I cracked into my memory bank and came up broke. "I didn't know I was making the reference."

"Shoot. Here I was thinking you had an appreciation for musical theater."

"I'm not *that* modern."

"Ugh. So macho all of a sudden."

"I try my best to be manly." I flexed. "Feel these guns."

Alexa reached over and ran her hands over my bicep, which I tightened for her benefit. She waggled her brows at me, which tightened something else on my body.

"Don't get carried away. I'm not a piece of meat."

I swatted her hand away, and she fell over the table cack-ling. "I see you've been getting in your workouts."

"I have. Although my new gym isn't as fun as my old one."

Her smiled softened. "I'm sorry about kicking you out. I overreacted. Probably out of jealousy."

Her admission sparked a shock of joy in my solar plexus. "I'd love to come back, if you'd let me."

"I think I still have your application in my files. I never processed it the first time. You were coming in for free."

"Send that baby through. I don't want to be accused of being a gold digger, getting by on my good looks and charm."

"Wouldn't think of it. I'll set it up on Monday."

She lifted her glass to toast our détente and caught her bottom lip between her teeth.

Relaxed and happy never looked sexier. The desire to protect her and to make sure she could have this feeling last hardened into resolution.

That's what I wanted for her—with or without me. All I wanted in the world was Alexa's happiness.

CHAPTER 62

ALEXA

*a*t five thirty, I tapped the incoming message alert, opening up a text message that contained nothing but a photo of Graham's bicep along with a sweating smiley face emoji. The background looked all too familiar.

Skipping out of my office toward the gym, I caught myself grinning uncontrollably.

Sure enough, he stood with a wide stance in the free weights area, watching his reflection for correct form on his hammer curls.

Guess he's gotta keep those biceps in shape.

Our glances crossed in the wall-length mirror.

"One hundred and one, one hundred and two…Oh, hey, Alexa. Pushing my reps today." He smiled through an exaggerated grunt.

"Really? A hundred curls? Impressive."

"Maybe for other guys. You know, just another day at the gym for me."

He lifted his shirt to wipe his face. His sweat-slicked abs flexing with each breath. My pulse kicked up, and I swallowed.

"FYI, I processed your application. The gym fee processes on the twentieth of every month. You should get an email with all the details."

"I'll check when I'm done here. Thanks. Are you teaching anything today?"

"Nope. I trained this morning and then subbed for a midday class, but I'm nearly done for the day. I have to get ahead. I leave town Thursday for Taryn's baby shower. It's Saturday."

"That should be fun."

"It will be. My parents are meeting me in Dallas, so I'll get to see how my dad's been doing."

"But he seems good?"

"He does. He's…my dad, you know. Always kidding around."

"He sounds like a great guy."

In some ways, Graham reminded me of Dad. The situation didn't exist that either of them couldn't joke their way through.

He positioned his weights back on the rack. Sweat streamed down his neck and disappeared into his muscle tee. He leaned over, dropping a hand on his knee as he huffed.

"Those curls really got to you."

He heaved a laugh. "No. I was only on, like, rep two, but I did some cardio intervals right before you came over. Either that or just seeing you renders me breathless."

I made eye contact with a non-existent client over my shoulder to keep from focusing on his sexy grin and my own sexy thoughts. After the whipsaw of Adam, then Graham, and then Adam again, I needed a break. "You're a charmer. That's for sure."

"I try. I don't suppose I can talk you into a drink."

My body screamed, "Yes," on a cellular level, but I resisted and shook my head. "Shower prep, then I've got to get home."

A flicker of concern flitted across his face, but he said nothing.

"Another time though. Maybe I can beat your ass in pool again."

"And you think I'm cocky."

"Is it cocky if it's true?" I tipped my head to the side with a smile. "Anyway, I just saw your text and wanted to say hello."

"Well, hello, then. I'll see you around."

"Yeah."

My affirmation floated toward his back as he scooped up his things and headed for the door.

～

GRAHAM

"Have you made plans to see her or what?" Jonah barked over the phone line.

"No. I'm playing it by ear. Besides, she's out of town this weekend."

I ran a hand through my damp hair and flopped onto my couch. I cradled the phone in the crook of my neck and pulled my computer to my lap. My favorite food delivery site gave me a lifeline to the best Thai food in the city, and my workout had left me famished.

"Playing it by ear, huh? What does that mean?"

"I'm giving her space to figure things out. The last guy was a crazy stalker. She's gun shy."

"She was gun shy before the stalker. I think that's who she is."

"Maybe."

Something slammed on the other end of the line.

"Not maybe. That's how she's been since you started up with her after New Year's. I don't know, man."

"She's gone through a lot—with her dad and the ex."

"All the excuses in the world don't explain why she's jerking you around."

"I'm not getting jerked around. If there's one thing I understand, it's cold feet. Not all of us fall instantly in love and imprint like ducklings."

"If she's who you want, I'm glad for you, but tick tock. You can't sit around forever waiting for her to pull it together. All while you stroke her ego. Women like that— they'll suck you dry. All they want is some guy to follow them around adoringly. Then, that gets boring, and they find a new puppy."

Jonah had always had my back, but his take on Alexa had me close to fury. "I'm not a lovesick puppy. I know what I'm doing."

"Fine. I'm just saying—"

"I know what you're saying. You don't know her. You can meet her at my Memorial Day party and see that she's not the devil. You and Shannon are still coming, right?"

I covered the ground between us fast, hoping to end on a point of agreement.

"Yes. We'll be there. How's your development project going?" he asked, sharply changing topics.

"Still delayed."

"That sucks."

"Yeah. We're making progress."

"How's your idiot partner holding up?"

"Idiotically as always. I'm really hoping Carmichael buys him out completely. He's going to need the cash. He's getting divorced. That's what happens when your wife finds out about your predilection for dominatrices."

"At least he'll enjoy the punishment of an expensive divorce," Jonah quipped.

We shared a dry chuckle, letting the air out of our argument.

"How are Shannon and the baby?"

"Both are good. He's kicking away, keeping her up at night."

"You know it's a boy?"

"Crap. That's supposed to be a secret. Don't say anything to anyone. Shannon will kill me."

I cackled. "Again with thinking that I have anyone to discuss your baby with but you."

"I don't know. You're getting so sensitive and caring these days. I thought maybe you'd be gossiping about it with your girlfriends over brunch."

"Funny."

"I have to go. Don't drink too many mimosas. See you in a couple of weeks."

I cursed at Jonah and hung up.

Like he was one to talk about getting all soft over love. The debut of "L" word in my mind straightened my spine, but I let it settle, waiting for a panic that didn't come.

Turning back to my computer, I brought up Amazon.com and searched for a book on women entrepreneurs I'd heard about on the radio. I plugged in Alexa's address, added a note for the gift card, and hit the ENTER key.

She'd enjoy it. Jonah didn't know what he was talking about.

CHAPTER 63

ALEXA

*O*ver the next week and a half, Graham wooed me with little notes and gifts that kept him on my mind every day. Nothing overtly romantic—just a slow drip of thoughtful moments sprinkled throughout my day.

His first delivery had my heart skipping. It arrived the day before I left for Dallas.

Heard this book reviewed on NPR, and I thought of you.
Graham

I opened the package and found a book about women business owners. Sweet. It was probably the first time a woman got gushy over a book with a forward written by an editor at *The Wall Street Journal.*

When I got back in town, he dropped by with a smoothie,

sent me a tin of M&M cookies, which I shared with the staff, and had a bottle of Pinot delivered to my house.

When Holly called me about another delivery, I tittered as I asked her to bring it back to my office.

"Here you go."

I took the UPS envelope. No sender name, and an Austin address I didn't recognize. There was a card inside, so I slipped it open with quick, nervous fingers. The rose petals falling out blew a chill over me like I'd opened an industrial freezer.

> Our two souls therefore, which are one,
>> Though I must go, endure not yet
>> A breach, but an expansion,
>> Like gold to airy thinness beat.

He didn't sign the note, but I recognized the taste in poetry. My belly convulsed. More John Donne. A sonnet for lovers whose hearts never part—even with distance.

I chucked the thick, peach-colored paper in the trash and swept the rosy detritus into the can after it.

Was this a goodbye? I held on to the idea that at least he was letting me know I didn't have to worry about seeing him around town. Still, no contact meant no contact.

A local phone number popped up on my mobile, and I answered it before I had time to consider who it might be.

"It's me, Adam. Don't hang up. Please."

I ran my finger on the edge of my phone, but didn't tap the red button. "You have sixty seconds."

"You got my note."

"How do you know that?" My throat closed up as the hammering accelerated in my chest.

"I got a text notifying me when it was delivered. I'm headed back to London."

"Okay. Glad to hear it."

"That's all you have to say?"

"Pretty much."

"I'd hoped you would know that I do care about you. It's so hard to reach you. All I wanted was to be in your heart like you're in mine."

"Don't make this about me. You broke into my house. I shouldn't even be talking to you. In fact—"

"Wait. Can't you let me apologize?"

I pulled the phone away from my ear and stared at it.

"I guess not." His sharp voice shot from the phone like a switch blade.

I heard him call me a word tossed around much more casually in England as I lowered the phone to hang up, which I should have done the second I heard his voice.

At least he was going back home.

I dialed the detective with whom I'd filed the complaint against Adam. All I wanted was him gone. With any luck, he'd have his happy ass back in London before the police could catch up with him.

My next call was as mandatory as the first. I needed his light humor and calm. I needed his reassurance. I needed him.

CHAPTER 64

GRAHAM

I arrived at Alexa's house before she did, so I waited in my car until I saw her electric blue BMW swing around me and into her driveway. She jumped out of the car and reached into her backseat, extracting a large paper bag. Our dinner, no doubt. The woman loved her takeout.

I strode over. "Do you need a hand?"

"Yeah. I will when I get to the door. Plus, I have a little twinge in my back."

"I'll take that."

I dropped my own grocery bag into the larger sack and followed Alexa to her door. She clicked open the double bolt —a new installation since my last visit—and turned off her alarm.

Despite Adam's claim that he was on his way back to England, I thought she still needed to be careful. The new security was a small step, but I didn't want to argue with her about telling her dad or doing anything else. She had her own mind.

"Thanks. Can you carry it into the kitchen?"

"Sure. Did you hurt yourself?"

"I don't know what I did. Maybe something happened when I was doing deadlifts the other day. I need to get a massage. What did you bring?" She led me to the kitchen.

"Wine and dessert."

"You may have to do dessert by yourself."

"You sure?"

I reached into the plastic sack and pulled out a family size pouch of Skittles.

"You're an evil man."

"I'm an angel. And you know it."

She smiled. The spread she unpacked on the table included two lasagnas and, of course, steamed vegetables.

"Pasta?"

"I felt like a little comfort food splurge."

"Then I did okay with the Skittles."

"Yeah. You did okay."

I reached for one of the containers at the same time that Alexa went to grab them both. My hand brushed hers, and I allowed it to linger. My fingers stretched, finding their way between hers.

A flush fell over her from her cheeks to her shoulders. The smooth skin of her chest deepened in color right down to where her cleavage disappeared into her cotton V-neck. Desire begged me to trace the deep rose brown with my lips.

She untangled her hand slowly from mine and gathered up the two trays of pasta.

"I'll heat these up."

I pulled out a chair and sat, scooting close to the table to conceal my arousal. "Oh, I wanted to ask you. What are you doing for Memorial Day?"

"Melissa and Kyle are cooking out, I think. I said I'd stop by. Why?"

"I'm having a party at my house with my partners and some other business associates. I do it every year. It may be a little stuffy, but it should be fun. I'm setting up tents in the yard. I can guarantee you good food and good booze. Jonah and his wife are coming down. You can meet her."

"Tents in the yard. Is this a fancy garden party?"

"Kind of."

"Okay. I may have to buy an outfit. I have workout clothes and go out clothes. Not much in between anymore."

"Most of the women wear sundresses or...I don't know. Nothing too fancy."

She crossed the room, shaking her head. "You don't understand the dress codes women have. You have to wear an outfit specifically for the occasion."

"That sounds like an excuse to spend money."

"Of course. But, hey, we didn't make the rules." Alexa slid our meals onto plates and popped them in the microwave.

"So, you're coming?"

"I'll be there."

"Great."

She gathered silverware, glasses, and napkins for the table.

I leaned back in the chair and put my hands behind my head—being back in her kitchen giving me a surge of satisfaction.

"How was the baby shower?"

"Fun. Since it was co-ed, we didn't have to be bored out of

our skulls with cutesy baby games, which was fine by me. I've tasted enough baby food and guessed the number of enough pacifiers in jars."

I made a sour-milk face. "I have never been to a baby shower a day in my life. Jonah's wife is pregnant, but no man shower for me."

"Men are included in the whole process now."

"I might want to go back to the time when our only job was to smoke the cigars in the hospital waiting room."

"That's not the only job the man has. There's a bit at the beginning."

Mischief sparkled in her narrowed eyes.

I grinned. "That's not work."

"Neither is smoking a cigar."

"Touché."

The microwave dinged loudly, disrupting what I thought was excellent progress in turning up the heat in Alexa's kitchen.

She arranged our meal on the kitchen table with the table settings and serving spoons while I opened the wine. I took advantage of her wine glasses' oversized bowls.

"Whoa. That's a heavy pour."

I set a half-empty bottle between us. "Go big or go home. I can drink yours, if you want."

I reached for her glass, and she shooed my hand away. "Back off."

"Yes, ma'am."

She tipped her glass back for a long sip. "It's really good."

"You saw your parents. Didn't you?"

"Yes." Her smile glowed. "My dad looks good. He's joking about all the time he'll have to fish once his arm is back in shape—after he retires."

"How's he handling that?"

"Hard to tell. My dad doesn't emote. He cracks jokes and pretends everything is okay, no matter what. My mom says he's a little depressed."

I dug into my lasagna. "How long has he been a cop?"

"About thirty-five years."

"That's a long time to find yourself suddenly having to do something else."

"I know, but I've never seen my mother so at peace. As terrible as the whole ordeal has been, it's like if this is the worst that it's going to be and now it's over, hallelujah. You know? She's been on edge for almost thirty-five years."

"And you too, I imagine."

Alexa chewed, poking her food with her fork, but I wouldn't let her get away with dodging the topic.

"You must have been scared growing up."

"He loved being a police officer. I dealt with it."

"You were a kid."

Her eyes misted over. "I was. The hardest part was helping my mom deal."

"You are allowed to be scared. Kid or adult. Having the threat of losing a parent looming constantly had to change who you are."

"It has. But I'm good at not thinking about it." A tiny smile changed the light in her eyes. "Which is what I'd like to do right now. He's on the mend. This is good news. I don't need to think about those things anymore. He'll find something new to do with himself, and we'll all move forward."

"Is that the power of positive thinking or avoidance?"

My question drew her eyes to mine in challenge. "Does it make a difference?"

"I guess not."

"What's going on in the world of wheeler-dealer real

estate?" She finally stopped pushing the lasagna around her plate and took a bite.

"Nothing earth-shattering. Construction has restarted on that project that stalled, which is a relief to one of my partners. He tends to overextend himself, and any hiccup sends him into a panic. It drives my other partner nuts. He's more of a 'slow and steady wins the race' kind of guy."

"And you? You seem like more of a risk-taker to me."

"Not in business. I take a more measured approach. I like to evaluate my options and make safe bets."

"Huh. I figured you for more of a wildcatter."

"No. I find the right deal and then focus and follow through. Boring, boring."

"I'll bet you find a way to make even real estate thrilling. It's in your nature."

I thought of Sierra's lackluster assessment of my straight-laced career in commercial real estate and laughed to myself.

"What's funny?"

"Oh. Nothing. I have a friend who disagrees. She called what I do for a living terminally boring. And—"

Alexa's eyes narrowed. "What? Finish what you were going to say."

"It's one of the reasons she decided I'm not boyfriend material. She's a creative type. Her hair changes color every other week. Her new guy is in a band. More her speed, I guess. His name is Larry."

"This is the woman you were out with when I called you."

"Yes."

"You said she was a friend. What does boyfriend material have to do with it?"

"Well, we...used to hang out occasionally. And that stopped."

"Recently?"

"When I met you. When she met Larry."

"No longer fuck buddies, huh?"

Heat spread from my cheeks to my earlobes. "No, but still friends."

"You think that's possible?"

"We're friends. And we're not sleeping together any more."

Her tongue flew to the corner of her mouth and hovered there between parted lips. "I'm not sure that's the best example."

"We're not friends?"

"I don't know what's going on between us, but it's not just friendship."

My heart thundered. Finally, an acknowledgement from her that this could be something more. "No. It's not. I've missed hanging out with you. I want to see you. More of you."

"How much more?"

I grinned. "As much as you'll let me."

"I've missed you, too."

My interest in my Italian takeout took a nosedive. "I never thought I'd hear you admit that, but I'm glad. Maybe I'll make it to first base tonight."

Alexa took a deep breath. "The coach may be waiving you around."

"How far?"

"The third base coach hasn't decided yet. I might be okay if you stayed the night."

"Third base and a sleepover?" I dropped my fork and rubbed my hands together, enjoying the new flush over-taking her chest. "I'll take it."

I reached across the table and took the fork out of her

hand, cradling her fingers in my palm. She tickled the center of my hand and withdrew.

"I'm eating."

Rather than respond, I piled my fork with pasta and took a colossal bite. I'd do whatever she wanted. Stop at first, stop at second, get waved home. It was up to her.

CHAPTER 65

ALEXA

$\mathscr{I}$ bypassed the line of cars in the circular drive in front of Graham's house. Young men in cropped red jackets jogged quickly between cars, spiriting them away to some unknown valet location.

Earlier in the afternoon, he texted me the code to enter the gated drive leading to the garage. I punched in the numbers and waited as the gate slid open. When I pulled beside the house, the drive curved around to the right. The garage door was up.

> **Me:** I'm here. Where should I park?
> **Graham:** In the drive.

I dropped the phone in the center console and parked outside the garage. The door to the house flew open, and he stood, leaning on the doorway in pressed linen pants with a checked button down.

"An untucked shirt. This is the casual you?" I lifted two bottles of champagne out of the back seat and nudged the car door shut with my elbow, careful not to brush against the car in my new, breezy, silk sundress. I walked through the garage to the door leading into his house.

He looked down at his ensemble and shrugged. "Summer casual me."

"So pulled together."

I squeezed through the doorway, my breasts brushing his chest as I entered the mud room between the garage and the kitchen. My skin tingled. Graham closed the door and walked close behind me, lightly resting his hand on the small of my back. Sensation swirled up my spine, and I shivered.

"Are you too cold? I dropped the air conditioning in the house since people are going to be coming in and out."

"No. I'm fine."

I stopped and Graham circled my waist, his lips hovering near my right ear. I turned toward him and found myself cheek to his freshly shaven cheek. A tiny bit of lather specked his jawline, which gave me the perfect excuse to run my fingers along the side of his face. I cleared my throat.

"You had a little shave cream."

"Thank you."

I started to pull away, but he spun me toward him and held on.

"You look lovely."

I snickered. "That's a compliment, right?"

"Yeah. So is this."

My lips parted and my eyes slipped closed, but instead of feeling his mouth on mine, I felt the brush of his chin down my cheek and the warmth of his lips in the tender spot below my earlobe. When I pressed closer to him, he upped his game.

The soft sweep of his tongue down the side of my neck ended with a suckling kiss on my collarbone. He drew his fingers over the tiny, tattooed stars, then scraped his teeth over my flesh, down to the bodice of my dress.

"Mmm. You taste good."

"Don't you have guests arriving?" I gasped.

"Right now, I'm only concerned with the one."

Without the heat of his mouth on me, my heartbeat slowed a little. "If that's how you're going to greet all your guests, you lips are going to chafe. That was quite a line of cars outside."

"That's a greeting for one guest only." Graham stroked my upper arms and pulled me in for a hug. "I'm thrilled you're here."

"I'm thrilled I came."

"Already? Damn, I'm good." He curved a hand over my behind and gave it a tap. Then, hand in hand, we passed through the kitchen to the back patio where wait staff circulated, passing out drinks to the throng of people. I leaned on Graham's arm, grateful I had more to support myself than my wobbly legs.

"Graham! So good to see you. And who is this?"

A trim, short, grey-haired man gestured toward me with a warm smile and sharp, blue eyes.

"This is Alexa Stevens. She owns the gym in the property we acquired a few months ago. Alexa, this is the principal partner in my firm, Walker Carmichael."

"Nice to meet you, Mr. Carmichael." I returned the man's smile and thrust out my hand to shake his firmly.

"Walker, please. You're going to make me feel like an old

man. My kids do enough of that already. Helena, dear, come say hello to Graham and his girlfriend."

Girlfriend? I immediately dismissed my knee-jerk panic and gripped Graham's arm tighter. I could do girlfriend. Why not?

A plump woman with crystalline blonde hair turned toward us, lips pursed. How had I already offended the woman?

I looked at Graham sideways, but he stared forward, smile painted on.

Then, I remembered. This must the woman who tried to set Graham up with Sequin Barbie at the benefit. What had Graham done?

The woman paused and swept her eyes over me. "Who is this?"

"This is my...friend, Alexa."

So, now, he backs off 'girlfriend' like bear trap?

"Aren't you an exotic beauty?" Helena Carmichael grasped my hand to shake it limply. "I suppose I'll have to take Walker's advice and stop trying to fix Graham up with every young lady I know. Such as shame. That he's off the market, that is."

I ignored any slight in her words. This was basically the boss' wife.

Graham stroked the hand I had curled around his bicep with his thumb. "I hope so."

"Oh, sweetie, if she doesn't have the good sense to snap you up, that's a *real* shame." Helena wrapped her words in a joking tone, but I felt their bite anyway.

"I know Graham's appeal to the women of Austin, and I'm glad he's here with me."

"You make quite the couple. Now, Walker, is that Amber

Sheehan over there? She's a friend of our eldest. We should go say hello."

Walker didn't have a chance to answer before his wife pulled him across the lawn out of earshot.

"I don't think she likes me."

"She likes picking winners and arranging people's lives. For a while there, I had to duck her suggestions that I take their daughter out. With her daughter engaged now, she thought she'd match me with one of her daughter's friends. Remember Candace?"

"Who could forget? You didn't like her daughter."

"Like mother, like daughter. She's a bit much. That's all I'll say."

"A woman with an opinion gets such the label."

"I can call Chelsea Carmichael if you want. Maybe I can knock off the fiancé."

"Absolutely not. You are one of the most eligible men in the city. Like Helena said, I should be clinging to you like grim death."

I poked Graham in the ribs and snickered. His smile congealed. I put my hand on his chest. "I'm only kidding."

"About which? My eligibility or wanting to hang on to me."

"Neither. I—"

Graham looked over my shoulder and cut me off. "Jonah. Shannon. You made it."

"We did. This is probably my last trip. The heat is really starting up. God, summer is tough."

The sound of the woman's voice jerked my head around. "Shannon? I didn't know you were...You're Jeff's ex-wife."

"I am. You're Taryn's cousin." Shannon ran a hand through her hair and looked away at Graham.

My eyes widened. "Sorry. I'm just now putting two and

two together. I didn't know the connection. Great to see you. I haven't seen you since…"

"New Year's Day. I came to drop off Olivia."

"Right. New Year's Day."

Jonah sighed and put an arm around Shannon's expanded waistline. "We were all over the place on New Year's. A lot has changed since then."

"It has." Shannon's shoulders relaxed, and she lay her head on Jonah's shoulder. "Especially my bladder. Sorry. TMI. Where's your restroom?"

"It's…I'll just show you."

Graham pointed toward the glass doors and followed behind Shannon. Her husband shook the ice in his glass and stared down at it before piercing me with an icy stare.

I was losing friends and influencing no one today.

"You're back with Graham?"

"We're talking."

"Talking?"

"Sorting things out."

Jonah snorted. "Graham's pretty sorted. I think you know how he feels about you."

I squared my shoulders and glared at Graham's friend. "I do. I guess. Is there a problem?"

"I don't like how you're stringing my friend along." Jonah's voice began to rise, but he caught himself and shifted to a low growl. "He's in love with you, and you keep waffling. 'I want you. I don't want you. I maybe want you. I'll take everything you have to offer and dangle a carrot in front of your nose.' He sticks around for it all. I'm sure it feeds your ego nicely."

I dropped my chin like a boxer ready to face off with an opponent. "You should really try to think before you speak.

You don't know anything about me, what I've been through, nothing."

"Does it matter? You either love someone or you don't."

"You don't know how I feel about him, and frankly, our relationship is none of your business."

"Graham is my best friend. He's my business. And you're right. I don't know how you feel about him, but neither does he. And I think that sucks." He knocked back whatever drink he had and turned around, scanning the yard. "I'm going to get another drink."

Tears swelled behind my eyes.

Damn.

I perused the previous weeks in my mind and saw the same growing happiness I'd felt when I got out of the car and saw Graham smiling at my from the doorway. We were seeing how things went, and things were going well.

Was he unhappy?

The thought took me by the throat, and I started toward the door to go find him. He was already heading back outside, smiling and chatting with another friend. Now wasn't the time. *Later.*

THE SUN HAD DISAPPEARED below the hills of West Austin before the last of the guests pulled away. The metallic slam of disassembling tables and displays rose up from the backyard to the second-floor movie room. The caterers had nearly cleaned and packed everything.

I curled up on the couch in my jersey pajamas, sipping a hot water with lemon. Prime rib, fried mushrooms, and cheesecake—my stomach roiled with the sudden departure from my clean eating habits.

Graham's feet thumped softly on the stairs as he brought up a bowl of popcorn.

"Air popped. No butter. I know you're recovering from the food explosion of today."

"I definitely overdid it."

In his left hand, he also had a small gift bag.

"What is that?"

"Open it."

My eyes misted over. He was doing it again—being irresistible. "You don't have to get me gifts."

"Just open it."

I looked in the bag and found another flat cardboard box. I pulled off the top and laughed. "A massage and facial at Starlight Spa. The spa's not open yet."

"But it's ready to open. I asked Melissa. She said Klaus gives a top-notch deep tissue massage, and I'm trying to put it out of my mind that I'm paying for another man to rub all over you. But, you said you needed a massage."

Graham moved closer, sliding a hand along my calf to my knee and bumping up my body temperature a few degrees.

"You didn't have to pay. I can probably swing that for free. I know the owner."

"No. No more freeloading. Besides, I want to keep things professional between you and Klaus."

He kissed me on the cheek.

"You keep giving me things."

He frowned. "The last thing I want is to make you uncomfortable."

"You're not making me uncomfortable. I feel…guilty."

"Why?"

"I haven't done anything for you."

"That's not true. And I like doing things for you. I like seeing you happy. Does this make you happy?"

He tapped on the gift certificate.

"Of course, it does. But...do you think I'm jerking you around?"

"Why would you ask that?"

Telling Graham what Jonah said might cause problems between the men, and I didn't want to pull an Adam, starting trouble between friends.

"Just today. We didn't finish our conversation about what I said. You seemed upset when I joked about Helena. It's simple. Do you feel like I'm toying with you?"

"Come here."

I fell into his arms, dropping my cheek against his chest. He squeezed me and spoke into my hair. "I think you have a hard time settling down, and your last boyfriend was a creep."

His understanding only drove Jonah's point deeper. I'd been unfair to him. So many times, I'd been angry with him. Then, I came crawling back, keeping him at arm's length, and he just accepted it.

"I'm taking advantage of you."

"How is it taking advantage of me? That I do nice things for you. I'm wooing you. Let me woo. Unless...you don't..."

Graham sat back, pulling his hand away. A grim veil cast over his eyes. "You don't feel the same way about me."

"I care about you."

"You care."

He stiffened. Panic trickled through my veins. That I cared wasn't all I wanted to say.

"This whole time, I haven't been able to get you out of my mind. Even when I was with Adam. You're there for me again and again, and I take you for granted. I wonder if I have anything to give."

"You make me laugh, and you challenge me on my bull-shit. And I have plenty."

As true as that might have been, lately, he'd done nothing but prove himself game for having a future together. I was the one putting up roadblocks. Graham tilted my chin up so I could look at him.

"Do you love me?"

I went still. I couldn't answer that question. I didn't know how to quantify what I felt for him.

"I want to be with you. Every day, I wake up with you on my mind. You're the best part of my day."

"That's not an answer."

I swallowed. "Do you love me?"

"Yes."

The word pulled me toward him as if it had gravitational force, our faces just inches apart. His was a love that shredded my control. Shredded and burned.

"You said you wanted to see if we could have more. You never said you loved me."

"The last thing I wanted was to be another guy putting pressure on you."

"I know you're not Adam." My defense of him flew from me in a sprint.

"Still. I don't want to scare you off by pushing for too much, too soon."

"Do you think I'm that much of a coward?"

"When it comes to love, I think you're scared."

"A coward."

"Alexa," he paused, reaching out to twirl a lock of my hair around his finger. "I wouldn't use that word."

"Because you're being nice. And I've been blind and stupid and narcissistic."

"I know you care about me. I can hear it when I talk to

you on the phone. I see a light in your eyes when you look at me."

"And that's enough for you?"

"No, but I see you opening up a little more every time I see you. It's not like being afraid to commit is a completely foreign concept to me."

"I can't tell you that I love you. I don't even know why."

"I know."

I couldn't say anything else—not with the openness and love in his eyes. So, I showed him.

CHAPTER 66

ALEXA

$\mathcal{M}$y eyes popped open at six a.m. Pale, early morning sunlight slanted through Graham's shutters.

He lay naked beside me. His dove gray cotton sateen sheet slanted nicely across his lower abdomen. He'd thrown his arms up over his head, stretching the muscles of his chest. Sexy asleep. Sexy awake.

I couldn't help but reach to the feel the prickle of his chest hair, drawing a hand down between his pecs to his belly. Happy trail indeed.

"Mornin', beautiful." My gaze flipped up to his half-open eyes and that familiar satisfied grin. The grumbling rasp in his voice did things to my insides. He rolled over and slid his hand along my hip.

"Good morning."

"What time is it?"

"Six-ish."

"Early. Too early. I'm going back to sleep," he mumbled.

I rubbed my fingernails over his stomach. He grunted, and his eyes slipped closed. In a snap, the rugged angles of his face softened with sleep. I traced the bones of the hand slackened at my waist with my fingertips. Leave it to Graham to have an impeccable manicure.

Soft brown hair flecked his arms from his wrist to his elbows, ending before the hard hills of his biceps and shoulders. He trembled, and his lashes fluttered. I withdrew my hand, so I wouldn't disturb him again—even though I now had no hope of getting back to sleep myself.

The kissable bow of his mouth taunted me. My belly tightened. What else would a man love more than to wake up to a woman ready for sex? I almost strummed his lips and slipped my hand under the smooth sateen sheet.

There was one other thing a man might want to wake up to, maybe not more than sex, but close to it. Could I still remember how to make my mother's biscuits and pancakes? How hard was bacon? I could do this.

I rolled carefully out of bed and padded downstairs. His refrigerator had nothing more than cold party leftovers, some eggs, and a half-gallon of milk past its best-by date.

After snagging a pen and slip of notepaper from a small nook in the kitchen, I scribbled a message and snuck back upstairs to leave it on his pillow.

Disappearing in a puff of smoke to the store, but I'll be
back. Be hungry. I'm cooking.
—A

He thrashed and turned over, but didn't wake up. I

decided to dress in one of the spare rooms and grabbed my overnight bag. Let him be surprised.

～

GRAHAM

I felt myself falling. The earth spun up toward me at an uncontrollable speed. My heart seized. And with a start, I snapped up straight in bed. The covers were half tossed to the floor, and the pillow from Alexa's side of the bed was missing—as was Alexa.

Gone. Again.

I shot out of bed and pulled the comforter back and forth, then snatched up the fallen pillow. Nothing.

Fuck. She was gone. Again.

The thought repeated itself over and over in a waking nightmare that made me want to hit the reset button, fall back asleep, and let myself splatter on the ground.

I searched for her overnight bag and her purse. They, too, were gone.

To call myself foolish would be a cruel understatement. I told her that I loved her—confident that my assurance would seep into her. She seemed to want to love me, to want to let herself be happy. I'd been kidding myself.

I stormed out of the bedroom, passing through the game room on my way to the stairs. Alexa's discarded lounge pants, T-shirt, and underwear were still strewn over the floor. So was the upturned bowl of popcorn—a casualty of our fervor the night before.

I closed his eyes and remembered how she'd reached for me and silently pulled her shirt over her head. Once she straddled me, my hands cupped her heavy breasts, which swung toward me. God, the way her nipples pebbled under the pads of my thumbs.

Even now, when she'd left me again, I wanted her. I'd never get her out of my system, but no matter. This game we played of who could run away fastest was over. I'd have to send her a trophy as a parting gift.

A headache put a vice grip on my temples, and I pounded down the stairs to make some coffee. The silence of the house imparted a sharp loneliness I'd never felt before.

I walked by the back door, which wasn't locked. Great. On top of everything else, she left my house unsecured so I could get robbed blind. I flipped the deadbolt with resolve.

Leaning on the cold granite counter, I waited with my face in my hands for the espresso maker to heat up and provide much needed caffeine.

A fast rapping on the back door made me jump.

Did she really drive all the way back here for her pajamas and underwear?

I crossed the kitchen, unbolted the door, and snatched it open. Her eyes and smile were as bright as the sun glowing behind her.

"Did you forget something?"

Her gaze roamed my face, and she stumbled back. "You didn't get my note."

"What note?"

"I left you a note. I wasn't leaving."

Only then did I notice the grocery sacks hanging at her sides—fury and hurt swirling inside me. "I didn't see it."

"I left it on my pillow."

I pinched my nose, eyes squeezed shut. "I must have... What did it say?"

"That I was disappearing to the grocery store and would

be back." Her arms flexed, lifting the bags to shoulder level. "I'm cooking you breakfast."

"You don't cook."

"Not often. No, but...I wanted to do something for you." The glossy brown of her eyes pulled my heart nearly out of my chest. "You thought I'd left you. God, the look on your face when you opened the door."

A tear spilled down her cheek, and she and her words flew at me in a rush. I shut the door behind her.

"I'm sorry. I should have just woken you up, but I wanted it to be a surprise. I thought you'd like it if I cooked for you. And...this is what I've done. You don't trust me. And you shouldn't. You look me right in the eyes and tell me that you love me, and I freeze up. I can't get the words out. You might not call me a coward, but that's what I've been."

Alexa swiped the back of her hand across her eye. The heavy grocery bag swayed against her as she dropped it back down to her leg.

"You looked at me like I was dead to you. Like you were lost to me forever."

Her voice was barely a whisper, her eyes full of fear and apology. I took the bags from her and set them on the counter. Then, I pulled her as close to my body as I could as if to eliminate all possibility of separating ever again.

"I thought you'd left again."

"I didn't." She pulled out of my arms and placed her palms on either side of my face, pressing her forehead to mine. Our brown eyes locked. "I'm not going to."

"Don't make me promises that you can't keep."

"I can keep that one."

Tentative and still sniffling, she brushed my lips with her own. Once. Twice. The light friction pulled all the anger out of my body, leaving nothing but how much I wanted her.

404 | KRIS JAYNE

I plunged my tongue in her mouth and gripped her tight until she moaned. Her yielding softness unleashed my relief and my joy. Alexa's hand wandered below the waistband of my sweatpants, gripping my bare ass.

She groaned and took her mouth and hands away. "Later. I'm making you breakfast."

"Forget breakfast. Who needs food?"

"I do. I'm actually starving."

I held her, not ready to let her go. Her hair was still slightly damp. "You already showered."

"I did. Why don't you go up and do that? I'll cook."

"Is there any point? I plan on getting sweaty again in an hour or so."

"You have a one-track mind."

"I do. And you love it. Admit it."

"Yeah. I do," she grinned and shooed me out of the kitchen.

EPILOGUE

ALEXA

I fumbled to roll over, extending an arm in search of my husband. I smiled. Instead of finding Graham, I found a note duct-taped to the pillow.

Happy anniversary! Making breakfast. Bring your appetite.
— G

One year. One year since Graham and I abandoned our wedding plans and flew to Vegas. My mother was only just now forgiving me because she saw how happy Graham made me. Dad missed walking me down the aisle, but as he put it, "I don't miss footing the bill, so we'll call it even."

I threw on a robe and walked downstairs. Graham stood shirtless over the stove. I tiptoed up behind him and ran my hands up his back to his shoulders and started the day the same way I had for over a year now.

"Mmm. I love you." My husky whisper in his ear carved a smile on his face.

"You love my cooking."

"That too. What are you making?"

"Omelets."

"With veggies."

"Yours with veggies. Mine with bacon and cheese."

"Remind me to nag you about a trip to the cardiologist."

"This is what it's like having a wife. Nag. Nag."

I slapped him on the rear. "This is why married men live longer."

Graham flipped the omelet onto a waiting plate and turned around. His mouth claimed mine. I nudged my hips against his, revealing my intentions.

"The omelets are getting cold."

His weak protest only propelled me on. I circled his nipple with my thumb and mumbled, "Since when do you care?"

"I don't."

He pushed me back against the kitchen island opposite the stove and untied my robe. His hands roamed as he knelt down, bringing my yielding body with him.

"The floor is impossibly hard."

Graham lowered himself onto his back. "Yeah, that's not the only thing. I'll be on the bottom. Never say I didn't sacrifice."

I laughed and climbed astride him. "I never would."

For news on upcoming books, join my mailing list at: https:// krisjayne.com/join

Continue the Thirsty Hearts series...
Enchanting You
https://krisjayne.com/enchanting-you

Turn the page for an excerpt!

PREVIEW ENCHANTING YOU

A psychic. A ghost. A hero with a sly secret... *Enchanting You* **is a delicious enemies-to-lovers tale with a touch of magic.**

Thirsty Hearts heads back to Dallas where another of Jonah's good friends, Jamie Wylde, finds new love.

∼

LILITH

Jamie lifted his chin to a haughty angle, but his evasive glance told me I was right. Preston was trying to tell me something. If I wanted to help Kali, I would have to set fire to the carefully reinforced walls at the edges of my psyche and listen.

"And you should be more careful of the truth," I snapped.

"No. Your sister should."

"What does that mean?" I edged closer to him.

"Ask *her.*"

"You're deflecting."

"I don't have to listen to this." He flipped the watch at his wrist to eye level. "Shit. I'm supposed to be somewhere."

"You can't run away. This isn't over, you know."

"Oddly, I do," he grunted with a grim smile. "You're relentless."

I took another step forward and poked the center of his chest. The grumble of my own voice through gritted teeth shocked even me. "You have no idea."

His gaze snatched down to mine as he took a half step back, trapped against the open door of his fancy car. The electricity between us crackled on my skin. My breath quickened.

The dim light of the parking garage played with the angles of his face. The perfection crumbled. A rogue curl of dark hair slipped to his forehead. The arrogant mask he wore fell away revealing confusion, trepidation, and hurt.

He straightened his shoulders, adding to his height as he stared down at me. His lip curled with revulsion as he spoke. "Is this your plan? You corner me in a parking garage and start touching me and giving me your best siren's eyes?"

"Siren's eyes?"

He cackled and lifted his hands up as if touching me might give him some incurable disease. "God, you and your sister *are* alike. But I'm *not* my father. I'm not going to let a little horniness make me lose my mind."

I covered my mouth and mockingly wretched. "Ugh. I'm going to lose my lunch."

"Really?" He snickered under his breath. "Yes. That's why you touched me."

"I was making a point. Your horniness is your problem." Still, I stepped away from him. "Understand this: I'm not going to let you railroad my sister."

I spun on my heels and stormed away, not totally sure

where I parked or if I was even on the right level of the parking garage, but I didn't dare risk looking confused. I kept walking to the other side of the elevator. Finally, the screech of his car down the exit ramp pierced through the roar of rushing blood in my ears. I closed my eyes, clenching and unclenching my fists to relax.

If I was going to fight for Kali, I needed to control my emotions. Because when *they* controlled *me*, that was a disaster.

ALSO IN THE THIRSTY HEARTS SERIES

Miss the other novels by Kris Jayne? Catch up now!

CHARMING YOU - BOOK 1

Micky Llewellyn has trusted men before—with disastrous results. Now, she's focused on her career, her friends, and making sure she doesn't let another charming man lie to her and break her heart. Nick Halden's life has unfolded according to plan—a career at a top law firm and an engagement to the perfect socialite (he hopes). Fate throws them together, and in their struggle to balance love and ambition, they have to decide what they want before they lose the one thing that matters.

CHOOSING YOU - BOOK 2

Taryn Lieber has a date set to marry a man beyond her dreams—Jeff McConnell. After a disastrous first marriage,

Jeff has his curly-haired daughter and the unfulfilled desire for a woman to stand with him as he conquered the world. The arrival of Jeff's ex-wife throws their relationship into chaos. Conflict, mistrust, and danger follow as Taryn and Jeff try to hang on and make it down the aisle.

CHERISHING YOU - BOOK 3

After missing most of the first seven years of her daughter's life, Shannon Clifton is getting her life together to be a good mother and prove to her ex-husband and the world that her past of drug addiction and crime are history. Jonah Moran hasn't struggled for much. He has a cushy job at his father's billion-dollar company, a string of socialite girlfriends, and anything money can buy. Drawn together in a novel passion, they find solace in each other's worlds even as their differences threaten them with ruin. Can Shannon and Jonah push through the barriers and find lasting love?

ENCHANTING YOU - BOOK 5

Lilith Carver will do anything to help her estranged foster sister—even tap into her repressed mystical gifts to uncover the secrets threatening their future. With one clandestine maneuver, Jamie Wylde can right the wrongs of his father and exclude the man's mistress from the Wylde fortune. Only Kali's provocative sister somehow senses the truth, and she's on a crusade to stop him. Equally matched and battling to win, can Lilith and Jamie triumph in love?

TWO TO TANGLE - BOOK 6

Delilah Johnston and Griffin Kelso ring in the New Year with revels and romance. But once the champagne runs dry, their differences--and some scandalous family drama--crash the party. Will their growing love be enough? Or will a disconcerting secret divide them forever?

ABOUT THE AUTHOR

Kris Jayne is a devoted writer, reader, and traveler. She spends her days blissfully sweating out the writing process in the Dallas area with her dog, Otis the Shih Tzu, Rocco the Terrier, and Red the Foxy Mutt.

Her passion for writing is only matched by her passion for the adventures of travel. In 2008, she let a friend talk her into sleeping outside for the first time in her life when she climbed Mount Kilimanjaro.

P.S. If you're buying her a gift, she has a penchant for single-malt Scotch and scarves.

Contact Kris at:
krisjayne.com
kris@krisjayne.com